always,
never,
still

Always, Never, Still

always, never, still

Rita Finch Pettit

*To Mama and Daddy, for love measured
in tablespoons and lightyears.*

CHAPTER 1

SOMETIMES MY LONGING for Sarah crashes into me like a wave, leaving me breathless.

I doubt she knows how much I miss her, how I ache to put my arms around her and hold her as I once did. Or the size of the hole in my life, now that I can't talk to my best friend, the one who can translate the shorthand of my cryptic movie references and even my silence.

I saw Sarah practically every day of my life up until five weeks ago, and now all I can hope for is a chance meeting. Even though I caught a glimpse of her in the stacks at Newman Library last week, I kept my promise and left her alone.

Yesterday on my folks' front porch, I watched as she arrived home for Thanksgiving and lugged her duffel bag into her parents' house. Maybe I'll sit outside to enjoy this crisp November day and just happen to see her driving off in her car. And then I'll decide to take a drive myself.

I've lost my mind.

Sarah said we should "take a break." What I heard was "break up." That's how it feels.

We started dating almost three years ago, in February of our junior year in high school, and I wanted to marry her from that first kiss. Sounds crazy, yeah, but I'd been in love with her for I don't know how long. We'd been friends since we were kids, and somewhere along the way we fell for each other. Yeah, she loved me too. Maybe she still does. I'm not sure of anything anymore.

Sarah suggested that this break last three months, then we would talk about where our relationship is going. That means the break should end approximately seven weeks and sixty-two minutes from now. Not that I'm keeping track or anything.

"Sam?" My mother has always called out to me like that, her voice rising at the end of my name, priming me for her question. "Honey, could you run to the Super Dollar for me? I thought I had enough butter, but I'm out."

"Sure, Mom." I need to get out of my old bedroom and its old memories before I get really loopy, anyway. As I walk down the stairs, I ask, "Need anything else?"

"I don't think so, but let me make sure." Mom's kitchen, pre-Thanksgiving dinner, looks like the secret hideout of a mad scientist: pots bubbling on every burner; both ovens going; bowls, spatulas, and measuring cups and spoons covering the countertop. I don't want to know how much butter she's used already.

And Mom herself? Somehow, perfectly put together—makeup pristine, not a hair out of place. Even her apron is clean. Dad calls this phenomenon one of her superpowers.

"I should be fine. Thank goodness the Super Dollar is open today. I would ask your father or Megan to go, but I thought you might like to get out. You've been spending too much time in your room." Mom gives me her intent stare, like she's putting all her energy into trying to read my mind. And me, I put all my energy into trying to block her, as if she can.

I smile, like that will ease her worry. "Okay. Back in a few."

"Sam?"

Almost out the door, I turn around. "Yes, ma'am?"

"I know she'll have dinner with her family, but Sarah's welcome to join us for dessert."

I swallow. Hearing Sarah's name is like a pinprick. I haven't said much to my parents and sister about the break, only that Sarah and I have decided to give each other some space. I'm sure my vague psychobabble made about as much sense to them as it did to me, but they left it alone. Until now.

I return to the kitchen. "Mom…"

She's wiping her clean hands on a towel. "I know, I know. I shouldn't get involved, your daddy said so, but I've been so worried about you. You're just not yourself these days and—"

She can't stop herself, so I do it for her. "I'm okay, Mom, really." I almost died three years ago. While it seems like ancient history to me, I don't think my mother's gotten over it. I wonder if she ever will. "I'm okay." I give her a hug—a real one, not the one-armed side-by-side see-you-later one. When I pull away, she has tears in her eyes.

Mom quickly turns and swipes at her face with a tissue. "I'm sorry, son, but I don't believe you." She gives me her direct gaze again. "I sat with Sarah in your hospital room for hours. I know how you feel about each other. Fix this."

Oh, how I wish I could.

*

Thanksgiving dinner is a true feast in the Russell-Wilson tradition. According to my mother, the Russells are known for meals hearty enough to keep a lumberjack going for a week, while the Wilsons— her side—create desserts capable of making an angel sing. She tries to bring the best of both traditions to every holiday gathering. Bottom line: food comas all around.

As a result, no one protests when I return to my room, presumably to take a nap. Having the extended family in the house has pushed my misery aside, at least for a little while. Grandma and Grandpa Russell are here, as is Mimi, my mother's mother. Pop, Mom's dad, passed away when I was five. It's hard to tell which of my memories of him are real and which are stories I've heard over the years.

Megan arrived yesterday and will stay through the weekend. Three years older than me, she works as an accountant in Charlotte. We had the usual sibling-rivalry stuff going on when we were younger, but we're getting closer now.

"How are you doing?" she'd whispered as we helped Mom clean up.

"Okay," I answered.

She raised an eyebrow in response. "Liar. Let me know if you want to talk."

Part of me wants to talk to Megan, but I don't know what I'd say. I've dissected that "take a break" conversation and the events that led up to it a million times, but I'm still not sure I truly understand what happened. I asked Sarah to marry me—not when we graduated from Virginia Tech but as soon as possible. And then everything fell apart.

My classes have been challenging this semester, so I've managed to prevent our break-up from playing in an endless loop. But here, with no distractions, I can't stop watching it. I might as well be tied to a recliner in my own little theater in hell.

The movie gets off to a good start—Sarah and I sitting in the back of my old Ford Ranger drinking hot chocolate, wrapped up in a blanket, and listening to a Tech football game on the radio. We could've watched the game on TV with our friends, but this way we can indulge another hobby—stargazing.

There's a spot outside town where we like to park and look at the stars. We stretch out in the truck bed and prop ourselves up with a couple of cheap pillows. I then proceed to point out constellations and Sarah pretends to see them. When pressed, she admits she can't see a single pattern and swears the ancients were high on berries or something when they saw a dog or a hunter in the night sky. It's a silly game we play, almost a ritual, but we like it. At least we did.

Anyway, after trying my best to outline Cassiopeia—for, like, the eighteenth time—I turned to look at Sarah as she stared up into the sky, her eyes straining to see the image of a conceited queen. I was struck again by how gorgeous she was, her long red hair flowing around her, framing her face and following the curves of her body. Unlike the mythical Cassiopeia, Sarah had no idea how stunning she was, which only made her more beautiful in my eyes.

She sensed my staring, turned and smiled. Her green eyes reflected the meager light of the waning moon and I fell into them. I kissed her mouth and tasted the lingering richness of chocolate.

We wrapped ourselves tightly around each other, two halves yearning to be whole. I wanted Sarah so much, I swore I might break apart at any moment, my cells unable to hold together.

Maybe that's why I said what I did, the question that changed everything. I pulled away and stroked her cheek. "Marry me, Sarah."

She laughed softly. "I like the question, but you're a little early. Ask me again in a couple of years."

I framed her face with my hands. "Marry me now."

Sarah sat up quickly and pulled her hair back, reserving one strand to twirl around her finger. "Come on, you don't mean…"

I was so overcome with love and/or lust that I didn't hear the warning bells going off. I knelt before her and took her hands. "Marry me now, or at the end of this school year at the latest. I can't wait to start my life with you. Three years is an eternity."

She jumped up so abruptly I was afraid she'd lose her balance and fall out of the truck. "That's…that's crazy. I mean, how would we… how could we?" She sat on the side of the truck and hopped down.

I was still kneeling there, drowning in rejection. Unable to speak, in my head I was shouting, "Stop talking! In the name of all that is holy, please stop talking!"

But she didn't.

"I love you, Sam," she said, throwing her pillow behind the passenger seat, "but we can't. It just won't work."

I finally managed to stand, fold the blanket, and grab my pillow. I must have gone into shock since I couldn't feel anything. I assumed the pain would come later.

In the cab, I sat with my hands on the steering wheel, trying to remember how to drive.

Sarah was looking at me. "Sam? Sam? Talk to me."

I stared through the windshield and searched for words. "I, uh, guess there's nothing to say. Maybe later."

She patted my hand like I was a child. "Yeah, later. We'll talk later."

I want the movie to stop there. Then I could write a better ending, one that doesn't involve three months of loneliness and longing.

But it continued.

I don't remember driving to Sarah's apartment or mine. I do recall sitting on the edge of my bed, then falling over and going to sleep fully clothed. I got about three seconds of normal when the sun blazed into my room the next morning, but then everything from the night before landed on me with a thud.

I hadn't been awake more than five minutes when I got a text from Sarah. *You okay? Worried. Need to talk. Lunch?*

Texting was okay, but I didn't know if I could handle talking to Sarah in person. I wasn't sure I was up to seeing the love of my life. Crazy.

Still. *Fine. Lunch at 12:30? The usual?* We have a favorite burger place we discovered our freshman year. From the looks of it, you would guess it passes inspections only through bribery, but the burgers are awesome.

Good. Can't wait to see you, was her perky reply.

"But you couldn't get away fast enough last night," I grumbled aloud.

My heart jumped when Sarah walked into the diner. She smiled at me and took a seat, knowing I'd already ordered for her. "Did we go for french fries or onion rings this time?" she asked, peeling the wrapper off her straw and dropping it into her Coke. So normal, so everything-as-usual.

I cleared my throat. "French fries. That okay?"

"Of course. I always trust your judgment."

I said nothing.

"So, uh, about last night…"

I waited and tried to look neutral, neither hurt nor angry. Although I was both.

Sarah played with the wrapper from her straw, folding it like she was going to create a tiny origami bird. She glanced at me, then returned her focus to the thin strip of paper. The silence stretched out—one moment, two, three, four, five—before she looked at me and spoke. "I'm sorry I freaked out. You surprised me, that's all."

"That's all?"

Sarah pushed the paper away and folded her hands. "What's that supposed to mean?"

I leaned in and talked just above a whisper. "What I saw last night wasn't surprise. I'm not sure what it was, but it wasn't that."

"Sam…"

A lump began to form in my throat and, God help me, tears skimmed over my eyes. "What I saw was a woman repulsed by the idea of marrying me. Or maybe terrified by the thought of getting locked into a lifetime with me. I don't know. Maybe you don't know. Call me when you find out."

Desperate to leave before I started crying, I put $20 on the table and walked out as fast as I could.

Sarah rushed after me, but I didn't look back. "Sam! Sam!" she called out. I was climbing into my truck when she grabbed my arm. "Please stop." Her voice broke. "I love you, Sam. You know I do. I want to marry you just as much as you want to marry me. But the timing…"

I moved her hand. "Is it the timing, Sarah? Because the way you acted…" The tears started flowing. I had to get away, fast. "Maybe we can talk another time, but not now."

She started crying and moved closer, her arms reaching for me. "Oh, Sam, I'm so sorry."

I pushed her away as gently as I could and closed the door. "Me, too," I said before driving away.

"Turn around, you idiot!" I yelled at the screen in my head. "Turn around and listen to what she has to say." I didn't want to stop the movie here. I wanted to erase it.

Sarah texted and called over and over that afternoon, the next day and the next. I never responded. The pain of rejection and my anger at Sarah congealed into a single mass, crowding out empathy and anything resembling a rational thought.

I didn't hate Sarah. I could never hate her. That would be like hating myself. But a dark shroud covered my feelings for her. I started to see everything that has ever happened between us through the prism of that starry night.

Three days after our non-lunch at the diner, I took a deep breath and answered my phone. "Hi."

"Oh, hi. I guess I was expecting your voicemail again." Sarah sounded fragile, like she was recovering from a long illness. I tried not to notice.

"Yeah, well, it's me." The ugliness in me couldn't resist a jab. "What do you want?"

I think she gasped. "I'd like to talk to you if you're available. Please. Sam, I…just talk to me, okay? I won't take much of your time."

I wondered when I became a man who forced the woman he loves to beg for a conversation. Dear Lord. I felt the darkness retreat. "Yeah, we need to talk. Just tell me when and where."

We met at the memorial for the thirty-two students and faculty killed in the April 2007 massacre. Sarah and I had always been drawn to this place, especially when we needed help putting things in perspective.

I got there first. When I saw Sarah approach, all my hateful impulses dissolved. I was left with love for her and a deep sadness.

I stood when she reached me and pulled her into a hug. When we moved away from each other, the circles under her eyes and the paleness of her face were obvious.

I held her hands as we sat on the bench. Decided to let her make the first move. Not out of stubbornness, but because she knew what she wanted to say. I didn't.

"Sam, I'm so sorry."

I opened my mouth to apologize for being a jerk, but she pressed her finger against my lips. "Please, let me finish."

I nodded.

"I'm so sorry for the way I acted that night. I would explain myself, but I can't. There's so much I don't understand."

I tried to speak again.

Sarah shook her head. "Please." She stared at my face like she was trying to memorize it. "I think…I think we could use a little break." She picked up speed as she talked, so her next sentence sounded like one terrible word. "We've been together almost three years now, and maybe it's time to step back and think about where we're headed."

As bad as I felt when she turned down my proposal, this was a thousand times worse. "This break—how long?" I managed to ask.

She moved from the study of my face to the study of my hands, tracing each one of my fingers with hers. "Three months," she whispered. Before I could reply, Sarah kissed my face and got up to leave. "Take care, Sam," she breathed against my cheek.

Then she was gone.

The movie ended. No soaring music, no funny outtakes. Just me on a bench, alone.

Of course, I called and texted and called again. I went to Sarah's apartment every day, but she refused to see me. When her roommate, Jessie, threatened to call the police, I realized I was losing it. That day I finally received a text from Sarah: *Please stop, Sam. Give this break three months, then we'll talk. Not before.*

I tried to pull myself back from the edge. It was a break, not a break-up. Sarah said so. We would talk in three months, and she would explain this separation and we would work everything out.

That would bring me some peace for five, maybe ten minutes. Then my heart would split wide open all over again.

My family went to Luray Caverns when I was five. Mom and Dad pointed to the cave's features as the guide described them: stalactites, stalagmites, how they were formed and how to remember which is which. I still remember the wide-eyed awe on the faces of Megan and our parents. I wasn't awestruck; I was terrified, certain one of those pointy things hanging from the roof would fall on me.

When the guide turned out the lights to show us how pitch black the caverns truly are, my fear almost became a kid-sized panic attack. Only Megan's hand reaching for me in the darkness kept my terror at bay.

But nothing stopped my slide into panic after Sarah pushed me away. Every night I begged God to change her mind. When that didn't work, I prayed that I would die in my sleep, just so the pain would end.

After a week, I woke up one morning with a word in my head: *still.*

"*Still* like *always*, or *still* like *motionless*?" I prayed.

Still.

I started talking to God a lot when I was comatose three years ago. Uh-huh, while I was in the coma. Sarah is the only person who knows that Jesus kept me company in that lonely place. Only Sarah knows a lot of things about me.

I didn't learn which *still* He meant, but the word was the beginning of the end of my downward spiral. I decided to act like my misery had an expiration date and poured all my energy into my classes.

The house is quiet now, a marked contrast to yesterday's Thanksgiving merriment. Mom, Grandma, and Mimi mapped out an elaborate shopping itinerary last night to get the best Black Friday prices, with breakfast at Denny's built into the schedule, of course. They planned to leave around 6 a.m., so I calculate they have spent the Gross National Product of Lichtenstein by now.

Dad and Grandpa are in Dad's workshop. Dad loves tools, especially those of the woodworking variety, but he never has time to use them. When Grandpa visits, he gives Dad the kind of guidance you can't find in an instruction manual or online. Grandpa has built beautiful pieces, including the cedar chest he gave Mom and Dad when they married.

Megan said last night that she planned to visit Skylar, her best friend from college, in Alexandria today. She probably won't be back until late.

So that leaves me, eating Cheerios alone. Welcome back to the pity parade.

I'm trying to work up the motivation to see if any of my high school friends are available, when my phone rings. I pick it up, thinking one of them is making the first move, but when I look at the screen, I almost drop the phone into my cereal bowl.

Sarah.

CHAPTER 2

"HELLO?"

"Hi, Sam." Those two words are a song, flying right into my heart. "Sorry to bother you. Do you have a minute?"

A minute? Sure. Or an hour or a century. "Of course." I hold the phone at arm's length so she can't hear me take a deep breath. "What's up?" Casual. Good.

There's a pause. Maybe Sarah is focusing on her breathing too. "So, uh, I know this is, uh, kind of awkward, but, uh, I got an email from Pastor Jeff a few days ago."

I've heard Sarah talk for hours without ever using *uh*. "Okay."

"And, uh, he wanted to know if we could help with the Christmas pageant again this year. You know, some extra hands at rehearsal, then stage managers like we've, uh, done in the past. You know."

I say nothing. On the one hand, I would give a kidney to stand within three feet of Sarah. On the other, being near her without being with her sounds like a special kind of hell. "Sure. I can do that if you want to."

"Yeah, I mean, I think it's the right thing."

"Okay."

I stare at my phone, willing Sarah to tell me to come over.

"Sam?"

Did it work? Please tell me the break has ended. Please. "Yeah?"

Another silence. "Good luck on exams."

I sigh and don't try to hide it. "You too."

"Bye."

"Bye." I dump out the contents of my bowl and go back to bed.

*

"Samuel."

I roll over and look at the clock. Eleven a.m. My father's voice could wake the dead, and I almost qualify. I shuffle to my bedroom door. "Yes, sir?" His using my full first name usually isn't good, although I can't imagine what trouble I could be in this time.

"I'd like to see you for a minute."

I brush my teeth and throw on some sweats. If I'm in trouble, I don't want to be cast out wearing my boxers.

Dad looks up when I walk into the family room. "Come in and have a seat, son." He gestures to Mom's wingback chair beside him. I feel like I've arrived for an interview.

Dad is a complicated man. I know he loves me. Mom says he rarely left my bedside when I was in the hospital, and Megan confided that he collapsed into Mom's arms and sobbed when the doctors said I might not make it. But I've never seen that kind of open emotion from him.

He is not cold or harsh, one of those soulless villains found in celebrity memoirs and James Bond movies. In fact, he has a terrific sense of humor and a huge circle of friends. "Chad Russell would give you the shirt off his back," I've overheard more than once.

Neither of us speaks for a few moments. Maybe this is Dad's interview technique.

I crack first. "So what's up?"

Dad turns so he can face me head-on. "I don't want to butt in…"

Uh-oh.

"But your mother and I are concerned about you."

"I'm fine, Dad, really. There's no reason to—"

He holds up his hand to stop me. "Son, we can see you're hurting, and it's not hard to figure out why."

I clasp my hands and stare at the floor. If I'm lucky, the wood will split and I'll fall through to the basement. What can I say?

I remain silent.

Dad takes off his glasses and starts studying them like he's never seen them before. "You know, sometimes things work out for the best, even painful situations."

I look up. "What are you saying?"

Dad clears his throat. "You and Sarah have been together for a while now—"

"Almost three years."

"And you both have big plans. You want to be a doctor, and isn't Sarah planning to become a counselor?"

Suddenly the chair seems to have three legs, not four. "Yes, sir."

"Okay, so post-graduate work for both of you. School for years to come. Freshman year was tough for you, Samuel, and your grades reflected it."

I think the chair's legs have been reduced to two. "I know, but I think I have a good chance of making the dean's list this semester, barring a total collapse during exams."

"Exactly." Dad points for emphasis. "You've focused on your classes this fall, and that's what you have to do to reach your goals. Sarah needs to do the same."

I'm balancing on one shaky leg. My father doesn't realize that I've worked so hard for those A's and B's not out of renewed dedication but as a distraction.

"So…so," I stammer, as that last leg gives way, "are you suggesting I have to give up Sarah if I want to be a doctor? I can't do that, Dad. I won't do that." Not if she will have me, anyway.

He shakes his head. "That's not what I'm saying, Sam. I only think that you and Sarah need to talk about your future. You need to focus on short-term pain for long-term gain."

Sarah and I have had enough pain for a lifetime. I stand up before my mouth says something I'll regret. "Is that all?"

Dad rises and puts his hands on my shoulders. "I only want what's best for you, son. You and Sarah."

I shake off his gesture. "Sarah's best for me." I return to my room and stop short of slamming the door.

*

As I battle the back-to-school traffic on I-81, I realize I'm giddy at the prospect of studying nonstop for the next two weeks. It will be (almost) impossible for that stupid movie to start playing again.

Dad has not said anything else about how my break from Sarah could be a good thing. What was he thinking? First, he said he and Mom were worried about me, since it's obvious I'm hurting. Then he started babbling about how this separation might be for the best. If he intended to deliver a pep talk, he failed.

I finally conclude the whole conversation was all about my becoming a doctor, Chad Russell's personal crusade for the past three years.

After I emerged from my coma, I was so thankful to the doctors and nurses who cared for me that I began to think about helping others in the same way. It might have begun as a pay-it-forward impulse, but as the idea took hold, I became certain that medicine was my calling. I've always been good with science and numbers, so becoming a doctor didn't seem like an impossible dream when I was in high school. But my freshman year at VT changed that.

I didn't fail any classes, but I did get my first C's ever. Making the dean's list, which I had assumed would be a given, was out of the question. Arrogant twit, welcome to the real world.

I questioned whether I could even be admitted to medical school, much less become a doctor. Although my grades have improved this semester, I'm still not sure I'm on the right path.

Dad doesn't seem to have these doubts. Megan and I grew up listening to him preach about the importance of higher education, and two seconds after I mentioned the idea of becoming a doctor, my career was settled in his mind. My high school schedule, my work ethic, my college choice—all were subject to Dad's med-school rubric.

But get this: my father never earned a degree, although he did spend a year at community college after graduating from high school. "But it was a delaying tactic," he often explained to Megan and me. "I didn't have a plan or motivation, so I wasted your grandparents' money instead."

Grandpa told him to learn a trade or join the military, so Dad became an electrician. An excellent one at that. Eventually he and Mom built a successful business, and now Russell Electric employs a brigade of electricians. "But I'll always regret not getting that degree, and I won't let you kids make the same mistake," he says. Dad enjoys his work, and he's a respected businessman, so I don't understand why he continues to focus on a piece of paper.

But what if the decision I made in high school was only a phase I was passing through? I might have missed my true calling in my—and Dad's—single-minded focus on med school. And if I'm not supposed to be a doctor, what am I meant to do? I wish I could talk to Sarah. Discussing things with her untangles my thoughts.

I'm certain that Sarah is meant to be a counselor. Not only is she a great listener, but she's also good at hearing what people aren't saying. That's why I've never been able to tell her a lie, even a white one. If only I had her skills, I would stand a chance of understanding why she wanted us to take a break. As it is, I'm left to create and cast aside a hundred different theories for why things went wrong.

A new thought comes to me. What if I wrote Sarah a letter telling her how much I love her and how empty my life is without her? She said we shouldn't talk until the three months were up, but she didn't say anything about writing.

Ridiculous.

But I might do it.

I spend the rest of the drive composing the letter in my head.

Given the stop-and-go traffic, I could type it up on my phone. Maybe seeing my words on paper—an email might be easier to ignore—will prompt her to reconsider the break. At the very least she might decide to give me a clue about why we're doing this in the first place.

Now I have two missions to occupy my brain: killing my exams and writing a letter to Sarah. Dad's grim take on my situation fades from my memory.

Almost.

My roommate, Gavin, returned yesterday in order to beat the post-Thanksgiving crush, so when I open the door to our apartment, I'm struck by the smell of pepperoni pizza. "Is there any left?" I call out.

Gavin walks out of his bedroom, trailed by the scent of soap and aftershave. "Of course. I thought you'd be back soon and deserved a reward for surviving the madness of I-81."

I drop my bag and behold two-thirds of a mozzarella-laden beauty. "You're a good man," I say and pretend to wipe away a tear.

"I live to serve," he answers, placing a hand over his heart. "But now I must be off."

"Kirsten?"

His face would break if his smile were any wider. "Indeed."

Gavin and Kirsten started dating last spring and have been inseparable this fall. Kirsten is a striking blonde who's fully aware of her beauty. The opposite of my Sarah.

Kirsten has stayed over at our place several times, and I try to give her and Gavin their space. But I returned from the library earlier than I anticipated one afternoon and heard them in Gavin's bedroom. I felt uncomfortable, but that was overshadowed by another, darker emotion: envy.

Sarah and I agreed early on in our relationship that we wouldn't sleep together until—it was never *unless*—we got married. We grew up in the same church, so we'd both heard all the reasons for *no*. But we also worked through the issue for ourselves, deciding that we wanted our first time together to be perfect—no sneaking around for fear of being caught and certainly no guilt. Getting married first seemed like the only route to make that happen.

But we had no idea how difficult waiting would be.

More than once in recent months, we've been only one kiss or one touch away from tossing the perfect someday in favor of the wonderful here-and-now. I've caught myself rationalizing that there's no reason we shouldn't be together, since we plan to get married anyway.

But that was before Sarah said we had to separate, back when I was certain she and I would grow old together and die in each other's arms. As much as I still think about making love to her, today I would happily settle for a kiss and the promise of a future together.

"How was Thanksgiving?" Gavin's voice brings me back to the present.

"Okay. Parents, grandparents, sister. You know."

"Nothing with Sarah?" Gavin knows about the break, but I have done my best to appear unfazed by it.

I shake my head. "Not really. She did call about working together on our church's Christmas pageant."

He sits down at the kitchen counter, no longer rushing out to see Kirsten. He and I are different in a lot of ways, but he has turned out to be a friend. "You're not going to do it, are you?"

"Why not?"

Gavin holds out his hands in a *duh* gesture. "You can't be serious. I watched you disintegrate for a week when you first broke up."

I guess I'm a lousy actor. "We're taking a break," I correct him.

"Whatever. And now you're thinking about working with her on a church thing, side by side, like nothing's going on? I don't see how you can do that without falling apart all over again."

Exactly. I sit at the counter and play with the edges of a paper plate. I want to say something light and cool, like this break is no big deal. But I'm still a bad actor. "I love her, Gavin."

He punches my shoulder lightly, a guy version of a hug. "I know. Women. Geez."

I work up a smile. "Hey, you better leave. Kirsten might think you're taking her for granted."

"Can't have that." Gavin puts on his coat. "I'll be back later tonight, if you want to talk."

I won't. "Get out of here, Romeo."

"Yes, sir."

I fight off an attack of self-pity with pepperoni pizza. I will get to work on that letter tonight. Sarah likes good stories, so I will give her one.

Dear Sarah,

I know you want me to leave you alone during this break, but I can't stand being cut off from you completely. That is why I am writing this letter. For all I know, you will recognize my writing on the envelope and throw it in the trash without ever reading these words. But I must try, if only to make myself feel better.

Not the most attention grabbing of beginnings, but I'm not a great writer, so the straightforward approach seems best. Plus, I acknowledge my selfishness, which Sarah's counselor side will appreciate.

Do you remember when I broke the strap on your new backpack in second grade? The one with the unicorn on it? I grabbed it and we wound up in a tug of war when you tried to take it back. Then the strap broke and you ran crying to your house.

You wouldn't talk to me for two days, and in a 7-year-old's mind that's equivalent to two weeks, at least. I can still remember how lonely I was. I sat on the wall at the playground, uninterested in playing football with Jack and my other friends. I watched you, Lissi, and Rebecca play tag and felt a deep ache inside. I didn't know how to describe it then, but I do now. Profound loss. Exile. Grief.

How honest do I want to be here? I make it sound like I was a disturbed seven-year-old stalker who grew up to be a nineteen-year-old one. The most generous take would be that I'm pathetic.

"Always choose truth." Sarah said that once when we were debating whether white lies are okay. "Okay, I'd never tell my mom she looks frumpy, but I might suggest she update her wardrobe," she finally admitted.

Truth it is.

That's how I feel now. I don't say this to make you feel guilty—I don't want you to end this break out of pity. I say it because it is the truth and I know you respect and expect that.

I think I'm on the right track.

I miss your presence in my life. I file things away under "Things to tell Sarah" that I never get to share. Like Mom and my grandmothers plotting their Black Friday mission. Or a weird conversation I had with Dad about med school and my grades. Even this stupid commercial about a kid sending a Christmas card to his father in the army, and how I know you would cry at the end when the family's reunited.

I miss running my fingers through your hair, following the curls all the way to the end. I miss the softness of your lips on mine and how you often taste like the peppermint candy you love. I miss the music of your laugh and how your green eyes seem to glow when you're happy and flash when you're mad.

I miss everything about you.

I love you, Sarah, with all that I am. I'm surviving without you, but it does not feel like I'm living.

Do I end there, or should I go on? Ms. Cochran, one of my high school English teachers, would say "What's the purpose of the letter?"

I can see now that I shouldn't have proposed the way I did, expecting you to turn your future upside down at the drop of a hat. And I was a total jerk afterward. I am so sorry. Please forgive me.

I hope (okay, to be honest, I pray) that you will read this and decide to end this break now. But if not, I will still be waiting when the three months are up. I would wait forever for you.

All my love always,

Sam

I click *Save* and close my computer. If I decide to send the letter, I'll make a handwritten copy. My father once told me that he lets important correspondence sit for a while before sending it. "That way the words can ferment in my mind and I can be sure I'm saying what I mean to say or even if I should say anything at all."

I'll leave the letter alone until tomorrow. And I'll probably edit it. But I have no doubt I'll send it.

CHAPTER 3

THE LETTER WENT in the mail this afternoon. I stopped short of kissing it before dropping it in the box, thank goodness. But I did say a quick prayer that my words would unlock Sarah's heart.

I didn't edit my first draft, but I held on to it for a couple of days. Now I feel certain that writing a letter was the right thing to do. It feels good to stop whining and moaning and act, even if nothing comes of it.

Dad would be thrilled with my academic focus. Between wrapping up assignments and preparing for exams, I'm as tightly directed as a laser beam. I've decided to set aside the question of whether I want to be a doctor. Soul-searching will have to wait until Christmas break.

Christmas break. Christmas. Christmas pageant. The thought of volunteering alongside Sarah makes me simultaneously excited and queasy. Gavin's probably right—I should have said no. I can't back out now, so I'll put that in the I'll-deal-with-it-tomorrow file too.

The past is a bad movie, and the future is a confusing and possibly heartbreaking mess. A present packed with books and reports and study groups and research is as good as it gets for me.

Really pathetic.

*

I feel good about my exams. Mom called last night to see when I'm coming home, and I heard Dad in the background asking about my grades. The man never lets up.

I wonder when Sarah's leaving Blacksburg. I thought about sending her a short text during exam week to wish her luck but decided against it. She hasn't contacted me about the letter, but I don't know if that's because she never read it or because she wants to talk to me in person or because...

Stop it, I tell myself, but not aloud. I'm not that far gone. Yet. I'm trying to accept the fact that I won't know anything about this break until Sarah chooses to tell me. I hate being completely powerless. If I didn't know her so well, I'd swear she is torturing me on purpose.

"Why do we let women torture us?"

Maybe I was talking out loud after all.

Having slammed the door to his bedroom, Gavin opens and closes the refrigerator and kitchen cabinets, apparently forgetting that we emptied them for the break. "I mean, they must go to secret classes to learn how to drive us crazy. I am not crazy, right? But look at me, searching the kitchen when I'm not even hungry. That's crazy."

"Gavin?"

He leans against the counter, stares at the floor, and shakes his head.

I move toward him slowly, as if he's a skittish animal or a man possessed. "Something happen with Kirsten?" Duh.

He nods, and when he looks up at me, tears begin to fall. I don't acknowledge them.

"So, last night she said, she said..." He pauses to blow his nose and stop the hitching in his chest. "She said she thought we had, uh, how did she put it? Yeah, 'run our course.' 'Run our course,' like our relationship was a drug trial or something." Gavin's in pre-med too. "'Run our course.' Can you believe that?"

I put my hand on his shoulder. "I'm so sorry."

"I called her just now, begging her for another chance. Begging her." Gavin walks over to the sofa and plops down, sobbing and covering his face. "I told her last night that I had fallen in love with her, but she said, she said…"

He doesn't have to finish. "I'm so sorry." I repeat. "When are you going home?" He's in no shape to drive.

"I'd planned on leaving this morning, but now…" Gavin shakes his head again. "How do I get through this, Sam? How did you?"

I start to point out the difference between taking a break and breaking up, but it strikes me that there is none, not where my heart's concerned. "I keep breathing, keep going to class, and well…"—I don't want to sound preachy, but I must be honest—"I pray a lot."

He looks up. "That actually helps you?"

I'm ashamed of my embarrassment. "Yeah, it does."

"Okay." Gavin stares at his hands as he considers my answer. "Could you, uh, would you pray for me?"

"Sure. Of course." Silence stretches between us and starts to become awkward. "Do you mean, like, now? Together?" My embarrassment is morphing into profound discomfort. Why did I have to open my big mouth?

"Isn't that how it works?" He looks like a little kid fresh from a beat-down on the playground. "I don't know, but I thought…"

"Most of the time I pray alone, talking to God in my head. But I've prayed with other people, and I'd be happy to pray with you." I hope God doesn't zap me with a case of hives for telling a lie, even if it is with good intentions.

"What do I do?"

I've never taught anybody to pray before. *Help me, please.* "I close my eyes so I can shut out distractions, but you can pray with your eyes open, especially if you're driving."

Gavin grins slightly. "Good safety tip."

I send up another silent plea for help before speaking. "Dear God, thank You for all that You are. You are awesome and powerful and mighty, and yet You take the time to listen to Your children." The words are coming easier now. "Please watch over Gavin and bring peace to his heart. Show him Your plan for his life and help him to follow it. And please bless Kirsten and lead her down Your path. In Jesus's name I pray. Amen."

When I open my eyes, I notice Gavin's are still closed. I wait as a stillness settles over us. God is here, so real that I expect to see Him out of the corner of my eye.

When Gavin finally looks at me, the desperation is gone, if not the pain. "That was not what I expected." He speaks slowly, as if he is taking something in. "I thought there would be a lot of words you've memorized and recited for years. That was more like a conversation, like you were talking to a person."

"I was." My discomfort has vanished. "I was talking to my Father in the name of His Son, Jesus."

"And I didn't expect you to pray for Kirsten too. Since you're my friend and all."

"Does that bother you?"

He shakes his head. "The funny thing is it doesn't. I'm not as angry with her as I was a few minutes ago. That's, that's..." He runs his hands through his hair as if to shake loose the right word. "Amazing. I never knew. How does that work?"

I wish Pastor Jeff were here to give the right answers. "I don't understand everything. I guess I never will." I sense the Lord's hand gently pushing me along. "But I do know that Jesus is my Friend. He can be yours too."

Gavin nods. "I'll think about it over Christmas. Thanks, Sam."

I pat him on the back. "Anytime." Neither of us speaks for a couple of minutes, and I realize it is time to get back to guy stuff. "So, since our cupboards are bare, how about I run to McDonald's and pick up some breakfast for us? My treat."

Gavin perks up. "With an extra-large coffee?"

"You got it. Back in a few."

After I get in my car, I say another prayer for Gavin. He and

Kirsten seemed so happy, but I guess you never know. His hometown is on the way to mine, and I wonder if he'd like a ride. He shouldn't drive if he's still upset, plus he might need to vent some more. I can be a good listener when I try.

My own darkness is keeping its distance. For now.

*

Gavin insisted he could drive home safely, but I refused to leave until I was sure he was okay. Not good, but calm. I feel for him. At least I have the hope that Sarah and I will wind up together. The way Gavin tells it, Kirsten saw his declaration of love as a neon sign urging her to move on.

Just north of Roanoke, I get a text from Kevin Carpenter, a high school friend who goes to James Madison University. Kevin's car has died, and he wonders if I could give him a ride back to Early. JMU is right off I-81, so it's no problem.

Early is a tiny town, but that doesn't mean I know every person who lives there. People who live in huge cities think that's how it is with small towns, but they're wrong. Having said that, it seems just about everybody in Early knows Kevin and his family, or at least knows of them. Jeff Carpenter, his dad, is the pastor at New Hope Fellowship Church, the church that Sarah's family and mine—and half of Early—attend.

I'm happy to give Kevin a ride, not only because he's been a good friend since high school but because he's a good guy. I know I could talk to him about the darkness and he wouldn't laugh or shrug it off. And he wouldn't tell anyone. Not that I plan to talk about Sarah and our break. It's all I think about now that exams are over, and enough is enough.

"Thanks so much, Sam." Kevin crams his stuff into the tiny space behind the passenger seat and buckles in.

"That's all?" I ask, looking at his duffel and backpack. "Guys usually pack light, but still."

He laughs. "Don't give me too much credit. I took some stuff home when I visited earlier this week." Early is only about an hour from JMU, so Kevin can make quick trips when necessary. "My dad needed help dragging the stable for the Christmas pageant out of Mr. Watkins's garage. That thing might look like wood, but it must be solid iron. I think it weighs as much as a real stable."

The pageant. Ugh. I start to sink into myself again.

"Sam?" Kevin doesn't miss much. "You okay?"

"Sure," I lie.

Kevin stares at me. "My dad said you and Sarah are going to help again this year. Does that mean you're back—"

"Together? No." For a millisecond I consider returning to VT as soon as I drop Kevin off. *Let it go, Kevin,* I plead silently. *Just let it go.*

He doesn't. "So are you guys still taking a break or have you, you know…"

"Broken up? No. It's complicated and I don't want to talk about it, okay? You wouldn't understand."

"Sure." Kevin leans back in his seat and stares out the window. "Sorry for bringing it up. I know some things are painful to talk about."

Of course. Kevin has his own heart trouble. Rebecca Nichols. What an idiot I am. "No, I'm sorry for being stupid. Have you seen her?"

A look drops over Kevin's face like a mask. I know that look. I see it every morning in the mirror: love tinged with despair. "No." He turns to me just as I shake my head. "But I've come up with a plan. Really."

According to my observations, Kevin has been in love with Rebecca since our sophomore year in high school. Six of us ate lunch together: Sarah and I; Lissi Stanfield, Sarah's best girlfriend; Jack Webster, who went by "Webs" back in the day but uses "Jack" now that he's Mr. University of Virginia Business Major; and Kevin and Rebecca.

Kevin and Rebecca were the shy, quiet ones. Each dated a little, but I could tell Rebecca was the one Kevin really wanted. It was obvious by the way he looked at her and listened to the few words she did say. I don't think anyone in our group missed it. Except Rebecca.

When both decided to attend JMU, I hoped Kevin would finally get up the nerve to tell Rebecca how he feels. But here we are, halfway through our sophomore years, and he hasn't even spoken to her.

But there might be hope yet. "So what's your plan?"

Kevin sits a little taller as excitement takes hold. "Okay, so there's the possibility that I'll see her over Christmas, at a party or something. If she attended our church, that would be easy."

I hope my doubt isn't showing.

"But here's the plan: I know some of her friends at JMU, and I think I can find out when she goes to the dining hall or library and then just happen to run into her. What do you think?"

I think you're sounding creepy, my friend. "Uh, Kev, have you considered just calling Rebecca and asking her to meet you for coffee? Even giving a note to one of those friends asking if Rebecca likes you would be more straightforward. Your plan sounds a little…"

Kevin slumps. "Creepy? Weird?"

"I didn't mean…" I lie for the second time.

"No, you're right. I guess I'm scared."

"Of what?"

"Of her pushing me away. Laughing at me. She's so far out of my league. It's easier to dream, I guess."

I don't get it. Rebecca is sweet and pretty, but Kevin's an awesome guy—he is super smart, and Sarah says he's cute. Although she has been quick to add that I'm cuter. I don't know what to say.

Kevin looks out the window again. "But she wouldn't laugh at me because she's such a good person. And, you know, sometimes I wonder if I'm in love with Becky or with this whole ideal girl I have made up in my mind. I'm messed up, Sam. Really messed up."

I get it. "We all are, buddy. Look at Jack. He and Lissi had a good thing going, then they split up when Lissi went off to Northwestern. But does Jack move on? Nope. He acts like he's a player, but I don't think he'll ever get over her." I pick up steam as things become clearer to me. "Look at me. I thought Sarah and I would be together forever, then out of the blue she says she wants to take a break. Now I don't know what will happen to us and I'm going crazy."

I glance at him. "Now look at yourself. You've loved Rebecca for years and you're afraid of what might happen if you reach out to her. We're all afraid of something, but you've got to put on your big-boy pants and step out and give life a shot."

Kevin is stunned. I doubt if I've ever said that many words to him at once. Then a smile breaks out. "Big-boy pants? Did those words really come out of your mouth?"

I laugh. "Blame my mom. I overheard her saying that to my dad once."

Kevin nods. "But you know what? Your mom was right."

Indeed.

*

I've gotten tired of hanging around the house, so I'm off to Winchester to do some Christmas shopping. *Shopping* probably isn't the right word for picking up gift cards for Mom, Dad, and Megan, but it's as close as I'll get this year. In the past Sarah and I have gone together, and she helped me choose things for my mother and sister. They loved the jewelry I gave them last year.

I don't like shopping. At all. And this time of year? Ugh. People rushing from store to store, filled with about as much Christmas cheer as grizzlies awakened early from hibernation. And the poor cashiers, trying to stay jolly even as old Mrs. These-Wrinkles-Didn't-Come-From-Smiling gives him or her a hard time about the twenty-five-percent-off coupon that expired yesterday.

I stop when I see a peach-colored sweater in a store window. It would look beautiful on Sarah. I start to walk in, excited about finding just the right gift, when it hits me. I probably won't see Sarah on Christmas Day, for the first time in…well, ever.

I'm standing there on the threshold, trying to figure out if this separation means I can't give Sarah a present, when I spot Kevin. He pushes his way across the mall's jammed intersection, using a couple of huge shopping bags to clear his path. He's almost out of breath when he reaches me.

"Impressive maneuvers out there, Mr. Carpenter. You could've had a career in hockey."

"Yeah, but I think being able to skate is a requirement. What's up?"

"Not much. Trying to do some shopping."

Kevin looks from one of my empty hands to the other. "Not trying hard enough, apparently."

"Hey, it looks like you're doing enough for both of us. You're going to give guys a bad name."

Kevin shrugs. "What can I say? I do love to shop. Sue me. But now I've come to rescue you."

"Huh?"

"The last time I saw eyes that glazed was when my dad brought home his trophy from the taxidermist."

I would protest, but there is no point. "And this rescue consists of…"

"A trip to the food court. Chick-fil-A awaits."

Did I mention that Kevin is super smart?

We're finishing up our waffle fries when Kevin's face suddenly turns grim. "Either Bigfoot is real or that's Dakota Crenshaw walking toward us."

Suddenly my appetite is gone.

Every high school has its bullies. As far as I know, Dakota never shoved anyone's head in a toilet or pushed a guy into the girls' locker room. His weapon was the perfectly timed hateful remark, a comment that lodged in your gut and festered for days. Dakota never seemed especially bright, but he was highly skilled in knowing which words would hurt the most. A savant when it came to cutting people down.

I don't know why, but Dakota despised our lunch circle and saved some of his best work for us. We weren't the super-popular celebrities of school, the kids you love to hate, but something about us drove him to new heights—or would it be lows?—of meanness. I remember vividly when he hurt Sarah's feelings one day on the bus. I wanted to knock him out. That would have taken a miracle, since he outweighed me by at least fifty pounds, but my anger might have given me a boost.

But maybe he's changed. Mellowed. Turned over a new leaf. Seen the light.

"Well, if it isn't two of my favorite losers."

Or not.

"Dakota," Kevin says. I think he would be more enthusiastic if he were greeting Satan.

Dakota smiles broadly and slaps each of us on the back. "So, did you finally give up on women and decide to, you know…" He seesaws a hand back and forth.

Definitely not.

"Still got that old charm, I see." It's the best I can do. My brain churns, scrounging around for a bit of information to strike him down with. I'm still thinking as he drags a chair to our table and straddles it. I think Kevin has gone to a safe space inside his head.

"You always were clever with words, right, Sammy?"

Only my mother is allowed to call me Sammy.

I return to my food, appetite or not, focusing on each fry as if it were a DNA molecule. Perhaps Dakota is like the boogeyman. If you don't pay attention to him, he ceases to exist.

"I heard that you and Sarah split up. I found that hard to believe, since you guys have been together since kindergarten."

Kevin emerges from his hiding place. "Back off, Crenshaw."

"Yeah, like I'm afraid of you, Preacher Boy." Dakota laughs softly.

I'm wandering around in my mind, frantically searching for my own safe space. Thinking of something—anything—to block Dakota's words. Chocolate cake. The velvety softness of Sarah's lips. The way I felt after I prayed for Gavin. Butterflies. Sarah's green eyes.

Dakota leans toward me, closing in for the kill. His eyes are cold and relentless, like a cobra's. "Then I saw them a couple of nights ago cozied up in a booth at Bailey's, talking and laughing. That's when I knew it was true."

I ask despite my heart's warning. "Saw who?" I croak.

"Sarah and Webster. Looks like your lady finally decided to hook up with a guy who might go places."

The outside world is slipping away from me, but I hear the anger in Kevin's voice and the screech of his chair as he stands. "Leave. Now."

"Sure." Dakota punches me in the shoulder. "Later, losers."

CHAPTER 4

I THINK I might be sick.

I've faced evil before—true, relentless evil—but I've never sensed it moving inside me. Until now. It burns its way through my belly, a low rumble that becomes a voice. *You didn't think Sarah was waiting around, did you? She called it a break just to let you down easy.*

Stop.

Jack heard she was free and made his move. They probably got together weeks ago. Chances are they're sleeping together.

Stop. Stop. Stop.

He knows her body in ways you never will. Holding her, kissing her, pulling her close. Sarah and Jack appear in my mind, their sweaty bodies entwined. Then they look at me and smile. *And they're laughing. Laughing at you all the time. Make them pay. Make them pay. Make them pay…*

"Jesus," I whisper.

The voice stops immediately, and I become aware of Kevin's hand on my arm, pulling me up.

"Let's get out of here. Come on, buddy. That's good. Let's go to my car."

I begin to reconnect with reality as we walk to the parking lot. A kid whines about needing to potty. A man talks loudly on a phone about which toy he's supposed to buy. A woman gives Kevin and me a funny look as Kevin pulls me through the crowd. I'm almost normal by the time we get to Kevin's car.

I lean back in the seat and close my eyes. I feel like a skydiver whose parachute didn't open until the last minute. Stunned but alive.

"Talk to me, Sam." Kevin's eyes are soft with compassion and concern, and I realize that he's the only friend I'd want with me right now. Except for Sarah, of course.

"What happened?" I finally ask.

"Dakota Crenshaw." Kevin's anger returns. "Dad talks about looking for the good in others, but Dakota…"

"No, I mean what happened with me?"

"You don't know?"

"I know what was happening on the inside, but what did you see? What did I do?" I almost expect him to say that my head spun 360 degrees and my eyes glowed red.

"You just stared straight ahead without blinking or showing any expression. It's like you were catatonic."

"Like Gregory Peck in *Twelve O'clock High*."

"Who?"

"Never mind."

"Anyway, it occurred to me that you might be having a seizure, so I was about three seconds from dialing 911 when you blinked and started to move a little." Kevin shudders. "You really scared me, man. What was going on?"

I close my eyes again. Back in third grade, a kid said that if you tell someone about a bad dream it will come true, so I keep my nightmares to myself just in case. And this? This was worse than anything my overactive imagination could ever conjure up. "I don't want to talk about it." Better to be safe than sorry.

I can sense the weight of Kevin's stare as he waits for me to come around.

I breathe deeply and look out the passenger window, fixing my gaze on a new oil change place being built. I can't face Kevin, good and decent Kevin, as I recount my experience. I tell him what happened, with one omission: I can't bring myself to describe my horrific vision. Only when I finish do I dare to look at him. I am already grieving the loss of our friendship.

But the compassion and concern are still there. "I can't imagine how awful that was." He shakes his head slowly. "It's like you were in a fight for your very soul."

Yeah, that sums it up perfectly. "But is the fight over? Or has he—or it, or whatever—made a home here?" I point to my heart. "I'm afraid."

Kevin nods. "Yeah, yeah, of course. You should talk to my dad. I'm just a stupid nineteen-year-old. But my gut tells me you'll be all right. After all, you're not fighting alone."

"You're right." Then I remember the comment that precipitated the...what should I call it, *attack*? Yeah, *attack* is the right word. "Do you think Dakota was telling the truth, though? About seeing Sarah and Jack together?"

Kevin shrugs. "I don't know. I mean, is it possible he did see them at Bailey's? Sure. But I think everything else he said was made up. We know Sarah and Jack. Does their getting together, even while you guys are separated, make sense? Of course not."

The terrible image of Sarah and Jack smiling at me returns. I squeeze my eyes shut, as if that will block it. "It doesn't make sense, but I have to know for sure. I have to speak to Jack." I can't risk approaching Sarah. I don't want to ruin whatever chance we have for reconciliation by accusing her of sleeping with one of my best friends.

"Of course."

"Kevin?"

"Yeah?"

"I need a big favor."

"Anything." I know he means it.

"Could you go with me when I see Jack?"

"Yeah, I'd be happy—"

I hold up my hand. "But that's not all. If that voice comes back and it looks like I'm losing it, you have to promise that you'll stop me. Whatever it takes." Kevin, quiet and kind, has been studying taekwondo since he was a little kid.

His mouth drops open. "I don't think that will be—"

"Please. Promise me."

Kevin holds out his hand and we shake on it. "I promise. Whatever it takes."

*

Jack answers on the second ring when I call. He knows something is up, since his usual happy-go-lucky tone ends shortly after "Hello."

Kevin follows me straight from the mall, and I'm thankful I asked him for backup. We'll arrive at Jack's house in around five minutes, and the idea of confronting him alone scares me. I haven't heard that voice since we left the food court, but I don't think I'll ever forget what it said.

"Hey! What's up?" Jack is an upbeat guy, but this afternoon he seems almost maniacally cheerful, like a clown without makeup. He opens the door wide to let us in.

"Yo, Kevin! I didn't know you were coming. Is this an intervention or something?"

"Or something," I say.

Jack drops his mask. I see uncertainty on his face. Or is it fear? He leads us into the family room. "The folks are out doing some last-minute shopping. Can I get you guys anything? Coke or chips, or I think my mom bought some pizza rolls."

"This isn't a social call." I sound like a detective interviewing a suspect. Chances are I heard that line in an old *film noir.* The observation would amuse me if I weren't on the verge of losing my girl and my oldest friend in the same day.

He takes a seat in a recliner while Kevin and I sit on the sofa to face him. I'm glad Kevin's close by.

"I didn't think so." Jack clasps his hands in front of him. "What is this about, Sam? We haven't seen each other in weeks, and I don't recall anything happening online."

"You don't know?"

Jack shakes his head.

I'm not convinced. "Sarah," I say in a neutral tone, letting the name do its work.

Jack nods. "Yeah, Sarah. What about her?"

"Really? That's all you have to say?"

Jack throws his hands in the air. "What can I say? I know you guys split in October, and she says you'll talk things over when the break ends in January."

I jump up and my newly acquired shadow quickly follows. "You have talked to her. What else have you talked about? When did you start seeing her? When—"

Jack stands and extends his arms, palms facing me. "Hold on, Sam. Hold on. I don't know what—"

I start to move around the coffee table toward Jack, but a firm grip on my arm restrains me. "Dakota Crenshaw saw the two of you in a booth at Bailey's the other night. He said you looked like a couple, that you were 'cozied up,'"—I use air quotes—"laughing and talking. Is that true or not?"

Jack steps toward me. "Come on, Sam! How can you believe anything that comes out of Dakota's mouth? He was, is, and always will be a nasty piece of work."

"But is it true?"

Jack nods, and the grip on my arm gets tighter. "It's true that I took Sarah to Bailey's for dinner. It's not true that we're a couple in any way, shape, manner, or form."

"Do you love her?"

"Of course I do," Jack answers immediately, and I feel sick again. But no rumble this time. I drop to the sofa and put my head in my hands.

"Not like that. I mean, I love Sarah like I love you guys." He gestures at Kevin and me. "You're the siblings I never had. But even if my feelings for Sarah were romantic, I would never, ever, *ever* act on them. How could you think I would, Sam? Don't you know me?"

I rub my eyes. Unless Jack is a consummate actor, he's telling the truth. "I'm sorry, man. I'm so sorry." But what about that dinner? "Then how did you guys wind up going out together?"

Jack sits back down. "I ran into her at the Super Dollar. We exchanged hellos and the usual how-are-yous, but I could tell something was wrong. Really wrong."

"How?"

He stares up at the ceiling for a moment. "It's hard to describe. She seemed, I don't know, breakable. Fragile. Yeah, that's it. Fragile, like that kite we made in fourth grade, the one that came apart the second we tried to fly it. Like that."

I've never thought of Sarah as fragile. She has faced evil too, and come out strong and whole on the other side. Sarah's not a hard person, not at all, but fragile? I'm skeptical. "You felt sorry for her?"

Jack shakes his head. "No. Maybe yes. I didn't think of it that way at the time. I saw a friend who was in pain, and I wanted to make her feel better. I thought maybe if we talked about some of the crazy schemes I came up with in high school, plus a few I've thought of since, I could make her laugh a little."

I've gone back into detective mode as I interrogate my witness. "You said Sarah seemed fragile, and now you say she was in pain. Which was it?"

"Both." Jack doesn't hesitate. "In the store Sarah asked me if I had heard from you. As soon as she said your name, she started twirling a strand of her hair, and when I said you seemed okay, she started crying. Not sobbing but tears quietly falling down her face. It broke my heart."

The image of Sarah coming apart makes me want to rush to her house and wrap her in my arms, "taking a break" be damned. But I don't understand. I thought she wanted this.

"Later, at the restaurant, she made me promise not to tell you that she became upset," he goes on. "I did, but that was a mistake. You should know what this separation is doing to her. I don't know why you wanted it, but it's time for it to end."

My grief gives way to astonishment. "You think I wanted this break?"

"Well, yeah. I figured it must have been your idea since Sarah's struggling so much."

"No." I'm fumbling around in the dark. "No. It was all Sarah's idea. We'd had…"—how much should I say?—"a blowup, but I didn't see the separation coming. We met to talk about things, but before I could say a word, she announced this break and walked away."

As Kevin and Jack stare at me, I realize I've never talked to anyone about the separation. I feel a sudden urge to tell them everything.

I choose my words carefully. If Sarah and I get back together— *when* we get back together—I don't want my friends to get the idea she was the bad guy in this story. And the really personal stuff, like my longing for her and the details of my letter, should stay personal. Otherwise, I give Kevin and Jack a full rundown of what happened.

After I finish, they're speechless for a few moments. Jack, the only person in the room who has seen Sarah recently, seems completely bewildered. "I don't get it. I believe you when you say this was all Sarah's idea, but none of this makes sense."

"Tell me about it."

"It doesn't make sense," Kevin echoes. "But maybe that's the key."

"Huh?" Jack says.

I agree.

Kevin starts gesturing with his hands, moving them about like he is putting puzzle pieces in their proper places. "Stick with me for a minute. Sarah wants you guys to split for a while. She won't see you, and she hasn't responded to your letter."

"Uh-huh."

"But when Jack sees her, it's obvious that she's completely miserable."

Jack and I nod dumbly.

"So…" Kevin waves at us like we should have the correct answer ready.

We don't.

"So, Sarah either didn't want the break to begin with or she's changed her mind. If she'd changed her mind, she would have called you as soon as she read your letter. She might have shown up on your doorstep. But she didn't. So…"

"She didn't want the break to begin with," I finish. I feel like the star pupil for two seconds. "But if she didn't want it, why suggest it?" We're back at square one.

Kevin lets out a long breath. "That, my friend, I don't know. The way I see it, you have only one option."

"You have to talk to Sarah," Jack says, pointing at me for emphasis. "Forget the three-month mark. Talk to her now and end this craziness."

Kevin nods in agreement.

The three of us share the chips and Coke offered earlier and rib each other about the success—or lack thereof—of our respective football teams. Kevin never tires of reminding Jack and me that JMU is the only one of our three schools to have won two national championships. For a few minutes, my world is sunny.

As Kevin and I leave, Jack taps Kevin on the shoulder. "Don't take this the wrong way, but why did you come over here with Sam?"

"To stop him from killing you."

"Oh. Okay."

"And if we'd found out you were hooking up with Sarah, then only my promise to Sam would've kept me from taking care of you myself," Kevin adds without a hint of a smile.

Jack pauses for only a second. "Okay. Thanks, Kev."

"No prob."

*

I know my friends are right. So why didn't I call Sarah as soon as I returned home? Why am I stretched out on my bed, staring at the ceiling? I can come up with only one reason.

Fear.

The only thing worse than living in limbo would be knowing without a doubt that Sarah and I are done. Of course, a conversation could lead to happily-ever-after. But optimism is not my default position these days.

My phone pings with a text message from Kevin. *Don't tell Jack, but he got me thinking. Time to end craziness. Called Becky's house. Coffee tomorrow. Your turn.*

That is the best news I've heard in weeks. *Congrats! Guess I should try on those BB pants myself.*

He responds immediately. *No Excuses!!!*

Kevin's right. But first, a slice of leftover pizza.

I'm surprised to find Mom in the kitchen. "Didn't expect to see you home already."

She jumps and almost drops the two shopping bags and gallon of milk she is juggling. "Good heavens, Sammy," she says as I grab the bags. "You scared me to death."

"Sorry." My eyes lock onto a package of chocolate chips. "Do I see cookies in our future? Please?"

"Soon, but not today." Mom starts unpacking groceries and pulling out recipe cards. "I just learned that Rob and Suzanne Reynolds are coming over tonight for dinner. Your father, bless his heart, invited them three days ago and forgot to tell me." She pulls back her hair with an elastic and puts an apron over her work clothes, going into full kitchen-battle mode. "Thank goodness my boss let me leave work early."

"Yeah," I agree. "I know he can be a pretty harsh guy."

Mom smiles and continues to work. That guy is my father.

"So, when is the big dress rehearsal for the Christmas pageant?" Mom asks in one of her out-of-the-blue comments that leaves me wondering if I've missed half a conversation. "I've heard they've been practicing during Sunday school, but you don't know what you're working with until those kids hit the sanctuary." Spoken like a veteran volunteer.

"Don't know. I haven't heard anything from…" My brain starts clicking. "Wait a minute. How did you know Sarah and I are helping out?"

Mom concentrates with a little too much intensity on blending her lasagna filling. "It's not a closely guarded secret, you know."

"Mom…"

She pivots to a straightforward approach. "Maybe when Pastor Jeff asked about your coming home for the holidays, I happened to mention that you and Sarah could help out. What's the harm in that? You've done it before."

"But you knew—"

"That you are separated, yes. I only want what's best for you. Sue me for being a loving mother." Mom turns away and crumbles ground beef in an industrial-sized skillet, apparently satisfied that this conversation is over.

"But you should have…never mind." I sigh. I'm trapped and we both know it.

Trapped. And maybe rescued.

CHAPTER 5

Suzanne and Rob Reynolds and my folks have been friends since Mom and Dad moved to Early fifteen years ago. When I was a kid, I would get confused sometimes, calling Dr. Reynolds Uncle Rob at his office and Dr. Rob at our house.

Uncle Rob is so calm and soft-spoken, I think it would take a tank driving through his office to rattle him. When I try to imagine myself as a doctor, I slip on his demeanor like a coat. I've never talked to him about my career plans but don't know why.

"How are you doing, big guy?" Uncle Rob started calling me this when I wasn't big at all. "Survived another semester, I see." He shakes my hand and slaps me on the back.

"Yes, sir. Good to see you."

Aunt Suzanne gives me a dainty hug and a kiss on the cheek. "Samuel Russell, I do believe you've grown six inches since we last saw you." She must practice perfect posture to claim a height of 5'3", so everybody seems tall to her.

"Not quite."

I run through a half dozen scenarios for my call to Sarah while my parents and the Reynoldses catch up with each other in between forkfuls of lasagna and salad. It's taken years, but I believe I've perfected the art of appearing to listen to a conversation without paying any attention whatsoever.

"So, how's pre-med going?" Uncle Rob asks as Mom delivers wedges of chocolate pie.

The term *pre-med* yanks me out of Sam World. Fortunately, I've also learned how to jump back into a discussion without hesitation. "Okay. I made the dean's list this semester." I wonder how much Dad talks to Uncle Rob about my becoming a doctor. Probably a lot.

"Yeah, Sam really turned things around this semester," Dad chimes in. "But he can't let up if he hopes to get into med school, isn't that right, Rob?"

It's time to excuse myself from the table. I need to make a call. Or go to a movie. Or wish on a falling star.

Uncle Rob shifts in his chair and clears his throat, as if he senses he's being drawn into someone else's argument, if not a war. "Well, yes, getting into med school isn't easy, that's for sure." He turns to me. "Why do you want to practice medicine, Sam?"

I almost bolt. I thought he'd throw in another layer of "Work harder. Don't get distracted. Blah. Blah. Blah." Instead, he's gone straight to the heart of things.

Caught off guard, I give the worst possible response. The truth. "I'm not sure that I do."

The room goes completely silent—even the forks are stilled. Dad's hovers above his slice of pie as he stares at me, his eyes wide. "What?"

I wonder if it's too late to take it back. I scramble for a few seconds, struggling for a foothold. But there's no point. "I've been thinking lately that maybe being a doctor isn't what I'm meant to do."

Dad shakes off his disbelief and goes on offense. "Of course it is. You had a rough start, and it hurt your confidence. But now—"

"Now I think I need to be sure of what I want before I go any further."

"I know what you want, but—"

Mom, who has been watching this little train wreck like a dazed bystander, stands and starts gathering plates. "I don't think Suzanne and Rob came over here for a *telenovela*." She's been working alongside some Latina ladies at the food pantry, and she's proud of the words and phrases she has picked up. "Next thing you know, somebody will start throwing my grandmother's china, and I won't be happy." She squeezes Dad's shoulder as she takes away his half-eaten pie.

He pats her hand, never taking his eyes off me. I can't tell if he is glaring with anger or disappointment.

Time to go.

"Can I help you with the dishes, Mom? I promised"—who should I throw under the bus? Kevin? Jack? If only I still had Sarah to call on—"Jack we'd hang out tonight." The lie comes easily.

"You go on, Sam," Aunt Suzanne answers. "Your mom and I do our best gossiping in the kitchen." She smiles as she tosses the lifeline.

"Thank you, Aunt Suzanne." I give Mom a quick hug. "And thanks for the meal, Mom. It was great as usual."

I'm on the porch, savoring my escape, when Dad opens the front door. He walks up to me and stands silently. He's good at this. "We will talk about this later, Samuel," he says finally. "I won't let you throw your future away."

I turn to Dad so quickly I startle him. "But it is my future, isn't it, Dad? Mine. Not yours." I walk away, with no destination in mind.

My phone pings as I turn on to Main Street. *What's up?* Jack has texted.

Not much, I respond. *Out for a walk.*

??? You okay?

Sure, I answer.

Coming to get you. Location?

No need. Really.

Shut up.

I give in. It's a clear night—I can make out Orion perfectly—so the temps are dropping. The lights of McDonald's are ahead, so I tell Jack to meet me there.

I order a cup of coffee and an apple turnover and settle in by a window. I'm adrift. I don't want to go home for an interrogation, and I can't turn to Sarah.

Jack's goofy smile brings some relief. He walks over with a little hamburger and some fries. Guys don't meet at a place selling food without getting any. Jack starts needling me immediately. "Once again, a UVA student must rescue a Hokie."

"Once again? I don't think so. Aren't I the one who saved you when your rust bucket died by the side of the road?"

Jack holds up a finger as he attempts to swallow the half-hamburger he jammed into his mouth. "Correction," he says. "My vehicle had a slight fuel-gauge malfunction, which caused it to register levels incorrectly."

"Just like a Hoo, using fancy words to cover up problems. You ran out of gas because you drive a rolling disaster."

Jack knows he's been defeated—this time—and doesn't bother replying. We finish our food in silence. But after he consumes his last french fry, he folds his arms and stares at me.

"What?" I ask, although I know the answer.

"So why was my oldest friend roaming the streets on a cold night like some homeless dude?"

"I was not roaming the streets. I was out for—"

"A walk. Yeah." Jack shakes his head and waits.

When will I learn that my friends can read me as plainly as a neon sign? "It's not a big deal, really. My dad keeps pushing me about med school, that's all."

Jack is unmoved. "That's all?"

"Yeah. I don't want to talk about it."

"You're sure?" He's going to drop it. Good.

"Yeah. Sorry again about this afternoon. This thing with Sarah has me turned upside down. I don't know what I was thinking."

He waves off my apology. "No problem. You had a lot going on already, then Dakota ambushed you. I'm thankful you didn't come to my house armed."

"Plus, I brought along Kevin…"

"Who would have taekwondo'd your butt if you had tried anything."

"Indeed."

We chuckle, but the laughter fades quickly.

"Are you sure you don't want to talk?" Jack asks. "About med school or…anything?" He could be a total goofball in high school, with his wacky schemes and dead-on impressions of everyone from local news anchors to fellow students. He became a little more serious when he started dating Lissi our junior year—although you would never call him dull—and we started having deeper conversations. I want the goofball back.

"Look, I know you want to help—"

He lifts his palm. "I get it. But I'm here for you, okay?"

My throat starts to burn, so I focus on the remains of my pie. "Thanks," I whisper, being careful not to look up.

"One favor."

"Sure," I say reluctantly.

"Are you gonna finish that pie?"

*

Jack gave me a ride home, and now I'm back on the front porch where I started. Unfortunately, the Reynoldses' car is gone from the driveway. They would've been an effective buffer between Dad and me. Maybe my folks have gone to bed already and I can sneak up to my room. I look at my phone: 9:45. They're not that old. I take a deep breath and unlock the door.

My foot is poised above the first stair when I hear it.

"Samuel."

I exhale and process. I could keep going like I didn't hear him, but that would only delay the inevitable. I turn and walk into the family room like a condemned prisoner.

Mom is sitting next to Dad. A tag team. Wonderful.

There's no doubt now that I'm a crummy actor, but I give it a shot anyway. "Hey. So, I thought I'd head on up to my room and read for a little while." Read? On Christmas break?

Mom enters the ring first. "We won't keep you long, honey." She's playing the good cop. Or should I stick with the wrestling metaphor? Wrestling cops? I grab hold of the distraction and hang on. If I pay attention to what my parents have to say, this conversation will not end well.

But I can't tune them out completely either, so I return my focus to my mother, who is mid-sentence. "...your father and I thought it best to talk about this now, before things have a chance to fester."

What things? Did I miss even more than I thought? Better stay quiet and let Dad say his part.

I throw him off balance with my silence, so Dad clears his throat to warm up. "How long have you had doubts about your career choice, son? Your mother and I had no idea how you were feeling until tonight."

Do I dance or tell the truth? But the truth's already out there. It's only waiting for clothes.

I can't read my parents' faces. Too many emotions are gliding over them at once. Not that it matters when it comes to what I have to say. "I don't know. I mean, I can't give you a date when things stopped making sense. The beginning of this semester, I guess."

Mom takes over. "Are you worried you aren't up to the work? Or is it a matter of your calling?"

Returning to VT and spending Christmas alone in my apartment sounds awesome right now. No awkward phone call to Sarah, no pain as I work alongside her at pageant rehearsal, no disappointed looks from Mom and Dad. But I'm stuck in the hole I have dug for myself. "I don't know." Come on. I must give my folks a real answer, one that doesn't make me look like a second grader who doesn't want to study for his spelling test. "It is true that freshman year made me wonder if I have what it takes to be a doctor."

Dad nods with satisfaction.

"But I also feel a...restlessness, like I may have overlooked my true calling all this time, that going to med school was a whim that got out of control."

Mom clasps her hands to her face, like she is praying with her eyes open. Dad's mouth is a straight line as he prepares his rebuttal.

"A whim? I never got that impression, Samuel." Dad leans forward as he makes his case. "You seemed quite certain from the spring of your junior year in high school on. I dare say you were at peace with your choice."

"But now—"

"But now you and Sarah have broken up," Dad interrupts.

I wish I had sat down. I'm feeling wobbly. "We're taking a break."

"Okay, you're taking a break, and that has knocked you for a loop. We understand that. But don't let temporary problems lock you into permanent choices. You must know that if you turn your back on med school now—"

"Chances are I'll never become a doctor. Yes." I refuse to add *sir* this time. "Is there anything else?"

Dad looks down and shakes his head.

Mom wraps up, "No, honey. Sleep well. Love you."

"You too." I do love my parents. But I don't like them much right now.

*

I do read when I get to my room. *A Tale of Two Cities*, of all things. There isn't much to choose from on my thinly populated bookshelf: a dictionary, a thesaurus, some graphic novels, a Bible, and *Tale*.

The beginning of the novel is familiar since it was part of English class in the fall of my junior year. I didn't get beyond the first couple of chapters before I wound up in the hospital. Mom and Sarah read aloud to me while I was in the coma, but anything I may have heard is trapped somewhere in my subconscious. I do remember Sarah crying over the ending when I woke up. I wanted to kiss her the instant I saw her beautiful face, but I didn't know how she felt about me.

Kind of like now.

Anyway, I like the book more than I did three years ago. I read enough to see that this Carton guy has some serious issues. He makes me feel a little better about myself. Sarah has never told me much about the plot, but I know *Tale* is one of her favorites.

I'll call her in the morning. I'll come right out and say this break has lasted long enough and that we need to talk. After all, there are two of us in this relationship, right? Where does it say Sarah gets to make all the rules?

*

The next morning, my phone rings. It's a local number, but I don't recognize it. Normally I would let it go to voicemail, but I decide to answer, if only to put off calling Sarah.

"Hi, Sam! It's Pastor Jeff." Our pastor, Kevin's father, is a great guy, but he has this annoying habit of talking at sonic-boom levels all the time. Occupational hazard, I guess.

"Good morning. How are you?" Did Kevin tell him about yesterday? No, he wouldn't do that.

"Fine. Fine." I hear some papers rustling in the background and a woman's voice in the distance. "Tell her I'll call her back. Thanks," Pastor Jeff answers her. "Sorry about that. Little fires pop up out of nowhere this time of year. Do you have a minute?"

"Sure."

"I tried to get in touch with Sarah this morning, but my call went to voicemail, so I thought I'd bother you this time." More papers. "Is it urgent?" Pastor Jeff calls out to Unidentified Woman, probably Mrs. Wilkerson, the church secretary. "Whew. Sorry again. Anyway, we're having a Christmas pageant rehearsal tomorrow night, and I wanted to check and see if you and Sarah can still help manage the chaos."

Talk about chaos. How can I turn him down? "Sure. What time do we need to be there?"

"Great. I hope 6:15 is okay. We've got to grab the little ones between supper and bedtime." Distant voice again. "I'll be right there."

"We'll be there. I'll call Sarah."

"Thanks again, Sam. See you then!"

I tap Sarah's number immediately.

She picks up on the first ring. "Hi, Sam!" Her voice is my favorite music.

"Hi. Pastor Jeff just called me."

"Pageant rehearsal time?"

"Yeah."

"When?"

"Tomorrow at 6:15." Should I? "Want to ride together?"

"Sure."

Does she sound happy? I think so. "Okay. I'll pick you up at 6."

Sarah laughs. "You live two doors down. I'll meet you at your house."

"Yeah, I guess that makes more sense. Okay. See you then!" I sound eager. I don't care.

"Great! Bye!"

"Bye." I hang up and stare at the phone. A simple conversation with Sarah and I'm lighting up inside.

Please let us get back together.

*

I haven't seen Dad much today. He and Mom left for work before I got up and he stayed late. I made supper for Mom and me. Okay, I heated the leftover lasagna and opened a bagged salad, but Mom appreciated it. She appreciates everything.

We eat in virtual silence, our conversation consisting of a how-was-your-day? exchange and my telling her about the pageant rehearsal. I still can't pin down how Mom feels about my vocational indecision, whether she's disappointed or angry or worried. And I don't want to ask.

The only words Dad and I say tonight are "Hello" and "Good night." When he's angry Dad doesn't become volcanic. He grows quiet and cold. I learned a long time ago that the softer my father speaks, the deeper my trouble. Tonight, he was almost whispering.

I go to bed early again and return to *A Tale of Two Cities*. Sarah would be pleased.

I need to figure out whether I really want to go to med school, but Dad is right about one thing: this separation from Sarah has knocked the wind out of me. I can't focus on much of anything until we sort things out. And what if sorting things out means the break becomes a break-up? I can't even imagine it.

I killed time today by finally doing the Christmas shopping I intended to do yesterday. Was it just thirty or so hours ago that I ran into Dakota Crenshaw—or, to put it more accurately, that he ran over me? Even thinking about that awful voice—the one inside me—makes me shiver. I should talk to Pastor Jeff about it sometime before I return to school, maybe after the first of the year. That guy has enough on his plate now.

I'm not sure how I'll get through the day tomorrow. I think it'll be like waiting for Santa combined with waiting for the SAT to begin, a mixture of excitement and dread.

Then it comes to me. Lights.

*

My parents are stunned when I stroll into the kitchen as they finish breakfast. "Good heavens, who is this?" Mom asks, slapping her hands to her cheeks in exaggerated astonishment. "It looks like our son, but it can't be!"

Dad looks up from his paper and almost grins, forgetting for a second that he is furious with me. "No, no. I think that's Sam Russell. Is this one of the signs of the apocalypse?"

"Ha ha," I respond. "You two are hilarious. Actually, I wanted to see you guys before you left for work so I could ask about our Christmas lights."

"Lights?" Dad puts his paper down. "We haven't put lights up in years. Not since you and Megan were kids."

"I know, and it stinks." I wave my arms about. "I mean, every year our house looks like it's owned by Ebenezer Scrooge."

"And your point is?" Mom asks.

"My point is, I have lots of time on my hands and I thought I'd put up some lights today. Are they in those big plastic storage boxes in the garage?" My parents organize their lives in containers. Christmas decorations in giant tubs, seven years' worth of taxes in brown accordion folders, Mom's current quilt squares in a reclaimed apple crate, Dad's fishing lures in a multi-drawer cabinet. They have accumulated a bunch of stuff, but at least they know where it all is.

They look at each other in disbelief, as if I've announced that I intend to clean the gutters, paint the house, and whip up some prime rib, all in one afternoon.

"I suppose so," Dad answers at last. "But I can't attest to their condition. Better test them first."

"And do we have any of those hanging clip things?" Clearly, I'm not fluent in homeowner-ese.

Dad shakes his head. "Hmm, I doubt it. Seems like something that I would have thrown away after a time. But they're cheap, as I recall."

"Okay. I'll head over to Early Hardware this morning." I'm feeling adult-ish all of a sudden, so I pour a cup of coffee instead of going back to bed as planned.

Mom and Dad turn in their chairs to watch me. "Sam?" Mom says.

"Yes, ma'am?" Don't tell me we're going to revisit the topic of med school.

"Thanks, honey."

Whew. "You're welcome."

*

The light strings are packed away in a box labeled—wait for it—*Lights*. Dad, ever the electrician, had carefully wound them around reels to keep them from tangling. Still, only about half of the strings work, leaving me enough to cover only the porch railing. Better than a dark house, but sad nonetheless.

I've been standing here for five minutes or so, trying to decide on my next move. I could go buy more lights, but I don't want to decimate my pizza/movie fund.

Then it hits me.

I haven't thought about pageant rehearsal all morning. Sarah has come to my mind, sure. She loves all things Christmas, so even a scattering of white lights makes me think of her. But I haven't been practicing what I'll say to her tonight, trying to figure out which smooth lines will pry open her heart.

I hope I haven't jinxed myself now that I've realized this. Back to work.

If you're going to do something, do it right. How many times have I heard Dad say that? And he's right. I probably eat too much pizza anyway.

I get in the truck, put it in reverse, and glance at the rearview mirror, only to see Dad pulling in behind me. "Checking up on me?" I ask as he gets out. "I promise I haven't broken anything."

"Good to hear." He opens the back door of his truck. Dad hasn't needed a truck for work for years, but he says it doesn't look right for an electrician to drive a tiny sedan. "Actually,"—he hands me three plastic bags—"things were slow at work today and putting up lights sounded like a better way to spend my time."

"But you hate outdoor lights."

Dad grabs two more bags and closes the door. "I do not hate lights. I procrastinate and whine about putting them up, but I like how they look. Besides, I can't have my son thinking I'm Ebenezer Scrooge." He smiles at me, and for a moment all the career pressure evaporates.

As we empty the bags of light strings and outdoor extension

cords—Dad said it would be bad for business if our house burned down in an electrical fire—the tension between us eases. I'm seven again and getting ready to go fishing with him for the first time, organizing rods and lures and talking about bait.

We don't talk much as we work, speaking only if necessary. I'd planned to cover only the first floor of the house, but Dad bought enough lights to cover the roofline too. We take turns climbing the ladder, attaching clips to the gutters and then the lights.

"Not bad, huh?" Dad slaps me on the back as we step to the sidewalk to admire our work. The lights are washed out by the sunshine, but you can tell they'll look great at night. "I think Clark would like it."

"Only if we cover the roof too," I reply.

Our family watches *National Lampoon's Christmas Vacation* every holiday season. Mom shakes her head and calls it "terribly inappropriate" before taking her place on the sofa and stifling her laughter as Clark Griswold's quest for the perfect Christmas unravels.

Dad figured out how to connect the strings so that the extension cords would be as unobtrusive as possible. Only two cords need to be plugged into the outdoor outlets every night. "That way your mother doesn't have to wander all around the house plugging things in when I work late."

"I could plug them in, you know."

"I suppose you could. I guess I'm used to you and Megan being away." He turns and squeezes my shoulder. "It's good having you home, son."

"It's…" Working alongside Dad has been nice. He has a peaceful, expectant look, with no trace of anger, and my own has subsided. "Good to be home."

CHAPTER 6

BRANDON WILLIAMS WAS the most hyperactive kid I've ever seen. He was in my third-grade class, and he had to visit the school nurse every day at lunch to take his meds. I didn't know anything about hyperactivity, but I knew the drugs were working by the way he acted when he didn't take them. Brandon would swirl around our classroom like an F5 tornado, knocking down everything in his path.

Our teacher, Miss Baker, would gently lead him to a chair and try to help him calm down. One time I stared as he bounced in place, and I thought lightning bolts were about to shoot out from his fingers, his energy levels were so high.

That's me right now.

Putting up the Christmas lights was a great distraction, but for the last couple of hours I've been consumed with thoughts of this pageant rehearsal tonight. You would think Baby Jesus Himself was going to show up.

I ate a bowl of cereal as an early supper, prompting Mom to put the back of her hand to my forehead to check for a fever.

"Leave the boy alone, Kathy," Dad admonished her. "He can eat something later if he wants."

I have tried reading, channel surfing, even video games, but the energy—and the nervous flutter in my belly—won't subside. I would go for a run if I had time.

5:45. Finally.

After I showered, I put on a light blue sweater and my best blue jeans. Sarah likes it when I wear blue. Dad is right. I do need a haircut, but it's too late to worry about that now.

"See you later," I call from the front door, like I'm heading out to just another date with Sarah. This isn't a date, of course, but I don't know what else to call it. A meeting? A reckoning?

I open the door as Sarah starts up our walk. The tiny white lights cast a glow on her face. She looks like an angel. "Hi, Red." I hide behind my old nickname for her. I'm such a good actor, after all.

"You haven't called me that in a while." Sarah smiles as I meet her at the foot of our steps. "I think I've missed it." She steps back to look at our house. "Nice lights."

We don't talk much on the drive to the church, just acquaintance-level chit-chat. The odds of a white Christmas, shopping for gifts, the health of our families. I glance over at her as she stares out the window at decorated houses, hoping she won't notice.

Gavin was right. This was a horrible idea. I am in the desert, with a glass of water two feet away. I am starving, inches away from a feast. *Help me.*

I focus on my breathing, on the Christmas decorations, on whether some kid will bite me tonight.

"You okay?" Sarah looks like she is going to check me for fever any second.

I keep my eyes on the road. "Yeah. Wondering how this rehearsal will go."

In my peripheral vision, I see her nodding. I don't dare look at her directly. Knowing her and the way she knows me, I'm certain she's unconvinced.

"Uh-huh. Want to hear something weird?"

Sure. Anything weird or odd or even horrifying. "What?"

"Every time I work with little kids, I'm terrified they're going to puke on me. Isn't that crazy?"

"I don't think so, considering I was thinking one of them will bite me. Are we going to be stage managers or zookeepers?"

"Maybe both," Sarah answers.

I stop at a red light and feel her looking at me. I take a chance and return her gaze. I'm surprised to feel my thirst and hunger easing—for now—and I relax into Sarah's company. Have I mentioned how much I've missed her?

When we walk into the sanctuary, Pastor Jeff greets us with an enthusiasm usually reserved for firefighters and lifeguards. "Sarah! Sam! So glad you can help us out!"

The scene before us resembles a prison riot without the shivs. One boy chasing another with his shepherd's crook. Another sitting on the steps of the platform digging so far into his nose I can't see his knuckle. A little girl crying at the end of a pew with two others patting her shoulder as a third, the likely perpetrator, watches the drama with her arms crossed. Two girls fighting over the doll standing in for Baby Jesus. Oh no. It's that antique thing Miss Lucille insists on the church using every year.

And right in the middle of it all is the helpless warden, Jane Singleton. She might have been a great ringmaster once upon a time, but she must be 108 now and coming undone. Her heart might give out mid-sentence. "Now, children. Children!" Even her exclamation is a wisp of smoke, carried away in the chaos.

"Listen up!" Pastor Jeff cranks it up to full volume, and the kids freeze. "This is Miss Sarah and Mr. Sam."

I'm a *Mr.* now? Nice.

"They're here to help out, and I want you to listen to them as well as you listen to me." He doesn't include Miss Jane. "Understood?"

"Yes, Pastor Jeff," a few kids answer, and they all nod obediently.

Sarah and I look at each other wide-eyed and open-mouthed. We will be lucky if the worst we have to deal with is puking or biting. I lean over. Her hair smells like coconut mixed with mint. "I'll distract Pastor Jeff so you can make a run for it," I whisper.

"No. We're in this together." Sarah beams at me, and it's like this break never happened.

I'm still drinking in the moment when I realize Pastor Jeff is talking to us. "So, I can't stay tonight, but I hope to make it for the next rehearsal. Thanks a bunch!" And with that the minister disappears through the door. Smart guy.

Sarah exhales. "Well. Have any inspirational quotes from one of your movies?"

"I've got nothing."

We watch Miss Jane for a moment, her thin, veiny arms waving about like a passenger from the *Titanic*. A passenger surrounded by pint-size sharks who smell blood in the water.

Sarah holds out her hand to me. "For Miss Jane."

I take it and feel a familiar zing. "For Miss Jane."

Sarah and I greet Miss Jane, who seems surprised to see us. She was probably underwater when Pastor Jeff announced our arrival. Then we split up to quell the riot.

Sarah tackles the junior soap opera while I stop the crazed shepherd from threatening the other kids with his hook. Then I toss a tissue to the nose picker as I head over to rescue the Jesus doll from the warring parties.

The taller girl—I think her name is Addie Baldwin—pleads her case first. "It's mine! I'm Mary, so I'm the one who gets to hold the baby."

The other girl—she must be a Yoder since she's got that super-blonde hair—doesn't let that stand. "It is not yours. It belongs to Miss Lucille. And Jesus belongs to everybody. Doesn't He, Mr. Sam?"

I have to give her points for a creative argument. I kneel, and as the two girls turn to me, I gently remove the doll from their hands. Smooth. I look at the theologian. "Actually, uh..."

"Bethany."

"Of course, Bethany. Actually, we belong to Jesus."

"Yeah, we belong to Jesus, Bethany," Addie repeats, with "Nah, nah, nah, nah, nah" implied.

I try to channel Dad. "Addie," I say in the deepest, softest voice I can muster, "would Jesus like that attitude?"

The voice works. "No, sir," she says, looking down.

Please don't cry. Please.

I notice Bethany is two seconds away from a victory lap. "Bethany, is Addie playing Mary?"

"Yes, sir."

"So, there's no need for you to hold the doll, right?"

Now Bethany looks down. No tears from Addie so far. I hope Bethany can hold it together too.

"Okay, girls, say you're sorry to each other." I'm going deep into grown-up territory now.

Addie and Bethany exchange a half-hearted *sorry* and return to their places on the platform.

Standing, I almost bump into Sarah.

"That, Mr. Russell, was very impressive."

"Aw, shucks, ma'am. It was nothin'."

Sarah places her hand on my arm. "No, really, you were great. You'll be a wonderful dad one day."

"Uh, thanks, Sarah—"

She's gone before I can finish the sentence, off lining up angels stage left.

"Sam! The shepherds!" I'm jerked out of a daydream by Sarah's voice and the sight of two shepherds dueling with their crooks. Considering the crooks are old wooden canes donated by a local nursing home, we're talking some serious put-your-eye-out potential.

"Hey! Stop!" I zoom over to them like a vampire on speed.

The boys—I would guess they're six or seven—stop and look at me like I am a vampire. I might be pretty good at this.

"Drop those right now and come here." I try on Dad again. "What's your name?" I ask the taller one, a bit of a chunk who I could see turning into a defensive lineman one day.

"Aiden," he answers in an almost whisper.

"And you?" I ask the shorter one, a little guy with glasses that overwhelm his thin face.

"Berkeley, sir." His voice is strong and confident.

"Would you rather be shepherds or angels?"

The boys give each other a where's-he-going-with-this? look.

"Because if you don't stop goofing off with these crooks, I have some beautiful white shiny robes that are just your size."

Aiden and Berkeley couldn't appear more horrified if I were a creature of the night. "No, Mr. Sam. I don't want to be no angel," Aiden says.

Berkeley nods. "That's right. Please don't make us angels. We won't play with our sticks anymore, will we, Aiden?"

Aiden agrees vigorously.

I stare at them like I'm trying to make up my mind. "Well, all right. I'll give you one more chance. Just one. If you fight again…" I point at the angel robes lying across a nearby pew. I feel like the title character in *The Godfather*.

I swear Aiden and Berkeley shiver. I don't know if God appreciates my tactics, especially in His house, but at least no one will lose an eye on my watch.

Sarah appears next to me. I think she's become a ninja since we separated. "Looks like somebody's on a roll."

"Beginner's luck. How are the angels?"

Sarah seesaws her hands. "Touch and go. As long as they're angelic by showtime, right?"

"Yeah, right." I wish I had an excuse to whisper to her again, so I could breathe in her scent. I'm trying to think of one when Miss Jane shuffles up to us.

"Sarah, Sam," she warbles. "Could you go to the supply room and get a few things?"

"Yes, ma'am," Sarah answers. "What do you need?"

"Here's a list I made earlier today." She hands Sarah a piece of paper covered with what appear to be hieroglyphs. Or maybe Chinese characters.

Sarah's unfazed. "We'll be right back."

I glance over my shoulder at the rioters, quiet for now. "Do you think Miss Jane will be all right?"

Sarah follows my gaze. "Better make this quick."

Our church's supply room is more like a walk-in closet. A walk-in closet owned by a chronic hoarder with no organizational skills. The sooner we can complete this mission, the better.

Sarah studies the list. "First we need the manger."

"You can actually read that?" Hebrew. It is definitely Hebrew.

"It's a gift." She laughs. "From years of reading my mother's shopping lists."

In a land of glitter and tiny pom poms, the wooden crib is easy to spot. "Next?"

"Any bales of hay over there?"

"You have got to be kidding."

"No, really. It says 'hay bale' right here. See?" Sarah points to some words.

"Sorry, but that's 'fay bade.'"

Sarah punches me in the shoulder as she tries to suppress a giggle. "Never mind."

"Don't have either one. Next?"

"Okay, Mr. Russell, how about little white Christmas lights?"

I see bins marked *Puzzles, Easter,* and *Ornaments.* There are a thousand tiny drawers with labels like *Brads, Sequins,* and *Glue Sticks.* However, the contents of said bins and drawers are scattered around the room. I guess people look for what they need, grab it, and never look back. "Where do I start?" I ask, slowly turning around the room.

Sarah puts her hands on her hips. "I have no idea. How about you start in this corner and I'll start in this one and we'll work our way around?"

"Deal."

We search in silence, and I'm so intent on finding those lights—is Miss Jane planning on stringing them around the stable or what? — that I'm startled when Sarah clears her throat.

"Find them?" I hope so. I think I'm developing claustrophobia. "No. I, uh…"

The hesitation in Sarah's voice redirects me completely. When I turn around, she's sitting cross-legged on the floor, twirling a few strands of that gorgeous hair. She only does that when she's nervous.

"You okay?"

Sarah appears to study the metal cabinet marked *Sunday School*, and replies without looking at me. "Yes. It's just that…"

Is she crying? "Sarah?"

When she looks at me, her eyes are filling with tears. I get up and sit beside her. I want to put my arms around her but don't know if I should.

"I, uh, wanted to thank you for your letter. It meant a lot to me." She turns her face up to me, and I must draw on every ounce of will-power I have—or ever will have—to stop myself from kissing her.

"I meant it, you know. Every word."

Sarah nods, struggling for composure. "I know."

"We have to talk, Red. Please."

She takes a deep breath and lets it out slowly. "You're right. I know you're right. But not here." She takes my hand and places it on her cheek. I think my heart is going to stop. "Come to my house tomor-row morning. My folks will be out Christmas shopping."

I finally manage to say, "Okay," before returning to my corner. I can't take her nearness for another minute.

"Sam?"

"Yeah, tomorrow morning. Text me the time." Don't look at her. Don't look at her. Don't look at her. I open a box labeled *Miscellaneous* and stare into it.

I hear Sarah rummaging around through the church debris. Then, "Found them!"

*

I don't know what Sarah told her family about our break, but when her dad answers the door, I can see he's arrived at his own conclusions.

"Sam," he says, his mouth a straight line and his jaw tight. Policemen greet criminals with more warmth. Daniel Winston is not a small man—6'2", I'd guess—and in pretty good shape for a guy his age. Truth is, I find him intimidating under the best of circumstances.

"Mr. Winston."

"Can I help you?"

I pull my hands out of my pockets so I don't look like a guilty five-year-old. "I'm here to see Sarah."

He starts to close the door. "I don't think…"

Sarah pulls the door open. "I invited him, Daddy." She smiles at me, and I pray for the millionth time that our break is over. "Come on in, Sam."

Mr. Winston moves out of the way just enough to let me pass. "Your mother and I can put off our shopping trip, honey." He talks to her but looks at me.

"Don't be silly." She takes my hand and leads me into their family room. I'm beginning to remember how breathtaking holding her hand can be. "You guys hunt for bargains. We'll be fine."

"All right." Mr. Winston reluctantly adds, "Call us if you need us."

Sarah and I sit on the sofa, not speaking until we see the Winstons' SUV pull out of the driveway.

I let out an exaggerated sigh. "So, exactly what does your father think about our break? I get the impression he believes I have besmirched the lady's honor."

Sarah grabs both my hands. "Your swashbuckling speech is my favorite."

A jolt of happiness passes through me. For years I would try to talk like the characters in whatever movie genre had me captivated at the time: Westerns, swordplay adventures, old gangster movies. But only with Sarah.

"All I told Mama and Daddy is that you and I decided to take a little break to think about our future. But Daddy is convinced you did something. You know how fathers are."

The happiness disappears like mist in the morning. "But we didn't decide, did we, Red? You did."

Sarah's face collapses as my words hit their mark. "You're right," she says softly, like all her energy has been drained away. She runs her fingers down my cheek, and familiar feelings re-emerge in a shiver. "Oh, Sam. I don't know where to start."

I cannot avoid the cliché. "How about the beginning? We've got to start talking. Please."

"Yeah, I know. But I need to ask you a question first."

"Sure."

"Have you dated much since we separated?"

I drop Sarah's hand and pull away from her. Surely she wasn't asking— "Have I what?"

"Have you dated much?" she asks again, in an almost whisper this time.

I stand, like that will give me the perspective to see where this is going. "You could have asked if I've dated at all and you'd get the same answer: No. What are you saying?" The logical follow-up cuts into me immediately. "Are you seeing someone?"

Sarah walks up to me, so close I think she can hear the hammer of my heartbeat. "No." She shakes her head. "Never. I can't imagine loving any man but you. But I thought…" She looks away, like she's trying to figure something out.

I gently turn her face back to me. "What did you think? What could you have possibly been thinking?"

A tear runs down her cheek. "I thought maybe this break would give you the chance to find someone better. Someone who's not as screwed up as I am."

Sweet Jesus. I wrap my arms around Sarah, and she returns my embrace. We stand there for a long time, melting into each other, soaking in each other's warmth.

When we finally part, I realize I've been crying too. I brush the tears from my face, then hers. "You're the most incredible woman—no, the most incredible *person*—I've ever known. How could you think you're screwed up?"

She leans her head into my chest. "But I am. Can't you see it?" Sarah looks back up at me. "Smiley...I'm afraid...he left some of his evil behind...in me."

No. *Dear God, no.*

CHAPTER 7

SMILEY WAS THE name Sarah gave John Perkins, the man who kid-napped her and another local girl, Emilia Gonzales, three years ago. He abducted Sarah after drugging her in her own front yard. I saw the whole thing and tried to stop him, and I'll never forget how angry and scared and powerless I felt as I tried to free her from his trunk. Then he backed into me, causing me to hit my head on the curb. Mrs. Winston found me when she came home from work.

Sarah told me everything about her ordeal in tiny installments, each memory a shard of glass. I didn't want her to relive that horror, but she said she needed me to know the whole story. "Sharing this with you makes it easier to carry somehow," she'd murmured through her tears.

Sarah decided to call Perkins "Smiley" because she thought he had a nice smile the first time she saw him. He had posed as a state trooper to draw her close. Later, when she awakened in his farmhouse, she saw that smile for what it really was: the mask of a monster.

Sarah and Emilia finally managed to escape and wandered all night in the woods before being rescued by an old man named Caleb Ryker. Mr. Ryker had a cabin nearby and was driving the girls back to town when Perkins found them. He ran Mr. Ryker's truck off the road and recaptured the girls, beating the old man after pulling him from the wreckage. The autopsy said Caleb Ryker died of a heart attack, but Perkins killed him.

Perkins forced Sarah to drive away, saying he planned to take them to his childhood home in Pennsylvania. "I knew without a doubt he planned to kill us," Sarah said. "And I was praying and praying and suddenly I knew what I had to do. It was like I was getting instructions whispered in my ear."

Sarah took the exit to a weigh station off I-81, catching the attention of a state trooper. She maneuvered Perkins's truck back and forth and finally rammed it into a semi heading back out onto the highway. Trooper Hathaway said trained law enforcement couldn't have driven any better.

In the chaos that followed, Perkins killed himself, but not before shooting and seriously wounding Emilia. Sarah emerged with a concussion and some bruises and recovered completely in a short time. Physically, anyway. She spent some time with a local counselor, working through everything that had happened to her. "Lindsay Donaldson led me out of the forest," is how she put it.

I had believed John Perkins was truly dead and gone, his shadow removed from our lives. Until now.

Maybe a barrage of words would show Sarah how wrong she is. Surely, I can convince her that she is really and truly good, with none of that monster occupying even a molecule's worth of space of her heart.

Then I hear it. *Still.*

I take Sarah's hands and lead her back to the sofa. "Talk to me."

She covers her face and shakes her head. "I can't."

I take her hands again. "Yes, you can."

She takes a deep breath and studies the rug at our feet. "Smiley never went away. When I say or think crazy things, I feel his darkness growing inside me."

I start to protest but manage to keep my mouth shut. I wait.

"I started to see it after we got to Tech. I started thinking awful things." Sarah keeps her focus on the floor, like her words are bubbling up from there. "Like how good it was to be away from my parents and their constant hovering. And how good it felt to be away from our high school friends—our friends, for heaven's sake—and the drama between Lissi and Jack and Kevin's pining for Rebecca over lunch every day but never speaking up for himself. I can't tell you how many times I wanted to reach over and shake some sense into him."

I bite my lip to keep from jumping in as Sarah builds up speed. "And how I never wanted to go home for a visit. I only wanted to be with you."

"But..." dribbles out before I can stop it.

Sarah shakes her head. "No. You don't get it. I mean, I wanted to be *with* you. I didn't want to wait anymore. I wanted you—I want you—so much."

"But all that's normal, Red. Every bit of it. And I want you too."

Sarah's tears are becoming sobs, muffling her voice. "But you have no idea how dark..." Her words come out in hiccups. "How dark I've become. I started thinking that maybe everything we've been taught is wrong, that maybe all the rules are stupid. That, that..." She runs her hands through her hair like she is about to pull it out. "That maybe God isn't real. Even after all He's done for me."

Oh.

I believed in God before Sarah was taken, but He became real to me while I was in the coma. When Jesus visited me in that in-between place, He appeared as a wolf with golden eyes and a British accent. He talked to me and gave me peace.

You could dismiss all that as a bunch of comatose brain cells going haywire except for this: Jesus visited Sarah too. Same wolf, same British accent. He came to her in her dreams during and after her ordeal.

And to top it all off, Sarah and Emilia experienced a straight-up miracle during their captivity. Back then Emilia was new to the U.S., having moved from Guatemala only a couple of months earlier. Her

English was broken at best. But she and Sarah were able to communicate freely even though neither could speak the language of the other. It still boggles me when I think about it.

So, how can Sarah question God's existence? Like she said, He has done so much for her, miracles even. I feel myself coiling up inside, ready to go on offense to defend God's honor.

Then the memory of a rumbling voice hits me like a blow to the head. It came not from Smiley or Dakota but from me. That voice slithered inside me like a snake, and only the name of Jesus made it stop. How dare I judge Sarah?

But what should I do? I scrounge around for the right response, but I am as dumb as a rock.

"Then I freaked out when you asked me to marry you. Even I didn't understand my reaction at first, then I got it. I knew."

I want Sarah to see herself through my eyes. I want to hold her and block the evil torturing her, even absorb its attacks myself. I want to do something, anything, to ease her pain. But all I can do is ask, "What did you know?"

Sarah slides to the floor, pulls up her knees to her chest, and begins to rock slowly, back and forth, back and forth. "That I wasn't crazy that night."

I strain to hear her.

"I had been pretending that I could have a life with you. But seeing the love in your eyes, I realized that I couldn't drag you down with me. I had to push you away in order to save you."

I move to the floor. *I don't know what to do. I don't know what to do. Please, show me what to do.* I encircle her in my arms and listen for an answer, helpless in the face of her pain. When I was a kid, I saw a butterfly trapped in a huge spider's web, flapping and flapping with no hope of escape. I wanted to knock the web down with a stick, but Dad stopped me. He said that was nature's way.

I thought I had been suffering since Sarah and I separated, but nothing prepared me for this. Seeing her trapped, hopelessness radiating from her, is unlike any torment I have ever known. And what is Sarah enduring? It must be hell itself.

Oh, God, help her. Please make it stop.

"The Lord is my shepherd; I shall not want," I hear myself say. I haven't recited Bible verses, much less something from the old King James Version, in years, but the words keep coming, pouring from me without any conscious effort. "He maketh me to lie down in green pastures: he leadeth me beside the still waters. He restoreth my soul: he leadeth me in the paths of righteousness for his name's sake."

Sarah stops rocking, and her body slowly uncurls as she leans into me.

"Yea, though I walk through the valley of the shadow of death, I will fear no evil: for thou art with me; thy rod and thy staff they comfort me. Thou preparest a table before me in the presence of mine enemies: thou anointest my head with oil; my cup runneth over."

Sarah's voice trembles as she finishes Psalm 23 with me. "Surely goodness and mercy shall follow me all the days of my life: and I will dwell in the house of the Lord for ever." She nestles into my shoulder. "Do you believe it, Sam? Do you really believe it?"

"I do," I whisper. "God is stronger than Smiley. He delivered you from evil then, and He will do it now. God will never abandon you. Never."

"Never," she repeats.

I nod, unable to respond. She faces me and combs my unruly hair with her fingers. "I love you, Sam. With every beat of my heart."

"And I love you," I manage to say before she kisses me.

Her kiss is tentative and tender, a first kiss. My desire for Sarah races through me, a drug traveling through my veins, burning away reason. It is my love for her, a river deep and cool, that pulls me back.

Silence falls over us. The house is as quiet as my heart. All the loneliness, all the turbulent back-and-forth of anger, guilt, and regret have retreated. At this moment I am at peace.

But not Sarah.

"Baby." Around a year ago I started calling Sarah that when I feel especially close to her, like we're one person occupying two bodies.

"What?" She sounds tired, like she has gone ten rounds with a dozen Dakota Crenshaws.

"I think you should see Ms. Donaldson again."

That wakes her up. Sarah moves away from me, and I see a familiar spark in her eyes. "But why? I feel better than I have in…well, I can't remember how long, thanks to you."

I hold up my hands to deflect any credit. "No, I delivered a message, that's all."

"Then you were the perfect messenger." Sarah smiles. "But, like I said, I feel fine now."

"Sarah…"

She told me that she lived in a state of denial for a while after the kidnapping, telling everybody she felt *fine*. Even now we use that word as code for *not fine*. Sarah looks like a kid caught with a stolen candy bar. "But I do feel…better."

I reach out and run my hands through her red curls. "And I'm glad. But I think the psalm was first aid, and you need…"

"A heart transplant?"

I almost smile at this flash of Sarah's temper. It is so much better than the raw pain I witnessed minutes ago. "No. A hip replacement, perhaps."

"A hip replacement?" She laughs. "What am I, sixty-five?"

"Come on. You know analogies aren't my strong suit."

"A hip replacement," she repeats. Her giggles ring through the house, taking me with them. "Okay. I'll call tomorrow. Satisfied?"

"Yes, ma'am."

She settles back into my arms. "Okay, then. I'll have to tell my parents, of course, and I only hope that Daddy…"

"Doesn't blame me," I finish.

Sarah nods. "Uh-huh. He is a good guy, but what is it about fathers and daughters? He acts like you're Mickey Corleone or something."

Guys don't giggle, but I almost do. "Michael Corleone, from *The Godfather* movies, only a series of cinematic masterpieces."

"Mickey, Michael, whatever." I often wonder if Sarah deliberately butchers movie titles and character names just to get to me. "You know what I mean."

"Yeah, but you still need to see Ms. Donaldson. Even if it does lead to your dad leaving a horse's head in my bed."

"A what?"

"Never mind."

Sarah and I didn't move from the floor until we heard the whir of the garage-door opener. We talked a little about small things: movies and football and Christmas cookies. Mostly we just held each other until even our breathing was in sync.

My daydreams about our reunion began with a succession of passionate kisses and ended with our making love. But considering what Sarah's been through, sitting together on a wooden floor, sandwiched between a sofa and a coffee table, was the best possible ending.

*

I plan to pick up Sarah in about an hour for dinner. When I told Mom, she gave me a hug and patted me on the back. "You fixed it!"

Then why do I feel like I haven't?

I guess I've spent so much time wandering around inside my head that I don't know how to stop. Sarah loves me. I need to grab hold of that truth and move on.

We're going to Bailey's, Early's best restaurant. Not that there's a lot of competition, but the food there is excellent, especially the mozzarella sticks. I have a thing for cheese.

I'm gobbling up my third stick when I realize Sarah's not eating. She's staring at me, chin in hand. "Sorry," I say as I wipe the marinara sauce from my mouth. "I didn't eat much today, but that's no excuse for being a greedy pig." I pick up the basket of fried deliciousness and extend it to her. "Would the lady like a mozzarella stick?"

Sarah smiles slightly and shakes her head. "No, sir. I was just thinking."

My appetite disappears. "About what?"

"The fact that you've barely spoken since you picked me up. What's going on?"

I grab her hand. "Nothing. I guess I'm still adjusting to the awesomeness of being able to hold your hand and talk to you again." Yeah, that must be it.

Sarah strokes my hand, studying each finger, and I'm taken back to that terrible afternoon at the memorial at VT. "I think there's more," she says at last, turning her attention back to my eyes, as if she will find an answer there. "To use your words, talk to me."

"Oh, it's nothing." I don't know why I bother to deflect. I've never been able to hide anything from this woman.

Sarah takes away her hand and folds her arms.

I would love to talk to Sarah. Every day of our separation, I've compiled mental lists of things I would like to share with her. But now that she's across the table from me, I don't know what to say. I am all tangled up inside and don't know why. "I'm okay. Don't worry about me." That is not a lie depending on your definition of *okay*.

She takes my hand again with both of hers. "That's like telling me not to breathe."

Maybe a little truth. "It's, uh, it's been hard, but you know that from my letter."

"But there's more."

Just how much quicksand should we try to cover in one day? "I'm okay, really."

Sarah stares at me, and I'm certain she's rifling through the file cabinet in my brain, looking for the thing or things that are not okay. I feel exposed, like those dreams where you accidentally run outside in your underwear. I raise my hand for the check. "Let's get out of here."

I drive to an abandoned apple orchard, long neglected and likely to be wiped away for a housing development. Once my truck is backed between the trees, I cut the lights. It's a moonless night, so we're invisible, wrapped in a cocoon of darkness and silence.

I never took the blanket and pillows out of my truck, so we bundle up and sit in the truck bed. Just like our last date back in October, when everything started to go wrong.

Sarah doesn't even pretend to look for the constellations this time. Instead she wraps her arms around me and holds me tight. "Talk to me, Sam," she whispers, her breath warm on my neck.

My eyes are still adjusting to the darkness, and I hope Sarah's are too. I can't hide when she looks in my eyes. "I'll be fine."

"*Fine?* Samuel Russell, you didn't just say…"

I don't need to see Sarah's irritation. I can feel it. "Okay, okay. You're right. But do we want to do this now?"

She moves so her face is inches from mine. "I made this mess by keeping things from you. Please, talk to me."

I stare at the skeletons of the apple trees around us, their gnarled limbs reaching up for rescue.

Sarah gently turns my face back to hers. "Tell me about the separation." Lindsay Donaldson 2.0.

"It hurt like hell." I'm surprised by the anger in my voice. "All the time. When I wasn't trying to figure out how I'd screwed up, I was trying to figure out how to make things right again. I thought everything was good until the moment it fell apart. I lost my best friend and the woman I love in the time it took you to say we should take a break."

Sarah backs away slightly. "I'm so sorry."

"And now we're back together, but are we? Are you going to draw me close just to cut out my heart again?"

I start to rise, but Sarah straddles my legs and pushes me back down. "No," she says in a voice that is both firm and thick with tears. "No. We're going to deal with this right now."

I try to turn away again, but Sarah holds my face with her hands. "You have every right to be angry. I thought I was doing the right thing, but I was a fool. If I had shared what was happening, we could have gotten through it together. Instead, I believed a bunch of lies." She leans in until our foreheads are touching. "I am sorry. I am *so* sorry. Please forgive me. Please, Sam."

My anger breaks into tiny pieces. "Only if you'll forgive me for being such a jerk at the diner that day. If I had listened to you, really listened…" The movie plays and I see myself driving off, filled with pain and fury.

"It might not have made a difference. I was so confused."

"But no more secrets, right?"

"No more secrets."

I pull Sarah in for a kiss, a lover's kiss, deep and lingering. *God, I need her more than air. Please keep us together.*

*

As I unlock the front door to my house, I feel like the title character in *Rocky* at the end of his fight—spent and exhilarated. I think I'll go to bed and sleep until lunchtime tomorrow.

"Sam?"

Not. Again.

Dad's in his recliner with some book about World War II on his lap. I can't remember the last time I saw him read anything other than military history.

Might as well get this over with. "Sir?"

"You and Sarah working things out?"

Is this a strategy he's borrowed from some long-dead general? If so, I'm not up to analyzing it, not tonight. "We're getting there."

Dad walks over to me and puts his hand on my shoulder. "Good. I'm happy for you, son. I really am." He smiles at me, and I think I feel something shift between us, like he's seeing me as I am and not as the little boy he coached in T-ball.

"Thanks, Dad. That means a lot."

He squeezes my shoulder and slaps me on the back, signaling that the moment is complete. "See you in the morning."

"Or afternoon."

As I trudge up the stairs, it hits me. Now that Sarah and I are back together, I must turn my attention back to what I plan to do for the rest of my life. The med-school question drops on me like an anvil.

I might sleep in until next year.

CHAPTER 8

As my eyes flicker open—at the semi-respectable time of 9 a.m.—med school is not the first thing on my mind. Sarah is. I press my fingers to my mouth as I remember our kisses yesterday. I can almost feel the velvet of her lips and taste her peppermint sweetness.

I realize I never thanked God for bringing the separation to an end. Sitting up I take my head in my hands and pray. *Thank You that we are together again. Please help Sarah recover.*

"Because if she doesn't..." I whisper.

I'm immediately filled with shame. *I'm sorry, God. Please help Sarah, no matter what that means for me.*

Better.

I decide to check in with Gavin. I'll reach out to a friend while putting off further consideration of my career dilemma. Win-win. *What's up?* I text. *Want to talk?*

Gavin replies immediately. *OK. Busy with family. Tonight?*

I answer with a thumbs-up emoji. Sarah's family goes to Lancaster, Pennsylvania, every year to see a big Christmas pageant with live animals and professional actors, not a bunch of kids with runny noses. They probably left thirty minutes ago.

I did not try to hide my pout when Sarah told me last night. "I don't want to go, but I have to," she explained. "It's a tradition."

I backed off from my spoiled-child reaction when I heard the stress in her voice. "No, I get it. I'm just a big baby."

Sarah squeezed me tight. "But you're *my* big baby."

I'm still smiling as I wash my face. I can make it through today without seeing Sarah, because I know I'll see her tomorrow. And the day after that. And the day after that.

The break is over.

*

I'm cleaning up after supper when Gavin calls.

"Go on," Dad says as he takes the dishcloth from me. "I can finish up." He hasn't mentioned med school for a couple of days. I don't know what's up, but as Uncle Rob says, you don't look a gift horse in the mouth.

I answer the phone as I head up to my room. "Hi! How's it going?"

"Okay." Gavin's voice sounds about three rungs below okay. "Trying to stay busy with Christmas stuff. How are you?"

I realize too late that this was a terrible idea. "Uh, all right. Christmas stuff too." Maybe Gavin is too miserable to even ask about Sarah.

Nope.

"Is working with Sarah on that church thing going okay? You're not falling apart again, are you?"

Hardly. "Uh, no." I would like to lie for Gavin's sake, but that would be stupid as well as wrong. "Actually, Sarah and I have been talking and I think we're going to work things out." There. I plunged in the knife, but I tried not to twist it.

"Wow! That's great, man!" The despair in Gavin's voice falls away. "That's the best news I've heard in a long time. You two belong together."

I'm stunned. My misery usually seeks company. "Thanks so much. I'm just sorry, you know..."

"Yeah, I know. But I have been thinking about it, and what

Kirsten and I had…it wasn't love. I can see that now. For me, but never for her."

This isn't the conversation I expected. Gavin and I have never been close. But I have learned that when love rips you open, it's hard to hide the bleeding. "Don't put yourself down." What else can I say? "The right one's out there."

Gavin laughs softly. "Maybe, but I don't feel like looking right now. But I'm glad you called 'cause I've got a question."

"Shoot."

"So, after we, you know, uh, prayed, I remembered a Bible my grandma gave me when I was like ten, and I thought maybe I should read it. But I started at the beginning, you know, like any other book, and felt like I was in over my head."

This ground is more familiar. I channel every Sunday school class I have attended since preschool. "Start with the four Gospels, the first four books of the New Testament: Matthew, Mark, Luke, and John. Each book gives you a little different take on Jesus and His ministry. What translation do you have?"

"Translation?"

"Yeah, look at the spine of your Bible and tell me what letters are stamped there."

I hear Gavin moving things around. "Okay. KJV. What does that mean?"

"King James Version. In 1604, King James I of England commissioned a more readable translation of the Bible. All good, but we don't talk that way anymore."

"Oh."

"Tell you what, I'll send you a more modern translation. I'll get it in the mail tomorrow."

"You don't have to—"

"Really, it's no problem. It seems like my parents and/or grandparents give me a new Bible at least once a year. I guess they're hoping it will all sink in one day."

"Thanks, Sam."

"No prob."

"Got any big envelopes or boxes?" I call out when I return downstairs.

"What for?" Mom answers from the family room.

"I want to send this to Gavin." Mom and Dad give me the same look Sarah's dog, Quigley, has when I howl at him. Yeah, I am strange.

"You're sending him a Bible?" Dad asks.

"The one Uncle Peter and Aunt Jackie gave you when you graduated from high school?" Mom adds. Another of her superpowers: remembering every gift everybody has ever given to anyone in her family. Heaven help you if you ever try to get rid of one at a garage sale. Ask Aunt Jackie.

"Yes, ma'am. I've already got a couple in this translation, and all Gavin has is a KJV."

"Might as well be reading Greek," Dad mutters as he returns to his newspaper.

Mom is horrified. "Chad! The King James is beautiful, especially Psalms."

"I'll give you that," Dad concedes from behind the newsprint. "But the rest is too fancy for a good old boy like me."

I try to break into the discussion. "So, about that box..."

Mom walks over to the bookshelves. "Well, for one thing, you're not going to give away a special keepsake. One day you'll look back and treasure the inscription."

I want to say, *You mean, Congratulations! Love, Aunt Jackie and Uncle Peter.* Dad knows what I'm thinking as he peeks out from the front page. We've both learned when to be silent. At least sometimes.

"Here you go." Mom hands me a Bible with a paperback cover. "We got this for donating to...somebody. I can't remember who. But it has no sentimental value."

Thank goodness. "Thanks, Mom."

"And we have some large legal-size envelopes in the bottom left drawer of the desk in the office."

"Okay," I say as I turn to leave.

"Sam?"

"Yes, ma'am?"

"We'd like to invite Sarah over for dinner tomorrow. It's been too long since we've seen her."

I know Mom and Sarah bonded while I was in the hospital, so it makes sense that she would like to catch up with her. So why do I feel like Sarah's being invited into an ambush?

*

Mom throws her arms around Sarah before Sarah even takes off her coat. "It is so good to see you," she gushes.

"You too," Sarah answers.

She and Dad do the side-by-side hug. I wonder if they'll ever graduate to the full-on bear variety. Maybe after we're married, since as far as I know Dad only hugs family members that way.

After we're married. The phrase lingers in my mind and spreads to my face.

"Well, don't you look like the cat that swallowed the canary." Mom pats my cheek, and I blush. I swear she can read my thoughts. Then again, I am Plastic Man.

"What a lovely poinsettia!" Mom finally notices the plant Sarah handed me when she came in. "You shouldn't have."

Mom went all out for dinner. Roast chicken, creamy macaroni and cheese containing at least four thousand calories per serving, green beans, candied yams, and homemade dinner rolls. She gives her standard reply when Sarah tries to compliment her. "Nothing gourmet, honey. Only plain country cooking."

Dad gives his standard response and pats Mom's hand. "Just the way I like it." The words don't change, but the feeling behind them never seems old and tired. I hope Sarah and I are like that after twenty-six years.

After dinner, we move into the family room for dessert. It's best to be seated on a chair or sofa when the final phase of carb overload hits. Just in case you keel over.

Mom finishes first since she gave herself only a sliver of carrot cake. "How was your fall semester, Sarah?" she asks between sips of coffee.

Sarah has a little cream cheese frosting at the corner of her mouth. I wish I could kiss it away.

Having read my mind, she dabs at the frosting before answering. "My classes went well, thank you. I think I'm finally getting the hang of this college thing."

I realize that I haven't asked Sarah about school since our reunion. I wonder if studying was a welcome diversion for her too.

"Good for you." Dad enters the conversation, and I go on alert. "Like we have been telling Sam, sometimes it takes a little while to hit your stride and then you take off. Are you still planning on becoming a counselor?"

I haven't told Sarah about the conversations I've had with my folks, so she has no idea she's walking into a minefield.

"Yes, sir. That's my plan, anyway."

"Graduate school too?"

Sarah rocks her head from side to side like she's weighing her options. "I'll have to eventually, if I want to have a practice like Ms. Donaldson. But I think I'll go for my certification so I can work as a school counselor first. I might like that so much I never go out on my own. Plus,"—she tosses me a quick smile—"I don't want to go to school nonstop for years. I'm not as disciplined as Sam."

Thud.

Sarah looks at me, then my parents, with a befuddled look on her face. One of us has to say something, and I guess that would be me.

"Well, uh…" Impressive start. "The thing is, I've been having second thoughts about med school. I'd planned to talk to you about it, but…" I let the sentence hang there, incomplete, as I stare at my father.

"But his nosy father opened up the topic before he had a chance," Dad finishes. "Sorry, buddy."

Yeah, I bet you are.

Mom jumps in. "How is your grandmother, Sarah? I heard she had a bit of a fall not long ago."

Talk turns from Sarah's Nana—who is not about to be stopped by a twisted ankle—to the rest of Sarah's family and on to various Early characters.

Thanks, Mom.

Dad stays quiet, as do I, and after a decent interval, I find an escape hatch. "Didn't you want to go to that late-night sale at Bentley's?" I ask Sarah.

It takes her only a moment to understand. "I almost forgot. Those gloves I want for Mama are going to be half price." She grabs her coat before turning to Mom. "Thank you so much, Mrs. Russell. The dinner was to die for, as usual."

"Thank you, honey, but what will it take for you to call me Kathy?"

Sarah laughs as she arranges her hair over her collar. "Reprogramming." She looks at me. "I know it's more shopping, but you're welcome to come, Sam."

"Sure. Let me get my coat. I'll drive so you won't have to go back to your house for your car."

"Great. Thanks again!" Sarah hugs Mom and Dad and we are out the door.

We climb in the truck, but Sarah grabs my hand before I can turn the ignition. "You've got some explaining to do, mister."

Oh boy. "Mad?"

She shakes her head. "Concerned."

*

"Just coffee for me, thank you." I hand the menu to the server. Her name tag says *Kayla*, a name that doesn't fit her level of, well, maturity. Kayla appears to be about the same age as my grandmothers, which means she should've been in bed for about three hours, not working at Denny's.

"Are you sure? The apple pie's pretty good." Kayla gives me the same indulgent look as Grandma, who justifies every dessert with a listing of its nutritious components: milk, eggs, whole wheat flour…

"No, thank you. Just the coffee."

She accepts defeat graciously. "Decaf?"

"Yes, please."

"And you, honey?" Kayla turns to Sarah. "You're a little bitty thing. Maybe you'd like some pie."

Sarah smiles as she returns her menu. "Just decaf for me too, thank you."

I unwrap my silverware and place the napkin in my lap, as if preparing for a four-course meal.

Sarah studies me. "What's going on?" she finally asks.

I smooth the napkin some more, like I'm paving a sidewalk.

She rests her chin in her hands, and our eyes lock on each other just as Kayla arrives with the coffee.

"Thank you," we say in unison. I get a reprieve as we add cream and sugar.

"Sam?"

"Okay, okay. I'm not sure what I want to do, that's all."

"You don't want to be a doctor anymore?"

There it is, in neon lights. "I don't know. My dad wants me to be a doctor, that's for sure. He doesn't let up about it, night and day." I share the story of the Worst Pep Talk Ever. I can almost picture myself in Sarah's office, surrounded by her degrees and licenses.

"Your dad said our break was a good thing?" Sarah drops her neutral counselor expression.

"Not exactly. He talked about med school for me and graduate school for you and said we need to stay focused on our classes."

She leans across and takes my hands. "That sounds more like your father. I've never gotten the impression he thinks our relationship is a mistake. And he's not a bad guy."

"I know," I admit. "But what about the whole short-term-pain, long-term-gain thing?"

Sarah tenderly strokes each of my fingers. "I think," she says at last, "that we'll always have other stuff tugging at us: school, then jobs, then children—"

"Redheads, I hope."

She blushes. "I'd prefer blondes with blue eyes, actually." Sarah says she loves my blue eyes, but they're blah compared to her green ones.

We stare at each other for a couple of moments, and my love for her washes over me like a flash flood. The miraculous thing is, I feel that same love flowing from her to me. I wish we could wrap this moment around us and live in it forever.

Sarah breaks the spell. "Where was I? You have a gift for derailing me."

"School, jobs, children…"

"Right. Isn't your father really saying that the balancing act begins now, while we're still in school?"

"I suppose. But what about you?"

Sarah tilts her head to the side and creases show up between her eyes. "What do you mean?"

"What if I don't become a doctor? I don't want to let you down…"

Sarah's eyes flash, and she squeezes my hands so hard I stifle an *ouch*. "Samuel Russell, I don't see how someone so smart could say such a stupid thing. Don't you know me?"

"But I…"

Her eyes soften, but her grip doesn't relax. "I love you for who you are, not what you do. As far as careers go, the only thing I want is for you to follow God's plan for your life. I don't need to be Mrs. Dr. Russell to be happy. Understand?"

I can never thank You enough. I find myself getting choked up, but

I subdue my tears this time. I've turned into a marshmallow. Kayla walks up to refill our coffees. "Doing okay?" She offers no commentary beyond a raised eyebrow.

"Yes, ma'am," Sarah pipes up. "I think we will share a piece of that pie."

Kayla smiles like it is Christmas morning. "Coming right up."

"With a scoop of ice cream," Sarah calls after her.

"Of course."

"Pie?" I ask. "You've got to be kidding."

Sarah shakes her head. "Nope. And you can't tell me you don't want some."

"You're right, as usual." We should have sat next to each other so I could pull her close. "It feels good to talk to you about all this, but I'm still so confused. I have no clue what I should do."

"What about Dr. Reynolds? Have you thought about talking to him?"

"Hmm. I never considered it. I'm not sure talking with him would help, but it wouldn't hurt. Unless…"

"Unless?"

I lean against the seat and close my eyes. "Unless he goes straight to my dad. Then all hell might break loose."

*

I hesitate before unlocking our front door. It's 1 a.m.—Sarah and I took our time saying good night—so I should be in the clear. But that's not the way my life works these days. Every encounter with Sarah has involved shoveling some emotional debris, and conversations with my parents tend to revolve around med school. I'm worn out.

I can't sleep out here on the porch, so I open the door. Inside, I stand still for a moment for my eyes to acclimate to the house's total darkness. Good. Mom and Dad will get up in around five hours, so I don't know what I was worried about.

"Samuel."

Really? I turn to the outline of my father standing in the doorway of the kitchen. He must have a secret life as a spy. "Yes, sir?"

Dad moves closer until I can see him clearly by the dim glow of the streetlight. "I couldn't sleep until I made things right." He reaches for the knob on the stairway banister and rubs it like a good luck charm. "I was out of line tonight and I'm sorry."

When Dad looks back at me, I'm surprised by sadness. He's waiting for my response, but I must pull some words together first.

"It's okay, Dad," I start. "No problem."

That would be sufficient for one of my friends. But not Dad. "No, I shouldn't have brought up the topic of careers and put you in an awkward position. Things okay with Sarah?"

Sarah. My mind drifts to our good-nights, and a shot of endorphins hits my system, the feel-good spreading through me. "She understands," I answer with a nod. "She says she'll support whatever choice I make, as long as I'm doing what God wants me to do." I don't add, "Unlike you," but I don't need to.

Dad seals his mouth in a straight line as he fights off his own words. "Good." He slaps me on the back and starts up the stairs. "Better get some sleep. Another early day. 'Night, son."

"'Night, Dad."

Great. Now I'm wide awake.

I flop down on the family room sofa and put my head in my hands. As usual, I have no fancy words to offer God. *Please show me what You want. I'm back with Sarah, but I'm still lost.*

The word boomerangs into my heart, but I have no greater understanding than when I first heard it.

Still.

CHAPTER 9

SHOWTIME AT LAST.

The Christmas pageant is tonight, and I think I'm more nervous than the kids. What if Aiden and Berkeley start a staff battle when they come forward to worship Baby Jesus? What if poor Miss Jane is overcome by the bedlam and succumbs right there in the church aisle? The possibilities are endless.

Sarah gives my shoulder a gentle shake. "Earth to Sam. It's almost time to start." She's cool and unrattled, of course.

"Yeah, I know. That's the problem. You're not worried about how this will go?"

She shakes her head and lights me up with a smile. "Of course not. Know why?"

I stare at her, no answer in my head.

"Because it doesn't matter to the congregation if the angels do nothing but twirl or the wise men spend the whole time picking their noses."

I grimace.

"It comes down to three words: *kids in costumes*. Every adult out there will come up afterward and say this was the best pageant ever. If the children manage to get through half a verse of 'Silent Night,' Miss Jane, you, and I will be covered in compliments for weeks, maybe months."

Ever the pessimist, I add, "We still have to prevent bloodshed."

Sarah offers me a fist bump. "We can do this. Saddle up."

A line from *The Sands of Iwo Jima*? How lucky can one guy get?

*

Sarah was right—the pageant was declared a success. Mr. Wilkins said that when Aiden and Berkeley went forward to worship at the manger, he was as moved as when "Brother Adams sang 'Rock of Ages' at my daddy's funeral." I have never met Brother Adams, although that isn't surprising considering Mr. Wilkins is practically petrified himself. But he's a nice old man, not crotchety at all, so my "Thank you" was sincere. I guess God does work in mysterious ways.

Christmas is only two days away, and it's going to be a much brighter holiday than I had anticipated only a week ago. So here I am at the mall yet again—it's starting to feel like I live here—in search of the perfect gift for Sarah. But nothing is special enough for my girl, so I'm shuffling toward the exit, resigned to defeat.

Then I glance over and see them in a glass case at Brubaker's Jewelers.

A huge display of engagement rings sparkle at me, like they're winking and waving me in. I walk over to check out how much they cost. Whenever I propose, I don't want to present Sarah with a stone so small you need a microscope to see it.

I'm staring at a king's ransom in diamonds, imagining that proposal and wondering if you can put a ring on layaway, when a familiar soft voice startles me from behind.

"May I help you find anything?"

Kirsten.

She's as surprised as me. "Sam! I didn't realize that was you. How are you?"

I shove my hands into my pockets to avoid a hug. "Fine. And you?"

"Good."

With nothing else to say, I start to leave, but Kirsten places her hand lightly on my arm. "How's Gavin?"

How is Gavin? After you broke him apart, I taped him together so he could make it home, and now he's working through the fact that you never loved him. Ever. He's a great guy, and you threw him out of your life like garbage. One day you'll realize you messed up. Big time. That's what I want to say. Instead, I answer, "Okay."

Kirsten nods. Something about her expression makes me think she already regrets the break-up. Too bad. "Are you looking for something for Sarah?"

I must get away from this woman before I say too much. But even as I shake my head, I see it: the gift I've been searching for. It's so perfect I'm even willing to tolerate Kirsten's presence for the time it will take to ring it up.

When she hands me the tiny bag, I smile politely and turn to go.

"Sam?" Kirsten calls after me.

"Yes?"

She stares at me for a beat, like she's looking for something. If it is a single drop of sympathy, she's out of luck. "Merry Christmas," she says at last.

"Same to you," I reply. And good riddance.

My phone jingles as I walk to the truck.

"Hello, gorgeous."

Sarah laughs. "Are you sure your caller ID is working right?"

"Absolutely." I unlock my door, climb in, and lean back in the seat with my eyes closed. I want no distractions from that musical voice. "To be accurate, the ID should read *Most Beautiful Girl in the World*."

"Charmer."

"Truth teller. To what do I owe this genuine pleasure?"

"Well, for one thing, I wanted to hear your voice. We haven't talked in...what, twelve whole hours?"

"Indeed."

"And for another, I wanted to remind you that I'm going to that mini Campbell family reunion tonight at some restaurant in Leesburg."

"Oh, yeah. This makes me sad." That isn't much of an exaggeration.

Sarah sighs. "Me too. What are you doing?"

I dangle the jewelry bag in the air and smile. "Finishing up my Christmas shopping. I'm quite pleased with the gift I found for my lady love."

"Oooh, I like the sound of that." Sarah gets excited about presents. I could wrap up a roll of paper towels for her and she would be thrilled. "Is it something I can wear?"

"No questions and no hints. Hey, you'll never guess who I ran into at the mall."

"Who?"

"Kirsten."

"Gavin's girlfriend?"

I forgot. Sarah doesn't know. "No, not anymore."

"Oh, I'm sorry to hear that. When did they break up?"

"Right before Christmas break." Me and my big mouth. The last thing I want to talk about right now is break-ups.

"How about coming straight home so I can see you, if just for a few minutes? I need at least a portion of my Recommended Daily Allowance of Sam."

I can almost feel her in my arms. "On my way."

My brain starts making a million random connections as I drive home. Like, I wish I were driving home to Sarah, to our home, even if it were a studio apartment with a table, a couple of folding chairs, and an air mattress. That sends me to the Big Question of how we can make it through another two and a half years of seizing moments here and there, wanting and never quite having.

Then I go into a dark place, a place my encounter with Kirsten summoned up. What might have been. What if Sarah and I hadn't gotten back together? And what if Smiley's hold on her never goes away and we break up again, this time for good? How could I live through a single day with no hope of having Sarah in my life?

I glance at my speedometer and see I have inched up to seventy-six miles per hour. "Breathe," I say aloud, easing my foot off the gas. If only getting my brain to slow down were that simple.

I make it home in record time. Mom and Dad are at the office, hosting their annual Christmas party for the company. They used to invite all their employees to a nice restaurant for dinner, but turnout wasn't that great. Now Mom brings in a boatload of calorie-laden treats and everyone receives a small gift with a not-so-small bonus attached.

I drop the bag from Brubaker's on the floor to keep it out of sight, lock the truck, and head to Sarah's house at an almost run.

The bell is still chiming as she opens the door. "Are your folks home?" I ask.

"Yeah."

Breathe. "Oh, okay. Want to come outside?"

"Sure."

While Sarah runs in for her coat, I grab the porch railing and gulp in as much cold air as my lungs can hold.

We start walking when she returns, in silent agreement that it's too chilly to hang out on the porch. "Are you sure you have time for this? Since you've got the big dinner and all?"

She intertwines her gloved fingers with mine. "I'm good. I don't have to spend a lot of time getting ready. It's not like I've got a hot date with my boyfriend."

"Who is this guy? I'll deck him." I shake the fist of my free hand.

She laughs. "I love it when you're silly."

Soon we arrive at our tiny neighborhood park. Sarah and I sit down on the lone bench, and I put my arm around her.

Silence settles over us, and I realize that I'm happy. No, *happy* doesn't cover it. It's a feeling that goes deeper than that, a feeling that I'm right where I'm supposed to be, with the person I was made for. Joy and peace swirled together.

Then I remember.

"Hey, did you ever call Ms. D for an appointment? I've been so consumed by my own stuff that I have been a slacker about nagging you."

I get my answer when Sarah slumps in my arms. I ease away from her and lift her chin. "Sarah…"

"I know, I know," she mumbles. "But I've been feeling…"

I raise my eyebrow in warning.

Sarah looks up at me and gives me a sheepish smile. "Better. A lot better. And I'm not sure I need to see her now."

I take her hands and stare into those emerald eyes. "Smiley almost destroyed us three years ago when he took you and ran his car into me. And now he seems to be reaching out from the grave, trying to take away everything we have. Call her." I pull out my high card. "Please. For me."

Sarah nods. "I'll talk to my parents tonight. And I promise to call Ms. Donaldson tomorrow. Maybe she can see me right after Christmas. Okay?"

"I only want what's best for you." Wow. I sound like my father.

"I only want what's best for you," she whispers. "I'd do anything for you, you know."

Bliss.

*

Mom and Dad were home from their party when I returned from Sarah's, so I checked in briefly before retreating to my room. I didn't want to run the risk of their deflating my euphoria before I got the chance to savor it.

The last of my doubts have fled. Sarah and I are together, for real and for always. We're going to get married. Probably not as soon as I would like, but it will happen.

I stretch out on the bed and begin designing our first home. We won't have much money, so our furniture will be a mash-up of stuff from our childhoods and fake wood junk that you have to assemble yourself. I wonder if Dad and Grandpa would help me build something, like a table or a chest. Then I could give it to Sarah as a wedding gift. She would love that.

I do a quick inventory of the things in our Blacksburg apartments: basic kitchen items, some linens, a couple of desks and chairs. I assume we would get a few wedding gifts, which would be great unless they're useless gadgets or dust collectors. I guess women like that stuff.

I skip over our wedding. I don't know much, but I'm aware that it's all about the bride, as it should be. Especially when the bride is as beautiful as my Sarah. If we end the day with her as my wife, I'll be happy. Much better than happy.

"Sam?"

A steel door clangs shut, with my imagination behind it.

I walk to the hall and see Mom at the top of the stairs. "Uh, yes, ma'am?"

"Are you eating dinner with your dad and me tonight?"

"Yes, ma'am."

"No plans with Sarah?" Worry glides over Mom's face for an instant. She's probably wondering if I've already made a mess of things.

"She's got a family thing."

"'Tis the season." Mom smiles. With relief, I think. "Speaking of family, Megan is on the road and should arrive around 9. I'd appreciate it if you'd make some time for your family over the next couple of days."

Whoa. Within thirty seconds, Mom has swerved from worrying that I'm not spending enough time with Sarah to worrying that I'm spending too much. "Message received."

Megan arrives right on time, not surprising for a CPA. Precision and accuracy are part of her genetic code.

"Little brother!" Megan's a tiny thing but a powerful hugger. "We've got some catching up to do," she whispers before letting me go. Her grin tells me she knows about Sarah. From Mom, of course. I should've told her myself.

"Sure thing," I answer.

After we help Megan bring in her suitcases and a sleigh's worth of gifts, Mom brings out her homemade hot chocolate complete with real whipped cream, not that artificial chemical junk. She makes it at least once every Christmas season.

"How's work?" is Dad's opening question. It's always about work with him.

"Good," Megan answers between sips. "I'm getting more responsibility, and I received an *Excellent* on my last evaluation. Plus, I'm fortunate to be on a great team."

"That's wonderful, honey." Mom dabs at her clean mouth with a napkin, and the rest of us take it as a sign that we need to use ours. We do so in unison. "But is there a special teammate these days?" Dad's about work and Mom's about love. A division of labor.

Megan manages to stifle a groan, but I sense it. "No, ma'am. If there were, I'd let you know."

Mom lets the matter drop, thankfully, and the conversation meanders from Tech's upcoming bowl game to changes in tax law, until Dad declares, "Time for the old folks to go to bed."

"Good night, Gramps," Megan teases.

"And good night to you, missy," Dad replies in a scratchy voice. He stoops over and waves an imaginary cane as he walks up the stairs.

"What a nut." Megan rolls her eyes.

"Dad? I can't see it." We're sitting on a couple of large pillows in front of the fireplace. The flicker of the gas logs spotlights a change in Megan's expression, but I can't define it.

"I know," she responds after a few moments. "And it makes me sad."

"What?"

She wraps her arms around her knees. "You and Dad have been so serious with each other for the last few years. Everything seems to be a matter of life and death."

I shift my eyes from side to side, like I'm looking for an answer to come creeping up over my shoulder. "Uh, I don't know about that."

Megan punches me in the shoulder. "You know exactly what I'm talking about."

"Mom told—"

"Yeah, I know you're having second thoughts about med school. But this stone-cold business with you and Dad goes back a long time."

"It does?"

She escalates by shoving me with both hands. "Jeez! How can a smart guy be so stupid?"

I barely manage to stop myself from falling over. I'm not sure it is from the shove or the recent consensus that I'm stupid. "Okay, tell me what I'm missing."

Megan puts her head in her hands and shakes it back and forth. "Try to follow me. After you came out of the coma and proclaimed you wanted to be a doctor—"

"I never *proclaimed* anything."

"Yes, you did."

"No, I didn't."

"Fine." She gives me her narrowed-eye stare before continuing. "After you *said* you wanted to be a doctor, your relationship with Dad changed. You weren't father and son anymore. You became, oh, what's the best word?"

I cross my arms and watch my sister struggle.

"Soldiers." Megan points at me. "That's it. Fellow soldiers on an urgent mission. It seemed like med school was the only thing on your mind or Dad's. Every conversation revolved around it. Still does."

"Not every conversation."

"Practically every conversation." She sits up taller—tall for her, anyway—and puts her hands on her hips. "Dad goes, 'Grr, keep those grades up, son.' And you answer, 'Yes, sir. Whatever you say, sir. I'm on it.' You usually don't say 'Grr,' but you throw in a salute."

"Do not," I protest, torn between laughter and indignation.

Megan tries to suppress a giggle. "Okay, I might be embellishing a little."

"A little?"

As silliness overtakes us, I feel every muscle unwinding and stretching out. "Grr," she repeats, her hands up like a bear.

"Yes, ma'am. Whatever you say, ma'am," I reply, wrapping up with a pitiful excuse for a salute.

When the laughter fades, I turn my attention to the flames licking the logs, burning but never consuming. "And now I'm having doubts."

"And I'm guessing Dad's not taking that well."

"Yeah."

Megan moves closer to me and her voice softens. "What do you want, little brother?"

"Other than Sarah? I don't know."

She sighs and stares into the fire with me. "I'm really glad you guys are back together. I look forward to having Sarah as a sister one day, although my brother is not half bad. Most of the time."

"Thanks, I think. I just wish…I don't know what to do. Go to med school? And if I don't, what do I do? I'm such a loser."

She puts an arm around my shoulders. "Samuel Russell, you are not a loser. You're a good person who's confused right now. Look at me, little brother."

I turn my head slightly, keeping my slumped position.

"You almost died three years ago. It's a miracle you're still here. That tells me that God kept you alive for a reason. And if He did, He'll be sure to let you know what that reason is."

Megan and I lean into each other, her head on my shoulder and mine straining downward to touch hers. We haven't sat like this since I fell off my skateboard and Dakota—yes, Dakota strikes again—called me a joke. That was so long ago, she was the taller one.

"I wonder…" she whispers. "Could it be that you and Dad are butting heads because you're so much alike?"

I back away. "No way."

"Stick with me here. You and Dad are bright, super conscientious, and selfless. Plus, both of you would jump into the fires of hell for the women you love."

"Maybe."

"I'm your sister, and I'm never wrong. Remember that."

"Yes, ma'am."

CHAPTER 10

EVERYONE ON BOTH sides of my family has converged at our house for Christmas this year. That means the amount of painfully personal advice being doled out and the level of general chaos have reached critical mass.

Mimi to Megan: "You can't be too picky, honey. You're not getting any younger."

Uncle Nick to me: "Are you enjoying your college days, boy? Don't get tied down like I did." He's divorced. No surprise.

Dad: "Has anyone seen my phone?"

Mom: "In the name of all that's holy, forget the phone."

We should call over someone to measure the madness, but I don't know if we need a rocket scientist or a paranormal investigator.

But me? I'm chill, the calm center. The only thing that matters is giving Sarah her present this evening. I should be fully recovered from my carb coma by then, with another serving of ham for additional energy.

You don't know if you've given someone the perfect gift until it's given. That's the way I see it, although I've never given the perfect gift to Sarah or anyone else. Some presents have come close but didn't quite make it.

Until this year. I've nailed it.

I hope.

I'm distracted throughout the afternoon by laughter, mild bickering (mild only because any discussion of politics is strictly forbidden), and some impromptu karaoke thanks to Aunt Jackie, who brought over her gift from Uncle Peter. Have I been permanently scarred by Uncle Peter's rendition of "I Will Survive"? Probably.

Grandma is warbling her way through "Stand by Your Man" when I check my phone. Seven p.m. at last. I find Mom in the kitchen—great detective work on my part—shining like a pearl amid a tsunami of casserole dishes covered in burnt-on food. I kiss her cheek and am stunned to find she's almost perspiring. What's next? Superman gets eczema?

"Mercy. Next time we're going completely disposable—pans, plates, silverware, the works." As if. "Off to see Sarah?" Mom dries her hands on a towel and appraises my attire.

"Presentable?"

She brushes off a piece of microscopic lint. "I suppose. Don't want the Winstons to think the Russells aren't civilized."

"Yeah, that's a big concern. Thanks for the food, for everything. Like Dad says, you're the Royal Highness of Holidays."

Mom beams. "A sweet talker like your father." She pushes me toward the side door. "Quick! Escape through the garage before they make you sing."

I'm not singing as I walk to Sarah's house, swinging the gift bag back and forth, but I am humming. Something I kept hearing on my multiple trips to and from the mall: "All I Want for Christmas Is You" by Mariah Carey. Makes sense, because Sarah is all I want for Christmas and for always.

As I wait for someone to answer the door, I hear laughter coming from inside the house. I allow myself to drop into my dream about our first home and how we will decorate it that first Christmas together. I bet Dad would give us some lights for the outside and Mom has enough ornaments to cover five trees. And we'll need a wreath.

"Hi there." Sarah appears suddenly, like a vision. I had traveled so deep into my daydream that I didn't notice the door opening.

She is breathtaking.

Sarah deserves more words, better words, but I don't think anyone has invented them yet. She's wearing jeans that follow her curves while still being family-gathering-appropriate, and her peach-colored blouse is buttoned a couple of inches below her collarbone, giving only the illusion of cleavage. Heaven help me, I want to drag her off right now.

"Did I get a glop of Mama's pumpkin pie on me?" Sarah pulls her blouse away to inspect it. "I'm such a slob."

"Stop," I manage to say. "You're perfect." I kiss her cheek, and her nearness makes me wobble. "Merry Christmas, Red."

"Merry Christmas, Sam." Then she leads me into the Winston Christmas.

Their Christmas seems much quieter than ours, but that might be because Mr. Winston has been known to spike the eggnog.

"Sam!" Mrs. Winston gathers me up in a hug. I would put her enthusiasm down to the aforementioned nog, but she's like this all the time. "So glad you could come over. Merry Christmas!"

"Thank you, ma'am. The same to you."

"Let me call Daniel away from the punch bowl. I'm sure you two are anxious to exchange gifts." She scurries over to the family room, but not before winking at Sarah.

"What was that about?" I ask, but Sarah only grins and shrugs.

I'm about to follow up when Mr. Winston steps into the foyer. It is Christmas, a time for good cheer and peace to all men. Surely I'll see Sarah's dad bathed in a soft, rosy glow.

Nope. Still intimidating. "Merry Christmas, Sam."

I try to give him the perfect handshake—not weak but not a bone-crushing show of force either. "Merry Christmas, sir." Is this how I sound with Dad? No wonder Megan was mocking me.

"No need to be quite so serious, Samuel." He gives me a shoulder squeeze. "You're welcome to come in and visit with the rest of the family."

Sarah jumps in. "Later, Daddy. I'd like to give Sam his gift first."

Mr. Winston gives Sarah a tender kiss on the top of her head. "Okay, baby girl," he says before heading back to the family room. "Now, Jacob, about that baseball card you took from me when we were kids."

Sarah rolls her eyes. "Every Christmas Dad and Uncle Jake argue about the mystery of the missing baseball card. It's become our little tradition, like singing Christmas carols or watching *It's a Wonderful Life*. What can I say? We're wacky." She takes my hand and leads me to a sunroom at the back of the house. "This is the only quiet corner of the house right now, except for our bedrooms."

"You do realize you're driving me crazy."

"Sorry."

"Really?"

A mischievous smile crosses her face. "No."

I clear my throat, as if that will clear my head. "So, I hear we have some presents to open."

"Me first!" Sarah stops just short of doing the quick half-clap of a little kid and rushes over to a Christmas tree in the corner of the room. Mrs. Winston shares Mom's love for Christmas trees, so she has three. This one is no more than three or four feet tall, but it's buried under enough ornaments to cover a forest. "I think there might be something under here." She pretends to search. "Well, look at this." Sarah hands me a small square box wrapped in red paper so shiny it looks wet.

I examine it carefully, knowing what the wait will do to her. "Hmm, nice wrapping job. The ends are neat, and I can tell no trimming was needed. The bow appears to be handmade from iridescent curling ribbon. From the size of the box, I'd guess—"

"For heaven's sake, open it."

"A baseball. That's it. A baseball."

Sarah responds with her own rendition of "Grr," followed by "Sam Russell, you are so impossible."

"Yeah, but you can't live without me." I give her my best wide-eyed innocent-little-boy smile.

Sarah shakes her head. "True."

I tear the paper to find a plain white gift box. Intriguing. In the past Sarah has given me an assortment of Virginia Tech items and video games. Inside is a mass of white tissue paper. It contains something small but substantial at its core, and for a moment I wonder if the gift is indeed a baseball.

It's a paperweight. No, a compass.

"Oh, Red, it's beautiful." The compass is about the size of a biscuit, around two and a half inches in diameter and one and a half inches tall. The face is surrounded by a gold metal frame engraved with leaves, and the side appears to be wood, covered with tiny carvings of animals and flowers and trees. The cardinal directions are feathery, like they were painted by an artist. It looks like something you would find in Ben Franklin's study or Captain Nemo's submarine.

"Is it an antique?" I ask. "I've never seen anything like it."

"I'm not sure," Sarah says slowly. "I mean, it looks old and the seller said it was from the late nineteenth century, but I don't know enough about that kind of stuff to be certain. I was shopping with Mama in Strasburg, and when I saw it, I just had to get it for you. I didn't have quite enough to pay for it, so Mama loaned me the rest."

"You shouldn't have."

"But look closer." Sarah leans over and pulls slightly on the compass, revealing its secret: it's the lid to a box. Inside is a tightly wound scroll about the diameter of a pencil.

I untie the red yarn holding it and strain to read the calligraphic letters written there. "'Trust in the Lord with all thine heart; and lean not unto thine own understanding. In all thy ways acknowledge him, and he shall direct thy paths.' Proverbs 3:5–6." When I turn to Sarah, my vision is blurry. "This is incredible." I hold up the scroll. "Did you make this?"

Sarah nods. "Mama helped me, but I did most of it myself. That's why it's not perfect."

I lean into her until our foreheads touch. "It is perfect. The best gift I've ever received."

Sarah pulls away. "I know you're struggling right now, and I wanted to remind you that God will always show you what direction to take. I used the King James Version because that's how we memorized it in Miss Jane's Sunday school class."

I welcome a distraction from the tightness in my throat. "Yeah, good old King James. Once he gets in your head, he never leaves."

"I thought you could put it on your desk or your dashboard or your surfboard or—"

"That's it. This Shenandoah Valley boy will become a world-class surfer."

"As long as you know I'll be right there, wherever you go."

I'm losing it again. "Me too."

A familiar bubble surrounds us, insulating us from the rest of the world. The arguing Winston brothers are muted and even the little tree dims. Nothing exists beyond Sarah and me and the feeling between us.

"Time for charades!" The voice of Sarah's grandmother punctures our bubble. She's not called *Little General* for nothing.

"And then there's that," Sarah says with a sigh.

"Yep." I lean back and hear the crackle of the gift bag next to me. "Well, look here. A gift for the lovely lady." I dangle the crushed bag in front of Sarah, keeping it just out of her reach.

"A present!" Sarah's eyes widen in surprise, as if she had forgotten that this is Christmas Day. "Gimme!"

I tease her with a couple more passes of the bag before allowing her to grab it.

Sarah takes her time removing the tissue paper despite her excitement. When she gets to the blue velvet gift box, her mouth opens into a perfect little O. She lifts the lid slowly. and when she sees the silver necklace, her hand goes to her throat. "Sam. Oh, Sam, it's…it's gorgeous." She runs her finger over the design and turns the box so I can see it. "What does it mean? It looks like a collection of symbols."

"It's an Irish claddagh. Mom's great-great-grandfather came over here from Ireland, so Dad gave her a claddagh ring years ago. When I saw this one in a necklace, I had to buy it." I trace the outline of the crown at the top of the design. "This is a symbol of loyalty. Whatever happens, I'll always be at your side."

Sarah nods. "I know. I'm sorry I wasn't—"

"Shhh. You didn't leave me, not really. Did you ever stop caring about me while we were separated?"

"Never." I see the tears forming in her eyes.

"Then the subject's closed." I better hurry, while I can still speak. "Below the crown are two hands holding a heart. These stand for friendship. You've always been my best friend."

"And you've been mine."

I point to the heart last. "And this stands for love, of course."

"Of course."

"Forever and always."

"Forever and always," she repeats, her tears finally escaping.

I remove the necklace from the box. "May I?"

Sarah nods and lifts her hair. My fingers feel like sausages as I fumble with the tiny clasp, but I finally succeed.

When she turns back around I lightly kiss one wet cheek, then the other. We're only a couple of rooms removed from her entire extended family, so I back off. "Guess we better see how that game of charades is going." I mean, who would want to miss that?

Sarah has her dreamy look, and I wonder if I should go home to a very cold shower instead.

"Oh, yeah. I guess. Do we have to?"

"Sarah—"

"Yes, sir," she answers, sounding like a beleaguered subordinate. "If you say so, sir."

I stand and offer my hand to help her up. "It's either charades here or karaoke at my house. You choose."

Sarah shakes her head, and her eyes grow wide. "Charades, definitely. I've heard your dad sing."

*

I'm sitting in Aunt Suzanne and Uncle Rob's family room, listening to the clink of ice being dropped into glasses and wishing I were back in my room reading *A Tale of Two Cities*. I stare at a Santa figurine left behind in the post-Christmas sweep and I can almost hear him say, "Run!"

I blame Sarah for this. She's seen Ms. Donaldson twice now, so I had no defense when she asked if I'd gotten around to talking to Uncle Rob about med school.

I haven't asked how her sessions are going, but she told me she's "gaining greater clarity." That's a Donaldson phrase if ever there was one. But Sarah does seem like she's dropping a heavy weight, ounce by ounce, so we're both willing to put up with the eyeroll-inducing psycho-talk.

"Suze has trained me well," Uncle Rob says as he hands me a glass of iced tea. "If a thief stole in during the night, she'd insist on giving him some hot chocolate and a cookie."

"But no cookie for me?"

"Afraid not." Uncle Rob settles into the chair opposite me. We're in his study, surrounded by shelves loaded with medical titles. Only a couple include novels and assorted nonfiction works. The tufted leather wingback chairs frame a fireplace. I can imagine Uncle Rob and Dad sitting here on a cold winter's night, sipping brandy and discussing politics like a couple of characters from an old Sherlock Holmes movie.

"Now that Christmas has passed, Suze has me on lockdown until further notice. That usually means waiting until the Super Bowl for anything approaching delicious."

"Sounds like my mom." I stare at the design of the rug at my feet, trying to decipher the pattern. I could apologize for wasting his time and run out of here, but that would be stupid. If Sarah's willing to confront Smiley again, the least I can do is talk to a man who has known me my whole life. Man up, Sam. "Thanks for seeing me, Uncle Rob." An unimaginative start, but solid.

"Happy to." He sets his tea on a side table, leans forward, and clasps his hands.

"I, uh, guess you know what this is about."

A half nod.

I take a deep breath. "The thing is, I don't know if I want to be a doctor anymore. Dad thinks this is just cold feet or lack of confidence or something. He can't imagine me doing anything else."

"I've gotten that impression."

"Yeah. I mean, yes. We keep butting heads over it. Sarah thought maybe you could help, so here I am." I realize I've been sitting on the edge of the chair, so I scoot back and sip the tea. Too sweet, as usual.

Uncle Rob walks over to the window overlooking their backyard and shoves his hands into his pockets. He seems to be watching something, but I can't imagine what the winter landscape would have to offer. I only know that if this silence stretches on for another minute, I will make my excuses and head for the door.

I'm rising from my chair when Uncle Rob finally speaks. "I give Suze a hard time about her bird feeders. I complain about refilling them and cleaning all that poop off the little statue of St. Francis under the tree." He smiles as he returns to his seat. "But I find that I do some of my best thinking when I watch those little guys fly back and forth. Don't tell your Aunt Suzanne that, though. A husband has to have something to whine about." He leans back in his chair and rubs its leather arms. "But you didn't come here to listen to me ramble, did you, big guy?"

I almost shake my head.

"I wish you needed advice on which courses to take as an undergrad or a pep talk about med school itself. I could rattle on for days. But this…this is getting into Lindsay Donaldson's territory, and I'm not sure I'm up to the job."

Uncle Rob leans forward, stares at the floor, and starts sliding his hands back and forth. I think he is about thirty seconds away from wringing them.

"I'm sorry, Uncle Rob. I shouldn't have dragged you into this." I rise and hold out my hand. "Thanks for seeing me."

He stays seated and gestures with his palm toward my chair. "Sit down."

I do as I'm told.

Uncle Rob's eyes are what I think you call hazel—sometimes gray and sometimes green—and I've had them trained on me for years. When he taught me to play chess. When he stitched up my chin after I sailed over the handlebars of my bike. When I woke up from my coma. But this look is different.

"Your dad and I, we're a lot alike. We don't say everything we should. Guess it's the way we were raised. But I think you should know how much…how much you mean to your Aunt Suzanne and me. You and Megan." Uncle Rob dabs at his eyes with his thumb. "You know, we didn't choose not to have children. It just wasn't in the cards for us. Tried adopting, but that didn't work out." He walks back to the window and clasps his hands behind his back. Clears his throat before continuing, keeping his eyes locked on the bird feeders. "We've tried to invest in the lives of other children, but you and Megan, you're special. We…we love you like you're our own." When he turns to me, I see the same softness I see in Mom's eyes and Dad's.

"We love you too."

He smiles and returns to his chair. "Well." He clasps his hands together. "So, tell me. Why did you want to become a doctor in the first place? What was going through your mind?"

Maybe I should watch those birds for some insight. Instead, I focus on the rows and rows of books staring down at me, hundreds—thousands—of years of knowledge poised above me, expecting something profound. "I don't remember."

Uncle Rob's raised eyebrow and tilted head tells me to try again.

"I guess it all comes back to how I felt during my rehab. I was overwhelmed by everything the doctors and nurses did for me, and I thought it would be cool if I could help someone like that. And then the more I thought about it—and especially after I told my parents—it felt like I had found what I was meant to do. Like a giant spotlight was shining on a path stretching out into the distance. Kind of like the yellow brick road in *The Wizard of Oz*. Does any of that make sense?"

He nods. "Certainly. You were helped, so you wanted to help others in return."

"Exactly."

"But you know, big guy, you don't have to be a doctor to help people. I wish we had talked about this sooner, but I guess I was more than a little flattered, thinking you wanted to follow in your old Uncle Rob's footsteps."

"I could do worse."

"Maybe," he says with a grin. "But this isn't about me or your dad. And it's not even about you."

"So…"

Uncle Rob reaches out, like he's giving me a gift. "It's about God and what He wants for you. He has a plan for all of us, Sam, but from the moment you emerged from that coma, I've felt strongly that God has something special in mind for you."

I should be grateful. Uncle Rob is clearly out of his comfort zone, opening up to me in a way he never has. Instead, one question is hammering against my patience: *What is the stinking plan?* I keep my eyes on the floor. Uncle Rob probably thinks I'm overcome with emotion. I am. Just not the one he thinks.

"Sam?" He speaks a half-level above a whisper.

I finally look up and hope he can't read my face. "Sir?"

"It's okay, you know."

I don't even try to hide my confusion. "I'm sorry, what?"

He walks over and touches my shoulder. "It's okay to be uncertain, to feel adrift. Not comfortable, that's for sure. But okay."

I feel like a little kid being consoled over the loss of a baseball game. I stand to tell it like it is, man to man. "I know all about not having answers. I had to face what happened with John Perkins. I get it. But I need to have some kind of clue about my future now, before my folks spend a lot of money on a dream that will never happen."

He backs away slightly, his face drawn downward by my rant. "I'm sorry, big guy. I was trying—"

"To help. I know. No, I'm sorry. I'm frustrated by this whole situation and took it out on you. You've given me a lot to think about, and I really appreciate your seeing me."

Uncle Rob's face brightens a little. "Come by anytime." He slaps my back as we turn to leave the room. "And it goes without saying that I'll be praying for you."

"Thank you," I reply, relieved that this utterly useless visit didn't do lasting damage to our relationship.

The doorbell rings. "Oh, that's probably the delivery of our newest bird feeder."

I grin.

Uncle Rob puts out his palm. "No judgment, please."

But when he opens the door, it's not a delivery guy.

It's Dad.

No.

CHAPTER 11

I DIDN'T SAY the word aloud, but Dad can see it all over my face. And I can see it on his.

He looks from me to Uncle Rob, then back to me. "I came over to drop off those lures I was telling you about," he says, still staring at me like he's trying to decide if I'm really there. "Sam?"

Uncle Rob valiantly leaps into the gap. "Sam and I were just catching up," he bellows, giving Pastor Jeff a run for his money. "Yep, we haven't had much of a chance to talk in a while."

"Catching up?" Dad's voice is flat, as unreadable as his expression. Except for me. I can read him perfectly.

"A bit of this and a bit of that, you know." Uncle Rob slaps me on the back again. "Thanks for the lures, Chad. Want to come in? I think Suze may have left some Brussels sprouts or cauliflower in the fridge."

"Uh, no. No, thanks. I've got to head on home." Dad's face has closed completely now, and even I can't tell what's happening behind it. "Coming home, Sam?"

I'll fix this later. I can't let my father's friendship with Uncle Rob become collateral damage. "Yes, sir." I shake Uncle Rob's hand again. "Thanks for seeing me."

"Always a pleasure." He gives my hand an extra squeeze. He knows what's coming.

Dinner's almost over, and Dad hasn't said anything about my visit to Uncle Rob's house. Mom has been prattling on about how she doesn't want to throw away the spoonful of mashed potatoes remaining, insisting that I finish them off. I push my chair back from the table. I told Mom I would wash the dishes tonight, and the sooner I start, the sooner I finish. Then I'll call Sarah.

"Samuel." Dad gestures toward my empty chair. I refuse to play this game anymore, so I remain standing.

Mom stops wrapping up the leftover meatloaf in foil and turns to him, then me. "Is something going on?"

"I ran into Sam at Rob's this afternoon."

"Okay." Mom's eyebrows draw together as she studies Dad's face. "And that means..."

Dad folds his arms across his chest and stares at me. "I'm guessing that means our son was talking to Rob about med school. I'm also guessing he was looking for an ally."

"Oh." Mom returns to her seat and looks at me. I don't think she would look any more concerned if Dad had told her he'd seen me hanging out behind the abandoned furniture store trying to score some opioids. "Sam?"

Enough. "So? I went to Uncle Rob for some advice. Sarah thought maybe he could help me sort out how I felt about med school." My heartbeat accelerates and I hear my voice rising. "I didn't go to him to line up an ally. This isn't World War II, Dad. But what if I did? It's not like I have any in this house."

"That's not true. You know that." His voice lowers. "Your mother and I only want what's best for you."

Mom nods and smiles at me.

"And you think becoming a doctor is what's best for me. How do you know that? Do you have a hotline to God or something? Why would He talk to you but not to me?"

"Sam..." Mom stands and reaches out to me.

I back away. "You don't know what God wants and you don't care." I fix my eyes on my father as he walks to Mom's side, his gaze cold and hard. "All you care about is living your life through me." My voice is shrill now as it vibrates through my bones.

"Please, Sam," Mom begs.

"You don't know what you're talking about, Samuel," Dad says evenly, the muscles in his jaw working. "You have no idea."

"No, *you* don't have any idea." I flail my arms as if tossing away every med school conversation we have had. "I'm trying to figure out what God wants from me, but do I get any help from you? No. All I get is this constant drumbeat of 'be a doctor, be a doctor.' I'm sick of it." A soft voice inside tells me to stop. "I'm sick of you pushing all your dreams on me. It's not my fault that you feel like a loser."

Dad moves toward me, and Mom jumps between us. "Chad, Sam, please stop." She extends an arm toward each of us to keep us apart. A part of me notices that she is crying, but I push that aside.

"All I've ever wanted is for you to fulfill your potential," Dad starts.

"No. All you ever wanted is for me to fulfill *your* potential. Sarah's the only one who cares about what I want. I'd marry her today if she'd say yes."

"No!" Dad thunders. "I knew it. I knew this all came back to her. I will not let you throw your future away for a sweet piece of—"

The words register in my body before they hit my brain. Mom cries, "Chad!" as I lunge for him. But I crash into her instead, and her *oof* as she hits the floor snaps me out of my rage.

"Mom?"

Dad crouches beside her and tenderly searches for injury.

"Mama?" The voice I hear is small and afraid.

"I'm fine, I'm fine." She brushes away Dad's hands as she sits up. "Just my usual clumsy self." She smiles at me. "Really, I'm all right."

Dad turns to me, his eyes dark. "Get out, Samuel."

"Chad," Mom protests.

"Get out," he growls, pulling Mom close. "Now."

I back out of the room slowly and stagger out the front door. *Dear God, what have I done?*

The cold slams into me, and I pull up the hood of my sweatshirt. I'm alone in the dark. No family, no home. My phone vibrates in my pocket—probably a text from Sarah or one of my friends. But they don't know me, not anymore. They don't know the guy who knocked down his mother as he tried to smash his father's face in.

Mom. I should call Uncle Rob about her.

"Hello?"

"Yeah, Uncle Rob, this is Sam. You need to come over. It's Mom."

"I know, Sam." He is quiet and calm, the doctor I thought I wanted to be. "Your dad just called me. Where are you now?"

"The porch."

"Stay right there, Sam. Don't leave. I'll be there in five minutes. Okay? Stay right there."

"Okay." I hang up and drop the phone on the porch. Mom will be okay. She smiled at me and everything. She'll be okay.

I sit on the top step and hug my knees to my chest. I want to run, I want to hide, I want to go to sleep for a thousand years. I'm back in the cave with a monstrous stalactite suspended above me, its hold on the roof tenuous.

I close my eyes to focus, to think, to come up with a plan, but I can't stop the buzzing in my head. *Help me, please.*

"Sam?" Sarah's voice settles over me like a cool compress. "What's wrong?"

When I look her, at her angelic face, Dad's accusation washes over me again, like the second wave of a tsunami. How could he talk about her that way? I want to go back into the house and finish what I started.

Looking down at my clenched fists, I try to open them. I take a deep breath and they uncurl in slow motion, only to close again.

Sarah covers both my hands with hers. "What is it? You're shaking. And your hands are so cold. Let's go inside and—"

I jerk out of her grasp. "No! I can't. I can't." I feel an icy trail forming on my cheek. "Leave. Please leave."

She strokes my face. "I won't leave you, Sam. Not ever." She wraps her arms around my shoulders and squeezes tight. I rest my head on hers, an involuntary reflex. I should make her go, but I can't.

Headlights blind me as Uncle Rob pulls into the driveway. He walks toward us, but he's closing in as if he's running. He nods to Sarah and me when he reaches the steps. "Good to see you're here, Sarah." He smiles slightly, the kind of reassuring grin you see in emergency rooms. "It'll be okay, Sam. I'll check back with you shortly."

After the front door closes, Sarah lets me go and turns my face toward her. "What's going on, Sam?"

I guess the leaving might as well start now, with the most important person in the world to me. "Dad and I, we, uh, had a fight." I feel more tears building in my throat, and Sarah hands me a tissue. "About med school. He said—we said—some terrible things and I tried to hit him. Mom got in the way and fell. She said she was okay, but I called Uncle Rob just to be sure. But Dad already had."

Sarah's face turns as pale as the moonlight, and I stand. I don't want to watch her go.

But she stands alongside me and holds my hand. "Is that all?" she whispers.

I shake my head. "No, uh, no." I am sobbing now, my anger and desolation pouring out. "When Mom fell, Dad, Dad said…"

Sarah hugs me and I hang on to her, burying my face in her hair. "Dad told me to get out. He hates me. He hates me."

"Shhh, shhh." She pats my back like I'm a child. "Your father doesn't hate you. He was angry, that's all. Just like you. You don't hate him, right?"

I hate what he said, as much as I've ever hated anything or anyone. Even John Perkins. But him? "I don't know right now."

Sarah's quiet. Maybe this is when she walks away. "It'll be okay. All shall be well."

God, make that so.

The creak of a door breaks Sarah's hold on me. "Is Mom all right?" I ask Uncle Rob.

He walks over and puts an arm around me. "Right as rain. Might have a little bruise on her back tomorrow, but nothing that will need attention."

Thank You.

He releases me and steps back. "I was thinking that maybe it would be good for you to spend the night with Suze and me, a little cooling-off period."

"Mom and Dad?"

Uncle Rob nods. "They agree. Why don't you head to your room and pack a few things? I'll wait here."

"But I can't—"

"Your dad has gone out to his workshop and will stay there until we leave."

"Can I help?" Sarah asks.

"No," Uncle Rob and I say at once.

Her mouth drops open. "Uh, okay. May I come to your house, then, Dr. Rob? Just to visit for a little while?"

"Certainly. But let your folks know first."

Sarah runs down to the sidewalk and continues to her house. "Do you know everything?" I ask Uncle Rob once she's out of earshot.

"I think so," he answers. "We can talk later if you like."

"Okay."

As I walk up to my bedroom, I hear the same creak on the same stair I've heard my whole life. The walls in my room are the same color, the T-ball trophies and cross-country ribbons are lined up on a shelf over my desk, and *A Tale of Two Cities* is face down on my bed, open to the last page I was reading.

Nothing has changed. But everything has.

*

Aunt Suzanne welcomes us with only a few soft words. She brings me some chamomile tea in a sturdy white mug and kisses the top of my head. Then she nods to Uncle Rob and slides the doors to his study shut.

Sarah sits with me on a loveseat across from the leather chairs. Only a few hours earlier, I sat in one of those chairs and squirmed about in a web of self-pity.

I'd had no idea.

Sarah doesn't try to make me talk. She alternates between rubbing my back and holding my hand. After half an hour or so, Uncle Rob looks up from the medical journal he's been reading and clears his throat. "Sarah?"

"Yes, sir?"

"After everything that's happened, I think Sam could use some rest." He tilts his head to me.

Sarah studies my face for guidance.

I attempt a slight smile. "I'll be okay. I'll call you tomorrow."

Sarah bites her lip, and I can see her eyes glazing over. "Promise?"

"I promise."

Uncle Rob returns to his reading after she leaves, and I use the silence to formulate a plan to make things better. Like that's possible. It would be more accurate to say I'm trying to come up with a plan to do something. Anything would be better than sitting here sailing back and forth between rage and regret. I drop my head into my hands and listen for God, but I guess even He's had enough of me for one day.

"Want to talk?"

I raise my head to see Uncle Rob staring at me, leaning forward with his hands clasped. "It might help," he adds.

I exhale slowly. "Do you really know everything?"

"I know that you and your father argued about med school, that harsh words were exchanged, and that your mother fell as she tried to separate you."

A bitter laugh slips out. "Harsh words? Is that what my parents called them?"

He draws back slightly, his face twisting with confusion. "It's what your mother said."

Of course. Mom would try to spin things as gently as she could, already feverishly working to repair the damage between her husband and son.

"Did you talk to my dad at all?"

Uncle Rob shakes his head. "Not really. Once he was assured your mother was fine, he went out to his workshop."

I feel my anger bubbling up again. "Dad was ticked off because I came to see you today. He assumed I was trying to make you my ally in this crazy med-school mess. Then I told him he doesn't care about God's will for me or what I want. I said he wants to live his life through me because he feels like a loser."

Uncle Rob's mouth drops open in shock, but he lets me keep going.

"I told him that only Sarah cares about me and that's when, that's when…" My voice rises as I fight for control. "That's when he said he wouldn't let me throw away my future for a sweet piece…" I can't finish Dad's sentence, just as I didn't let him finish it.

Uncle Rob looks like he's been punched in the stomach. "Dear Jesus."

Now the regret rises and the tears return. "Then Mom fell, and Dad told me to get out. Not like 'get out for now,' but 'get out forever.' I can't go home—I don't think I have a home anymore—and I can't look at Sarah without thinking about what Dad said." I drop my head in my hands again.

"'When sorrows like sea billows roll,'" Uncle Rob whispers, his voice cracking.

"Excuse me?" I manage to croak.

"A line from an old hymn. Don't worry, I won't sing it."

I turn to him and wipe my eyes with the back of my hand. I almost grin. "Thank you."

He walks over and ruffles my hair. "I figure you've gone through enough for one day. And you do need to get some rest. Doctor's orders."

"Yes, sir."

*

The little clock on the nightstand says 3:30. I went to bed around 11 p.m. and have dozed off and on. Each time I awake, I spend a few seconds trying to figure out where I am. The nightlight in the corner is enough to reveal a space of perfect order and complete girliness. A figurine of a woman carrying a basket of flowers is flanked by four framed pictures on the dresser, a man-sized silk tree stands guard in one corner, and a teddy bear is watching over me from a floral wing-back chair in the other. In addition to the clock, the nightstand holds a lamp with a crystal base and a small leatherette copy of the New Testament, like the ones those guys give away at the fair every year.

There's no relief when I remember that I'm in the Reynoldses' guest room, because then I remember why I'm here.

I spent a lot of sleepless nights when Sarah shut me out, but this is different. Back then I could tell myself that everything would work out, that at the end of three months Sarah and I would be reunited. Okay, so maybe I was being a deluded fool, but those pep talks pushed me far enough from the edge to give me a few hours of rest.

But I can't see how things will ever be right with my parents. I think Mom and I will reconcile one day, maybe sooner than later. But how will I ever be able to look Dad in the eye again, knowing what he thinks about the woman I love? Knowing what he thinks about me?

I feel a sudden pain in my gut. What about what I said to Dad? I didn't call him a loser, but I did say he feels like one. Did he take it one step further and assume I see him that way?

Sometimes, right before sleep overtakes me, I feel like I'm falling and I jerk to wakefulness. I feel the same way now, only the fall doesn't stop when I open my eyes.

My phone lights up and vibrates.

Sarah. *Awake?* she texts.

Yeah, I answer.

The phone hums again, this time with a call.

"Hi, Red."

"Hi, baby." Sarah's voice breaks my fall. "I couldn't sleep for thinking about you. How are you?"

"Okay."

"Sam—"

I sigh. I'm too strung out to pretend, anyway. "Everything's so messed up, Red. Everything. We separated because you thought I deserved better than you. But the fact is, you deserve better than me."

"No, honey, no." Sarah's voice breaks. "Don't say that."

I push on before talking becomes impossible. "No, it's true. Tonight showed me how screwed up I am. Move on, Sarah. Please."

Sarah shifts into anger. "No. Stop it. I'm not leaving you, and you know it. Whatever is going on, we are going through it together. Do you hear me?"

I am crying full-out now.

"Sam? Do you hear me?"

"Yes," I gurgle.

"All right then." She sounds strong and confident, and I hang on to every syllable. "Here's what we'll do. I'll pick you up at eight and we'll go to breakfast. Then we'll sort all of this out. Things will look better in the morning."

"Okay," I manage. "Sarah?"

"Yes?"

"I'm scared."

"I know." Her voice softens into a lullaby. "But everything's going to be all right."

"Tell me how."

She takes a deep breath. "So, once upon a time there were these two kids, Sam and Sarah—"

"Sarah and Sam."

"Shhh. My story. Anyway, Sam and Sarah grew up together and became best friends. Then one day they both realized they were more than friends. They had fallen in love."

My muscles unwind and my crying eases.

"Sam and Sarah were deliriously happy. Then Sarah began to believe some lies and pushed Sam away. But Sam didn't give up on her, and they came back together again."

My mouth turns toward a smile.

"Time passed and they got married. They didn't have much at first: a dollhouse-sized apartment with a bed, a table and chairs, and a sofa. But they had all they needed. They had each other."

The smile has arrived.

"Sometimes, on a rainy weekend, they'd spread a quilt on the floor of their tiny family room and make love. Their favorite place in the world was in each other's arms."

Oh, God, make it so.

"After a while they welcomed a son, then a daughter, both with brilliant blue eyes and blond hair, like their father."

"Red hair and green eyes, like their mom."

"Shush! *My* story."

"Yes, ma'am."

"Sam and Sarah lived happily ever after, all the way to their last day. Then they danced into heaven."

The tears are back, but only because my love for Sarah is consuming me. "Oh, Sarah…" I say.

Her voice breaks again. "I believe it, Sam. If I need to, I'll believe it for both of us. Sleep now, and I'll see you at eight."

I disconnect and drop into unconsciousness.

CHAPTER 12

IT FEELS STRANGE, riding shotgun in Sarah's car. "Uh, I know this sounds sexist, but I'm used to driving when we go out."

Sarah grins at me. "You're right, it does sound sexist. But I'll give you a pass this time." She reaches over and pats my arm.

"Yes, ma'am. Whatever you say, ma'am."

She sticks out her tongue at me, and I respond in kind. "Besides," she continues, "I know where we're going and you don't."

After twenty minutes or so, we stop in front of a building that has seen better days. Like, maybe forty years ago.

"Is this it?"

"Yep." Sarah unbuckles her seat belt. "I know it looks like a dump, but the food is awesome. Trust me." She smiles, and for a moment all the craziness of the past twelve hours evaporates, leaving only us, back in our bubble.

I wish we could keep driving, on to the end of the world.

She opens her door and fakes annoyance. "Don't make me come over there, Sam Russell."

"Or what?" I ask, shaking off the moment.

"Sheesh! Men."

We're welcomed like visiting dignitaries by the lone waitress in the place. "Well, if it isn't Jerry's granddaughter! Sarah, isn't it?" The woman wraps Sarah in a hug before turning her attention to me. "And who's this?"

"This is Sam. Sam, this is—"

"Roberta, although my friends and best customers call me Robbie. Nice to meet you, Sam. Come on over. Jerry's favorite booth is open. We must have been expecting ya."

"Wow," I whisper after Robbie walks away. "I had no idea I've been dating a celebrity all this time."

Sarah laughs softly, then straightens her mouth and lifts her chin. "I am a woman of mystery, sir."

"Clearly." My girlfriend is so stinking cute. "How did you find this place, anyway?"

Sarah stares out the window as she calls up the memory. "Grandpa and Grandma discovered it years ago, and he brought me here back when I was 'fine.'" She uses air quotes.

Oh. After the kidnapping.

She turns back to me. "After we ate here, he took me on that hike I've told you about, to Hawksbill Summit in Shenandoah National Park."

"The one where you—"

"Went a little crazy, yeah."

"I wasn't going to say that."

Sarah reaches for me, and we hold hands across the table. "No, you wouldn't. But it's true. But my going crazy turned out to be a good thing, because that's when I stopped pretending I was fine. That's when I started to heal."

I nod, but no words are necessary.

*

Sarah and I ate our plate-sized blueberry pancakes, sausage, and eggs in silence, but it wasn't awkward. More like recharging.

But now it's time. I wrap one hand around my warm mug and reach for Sarah with the other. "I don't know where to start."

She squeezes my hand. "Let's leave. I know a better place to talk."

We drive on and turn off Route 11 near Mount Jackson. I don't bother to ask where we're headed. It feels good to shift into neutral and go along for the ride.

I'm surprised when I see we're approaching a covered bridge over the Shenandoah River. "Is this—"

"Meems Bottom Covered Bridge? Yes, sir. The place where Grandpa and I had a picnic after my hiking meltdown."

"Is this a tour, something like 'Walking in the Footsteps of Jerry and Sarah Winston'?"

Sarah parks the car. "Come to think of it, I believe we are on the list for our very own historical marker."

I grab her hand and pull her to me as she reaches for the door. "Thank you," I whisper against her ear.

She pulls away and combs my hair with her hands, her brows drawn together with concern. "For what?"

"Everything."

Sarah and I perch on a huge rock—the Shenandoah Valley has no shortage of those—and I let the whole story of my fight with Dad spill out. Almost the whole story. I can't share Dad's unfinished sentence. I may have to live with those ugly words gnawing at my insides, but at least I can spare Sarah.

She takes both my hands and holds tight, like she's pulling me out of quicksand. "I know darkness, Sam. I saw it in Smiley, but I've also seen it in myself, and that was even more frightening. You can't shock me."

I shake my head. "Please leave it alone."

Sarah gently rubs my knuckles. The same hand that almost struck my father. She has no idea what kind of man I am. A shiver surges through me.

She leans into me, and I hold her tightly, like I'm trying to stop her from blowing away. She's so good, and her love for me so pure that I feel my anger toward Dad building again. But I refuse to let him spoil this moment. I refuse to allow him to spoil any part of our relationship.

"Have you heard anything from your folks?" she murmurs, her voice soft and soothing.

"Mom texted around six thirty, asking if I was ready to talk."

"Did you answer?"

"Yeah. I told her not yet." I smooth her hair and realize my rage is dissipating. "But I guess I'll have to talk to them soon." The enormity of the argument opens before me, like the mouth of a blue whale. "For all I know, Dad will disown me. I may never see him again."

Sarah leans away to look at me. "Don't say that."

The rage in Dad's eyes flashes back into my memory. "You didn't see him, Red. You have no idea how much he hates me." I'm surprised by a sudden stab in my gut.

Sarah places her hands on my cheeks. "I know your dad loves you. Just like I know you love him."

I try to wriggle out of her grasp, but she holds on. "I'm not sure—"

"I am. You're angry now and I guess your dad is too, but the love is still there."

That is Sarah, forever looking for happy endings.

But this is no fairy tale.

*

We're a few minutes away from Early when I get a text. Pastor Jeff wants to call.

"It couldn't hurt," Sarah says. "I mean, pastors are supposed to help with this kind of thing, right?"

I sigh and lean my head against the window. If only we'd kept heading south. "Yeah, I know. But I don't want to talk to anyone besides you right now. Not Pastor Jeff and especially not my parents."

She reaches over to squeeze my hand. "You can't hide out forever."

I take in a deep breath and let it out slowly. "Okay." I redial and wait for Pastor Jeff to pick up.

"Hello, Sam." His voice has dropped to a normal human level, not the amped-up boom of Sunday morning.

"Hello, Pastor Jeff." Let him do all the work in this conversation.

"No point in dancing around things, is there? Your parents are worried about you, Sam."

"My parents or my mom?"

That seems to catch him off guard, and he's silent for a moment. "Your mother called me, but I've known your mother and father for a long time, so I'm sure they're both worried."

Or not.

"What do they want?" No *sir* or *please* or *may I ask*. I'm not up for it.

"They want to see you, Sam. They want to make things right."

"Hang on." Sarah glances at me and stops on the shoulder of the road.

I put down the phone and rub my face, my lack of sleep catching up with me all at once. She turns to me and nods, mouthing, "You can do this." I feel her love wrapping around me like a blanket.

"Okay," I finally answer. "When?"

"Would four o'clock work for you?" Pastor Jeff's voice picks up a bit of its usual volume.

"Where?"

"I thought we could meet at your home. It would be more... private, since I never know who might pop in at the church office."

"Okay." I hang up without a *goodbye*.

Sarah leans across the car's console and pats my cheek. "I know it's hard, but you're doing the right thing."

I nod, but my heart is cold and heavy.

*

I wish Sarah could be here.

I'm sitting in the family room of the house I grew up in yet I feel like a stranger. Mom is seated in her wingback chair, and Pastor Jeff is on the sofa with me. Dad isn't here yet, and his massive recliner seems to be waiting for him, like a throne.

"Y'all are sure I can't get anything for you? A piece of cake or some coffee or tea?" Mom has made a valiant effort to be a good hostess since Pastor Jeff and I arrived. She's trying so hard to appear normal—*fine*, as Sarah and I would say—that I'm afraid she'll snap like a rubber band stretched a bit too far.

"No, thank you," we say in unison. Pastor Jeff studies his fingernails, I the carpet, and Mom the grandfather clock. Its tick-tocking is the only sound in the house.

Where in the world is Dad?

"I can't imagine what's holding up Chad," Mom says to no one in particular. "He's not answering my texts, and calls are going right to voicemail."

"Maybe he left his phone at his office and now he's stuck in traffic," Pastor Jeff suggests. He might as well have theorized that aliens had kidnapped my father and asked for help with their wiring. Chad Russell is always within an arm's length of his phone.

Mom doesn't bother to respond. "I don't know. It might have gone dead, but he has a charger in his car." She twists a tissue in her hands as she walks to the window. "Maybe…" She stops, the color draining from her face. "No," she whispers. Then, "No!" as she runs to the front door.

"Mom?" I'm behind her as she opens it.

For a moment the scene freezes, like a still taken from a movie. From my perspective, it is framed by the "L" of my mother's neck and shoulder. A state trooper stands in the doorway. His nameplate says *Hathaway*. Is this the same man who helped rescue Sarah and Emilia? He seems kind of old, his eyes soft and kind, like a grandfather's.

Mom brings her arms around to hug herself, and I rest my hands on her shoulders. Pastor Jeff comes alongside us. He, Mom, the trooper, and I seem to be waiting for a cue, a director's call to action.

It comes from Mom. "Who is it?" I can't see her face, but I'm surprised by the calm and evenness of her voice. "It's Chad, isn't it?"

"Mrs. Russell," Trooper Hathaway starts.

"Where is he?" Mom turns to me. "Sam, we'll ride together. You drive and I'll call Megan." She looks back at the trooper. "Where is he? Which hospital?"

Mom and I gasp when we see Uncle Rob trudging up the porch steps. He moves around the trooper and takes Mom's hands. "Kathy."

Mom falls back into my arms, but she doesn't faint. She dissolves.

I turn her into my chest and wrap my arms around her. I feel her words before I can understand them, thrumming against my rib cage. "No, Jesus. No. No. No." Each word builds on the last, like a storm rolling in over the mountains. "Please, Jesus. Oh, God. Oh, God, no."

This is a bad dream. God is telling me to make things right with Dad. *Okay. I'll call him when I wake up. This is a dream, isn't it, Jesus? Just like with the wolf. Right?*

My body shudders with the answer. *No.*

A spike made of stone drills into my head, splitting me in half. I hold Mom tighter to keep from doubling over.

Why didn't you take me instead?

Then I hear it. Not the dark rumble I heard with Dakota, but something clear and deep.

Take heart. I have overcome the world.

I pick up my mother—she suddenly seems so tiny, like she's been cut in two—carry her inside, and place her gently on the sofa. Our pastor, our friend, and the trooper follow us into the family room in a silent procession and wait. Mom leans into my side and her keening subsides as I stroke her head.

"What happened?" It's my voice but not me. I have been picked up too, and gently settled in a quiet place.

The trooper works at the brim of his hat as he sits at the edge of Mom's chair. "Mr. Russell was traveling southbound on I-81 when he saw another motorist, Ms. Houseman, on the shoulder. She said he pulled over and asked if she needed help. Ms. Houseman told him she had a flat tire. She had left voicemails with her boyfriend and her father, and was sure one of them would get back to her soon."

Mom focuses on the trooper, her hands covering her mouth.

"Ms. Houseman told us that Mr. Russell insisted on changing the tire, saying he wouldn't want his wife or daughter stranded on the side of a busy interstate."

"That's just like Chad," Mom whispers. "He always…" The tears return, quietly this time.

Trooper Hathaway nods. "Mr. Russell and Ms. Houseman were removing the spare and lug wrench from the trunk when Mr. Russell noticed a car coming toward them. Ms. Houseman said it was like he sensed it more than saw it, because the next thing she knew she felt a strong shove as she was pushed into the grassy area by the roadway. She looked back just as…" The trooper hesitates.

"Go on," Mom says.

"She looked back just as the car hit Mr. Russell."

Mom turns into me again and whimpers like a child.

Dear God.

"Did he suffer?" I ask.

The trooper shakes his head vigorously. "No. No. We're certain of that."

"What about the person who hit him?" Uncle Rob's voice trembles with anger.

"The driver had minor injuries. We're questioning him now." Trooper Hathaway's cool, professional tone has an edge to it.

Mom turns to me. It's the first time I've looked into her eyes since she walked over to the window only a few minutes ago. But in that short span of time, she's been hollowed out, like a cancer patient who has been burned and cut and poisoned in a vain attempt at survival.

Dad's gone. And so is Mom.

"What will I do without him, Sammy? Sweet Jesus, what will I do?"

I pull her close. *Help her, God. Please. Help us all.*

CHAPTER 13

MOM IS IN her bedroom, resting. Well, not really. Uncle Rob finally persuaded her to take a sedative, so she's quiet now. But I don't know when she'll rest again.

I've been on the phone, caught up in the machinery of loss. Uncle Rob and Pastor Jeff suggested that family be notified in person if possible, so we enlisted friends for that duty. We divided up the list. I'm grateful I have had only a couple of these terrible conversations.

My first call was to Uncle Peter, and I didn't know if I would be able to make another.

"What?" he said when I told him Dad was gone.

"There was an accident. Dad is gone," I repeated.

My cool, articulate, always-in-command uncle fell apart after that. We did discuss, through breaks in his sobbing, who should notify Grandma and Grandpa, since Uncle Peter and Aunt Jackie live in Maryland. Uncle Peter said he would enlist Isabel and Joe Patterson, who have lived next door to Grandma and Grandpa for ages. I pray he can make the call.

I also spoke with Brittany, Megan's roommate, and told her that Aunt Suzanne would be coming to Charlotte to bring Megan home. "Thank God for that," was her response. "She's going to be devastated."

Clara Carpenter and Mrs. Winston came over shortly after we got the news. I hear the clank of pots and pans in the kitchen as they cook food no one feels like eating. I guess they're also clearing the decks for the casseroles and cakes and pies soon to be delivered from ladies at church.

And Sarah is with me. We've spoken little, but I need her touch more than her words right now. She has released my hand only to get me a glass of water or when I've needed to look up a number or write something down.

When I opened the door and saw her standing there, her face wet with tears, I felt her hug even before she wrapped her arms around me.

"How are you doing?" she whispered against my chest.

"Okay," I murmured.

She pulled away and touched my face.

I preempted her question. "I'm not saying I'm fine. But I must focus on Mom and Megan now. I need to do this for Dad."

"All right. But I'll be here when it's time for you."

I squeezed her tighter. "I know, baby. I know."

The front door opens—nobody's bothering with the bell any-more—and Grandma and Grandpa stagger in. Grandma is glued to Grandpa's side, his arm the only thing keeping her from falling to the floor. Grandpa's eyes latch onto mine for a fragment of a second, and I recognize the invisible thread holding him together.

"My sweet boy," Grandma says as she reaches for me. I walk into her arms to offer comfort, but realize too late that she intends to care for me. "My sweet, sweet Sam. Your daddy loved you so much. He was so proud of you…" Her voice breaks just as I feel myself giving in to her sympathy.

I take a deep breath and release her into Grandpa's embrace. "He loved both of you too. Dad said you kept him on the right path."

Grandpa's mouth lifts slightly into a half grin, even as he starts to cry. "That took us and the Lord. That boy could be a handful."

"Olivia? Richard?"

We turn to see Mom clinging to the stair rail, and I rush to her side. "Go back to bed, Mom."

She pushes me away, but her touch feels as insubstantial as a breeze. "No. I need to visit with your grandparents."

"Mom."

She runs her fingers through my hair, much as Sarah did earlier this afternoon. "You'll need to get a haircut tomorrow, Sammy. You know how much your father likes a neat haircut." She continues down the stairs, holding on to the rail like old Mrs. Smith at church. "Olivia, Richard," Mom repeats.

Grandma and Grandpa welcome her into their embrace.

The house is still, as quiet as snow in the middle of the night. Even the busyness in the kitchen pauses and the ladies glide into the foyer. All of us stand by reverently and watch as the three people who knew Dad best cling to each other, adrift in a dark sea.

Oh, dear God, I cannot do this.

Remain in Me.

My heart returns to the quiet place, and I lead my mother and my grandparents to the family room. "I'll be right back with some tea, okay?" I pat Mom's hand.

Sarah grazes my arm as I walk into the kitchen, and I see she's holding my phone. I didn't even hear it ring. I don't have to see the screen to know who's calling. One glance at Sarah's face tells me. Megan.

My sister's voice sounds broken by static, although the connection is clear. "Brittany got it wrong. I'm sure she did. Tell me she got it wrong, Sam. Tell me she got it wrong."

"Honey, she didn't," I start.

"No, no, no, no, no." Megan says the word until it becomes a single sound. I hear rustling, and Brittany comes on the line.

"Your aunt is coming to get her, right?" Her voice is strained, desperate. "Because it's all I can do to keep her here, and she's in no shape to drive."

"Thanks, Brittany. Try to get her back on the phone, okay?"

There is more movement, then a faint, "Yes?"

"Megan." I move outside to our back deck, but I still lower my voice. "Mom's in bad shape. So are Grandma and Grandpa."

The voice becomes stronger. "Of course."

"I need your help, Megan. I can't do this without you."

"Yeah, yeah, sure." She's beginning to sound more like my big sister. The one who looks out for her brother.

"Can you hang in there for me, sis? Please?"

She clears her throat. "Yeah. We'll get through this together, Sam. You and me and Mom." The resolve in Megan's voice almost melts the resolve in mine.

"Wait for Aunt Suzanne, okay? Mom will worry if you try to drive home alone."

"Of course. I'll start packing now. Sam?"

"Yes?"

"I love you."

"Love you too." I hang up before she hears my tremble.

Only then do I realize Sarah's fingers are interlaced with mine.

*

I spent last night in the Reynoldses' guest room, consumed with thoughts about myself. My anger. My hurt feelings. My future. But I don't have time to rifle through my dirty laundry. I've been given the mission of carrying my mother and sister through this fire. Perhaps this is the beginning of my penance.

I turn to face my bedroom door, as if a change in position will bring sleep. I thought about asking Uncle Rob for a sleeping pill but decided against it in case it left me foggy. But I'm glad Megan took something.

Sweet Megan. She arrived with a brave face and consoled Mom with tender words and a gentle touch. It wasn't until Mom went upstairs to bed that she fell apart in my arms. "This isn't right, Sam," she gasped between sobs. "It isn't right. Mom needs Dad, we need Dad, and God knows that. How could He take him away from us?"

"I don't know, Meg. I don't know." I swayed slightly as I held her, like I've seen mothers do with their toddlers at church. The movement quieted her, so I kept it up. We sat like that on the sofa for a long time, neither of us speaking, until I began to wonder if my sister had fallen asleep. "Megan?" I whispered.

"Uh-huh."

"You should get some rest. We've got a long day tomorrow."

She sat up. "You're right. We've got to be there for Mom."

"Yeah. For Mom."

Megan started to rise but stopped and stared at me. "You're just like him, you know." She kissed the top of my head. "Just like him. Love you."

Remembering Megan's words pushes aside any hope of rest. I might as well go downstairs and get a cup of herbal tea or a glass of milk. Anything will be better than turning back and forth in my bed, chasing sleep.

When I reach the foot of the stairs, I hear the squeak-squeak-squeak of Dad's recliner rocking back and forth. I rush to the family room, convinced for a millisecond that I'll see him there, waiting to talk to me about med school or Sarah or Christmas lights.

But it's Mom. She's curled up in the chair, as if in Dad's lap, and is stroking the cushions tenderly with the back of her hand. For another millisecond I think Dad is there, and I can almost see his pale outline.

I shouldn't be here.

This is too raw, too intimate. My mother's loss laid bare. I try to back out of the room quietly.

"I didn't kiss him goodbye yesterday."

I freeze, uncertain whether to respond. Mom might not even know I'm here. The only light in the room comes from the Christmas candles still glowing in the windows. They're the first decorations set out and the last put away, because Mom likes them so much. Dad bought nice ones with timers a few years ago, so she would see them throughout the long winter night.

"I didn't kiss him goodbye," Mom repeats, and I kneel at her side. "I always do, you know. Always have. But I was still mad yesterday morning, so when he came and put his arms around me, I turned away." She covers her face with her hands. "Oh my God, I turned away. That was my last moment with him and…oh, God."

Oh, God.

The fragments of my heart break apart into even smaller pieces, but I must tend Mom's bleeding, not mine. "Dad knew you loved him, Mama." I run my fingers down her arm and try to keep my voice soft and even. "He wouldn't want you to worry about that. He knew, Mama. He knew."

Mom stares at me like she's only now realizing I am there. "I'm so sorry, Sammy. I'm so sorry."

"Why?"

She sits up and takes my hands. "I'm your mother. I should be the one comforting you and Megan, not the other way around." Even her eyes are pale, like the tears have washed out the blue in them.

I hug her tightly. "No apologies now," I whisper. "We're going to get through this as a family, taking care of each other."

"Like your daddy would have wanted."

"Yes, ma'am."

*

There is no manual for death. No how-to books, no checklist, except what the guys at the funeral home and your pastor tell you.

Mom and Dad had new wills drawn up five years ago, but they hadn't talked about cremation or burial plots or obituaries. Mr. Burrell, the director at his family's funeral home, is asking Mom if Dad would have preferred burial or cremation.

"Burial, definitely. Chad hates being hot."

Mom, Megan, and I stare at each other for a beat before we start giggling, which leads to full-on laughter. Mr. Burrell looks at us with a neutral expression, something they probably teach at funeral school.

The laughter feels right and good. I swear I feel Dad laughing with us, and the throbbing in my chest subsides for a few moments.

We leave with two plots purchased—Mom said she didn't want to wind up next to some stranger—and all the arrangements made. Mr. Burrell asked us for photos of Dad to be used at the visitation, and Megan and I agreed to handle that.

"Our meeting with Pastor Jeff isn't until two, so we have plenty of time for me to make you some lunch." Mom seems to have returned to herself outwardly—planning and organizing Dad's funeral with the same efficiency she displays with dinner parties and company balance sheets. But when I woke at dawn, I heard Dad's recliner creaking again.

"You don't need to fuss over us, Mom." Megan reaches from the back seat to squeeze her shoulder. "Sam and I can cook, can't we, bro?"

I'm driving, and as I glance at my mother and sister, I can almost hear Dad in my head: "You're the man of the house now, son. I'm counting on you."

I rest my hand on Megan's. "Sure. Grilled cheese is my specialty. And spaghetti for special occasions."

Mom smiles slightly. "Oh, for goodness' sake, I'm not an invalid. Anyway, we might not have to cook anything, considering how much food has been delivered to the house."

"Just don't force me to eat Mrs. Dawson's chicken casserole," I plead. "It's got about five pounds of mushrooms in it."

Mom rolls her eyes. "You and your dad and mushrooms. I'll never understand." The smile brightens and then collapses, like a dying star, and she turns to look out the window.

Stupid mushrooms.

*

We had a buffet for lunch, spooning up dollops of chicken casserole (the good one brought by Aunt Suzanne), lasagna, and shepherd's pie onto our plates, then zapping them in the microwave.

Sarah texts as I slide the last casserole dish back into the refrigerator. *Home?*

Yes. You? I step outside and look at her house.

Sarah responds by walking out onto her porch. Her red hair captures the weak winter light and throws it back to me, like a lighthouse.

Oh, Jesus, she is so beautiful. Not an exclamation, but a prayer.

I'm walking—almost running, actually—to meet her when I feel something tugging at me. Megan and I need to get going on those photos of Dad, and I should talk to Mom about our meeting with Pastor Jeff. He'll be here in about thirty minutes, and we haven't discussed the funeral service at all—what songs to sing, Bible readings to include, nothing. What was Dad's favorite hymn? I can't remember.

Sarah reaches out for an embrace, but I take her hands instead. She studies my face as I hold her literally at arm's length. "How are you doing?" she finally asks. Her face is drawn downward with sadness, but her brows are knotted with worry.

"All right, I guess." Now I remember. "It Is Well with My Soul."

"Sam?"

"What?"

"You're not all right."

I let go of her hands and shove mine in my pockets. "Maybe all right isn't the right word, but I've got stuff to do, especially until we get through the funeral. A lot of decisions to be made. You know."

Sarah removes one of her gloves and caresses my cheek. Her touch is delicate and warm. And treacherous. God is holding me together for now, but Sarah's tenderness could make me come undone.

I gently move her hand away. "I'm sorry. But I can't get...distracted. I realized today how much we have to do in a short time."

Sarah's green eyes glaze over, with pain this time. "I just want to help," she whispers. "Let me help, Sam. You don't have to carry everything alone."

She doesn't understand, but that's not her fault. She can't understand. "I know you want to help. And you will. Later."

Sarah leans into me, her head against my chest.

I crave her comfort, holding her in a light embrace.

"Promise me," she murmurs.

"Promise what?"

Sarah steps away and clasps both of my hands. I'm stung by the sight of her tears. "That you'll let me help soon. Or if not me, somebody else. Okay?"

I tuck one of her curls behind her ear and kiss her cheek. "I promise."

But I have work to do first.

*

"The bottom line is that every family is different. How much you want to participate in the funeral is up to you. Don't let anyone pressure you to do anything you're not comfortable with." Pastor Jeff's booming voice has been replaced by one so soft, I strain to hear it. I suppose that's how he usually talks to those in mourning, but there's nothing insincere or practiced about it. He seems to be hurting right alongside us but fulfilling his calling nevertheless.

Mom, Grandma, Grandpa, Mimi, Megan, Pastor Jeff, and I are gathered around the dining room table. I've never sat in here without a week's worth of food before me. Now the table is empty, as are we.

We've talked about songs and Bible verses Dad liked, and Grandma and Grandpa shared a couple of funny stories from his childhood. Mom insists that the funeral include glimpses of Dad's humor—"his playful nature," as she calls it.

Now we need to decide if any family members will speak at the service. The silence is stretching out as each of us pictures ourselves at the pulpit.

Grandma speaks first. "Peter told me this morning that he'd like to say a few words. He used to follow Charles around like a little puppy when they were children, but Charles never..."—Grandma's voice skitters as she begins to cry—"never lost patience with him. He was such a good big brother." Dad decided he wanted to be called "Chad" when he was seventeen, but he never stopped being "Charles" to Grandma.

We nod in unison. Uncle Peter will do a good job.

"I want to speak."

We all turn to Megan, who works hard to remain out of the spotlight.

"This is the last thing I can do for my daddy, and I need to do it."

Mom puts her arm around her. "You're sure, honey?"

"Yes, ma'am," she manages to whisper.

I have no choice. "Then I'll speak too." Maybe Megan and I can draw strength from each other.

Mom is sitting between us, and she grabs my left hand and Megan's right. "Your father would be so proud of both of you."

Grandpa clears his throat. "He was proud of his children." He stares at me. "Very proud."

I should add, "Until his son turned on him." Does Grandpa know what happened? No, no, he must not. I wish he would turn away.

"I think that covers everything." Pastor Jeff zips up the cover holding his Bible and closes the folder with his notes. "Of course, you can call me anytime. Shall we pray before I leave?" He reaches out to Megan on one side and Grandma on the other, and we all join hands and bow our heads. "Dear God," he begins, his voice rising from counselor softness to a light version of his sermon tone, "You know what this sweet family is going through. You know what all of Chad's friends are going through. He was a good man, taken from us too soon."

I squeeze Mom's hand as it starts to tremble.

"We don't understand this, Father. It doesn't make sense to us. But we put our trust in You, the One who brings light out of darkness. And we thank You for Chad Russell, for giving us the opportunity to share this journey with him."

I drop Mom's hand and put my arm around her.

"I pray that you'll cover Chad's loved ones with Your peace, the peace that surpasses all understanding. And I ask that You give Megan and Sam Your words when they speak at the service, that they will be filled with Your power, so that others will see Your glory in them. I ask all this in Jesus's name. Amen."

I take a deep breath before opening my eyes. *Please, Jesus. Please.*

CHAPTER 14

THE PAST FIVE days have been a blur. Funeral preparations, the arrival of Aunt Jackie and Uncle Peter, and visit after visit from Dad's friends and colleagues. Each new expression of sympathy has been bittersweet, reminding us of Dad's impact on others while ripping the scab off our loss. I guess there's no way around that. It would be horrible if no one came forward to share our grief, if Dad's death didn't even show up on their radar.

Megan and I have struggled to come up with the right words for our eulogies, so we stayed up late last night brainstorming together.

"It's so hard to come up with the right balance." She pulled her knees up to her chest and stared into the fireplace.

"What do you mean?"

"You know. Between funny and serious. And keeping it real."

I was lost. "Keeping it real?"

Megan turned to me. "We had an awesome father. But he wasn't perfect." She reached out for my hand. "I know, Sam."

My breath caught. How could she know? She must be talking about something else. Better to play dumb. "Know what?"

Her eyes filled with tears. "I couldn't sleep last night and came downstairs. Mom was in the kitchen and we talked. She's worried about you."

I shook my head. "She shouldn't be."

She took my other hand. "But she is, Sam. She told me that you and dad had a huge fight the night before the accident and terrible things were said. Now she's worried that you're carrying that fight around in your heart."

I closed my eyes to block the memory. "I can't...not now. Please, Meg. Just let me get through tomorrow."

She squeezed my hands before letting go. "Okay, Sam. Okay. But don't forget that we love you and we're here for you."

I nodded even as I thought that my sister has no idea who I am. "Thanks, sis."

Now we're all lined up in a pew, waiting for the service to begin. It feels strange to be up front. The middle rows are our comfort zone. Mom is seated between Megan and me, her tight grip on our hands the only sign that she's struggling.

I saw Sarah when I walked in, and her soft smile almost undid me. I love her so much, and when this is all over, I will tell her so. I will take her in my arms and kiss her and we'll return to planning our future.

When will this be over?

Sarah and I spoke at the visitation, then she kept her distance. I know I hurt her by pulling away, but she isn't holding a grudge. She doesn't do that. Instead, she's giving me the space I asked for, a request that feels incredibly stupid right now.

We had the visitation right before the service in the little chapel that served as our church's first sanctuary. Our family stood in a receiving line, accepting hugs and handshakes and condolences from a continuous stream of people. It felt like all of Early and half of the Shenandoah Valley showed up.

Over and over, I heard words of comfort, all around the same theme: Dad was a good man.

"There was no better friend than your dad."

"Your dad gave me my first job when other folks wouldn't."

"Your dad jumped in and got our food pantry going."

"Your dad led me to Christ."

Lissi, Rebecca, Kevin, and Jack came through the line, all giving me bear hugs, even the guys. I was surprised when I saw Gavin walk through the door. He gave me a real hug too, and thanked me for the Bible.

I didn't know if I would make it.

Mom was beautiful and composed, offering consolation to those who came to console. I'm not sure how she's hanging in there. It must be a God thing.

Pastor Jeff is talking now, but I'm not following him. I'm scattered between past, present, and future—fighting the current drawing me back to that awful night even as I dream of a life with Sarah. I'm incapable of standing still in time.

Still. God's message is not any clearer to me now than it was back in October. Maybe I'm too dense to get it.

I drag myself back to the present as we stand to sing "It Is Well with My Soul." Our church doesn't use traditional hymns much anymore. Mostly praise songs that go on and on for, like, a dozen verses, with only a word or two of variation between them. A lot of people get into the repetition—Megan, for instance—but I find it boring.

I like the old songs better. Each verse forces me to focus if I want to understand what I am singing. Autopilot doesn't work.

> *When peace like a river, attendeth my way,*
> *When sorrows like sea billows roll*
> *Whatever my lot, thou hast taught me to say*
> *It is well, it is well, with my soul.*

Mom leans into me, her eyes closed. A single tear flows down her face, and I can feel her anguish. It is tangible—a dark, thorny thing sinking its roots in deep.

Sorrows like sea billows. Yeah, that writer understood pain.

> *Though Satan should buffet, though trials should come,*
> *Let this blest assurance control,*
> *That Christ has regarded my helpless estate,*
> *And hath shed His own blood for my soul.*

Some of the tension leaves Mom's body, and she stands straighter. She's pulling it together now. She'll make it through the service.

Will Megan? Will I?

*

Uncle Peter is shuffling to the pulpit. He's five years younger than Dad, but today he looks ten years older, at least. He locks on to us with his red-rimmed eyes and smiles slightly. "Kathy, Megan, Sam. Mom, Dad. There are no words for this moment. We never imagined coming together to remember Chad. Not now, anyway. Not for many, many years. My big brother used to tease me—that is what big brothers do, of course—about our different levels of fitness. How he was fit and I wasn't."

A low chuckle vibrates through the sanctuary.

"I'd respond that I planned for him to outlive me so he'd have to give a big speech saying how awesome I was. He'd roll his eyes and answer, 'But I'm no good at creative writing.'" Uncle Peter stares down at his notes and takes a deep breath. "I'm not either. But when it comes to Chad Russell, I don't have to be."

I want to crawl back inside my head. I can't.

"I'm not here to list my brother's achievements. You know about them already. As you can guess, the one he was most proud of is sitting in the front pew." Uncle Peter looks at us again, his lower lip trembling.

Please hold it together, I beg him silently. *If you don't, there's no way I will.*

Uncle Peter stares right at me, like he heard my thoughts. His voice is steady when he speaks again. "Chad and I joked around most of the time, but I'll never forget a conversation we had years ago, when I was going through a rough time."

A rough time? I never heard about any rough times for Uncle Peter. Dad called his little brother "Golden Boy," since he seemed to glide from one success to another: college, law school, marriage, a prosperous practice. At Christmas I overheard Dad talking to Uncle Peter about the possibility of his becoming a judge.

"Chad told me that I'd be okay as long as I kept my priorities in the proper order: God first, followed by family, then friends, with worldly success at the bottom of the list. I will never forget what he said: 'Pete, nothing I do is worth a damn if I fail as a husband and father.' I think it's clear that my brother did not fail."

Mom, Megan, and I nod in unison, and I sense those around us doing the same. *Oh, God, please keep us going for a little longer.*

"Chad Russell was uncomfortable with praise, so I'm sure that if he were here, he'd either try to drag me away from this pulpit—and, as I've noted, he was stronger than me—or run from the sanctuary. My brother managed to deflect every compliment I ever sent in his direction. But I hope he knew this: I always wanted to be just like him."

Uncle Peter looks up to the corner of the ceiling and closes his eyes for a moment. I see the change come over him. He's not trying to power through in his own strength anymore. When he returns his gaze to the congregation, he looks calm and confident, like the judge he's likely to become. "Chad Russell lived and loved with his whole heart, with nothing held in reserve. He put all his resources at the disposal of his friends and family: time, money and talents. If you needed him, he was there, without complaint."

I hear a soft "That's right," from the back.

"And Chad's wholehearted approach to life was reflected in his devotion to Jesus Christ. He loved his Savior with all his mind, all his heart, and all his spirit. Chad would tell you that his relationship with Jesus made his bond with us possible."

He swallows. "When I got the news about the accident five days ago, I was shocked and saddened to the core. But I wasn't surprised. Of course my brother, Charles Timothy Russell, would sacrifice himself to save another. That was his nature."

Mom, Megan, and I squeeze in close to each other as a fresh wave of grief approaches.

"I know,"—Uncle Peter pats his chest as his tears return—"I know that when Chad showed up in heaven the other day, Jesus wrapped His arms around him and held him tight. And I know that the Savior whispered the words my brother had waited a lifetime to hear: 'Well done, good and faithful servant.'"

As Uncle Peter returns to his seat, he stops at our pew. He bends down to kiss the top of Mom's head and Megan's and ruffles my hair, just the way Dad used to. My longing for one more hug—one more light punch to the shoulder—tears through me, squeezing the breath from my lungs.

Uncle Rob is up next, but I manage to tune out his eulogy.

Then it is Megan's turn. I can't disengage now. My sister needs all the silent encouragement I can give her.

There's a fragile beauty to Megan today, like an iridescent bubble floating upward. I wrench my focus from myself and begin praying for her. As I do, I realize, maybe for the first time, how much I love her.

Megan clasps her hands and rests them on the pulpit as she looks out over the congregation. Although she has never wanted to be the center of anyone's attention, she appears...not comfortable exactly, but resigned. No, that's not right. More like ready. "Over the last few years, every time our extended family has gotten together, I've been asked if I'm seeing someone special. This Christmas I finally came up with a good response: 'Every guy I have ever dated has known that Chad Russell is an expert marksman.'"

Megan waits for the laughter to fade. "Dad pretended to be offended. 'What is that supposed to mean?' he asked. 'Well,' I answered, 'Maybe it's a coincidence, but my last boyfriend actually moved to the West Coast when our relationship ended.' Dad just shrugged and said, 'He wasn't good enough for my baby girl anyway.'" She looks down and rubs her notecards between her fingers.

Come on, Meg, I plead silently. *Just a little longer. Hang in there.*

She squeezes her eyes shut before returning her gaze to us. "And you know what? He was right. Not about the guy being unworthy of me, but about his being good enough. Because he wasn't as good as my father." Megan looks at me and smiles. She will hold it together now. "Sam and I were blessed to have Chad Russell as our dad. He had high expectations for us— 'You can't let your gifts go to waste,' we heard more than once—and we chafed at that from time to time. But we never doubted that Dad loved us and wanted only the best for us."

But I did doubt. *God, help me.*

Mom drops my hand, wraps an arm around me, and holds me tight. My darkness subsides, and I return my focus to Megan.

"Dad wasn't perfect, but I can't imagine a better role model. He loved Mom without reservation, and I refuse to settle for a husband who doesn't look at me the way he looked at her."

Mom rests her head on my shoulder, and I feel her composure collapsing.

Megan pauses when she sees Mom crying, but manages to keep going. "And Dad never failed to make time for us, whether joining me for a tea party, crouching in one of my child-sized chairs, or playing catch with Sam and me in the backyard until it got dark." Tears are sliding down Megan's cheeks, but her voice remains steady. "But the greatest thing he ever did was to introduce us to Jesus Christ, and to show us how to live for Him. When I see Dad again—he'll probably be rewiring heaven's streetlights—I'll thank him for showing me what's really important." She looks down at the casket. "I love you, Daddy."

I rise when Megan returns to the pew and hold her close. She's shaking as her sobs take over. "You were great," I whisper.

It's my turn.

My legs have turned to jelly. The three steps to the platform might as well be three hundred. I'm not sure if I am going to faint or be sick. I take deep breaths, forcing oxygen into my system.

When I finally reach the pulpit, I place my notes in front of me and carefully smooth out the paper. I scan the congregation, but only Sarah's face is in focus. She's staring at me with such intensity that I can almost see a beam of white light traveling between us, a bond of love and trust that has been damaged but not destroyed. She nods slightly, and I hear her message as surely as if she had shouted it: *You can do this.*

Okay. Here we go.

I glance at my notes again, but they're trash. Nice words that could be said at anyone's funeral, changing the name and details as necessary. *Fill-in-the-blank was a good man/woman and a great dad/ mom. Everyone knew you could count on him/her,* etc. I fold up the paper and put it in the inside pocket of my coat.

"I was told recently that I'm just like my father. At the time, Dad and I were not seeing eye to eye on some things, so I wasn't sure how to take the comparison. But today, listening to Uncle Peter, Uncle Rob, and Megan speak, I realized something."

Mom and Megan are huddled together, fingers interlaced, like they're trying to get warm. They smile slightly at me.

I clear my throat. "I realized that I'm not just like my father. But I want to be." The sick feeling has disappeared. "I can see things we have—had—in common: a love of Virginia Tech and my mother's cooking and a distaste for mushrooms."

My mother and sister laugh softly, and my strength starts to return.

"We're both hard-headed and determined, so I guess that explains our recent disagreement." I hope understatement is not a lie, especially in a church. "But I have a long way to go before I'll be just like my father: selfless and generous to a fault, slow to anger, and walking close to the Lord daily."

My throat starts to burn. *No, no, no.* "I hope…" I take another deep breath. *Please.* "I hope that when I see Dad again, he'll be proud of the person I became." Another breath. "Love you, Dad."

Mom and Megan wrap their arms around me when I return to the pew. It's over. Thank God, it's over.

*

Our church holds luncheons in the fellowship hall after funerals, and I was worried this would turn into yet another receiving line. But fried chicken, Mrs. Peterson's potato casserole—the one with all the cheese in it—as well as a runway of other vegetables and desserts have distracted people from further expressions of sympathy. I'm okay with that.

I've managed to step away from the crowd to a corner by the window when I feel a familiar touch on my shoulder. Before she can say a word, I pull Sarah into my arms.

You can let go now.

Sarah holds me tight, and we're back in our bubble. "I'm sorry," I whisper.

She moves away to look at me, as if I just announced I'm a Martian. "For what?"

I pull one of her curls through my fingers before tucking it behind her ear. "For pushing you away."

She shakes her head. "You did what you had to do to get through this. But now…"

I can't let go. Not yet.

I take her hand in mine. "I still need to help Mom. You know, insurance and the estate and everything. I'm…" I look away as a new idea settles on me. "I'm beginning to wonder if I should go back this semester."

Sarah grabs both my hands and stares at me, her eyes narrowed.

"Have you talked to your mother about this? I can't imagine she'd want you to quit school."

I glance at Mom. Mrs. Peterson is trying to hand her a plate filled with food, but Mom is shaking her head. I know Mom doesn't feel like eating, but she looks like she's about to fall over.

"Sam?"

I study Sarah's long, thin fingers wrapped around mine. "It wouldn't be quitting. I could go back at any time. It's not like I know what I'm doing anyway."

She laces her fingers through mine. "Just don't make any decisions without talking to your mom, okay?"

I give her a gentle kiss on her forehead. "I promise."

She wraps her arms around me. My grief and regret are joined by a sudden rush of love for Sarah, for my mother, for my sister, for my friends, and the rest of my family.

For Dad, who will never know how I feel.

CHAPTER 15

MOM AND MEGAN insisted that I return to school for the spring
semester. Mom wasn't pleased when Megan announced she was taking
a leave of absence from her job to help her with the estate details and
decisions about Russell Electric, but Megan didn't back down, and I
feel better knowing Mom isn't alone.

I know it's selfish, but focusing on my classes has tamped down the
pain in my chest, bringing it from a constant stabbing to a muted ache.
Still, sometimes, right before I go to sleep, I feel like I've wandered back
into the caverns, and the guide's hand is poised over the light switch.

I go home every weekend, so I don't see Sarah much. She went
with me the first couple of times, but stopped when I told her I had
to focus on my family during those visits. She said she understood.

Sarah and I talk or text pretty much every day. Nothing deep. She
knows my classes and Mom and Megan are my top priorities now.
I must stay in my lane and keep swimming. There will be time for
Sarah and me later.

"Want to talk?" Megan's voice startles me. I didn't even hear her
walk into the room. "Or should I call Uncle Rob for a tranquilizer?
You're as jumpy as a cat." She smiles, but her eyes give her away.

"Very funny, sis." I give her shoulder a light tap. "Just thinking
about stuff." Returning my gaze to our backyard, I wish we had a
birdfeeder village like Uncle Rob and Aunt Suzanne.

Megan turns me toward her with gentle pressure on my arm. "Sam, we need to talk."

When I give her my full attention, I realize she has grown up a lot in the past six weeks. Not that she was ever flighty or immature. I once overheard Dad say she was born middle-aged. But there's a greater depth to her now, like she understands things she didn't even think about before. I guess death does that.

"What do we need to talk about?" My mind goes to its usual place. "Is it Mom?"

Megan shakes her head, takes my hand, and leads me to the sofa. "You're kind of scaring me, Meg. What is it?"

She takes my other hand. "It's you."

My mouth drops open and I jerk backward, like my sister has punched me in the gut. "What do you mean?"

She pulls me back toward her. "We're worried about you."

"We? Like you and—"

"Me." Mom walks in and sits beside me. "Megan, I said both of us should talk to your brother."

"I know." I hear the same I'm-caught tone in Megan's voice that I've heard since we were kids. "But I thought that this was something I could take care of for you."

"Excuse me. I'm right here." I look at my mother on one side and my sister on the other, and it strikes me that this is an intervention. Like I'm an addict or something. "Whatever this is, I don't have time for it." I rise and start walking toward the stairs. "I know you mean well, but I need to do some work for chemistry class. I'd also like to go around and switch out the air filters today."

"That's it, honey." Mom and Megan look at each other.

Forget the intervention. I've stumbled into a meeting of a secret society.

"What?" I shove my hands in my pockets so I won't start waving my arms around like a crazy person.

Mom crosses the room and places her hands on my shoulders.

"That's it," she says in an almost whisper. "You're coming home every weekend—without Sarah, I might add—and studying or working around the house every minute you're home. Megan and I are worried that you're burning yourself out."

My heart has started to hammer. "I'm not. I'm trying—"

"To take care of us," Mom says. "But what about you, son? Who's taking care of you?"

I remember holding Sarah's hands after the funeral. She wanted to take care of me. My throat starts to burn.

Megan joins Mom and me in the doorway. "Mom and I will be fine if you spend some weekends at school. Take Sarah out on a date. Go to a basketball game. Live your life."

"But you've given up your job and moved here."

Mom appears stricken, like I've slapped her. "And I begged her not to do that."

Megan narrows her eyes at me, then goes soft when she turns to Mom. "My job will be waiting for me once everything's settled. I want to be here." The narrowed eyes return. "And Sam, my situation is different. Because of my leave, I can focus on Mom and the company. I'm not torn in a dozen directions like you are."

I clench my fists in my pockets. Time to wrap this up. "I'm not torn. I'm prioritizing, that's all." On that weak exit line, I head to my room.

But I feel the eyes of my mother and sister following me.

*

I'm thankful Mom and Megan didn't restart their intervention. I know they love me, but they don't understand how I have things lined up. I'm still unsure about med school, but if I don't get good grades, I'm shutting down the possibility entirely.

I'm sorry I brought up Megan's moving in with Mom, even if it is temporary. Mom feels really guilty about that. But the fact remains that I need to do my part. Basic home maintenance, getting the cars inspected, that sort of thing. I didn't realize how much I observed Dad over the years. I wonder if he did.

And Sarah. Yeah, I have put our relationship on a back burner, and I don't feel good about that. But she understands how I feel about her, and once everything stabilizes, we'll pick up where we left off.

I'm jolted out of autopilot by the hum of my tires on the shoulder's rumble strip. "Get it together, Russell," I say.

Great. Mom and Megan did such a number on me that I've started talking to myself. Maybe by the time I reach Blacksburg, I'll have my head on straight again.

I read a text from Gavin when I stop to get gas. I didn't text much while driving in the past, but I never do now. He came down with a stomach bug while visiting his folks this weekend, so he won't be back until Tuesday at the earliest. I send my sympathies, but the fact is I can get more work done when I'm alone. If I have a couple of extremely productive days, maybe Sarah and I can get together for lunch Wednesday.

I'm trying to figure out when Sarah and I can go on an actual date—dinner and a movie, with some stargazing thrown in—as I pull into my usual parking spot at my apartment. And then complete and utter confusion hits me. Sarah's car is parked next to mine. And she's in it.

We emerge from our vehicles at the same time, and for another moment it's like I've never seen her before. Her long red hair, that smile that zings right through me, those gorgeous green eyes. She's perfect.

"Talk about great timing," she says in her musical voice. "I just got here maybe five minutes ago."

I shake my head to restart my brain and enable speech. "I didn't expect you. I mean, this is a surprise."

"Your excitement is overwhelming." I'm still standing behind my open door, so Sarah walks around my truck as a mischievous smile begins to play on her face. "Your flattery will cause my head to swell, dear sir." Then she hugs me and holds on tight, like she hasn't seen me in months.

I return her embrace, and for one more moment I wonder why I've kept her at a distance. Again. Then I remember. "I've got some stuff to work on tonight, but would you like to come in for a minute?"

Sarah drops her arms and moves away from me, taking her warmth with her. "I was hoping for more than a minute." She is twirling a few strands of that beautiful hair. "I know you've got a lot going on, but—"

I'm an idiot. "I've got lots of minutes for you." I try to bring back the funny guy I think I used to be. "Let me drag in my stuff, and we might even find some food in the refrigerator. But don't count on it."

"Lead the way, Mr. Russell."

I grab my duffel and my laundry basket of clean clothes. Sarah picks up two bags of groceries Mom insisted I take. "Looks like you were holding out on me," she accuses, glancing down at the bags.

"Not intentionally. I forgot about the stuff Mom sent." I lift my hands in self-defense as much as my luggage will allow. "Really."

"Uh-huh." Sarah's tone is skeptical, but her smile gives her away.

"Would it help my case if I let you take some of Mom's chocolate chip cookies?" I ask as I unlock my door.

"Make it six and we'll have a deal." Sarah follows me in. "Plus, we open up these cheese puffs tonight."

She's not afraid of junk food. I love that. "Deal."

Sarah puts away the groceries as I unpack. This all feels so common, so everyday, so...normal. She's folding the cloth bags as I return to the apartment's family room/kitchen/dining area. I'm glad Gavin and I finally did some cleaning Thursday night. The place had started to look disgusting.

"How was your weekend?" Sarah takes my hand and leads me to the sofa. "Get a lot done?"

"Yeah. Finally changed the filters around the house, worked on chemistry, talked with Mom and Megan about the company. You know, miscellaneous stuff."

She brushes my hair out of my face with her fingers. "Does your mom know what she wants to do about the company yet?"

I shake my head. "No. Russell Electric is stable, so there's no need to rush any decisions. One thing at a time, you know?"

"You're right." Sarah moves her hand from my hair to my face, her fingers barely touching my skin. Our eyes lock on each other and something passes between us, but I can't translate it. I'm out of practice.

"I've missed you," she whispers.

All I can do is nod.

"I've been, I don't know, not consumed or desperate, but I've had this strong feeling that we should talk." Sarah continues her barely-there caress of my cheek. "This weekend lasted forever. I didn't think Sunday would ever come. I even texted Megan about your possible ETA so I could meet you when you arrived."

I move her hand and back away. "You texted Megan?"

Sarah tilts her head and studies me. "Yes."

"So I guess you're part of the intervention too." I walk to the kitchen counter and grab its edge, leaning in and breathing deeply.

"What is it?" Sarah comes to the counter, careful not to touch me.

I turn to her. No, I turn *on* her. "Mom and Megan ambushed me yesterday, saying I'm burning myself out, but I'm only trying to do my part. And now you're in on it." I see Sarah wilting with each word, but I can't stop myself. "I know what I'm doing. I know what I need to do. And I don't need anybody's help. And I don't want to talk."

"I don't—"

I step away from the counter and begin to pace around the room as I sort myself out aloud. "I know all of you are worried about me, and that's sweet and everything, but can't you see that I have to make things right? I have to do a better job at school, and I have to take care of Mom and Megan, and I have to do everything that Dad would want..." My throat is closing and my heart is racing, each beat blending into the next. "That Dad would...that Dad..." I don't have enough breath for speech. I stagger and fall back into the old rocker recliner Gavin's mom passed on to us.

I think I'm dying, so I close my eyes and wait.

"Sam!" Sarah sounds far away, but I feel her warmth as she kneels before me. I realize I'm not dying when the first tears slide down my cheeks. Then something breaks lose inside.

"Dad's gone. He's gone and he died thinking I hated him." The words are flowing now, each a confirmation of my darkness. The lights in the cavern have been switched off and I'm utterly lost. Utterly alone. "And I did hate him when he said those things. God help me, I hated him then. But I didn't hate him after that. I did not hate him, and I did not think he was a loser. But, oh my God, he thought I did. And now he's dead. He'll never know…oh, Daddy, Daddy." My body convulses as every tear I've held back crashes through my defenses.

Sarah climbs into my lap and pulls my head to her chest. The chair begins to rock as she strokes my hair. I cling to her as I repeat a name I haven't said out loud since I was five years old. "Daddy's gone, and it hurts so bad. It hurts so bad," I whimper. The cave is collapsing, crushing me beneath the weight of the world above.

"I know, baby, I know," Sarah coos. "But your daddy knew you loved him. He knew. He knew." She sings the words to me until the shaking stops.

In the haven of Sarah's arms, the sharpness of the pain eases and my sobbing ebbs. We say nothing for a long time, only hold fast to each other as we rock back and forth.

I start snuffling and wipe my face with my hands. Sarah digs into her pocket and pulls out some tissues. "Here you go."

"Thanks. I'm sorry—"

"Hush." She places a hand on either side of my face. "There is no need for *sorry*." She leans in until our foreheads are touching. "You and me. Always."

"Always," I whisper.

Sarah gives me a tender kiss, a slight brush of her lips against mine. When she pulls away, I press my hand to her cheek and she leans into it, closing her eyes. I close mine too, and feel a powerful current flowing between us. It carries all our history, from childhood on, the pain we've inflicted on each other as well as the joy we've shared. It is so clear now: Sarah-and-Sam is bigger than Sarah or Sam.

We're speaking without words again. But this time I understand.

I draw her in and kiss her hard, starving for another taste of her. I feel Sarah's hunger too, as she shifts in my lap to face me and runs her hands through my hair.

Her soft mouth travels from mine, across my face and throat. "I've missed you so much, Sam. So much," she murmurs.

"Sarah," I manage to say before returning to her lips. I can't kiss her enough or touch her enough. I'm out of my mind with need. She's warm and alive, a light I must claim. I slide my hands under her shirt, and when they skim past her breasts, she sighs.

My universe is shrinking to the size of this apartment. Nothing outside exists. Nothing else matters.

Sarah rises from the chair, then turns and extends her hand to me. I take it and we walk to my bedroom.

At my door, I pull her into my arms again. "Is this what you want?" My voice has turned raspy, each syllable an effort. "If we go there, I might not be able to stop."

"Then don't." Sarah's mouth comes to mine, and I press against her. We go in.

My universe is now contained in Sarah's body: the long, lean muscles of her arms and legs as she wraps them around me, the curve of her waist, the softness of her breasts, the flash of her green eyes, the lush red hair draping around us.

Everything else has fallen away, and we are together at last.

At last.

At last.

*

Sarah is resting her head on my chest, her body curled into my side and my arms around me. A cold rain is now falling, which makes our nest that much cozier. I could lie here with her for a thousand years and still beg for more time.

"I love you so much, baby," I whisper as I hold her tighter.

"I love you," she answers, but I hear a catch in her voice.

I quickly move to my side so I can see her face. She's crying, just as I thought. "What is it, honey? Did I…did it hurt?"

She smiles slightly. "A little. But I'll be all right."

I wipe her tears away with a caress. "But what's wrong?"

Sarah looks away, but I gently turn her gaze back to me. "I don't know. I'm kind of overwhelmed, I guess."

"Want to talk about it?"

Sarah shakes her head. "All I want right now is to lie here and listen to the rain with you. Well, there is one other thing."

I give her a soft kiss. "Anything."

"Tell me again that you love me."

"Oh, Sarah, you know I love you. I've loved you since we were kids, and I will love you until I leave this world. Like we said before, always."

Sarah smiles, full-on this time, and holds me tight. "Always."

*

The sun set some time ago, but we're still in my bed. We've found an oasis, and neither of us wants to return to the desert. We've moved only to shift positions. When I'm on my back, Sarah keeps her head on my chest. When either of us turns to the side, the other scooches in like a spoon.

It is almost as sweet as making love.

I'm startled when Sarah speaks. "I don't want to go."

"So stay," I answer, pulling her closer. "There's no reason you can't."

Sarah turns to face me, her smile enough to light up the whole world. "Go on, sir."

"Well, madam," I reply, dropping my voice as I typically do when we adopt our formal language, "is it not true that your first class of the day tomorrow does not commence until twelve fifteen p.m.?"

"Indeed."

"And my roommate is not scheduled to return to our abode until Tuesday, due to an illness that befell him this weekend."

Sarah's hand flies to her mouth in exaggerated horror. "Oh, no! How dreadful. The illness, that is, not his late arrival."

I struggle to keep my formal demeanor in place. "Truly. Therefore, I see no reason why you cannot remain here with me until the morn."

Sarah's smile slowly dims as she turns to her back and stares at the ceiling.

I prop myself up on my elbow and brush her hair away from her face.

"Would we, you know, sleep together tonight?" she asks.

"Of course." I'm totally lost.

Sarah sits up and pulls the sheet practically to her chin. I find her sudden modesty touching somehow. "I don't know where we go from here."

A familiar knot reappears in my gut. "What do you mean?"

She gives me a peck on the cheek. "It's okay, honey. We'll get dressed, I'll call Jessie to let her know I'm staying here, then we'll talk."

The knot loosens a bit. "Okay."

I stare at Sarah as she gathers her things. I can't help myself. She's a Renaissance painting come to life, the hair flowing down her back a stark contrast to her silky porcelain skin. The curves of her body are accentuated as she glides across the room.

She is flawless.

The knot disappears when she glances over her shoulder and smiles at me. "Come on, Mr. Russell. Are you going to stay in bed all day?"

I run my hand over the sheets, still warm from Sarah's body. Then I force myself to think about chemistry and cleaning gutters and getting cars inspected, anything but staying in bed all day.

With her.

CHAPTER 16

We have grilled cheese sandwiches and tomato soup for supper. Sarah insists that I make the best grilled cheese sandwiches in the world, with the perfect amount of butter and my unique combination of cheddar and mozzarella. This fact has not been independently verified, but that's only a formality.

"Mmm. So good," she mumbles as she eats the last corner of her sandwich.

I reach over and wipe a few crumbs away from the corner of her mouth.

"I'm such a mess." She grabs her napkin.

"I love to watch you eat."

Sarah giggles. "You're weird, Sam Russell. But in a good way."

"Thanks for throwing that in." I pick up our bowls, plates, and spoons and take them to the sink.

She appears at my side. "I'll take care of these. It is only fair since you cooked."

"I don't know if I'd call it cooking."

"You're too modest." She takes over the rinsing. "Best grilled cheese ever."

Like I said.

I back away and watch her, falling into my familiar fantasy. Sarah and I will come home from work tomorrow and talk about our days and watch some TV or curl up on the sofa and read and then she'll turn to me and…

"Earth to Sam, do you copy?"

"Sorry." It takes a second to reorient myself to reality. "Drifted away for a second."

She puts her hands on her hips in mock annoyance. "You're so bored with me already that you have to resort to daydreaming?"

I grab her around the waist. "Actually, I was thinking about…" No, I better not go there. Not yet. "About how nice it would be if you were here all the time." That is the truth. More or less.

"I'd like that." Sarah looks up at me, and her eyes have gone dreamy. "I'd like that a lot."

I kiss her cheek, then her mouth, and the moment my lips touch hers, my desire roars back, like a glowing coal doused with gasoline. But this time I stop. "Red," I whisper.

She lets out a deep breath. "I know. It's time."

The steady rain has become a downpour. We bundle up in a Virginia Tech blanket when we sit on the sofa, even though my apartment is warm and dry.

"What were you saying?"

"What?" Sarah answers, creases forming between her brows.

"What were you saying while I was off in Sam World?"

"Oh. I was wondering where you keep your mugs, since I found some hot chocolate when I unpacked your groceries."

"Want me to boil some water?" I start to get up. "Or I could even heat some milk, make it really rich. It won't take long."

She grabs my hand. "Sam."

"Yeah?"

"You're avoiding." She pulls the blanket back over me.

"Yeah." I look down at the carpet.

Sarah rubs my arm gently. "Why?"

When I look at her, all the sleepless nights and hopeless days of last fall rush back at me. I'm being drawn into that awful movie again. "I'm afraid." I take her hand.

She covers my hand with hers. "Of what?"

Of so many things. Of letting my mother and sister down. Of never figuring out what I'm supposed to do with my life. Of not becoming the man Dad was. But one thing most of all. "I'm afraid that somehow I'm going to lose you again."

Sarah's face crumples. "I still can't believe how stupid I was. I'm so sorry."

I quiet her with a light kiss.

"But that's not going to happen again," she continues, her breath warm on my face. "I'm not going anywhere. I promise."

I exhale slowly. When I put my arm around her, she leans into me.

"I've changed my mind," she murmurs. "I want to keep this day perfect, without any discussion or conversation or sorting things out. Only you and me savoring the beautiful glow of this afternoon."

I bring my other arm around her. "It was beautiful, wasn't it?"

Sarah puts her arms around me, making our circle complete. "Better than any dream I've had."

A lump grows in my throat. The current between us is calm now, and deep. I want to live here for the rest of my life.

I stroke Sarah's head and breathe in her scent. "I never answered your question."

"About?"

"About tonight. About sleeping."

Sarah fixes me with those green eyes. "And?"

"And I think we should just sleep, that's all. Is that okay?"

A slight smile breaks across Sarah's face, but her eyes remain intense. "I think that's best. Unless…"

"Unless what?"

She scoots over, her retreat from my arms as shocking as a cold shower. "Unless I go home. If I stay, we might do more than sleep. And we haven't decided if that's our new normal. Not yet."

I gently rub my thumb over her lips. "You're right. But please don't go. I'll sleep on the floor if I must, but I can't face tonight without you. Please."

Sarah moves back into my arms. "I don't want to go." She squeezes me tight. "How about a movie? Everything can wait until tomorrow."

Tonight is for Sarah and me.

*

Sarah and I fell asleep on the sofa watching *Singing in the Rain*. I think we nodded off right before Lina Lamont's sabotage of Kathy Selden was revealed. I dreamed about dancing in the rain with Sarah, both of us splashing with abandon.

I've been awake for a while now, listening to Sarah breathe. I wish I could see her face—I can only imagine how beautiful she is as she sleeps—but I don't want to wake her. One of my arms is tingling, but I don't mind. For the first time in weeks, maybe months, my brain is quiet.

Finally, I reach for my cell on the coffee table. 8:15. I can't remember the last time I've slept this late. I can't remember when I've slept.

"Time to get up?" Sarah asks.

"You can sleep a little longer."

She slowly moves to a sitting position and stretches, scissoring her legs back and forth. I have discovered another thing I love about being with Sarah: watching her wake up.

"Do you do that every morning?"

"What?"

"That whole calisthenics thing with your legs."

Sarah bites her lip and looks down. "It's annoying, isn't it? Rachel says so."

I run one of her curls through my fingers. Silky, just like her skin. "Your sister doesn't know what she's talking about. It's beyond adorable. Like everything else you do."

She pulls out one of her mischievous smiles. "You'll change your mind about that after we've lived together for a while, Sam Russell."

I pull her into my arms. "I doubt it. But I'm willing to take the risk."

She hops up and starts for the bathroom, then stops suddenly and clamps her hands over her mouth. "Oh, no! I don't have my toothbrush," she says from behind her screen. "I can't walk around with nasty breath."

I walk toward her. "Don't worry. I'll run—"

Sarah stretches out her arms like she's warding off a vampire. "Stay back! I don't want to breathe on you."

"I'll keep my distance," I say with a grin. "Walgreens is only five minutes away. I shall buy you their absolute best toothbrush. Does the lady require anything else?"

"Make sure the brush is soft, please. And floss too. The waxed kind. I think that's all since I'll take a quick shower at my place."

Sarah in the shower. I shake my head to focus.

She touches my arm as I walk to my bedroom to change out of my rumpled clothes. "And do you need to replace, uh, you know, what we borrowed?" Pink is spreading across her cheeks.

Mine too, as I recall ransacking Gavin's room yesterday. I finally found a precious foil-wrapped disk in his nightstand. Only now do I feel bad about invading his space. "Yeah, yeah. I'll do that too."

An awkward silence settles between us, and we feel less like lovers and more like co-conspirators.

Yesterday's gone.

*

While I was out on my Walgreens run, I stopped by McDonald's for some breakfast. Sarah is dressed and waiting for her toothbrush when I return, which she insists on using even before we eat.

We don't talk much before she leaves for her place. There isn't much to say, since neither of us seems to have had any revelations about our "new normal." I give her a quick kiss at my door, along with a "Love you." She turns to go, then grabs me around my waist and nestles her head into my shoulder, her face turned to my neck. She fits perfectly there.

"Tell me everything will be all right," she whispers.

I cup her face and kiss one cheek, then the other. "Of course it will, Red." When her eyes hold mine, I see that she needs more. "We're back together now. Really together, with no more going off on our own. Everything will be all good."

She returns her head to my shoulder. "All good."

We're together now. Does anything else really matter?

*

I've been sitting here on the side of my bed trying to answer that question. I came in here to change for class a while ago, but this is as far as I got. My coffee has gone cold, and I'm as clueless as I was when I walked in.

I didn't think it would be this way. In my daydreams we would make love for the first time and never look back. I never guessed that we would need to sort out anything.

I take the logical approach, cost versus benefit. I race by the costs to reach the benefit. There is only one, but no more are needed. I close my eyes and a new movie appears, the one with Sarah and me yesterday afternoon. I absentmindedly run my hand over my sheets and realize that now and forever this will be Sarah's side of the bed.

Sweet Jesus, it was perfect.

I feel a twinge at the use of His name. I have not asked what He thinks of all this. I should, but I don't want to.

"Anybody home?" Gavin's voice startles me.

"Yeah, in here." I walk to my bedroom door. "Wasn't expecting to see you yet. How are you?"

He holds up a bottle of Gatorade. "A little dehydrated, but the worst is over. I started feeling human again last night, so I decided to give my afternoon class a try."

I do a lousy job of concealing my apprehension, because he rifles through a bag and pulls out a container of disinfecting wipes. "Never fear. I'll keep this place as sanitized as an OR, plus I'll keep my distance for a couple of days."

"Appreciate it."

Gavin puts away a half dozen bottles of Gatorade, a couple of ginger ale cans, and a box of crackers. It looks like a stomach bug first aid kit. "Yeah, my mother went a little overboard," he chuckles. "She didn't want her little boy to come back yet. How was your weekend?"

I'm surprised that I want to tell Gavin everything. Not every detail, of course, but that Sarah and I slept together. I don't know where that impulse comes from, since I never talked about our relationship at all until our break, and even then I kept things vague.

I hesitate so long that he stops his unpacking and stares at me. "That bad, huh?"

"No, not really." Another understatement/lie. "Busy at home. Spent some time with Sarah when I got back." Now the line has been crossed.

Gavin looks at me for a couple of beats before returning to his grocery bags. "Good. My roommate gets cranky when he neglects his girl."

"I do?"

Gavin laughs. "Uh, yeah."

"And you think I've neglected Sarah?"

Gavin crosses his arms and his mouth drops open. "You can't be serious. As far as I can tell, you've barely seen her since…" He reaches out, palms up. "I'm sorry, man. I didn't mean to… I'm stupid."

The familiar ache asserts itself, but I'm distracted by Gavin's apology. "It's okay. And you're right. I have put my relationship with Sarah on the back burner, but I think I've finally gotten my priorities straight."

He nods. "Good for you." As he hauls his duffel back to his room, I wonder if he regrets having slept with Kirsten. Maybe that's why I want to tell him what happened, so he can tell me what we should do.

Not that that sounds desperate or anything.

I'm pulling some jeans out of my closet when Gavin appears at my door. "I've been so focused on my medical condition that I forgot to tell you what happened Friday night."

"What?"

"Kirsten called."

I plop down on my bed in shock. "No way."

He leans against the door frame and shakes his head. "That was my reaction."

"So?" I wave my hand for more information.

"So she wants to see me." My roommate's mouth is inching closer to a smile, and that worries me. I work to keep a neutral expression.

When I don't respond, Gavin shoves his hands in his pockets and stares at the floor. "And you think that's a lousy idea," he mumbles.

"It doesn't matter what I think."

When he looks up, his mouth is set in a hard line. "Sure it does. You really helped me when she dumped me, and I need another set of eyes on this."

"I think..." I breathe a quick prayer. "I saw her over Christmas break, when I was out shopping."

"You did?"

"Yeah. I was in a jewelry store looking for a gift for Sarah and there she was, working behind the counter. I didn't say anything about it because, well, you know."

Gavin nods.

"Anyway, she asked about you. For a minute I thought she was going to start crying. I'm not proud of this, but I thought she deserved it after all she put you through." I remember my frantic drive back to Sarah, my need to take her in my arms after glimpsing what could have been our future.

His face holds a mixture of surprise and disappointment.

"I'm sorry. I should have told you. But I didn't want you to get hurt again. I still don't." I feel a nudge. "Do you still love her?"

Gavin turns away, but not before I notice his eyes misting over. "God help me, I do. And I mean that, Sam. About God. I've been reading the Bible you sent me, and I've been talking to Him. God, that is."

I pushed Jesus away earlier, but He is back, right between Gavin and me. "That's great, man. What do you think God is telling you to do?"

He wipes at his eyes before talking to the wall. "I think I should see her, hear what she has to say, then take it from there."

"Okay. I'm here to talk anytime. You know that, right?"

He smiles at me. "Sure thing. Goes both ways."

Right. But not today.

*

I had to work so hard to focus on my classes this afternoon that I wouldn't have been surprised if beads of sweat started dripping down my face. Every neuron, every synapse is occupied by Sarah: Sarah yesterday, Sarah this morning, Sarah whenever I get to see her again. I am possessed, addicted, consumed.

An ecstatic, muddled mess.

I text her before leaving my last class of the day. *Meet for dinner?*

She responds immediately. *Sure. Burgers?*

I insert a smiley-face emoji followed by *See you in 20?*

She sends a GIF of a dancing bunny in return.

When I arrive at our place, it's busy. Servers wind their way through the tables, their trays of milkshakes and hamburgers and fries held above the crowd, balanced better on one hand than I could manage with two. Students and locals fill the seats, and their laughter bounces off the walls.

But it all disappears when Sarah walks through the door.

She scans the restaurant, and when her eyes land on me, my heart seizes up. Not the painful squeeze I felt the last time we were here, but a reaction to so much joy hitting me all at once. The light in Sarah's face leads me to think she feels it too.

"New booth?" she asks after I rise to greet her.

"Yeah. New year, new booth."

"Change is good." She takes her seat on the opposite side. I would like to feel her next to me, but this way I can spend the whole time staring at her, taking her in.

We say nothing for a few moments.

I reach across for her hands. "It's so good to see you."

Sarah runs her fingers across my knuckles, her smile growing wider with each caress. "You too. But it is crazy, isn't it? We saw each other only a few hours ago."

"Feels like days."

She squeezes my hands. "Yeah."

"Ready to order?"

I jump at the sound of the server's voice. I'd forgotten we're not alone.

Sarah and I haven't cracked open our menus. I don't know why we bother taking them anymore. "Two #4 combos, please. No onions for the lady, and Cokes for both of us."

"Got it." The server grins at us before walking away, like she's in on our secret.

"She knows," Sarah says softly. Her eyes widen as she tries to pull off an expression of amazement mixed with reverent awe. But she quickly succumbs to a fit of giggles, taking me with her.

We finally stop laughing when we notice an old couple—I'd guess they're in their sixties at least—staring at us.

I lean toward Sarah. "Probably haven't laughed in years."

She sputters but manages to squelch the giggle, then leans toward me. "Know what?"

"What?"

"I love spending time with you. Laughing, talking, everything. Not only when we...you know."

I wish I could hold her right now. "Me too. How did I ever get so lucky, falling in love with my best friend?"

"But we're not lucky," she corrects me. "We're blessed."

Jesus is back. He must have slid into the booth when I wasn't looking. "Yeah, blessed."

Sarah's smile has faded. Her face is quiet, at rest—her green eyes steady and cool like a deep mountain lake, her forehead unlined by concern, and her mouth lightly closed, not sealed tight with hurt or anger. "You feel it, don't you?" she asks.

I used to think Jesus only showed up in a big way at church, with Pastor Jeff at full roar and the choir at full strength. Smiley's attack taught me that Jesus can work anywhere. Even in a busy diner that's as loud as an elementary school cafeteria.

I nod. "It's not what I want."

Sarah reaches for my hands again. We dropped them amid our giggles. "Me neither," she sighs, "but it's the right thing."

I breathe out slowly as I fold up my desire and lock it away. "I know. We'll make it work. What matters is that we're together, right?"

"Right." She rubs my arm. "I really wish I could kiss you right now."

Lord, have mercy. Really.

CHAPTER 17

IT'S BEEN A week since we decided that our "new normal" should be our "old normal." When we met at the diner that day, I had no idea we would walk away with everything sorted out. I assumed we would have a series of conversations about pros and cons. Tears would likely ensue, but when the dust settled, we would have a plan in place. I would go through all that talking for Sarah's sake, but I had made up my mind already. I wanted to make love to her at every opportunity.

And yet here we are.

I wasn't lying when I agreed with Sarah that we shouldn't sleep together again until we're married. I didn't need lists or discussions to conclude that the love we made, incredible as it was, was outside the lines.

Because I had known it all along.

On one level I'm thankful there will not be another drawn-out drama starring Sarah and me, with too many words and not enough. On another, I wish we could've played this out a little longer so I could've gone on pretending we would be together again in a matter of days. Not years.

It was difficult to wait before, when I had only half-formed dreams of making love to Sarah. Now I know those dreams were only guesses, pale imitations of reality, like a child's drawing of a rainbow.

I stand and stretch. I've been trying to study, but my brain's not cooperating. Maybe I should go for a run. The fresh air might stir up some motivation.

I ran track in middle and high school, but when I came to Tech, I let it go. Not that I was good enough to run at the collegiate level, but I stopped running completely. I didn't decide to give up something I had enjoyed. I let it slip away from me, one day at a time.

One day at a time. The words bounce in my head to the beat of my feet on the pavement. After only a few minutes, my lungs are burning in the cool, not-quite-spring air, and my heart is pounding. I slow to a jog and push on, but the words don't disappear. Instead, my winded brain breaks them apart. *One.* Inhale. *Day.* Exhale. *At a.* Gasp. *Time.* Wheeze. It's a playlist consisting of only one song.

I accept defeat about twenty-five minutes in and start walking. At least Webs isn't here. I'd never hear the end of it. I resolve to try again tomorrow and the day after that, until I'm back in shape. One day at a time.

I freeze when the words finally hit their mark. I can be so dense sometimes.

I limp back to my apartment and start packing for my trip home. I stayed on campus last weekend, with the hearty approval of my mother and sister. Mom started to argue when I told her I would be visiting this weekend, but backed down when I told her Sarah would be coming with me. "Well then, that's different," she practically sang. Mom is still all about love.

Like mother, like son.

*

Mom greeted Sarah like a movie star, or maybe a princess. She was practically giddy when she saw us together as I pulled into the driveway. Mom hugged her and complimented her shoes (what is it about women and shoes?) and went on and on about how much she has missed seeing her. I walked with Sarah to her house, and Mrs. Winston's greeting was comatose by comparison.

I was a little embarrassed by Mom's fawning, but then I noticed something I haven't seen in weeks: Mom's smile. A real smile, not the pasted-on thing she has been pulling out to convince Megan and me she is fine. Seeing Mom happy made me happy, of course, but I still don't understand her over-the-top reaction to seeing Sarah again.

"What was that all about?" I ask Megan when Mom retreats to the kitchen to make chocolate chip cookies, Sarah's favorite.

Megan leads me out onto the porch for greater privacy. "Yeah, a little scary, right? I think I have a theory."

"Shoot."

Megan sits down on the top step and pats the space next to her. She glances over her shoulder at the door before continuing. "I think," she whispers, "that Mom wants you to be happy."

I stare at her and wait for the rest. "And…"

"And that's it." Megan holds out her hands, palms up. "Mom is dealing with Dad's death by focusing on you and me." She pushes me with her shoulder. "How are you and Sarah, anyway? I've got to confess, I was relieved to see you together today."

My smile gives me away.

"That good, huh?" Megan grins and shoves me again. "I'm glad."

My thoughts drift back to a rainy afternoon two weeks ago, and I scan the yard, looking for anything to distract me. My eyes land on Dad's old parking spot. I almost expect to see his truck there. "Megan?"

"Yeah?"

"How's Mom really doing?"

My sister follows my line of sight, and we say nothing for a couple of minutes. We've stumbled upon a black hole, and we can't escape its gravitational pull.

Megan wipes her eyes with the back of her hand. "Mom works so hard every waking minute to convince me she's getting better. We talk about the will and probate and the business, and she's very calm and matter of fact, cool and collected. But she drops the mask when she thinks I'm not looking. Yesterday I ran into her at the coat closet, hugging Dad's old hunting jacket like he was still in it."

I put my arm around her shoulders.

"I still don't get it, Sam." Her words are muffled by tears. "I don't understand why God had to rip Dad away from us like that. Sometimes it feels like we're losing Mom too. And I can't stop it. I feel so helpless."

I lean my head into hers and kiss her forehead. I need to be strong and good, like Dad. But I'm not. I am weak and self-absorbed, with no wise counsel to offer. "I know. Me too." I give her shoulder a squeeze. "None of this is right, and I don't know what to do to make it better."

An image burns its way across my brain: Dad on the kitchen floor next to Mom, glaring at me, scalding me with his anger. *If You wanted to take him, why didn't You give me a chance to make things right first? Why did You leave me with this?* I make a frantic effort to return to the memory of holding Sarah in my arms, desperate for cool water to ease the burn.

"It's okay, little brother," Megan whispers as she takes my hand, unaware of how deep the darkness goes. "Everything will be okay in time."

If only.

*

The weekend got better after that. I guess it had to. Mom chilled out considerably, and Sarah and I fell back into our old routine, with Friday night spent catching up with our families, Saturday for us, and then back to Tech after church Sunday.

We didn't talk much for the first half hour or so of the drive, and the silence was familiar too—at first. But then it became a presence between us. Sarah withdrew more with every mile.

"You okay?" I ask when we stop for gas near Staunton. "You haven't said much since we left."

"Yeah," she answers, never taking her eyes from the tractor trailers rumbling toward the diesel pumps. "School, other stuff. You know."

A guy in a pickup towing a massive fifth-wheel trailer pulls behind me and flashes his lights.

"Okay, okay," I mutter as I drive away. But instead of returning to I-81, I park in front of the adjoining McDonald's. I reach over and stroke Sarah's arm lightly. "Red."

She gives me a half smile and places her hand over mine. "Sorry. Feeling a little blue, I guess. I'll be okay."

I squeeze her hand and think about pressing her for more, but I know I'll get nowhere. She'll talk to me when she's ready. But apparently, not yet.

*

Since then, we've been in touch every day, with each conversation a little shorter than the last. Our call today, three days after the trip back to college, went like this:

Me: "Hey, Red, how are you doing?"

Sarah: "Okay."

Me: "So, I know this week has been pretty busy for you, but I was wondering if you would like to go out for dinner tonight."

Sarah: "Sorry. Another time."

Me: (Huge sigh) "Tomorrow, then?"

Sarah: "We'll see."

Me: "Okay. Love you."

Sarah: (Pause) "You too."

Me: "Bye."

Sarah: "Bye."

She hesitated when I said I love her. What's that about? What did I say or do this weekend? How did I mess up this time? I comb through every moment of our visit, looking for clues, but I wind up empty-handed.

But maybe it's not me. Maybe she got into a fight with her parents. But she would tell me about that. I think so, anyway.

All I can do is wait. And I hate that.

No. I'm not waiting this time. Waiting leads to quicksand for Sarah and me. I'm going to her apartment and not leaving until she tells me what's wrong.

My place is only about fifteen minutes from Sarah's, but that's long enough for anxiety to take root. I don't hear the dark voice that came to me that awful afternoon at the mall, but I feel like I'm skating along the edge of the pit where it lives. The familiar litany returns. I'm a loser and Sarah's done with me for good this time. She doesn't love me and she never will again.

I park and rest my head on the steering wheel. *Help me.*

My heartbeat slows and my breathing becomes more even. I'm not at peace when I ring Sarah's doorbell, but I'm not crazed anymore either.

Jessie scowls when she opens the door, and her disdain settles me further. Irritation replacing fear, I guess.

"Hi," I say, trying to sound as friendly as possible. "Is Sarah home?"

She stares at me for a beat. "Let me see." Then she closes the door in my face. I must be sleepwalking through the world, offending people with no memory of it.

When the door reopens, Sarah's standing there. At least, I think it's Sarah. This girl has red hair, yes, but it's uncombed and floating wildly around her head. Her face is pale and there are dark circles under her eyes.

"Baby," I say, moving forward to hold her before she falls over.

But she steps back as I walk inside.

Jessie appears beside her. "I can stay if you want," she says, smiling at Sarah before glaring at me.

"No." Sarah pats Jessie's shoulder. "Go on to your study group. I'll be fine."

The word *fine* vibrates through my brain. *Dear God, what is happening?*

I stare as Sarah shuffles over to the sofa like a patient in hospice care. *God, no, is that it? Is she sick?*

Jessie bumps into me as she heads for the door. "You've done enough. Leave her alone," she whispers—no, growls—into my ear.

I would ask what she's talking about, but I can't focus on anything but Sarah. My sweet Sarah who's falling apart. I sit down, careful not to touch her, the one thing I desperately want to do. "What is it, Red? Please tell me. Please."

She rubs a hand over her eyes and shakes her head. "Oh, Sam," she begins, hugging herself before twisting to look at me. "I don't know how to tell you this."

The nightmares I thought I'd buried come to life and unfold before me. I see everything clearly now. I've been living in a dream world where Sarah and I live happily ever after. When she took my hand and led me to my bedroom, it was an act of pity. That's why she cried afterward.

We ended last fall, but I didn't realize it until now.

"Is…is there someone else?" I ask, the words acid on my lips.

The downward tilt of Sarah's head is so slight that the motion is almost imperceptible. But it's there.

I need to get out of here and find a corner where I can wait for my heart to stop beating. But my legs are filled with lead, and blood is thrumming in my brain. All I can do is rise and back away, one foot stumbling into the other. I want to cry out for help, but I'm bound and gagged by fear.

"Sam." Sarah follows me and grabs my arm. I don't have enough strength to fight her off.

"Let me go," I beg. I want to die alone.

"You don't understand." She's crying, and I can't imagine why.

Then she places my hand against her stomach.

It is like touching a live wire. I jerk my hand away, but not before the electricity has started flowing through my body, pushing out every thought in its wake. Even the mocking voices are gone. Only one word manages to escape my mouth. "You're…"

"Pregnant? Yes." Sarah is still crying, but her voice is strangely calm.

My brain starts to come back online and make connections, trying to make sense of what she's saying. "But I used protection."

"Well, it didn't do its job."

I take her hands in mine and scan her face, hoping I'll find uncertainty there. "You're sure?"

"Yeah. I should have started last weekend, and I've taken a couple of tests."

"They couldn't be wrong?"

Sarah grabs hold of my shoulders and stares at me, her green eyes deep and still. "I'm pregnant, Sam. I'll go to a doctor, but I'm sure."

I stagger out of her grasp and begin to pace. "One time. We're together one time and you get pregnant." My voice rises as the news finally hits home. "Idiots have sex all the time and don't get pregnant."

Sarah blocks my path, her hands clenched at her sides. "So what are you saying? That this is my fault or that I'm an idiot or both?"

Suddenly I see myself through Sarah's eyes—a stereotype, the worthless father blaming the mother of his child. *Jesus, what am I doing?* "No, no. I'm the idiot. I'm so sorry. I just meant—"

"That this is my fault. I get it." She marches to the door and opens it. "You can go now."

I push it closed. "Of course it's not your fault. But I couldn't help but think—"

Sarah turns the knob frantically, her eyes now wild. "That it's my fault. Jessie said you would try to turn this around and blame me before walking out. I said you'd never do that, but she—"

"Wait. Jessie said what? She knows?"

My distraction gives Sarah the chance to reopen the door, but I close it. When she looks at me, I still see the love there, but there's anger too. Even worse, disappointment.

"I ran into her at the drugstore and wound up telling her everything. She said she knows how guys are." I feel Sarah's anger dissolving into pain. "She said—"

"But does she know me? You do, Sarah. You've known me your

whole life. I say and do stupid stuff, but have I ever done anything that would cause you to think I'd abandon you?" My emotions are crushing me from the inside. "I love you, Red, and I always will."

She falls into me and begins to sob. "What are we going to do, Sam? Oh, dear God, what are we going to do?"

I wrap her up in an embrace and rest my head on hers. Gentle shushing noises come from my mouth as we stand together, shifting our weight in a rocking motion.

When Sarah's crying subsides, we return to the sofa. We nestle there together and say nothing for a long time.

"Sam?" Sarah leans back and studies my face like she has never seen it before.

"What is it?"

"Why did you ask if there were someone else?"

The possessed guy fighting off his nightmares vanished the moment Sarah grabbed my hand and pressed it against her stomach. Maybe he's gone for good. Maybe not. I take a deep breath. "You remember my telling you about running into Dakota at the mall and how that kind of sent me off the deep end?"

"Of course I do." Sarah closes her eyes and shakes her head. "If only I hadn't pushed you away—"

"All of this was on me." I run my hand over her cheek, so smooth and perfect, and wish I could take back so many things. "Anyway, when you wouldn't talk to me today, I assumed you slept with me out of pity. It's like my head has a mail slot and all this disgusting stuff keeps getting dropped in there."

She pulls me close and brings my forehead to hers.

I try to turn away, but she won't let me. "You deserve better than me," I manage to say before my throat closes.

"Stop it." She's whispering, yet her voice is strong, almost stern. "I believed a lie myself, thinking you'd walk away from me. We can't give in to the darkness. We've got to fight it." She kisses me tenderly, as if sealing a promise. "We've got to fight it together."

I start to run my hands through her hair, but my fingers get caught in the tangles. "How do you feel? Physically, I mean."

Sarah pulls her hair back as if to hide it. "I'm a mess, aren't I?"

"You're beautiful," I answer, and mean it. "But how are you?"

"I haven't been throwing up, not yet anyway. But I can't sleep." She looks away and bites her lip as her eyes glaze over. "You're right. It doesn't seem fair that I get pregnant the one and only time we make love. Every night I've told myself that I would start in the morning and everything would be normal again."

"But you haven't."

She shakes her head slowly. "And nothing is normal."

I lace the fingers of our hands together and stare into her green eyes, now puffy from crying. Sarah's pain is hitting me like waves on a beach, and I don't know how to make things better. "What do you want to do?"

"I don't know. I'm so mixed up," She leans against me and stares at the opposite wall as if there's a list posted there. "I guess we have three options. I can have the baby and we raise her—"

"Or him."

"Okay, or him, together."

"You know I'd marry you tonight, Red. I'd only be doing something I've planned to do anyway."

"I know. And I want to marry you." She swallows. "Or I can have the baby and we can put her or him up for adoption."

"Give up our baby to strangers?"

She nods. "To good people, but, yes, strangers. Or..."

"Or what?"

"Or I don't have the baby at all."

I shiver as if the front door has blown open, exposing us to a blizzard. The cold comes to rest in my heart, and I move so I can look Sarah in the face. "But we've said—"

"That abortion's wrong. I know." Sarah rises and walks to the window, careful to avoid my stare. "But maybe it's a matter of degrees. Like Jessie said—"

"Jessie again." I hear the edge in my voice.

She finally looks at me. "Yeah, Jessie, but she made some good points. What's inside me now is just a clump of cells without a heartbeat. Is there really any difference between termination and an appendectomy at this point?"

"*Termination*? Sounds better than *abortion*, doesn't it?" Even as I ask the question, I feel myself wavering. "I can't deny that it's the simplest way out."

Sarah sits beside me and grabs my hand. "Exactly. This would be the end of it, and we'd walk away free and clear."

It's her decision, really. My only job is to stand by her. "What do you want, Sarah?"

She rests her head against my chest. "I want you to follow your dreams, whether that's becoming a doctor or going on to do other great things. I want you to be happy. What do you want?"

"To be with you."

We settle back into each other's arms, quiet but not at peace. I can almost feel the turbulence between us, like high winds accompanying a change in the weather. Sarah loves me and I love her, but now… what? In my mind I picture three paths before us, each curving just enough that we can't see where it's leading.

I guess we should be talking, but I don't know what else to say. I'm relieved when Jessie returns home, and that fills me with shame.

"You're still here," Jessie accuses as she drops her backpack by the door. "Are you okay?" she asks Sarah while keeping her glare fixed on me.

Sarah and I rise from the couch in unison. "Yeah, yeah, I'm fine," she says, pasting on a semi-smile to prove her point.

Fine again. I should grab Sarah's hand and take her to a justice of the peace right now.

I ignore Jessie and kiss Sarah's cheek. "Want to get together for breakfast tomorrow?"

"Sure, yeah. Call first in case I'm not feeling…you know." Sarah embraces me and gives me an extra squeeze. "I love you, Sam. Always."

"And I love you too," I answer, scenes of movie farewells crowding my brain.

CHAPTER 18

I DIDN'T THINK I would ever get to sleep last night. My thoughts swiveled between the three options before us. Plus, I couldn't shake the sense of foreboding that settled on me as Sarah and I said goodbye.

Now I wish I hadn't slept at all, considering the nightmare that just jolted me awake. Sarah and I were walking down a beach, soaking in the sunshine of a perfect summer day, when a storm rolled in out of nowhere. The wind whipped around us, so loud we couldn't hear each other speak, and rain stung our faces.

I held tightly to Sarah's hand, but she was blown out of my grasp, toward a gaping black hole that appeared in front of us. I saw her form the words *I love you* right before she was swallowed by the void.

I ran toward the hole, screaming for her. But it disappeared, taking Sarah with it, leaving me alone. So alone.

My heart is still hammering away. It's 6 a.m. Still too early to text Sarah. "It was just a dream, just a dream," I repeat aloud to myself. I could try to go back to sleep—my alarm's set for 7—but it's pointless. Besides, that nightmare might return.

I stagger into my bathroom and splash my face with cold water. "Get it together, Sam," I say to my reflection. "It was just a stupid dream." Back in my bedroom, I plop down on my bed and rest my head in my hands. I should pray. Yeah, that's what I should do. *Dear God...* I can't go on. My mind is filled with the sight of Sarah disappearing before my eyes.

I'll go ahead and text her. I would rather apologize for the early wake-up call than sit here obsessing over a nightmare.

How are you? I ask.

No response.

I'll give it five minutes. Maybe she's in the bathroom.

Still nothing.

I call.

But the call goes straight to voicemail.

"Come on, Red, why aren't you answering?" I ask, as if she can hear me.

This is ridiculous. Maybe Jessie came home and filled Sarah's head with more crazy advice and now I'm being frozen out. Yeah, that's probably it. But the nightmare won't leave me alone.

I throw on some sweats, brush my teeth, and grab my keys.

"Hey, man. Where are you going so early?" Gavin asks when I pass the kitchen. "What's up?"

"It's Sarah." I look for my jacket and find it on the chair where I threw it last night. "I'm worried about her. She's not answering my texts or calls. Do me a favor?"

Gavin sets down the coffee pot, his face clouded with concern. "Sure."

"I don't think Sarah will come over, but can you let me know if she does? And keep her here until I get back."

"Yeah, sure, but what's going on?"

I hesitate, not wanting to say the words, as if doing so will make everything more real somehow. "She's pregnant."

Gavin's mouth drops open. "Oh. Sorry, man. I'm here for you, anything you need."

I'm almost out the door when he calls out, "Hey, Sam!"

"Yeah?"

He jogs to the front door and leans on the jamb. "I'll say a prayer for you guys, okay?"

A part of me—the very tiny part not being flooded with panic—is touched. "Thanks."

Traffic is light as I drive to Sarah and Jessie's apartment, but it feels like my wheels are mired in mud. By the time I ring the doorbell, I'm in full fight-or-flight mode.

Jessie answers the door and I prepare for another attack, not that I care at this point. Instead, I get a question. "Where's Sarah?" She's confused, but so am I.

"What do you mean?"

Jessie leans out and looks around like I'm hiding Sarah somewhere. "She's not here. I thought maybe she was with you."

"I haven't seen her since yesterday." Calm. I need to stay calm if I'm going to figure this out. "When was the last time you saw her?"

I don't know what my expression tells Jessie, but she flips from enemy to ally in a heartbeat. "Around eleven thirty last night. I was headed to bed and she said she was going to stay up for a while. To think, I assumed." Her brows knit together. "Where could she be?"

We exchange numbers. "Call me if she returns, okay?" I ask. "And I'll call you if—when—I find her."

Jessie flips her phone back and forth in her hand. "Find her, Sam. She's the only real friend I've ever had."

I nod and get back in my car, with no destination in mind. "Where are you, Sarah?" I wonder aloud. "Come on, baby, let me know."

I start driving toward campus because I don't know where else to go. I try to recall her favorite places around town, but my mind is blank. Anxiety has wiped it clean.

I jump when my phone rings and pull over to the curb. It's Emilia Gonzales. She and Sarah became close when Perkins held them captive three years ago, then drifted apart until Emilia became fluent in English. Sarah tried to learn Spanish, but Emilia was a quicker study. Talking to her now, the only clue that Emilia wasn't born here is her slight accent.

"Sorry, Emilia. I can't talk right—"

"It's Sarah."

Hope at last. "Have you heard from her?"

"No, no, but—I know this is going to sound crazy—but I was getting ready for class when all of a sudden I had this terrible feeling about her, like she was—I don't know how else to put it—being consumed by something terrible. Something dark. And then I couldn't reach her. What's happening, Sam?"

Sarah has described Emilia as being a devout Christian, almost a mystic. "I'm not saying she's a prophet or anything," Sarah once said, "but she seems to know things."

So this vision of hers fills me with dread. "I don't know, Emilia." Now isn't the time to share about the pregnancy. "I'm trying to find her now. Pray for her, okay? Pray hard."

"I already am," she says with a break in her voice. "Please let me know when you find her. *Vaya con Dios.*"

I hang up and finally pray myself. *God, I don't know what to do. Please show me what to do. Please.*

I dreamed about Sarah vanishing into a black hole. Emilia had a vision of Sarah being swallowed up by something terrible. But just last night Sarah almost scolded me, telling me we must fight darkness together. "Did you try to fight it on your own, Red? Why would you do that?" An answer plays on the edge of my mind, but I can't bear to search for it.

I drive aimlessly, hoping for a sign. A name drops into my mind: Lissi.

Of course. Lissi is Sarah's best girlfriend. Maybe Sarah would tell her something she wouldn't want to share with me.

Lissi is a student at Northwestern University, outside Chicago, so it's only 6 a.m. there. Her phone rings a couple of times before she answers. "Sam?" She sounds groggy, so I must have awakened her.

"Yeah. Have you heard from Sarah lately?"

Lissi is instantly alert. "Just last night. What is this about, Sam?"

No time. No time. "What did she say?"

"It was personal. I don't know if I should—"

"You have to tell me, Lissi." I have known her forever, almost as long as I've known Sarah, and she doesn't respond well to being told what to do. But I don't have time for persuasion.

"Now you're scaring me, Sam. What's going on?"

I plunge in. "Sarah's missing. What did she say?"

"Missing?" Her defenses collapse. "For how long? Have you called the police?"

I hadn't thought of the police. "I don't think she's been gone long enough for them to get involved. Her roommate last saw her at eleven thirty last night, and I've been trying to reach her since six fifteen. I'm hoping Sarah said something to you that will give me a clue about where she has gone."

The line is silent for a moment. "Sweet Jesus. I'll tell you what we talked about, of course, but this has to stay between us."

"Sure," I almost yell into the phone. "What did she say?"

"First, she asked me if I still love Jack. I said I'd probably always love him, even though things didn't work out between us."

"Was that all?"

"No. Then she asked me if I could do what's best for Jack even if it were bad for me, even if it meant Jack might hate me. I said I'd hope so and then asked her what was going on."

My mouth gets dry as Sarah's thinking becomes clear. "So, what... what did she say?"

"Well..." Lissi struggles to speak. "She thanked me for listening and said she'd be in touch soon. I begged her to open up, but she refused to talk and rushed to disconnect. I should have pushed her harder for an answer. This is bad, isn't it? Really bad."

Breathe in. Breathe out. Calm. "I hope not, not if I'm in time, anyway."

"Oh my God. What can I do?"

"Pray."

I search the net until I find what I'm looking for. Then I inch my way through morning traffic until I get to I-81. Once on the interstate, I drive as fast as I dare, praying I'll get there in time.

To save the baby.

To save Sarah.

*

I don't see Sarah's car in the parking lot, but I go into the clinic anyway, just to be sure.

The women in the waiting room stare at me like I'm a COVID-19 carrier. "Excuse me, but I'm looking for my girlfriend."

The receptionist doesn't even bother looking up. "I'm sorry, but privacy laws prohibit us from disclosing patient information."

"But I just want to know if she's here." I try to tamp down the panic leaking out of my voice.

She glares at me and repeats her standard answer. "Privacy laws prohibit…"

I leave before she can finish, since it's clear I'm getting nowhere. I'm deflated, empty of ideas and hope. I lean against my car and close my eyes against the cold March sunshine.

I ruin everything. I lost my temper with Dad and he died thinking I hated him. Now Sarah's out there alone, trying to figure out what to do, all because I failed her. I told myself I was being supportive, but I might as well have said, "I love you, but this is your problem."

Jesus, I don't know what to do. I know You love Sarah and our baby, so please keep them safe. Please, God, watch over them. I don't care what happens to me.

A melody plays in my head, scratchy and distant. Grandpa showed me his father's radio when I was a kid. I watched him turn the dial slowly, navigating the static to coax a station into clarity. I can't do the same thing with this music, but my breathing steadies and my heartbeat slows nevertheless.

"Okay," I say as I open my eyes. "Okay. You drive."

Instead of returning to the highway, I meander through Roanoke.

I slow slightly at each cross street and intersection, waiting for direction. I've never done anything like this before, but I assume I'll feel a nudge of some kind when I reach my destination.

I finally park at a convenience store. The only prodding I've experienced is a need for a bathroom. Still, I look around in case a neon sign drops down from heaven.

No sign.

Might as well go in.

I feel obligated to buy something after using the restroom, so I head over to the coffee bar and pour a cup. I flip the levers for several dispensers to mix the various roasts offered, something Sarah and I do. Such a small thing, a ritual for getting a cheap cup of coffee, but it's our thing.

Longing washes over me, just as it did when Sarah and I were separated. *Oh, God, I love her so much.* I sway slightly, burning my hand as the coffee splashes out.

"Here you go." Leathery, filthy fingers reach out to me, holding a sheaf of paper napkins. "Happens to me all the time."

"Thanks." My eyes travel from the hand to a flannel sleeve that may have been red plaid years ago, to a face that has been around longer than the flannel shirt. Longer, perhaps, than Eli Whitney's cotton gin. The man is old—either that or he's had a hard life. Probably both. His skin is deep brown, with wrinkles inside of wrinkles. He has a significant lesion on his cheek, possibly a basal cell carcinoma, but its ragged outline is concerning. Either way, it needs to be checked out. Too bad it won't be.

His beard and mustache are surprisingly neat. Unfortunately, they encircle a mouth with roughly the same number of teeth possessed by your average one-year-old. His nose is bulbous, likely from rosacea. But his eyes—nothing amiss there. A striking blue, almost violet, and as clear as a child's. No indication of alcohol abuse or illness of any kind. I forget about the coffee dripping from my hand as well as the mess on the counter as I stare into those eyes. Sarah's gaze is the only one that can mesmerize me.

Until now.

I have seen those eyes before. Maybe a movie. Or maybe an illustration of Santa Claus. I see a sparkle there, even merriment.

The crow's feet at the corners deepen even further as he smiles at me. "Everybody has a little spill now and then." The man starts cleaning the counter, and my embarrassment breaks the spell.

"Oh, no. I'll do it." I grab a few more napkins and finish the job. "Thanks for the help, Mr..."

"Mr.?" The man laughs as he pulls a cup from the dispenser. "Ain't nobody called me Mr. anything for a long time. It's Josh. Just Josh." He sets down the cup and offers me his hand.

The moment we touch, I make a mental note to use sanitizer as soon as I return to the car. But that thought evaporates as I fall back into his eyes. "Thank you, Just Josh."

"Good one, boy!" He slaps me on the back and fills his cup. "Just Josh," he repeats to himself with a chuckle as he walks to the cashier.

"That'll be one fifty-nine," the cashier says in a flat, robotic voice.

Josh scans the rack of snacks at the register and selects a small bag of peanuts. "These too, please."

"Okay," Miss Personality answers, drawing out the word to signal her exasperation. "That'll be three dollars even."

Josh pulls out a small floral change purse from the front pocket of his jeans. I have seen old ladies use them, the kind that close with two metal knobs that click together. He studies the contents, then returns the peanuts to the rack.

I grab them and plop them back on the counter. "Let me," I say before he can protest. "And let's get..." I look at the snacks, searching for anything remotely healthy. Peanut butter crackers and packages of pistachios and mixed nuts will have to do.

Josh places his hand on my arm. "You don't have to do that, son."

The word *son* crashes through my heart, stirring up my shame and grief. I shake my head, not trusting myself to speak. I don't hear the cashier give me the total, so I pull out a twenty.

She rolls her eyes and exhales loudly.

I wish I could pay her in pennies.

I should be jumping back in my car, but instead I'm standing in front of a store with a nice old homeless man. I can feel his eyes on me, but I fix my gaze on the busy road before us. Then I sense Josh turning his attention toward the road too. We shuffle away from the entrance, the only move we make.

I need to go. I must go. Finding Sarah is all that matters. But I can't move. I can't explain it, but I feel compelled to stay with this broken-down guy I met less than ten minutes ago. Then I hear Josh humming the same tune that's been stuck in my mind since I left the clinic. I finally look at him. "What's that song?"

"Oh, it's an old one, maybe older than me." He grins, and the smile moves to his eyes. "'Turn Your Eyes Upon Jesus.' One of my favorites."

I remember now. Our church choir sang it ages ago. I can still hear Mrs. Rankin's soprano soaring above the rest of the group. As the lyrics drift back to me, Josh begins to sing softly.

Turn your eyes upon Jesus,
Look full in His wonderful face.
And the things of earth will grow strangely dim
In the light of His glory and grace.

Everything around us falls away—the traffic noise, the customers entering and leaving the store, the bite of the morning air. Josh and I are in church, a congregation of two.

He stops after finishing the first verse, then taps my arm gently and studies me with those blue-violet eyes. "Focus on Him and you'll be fine, son. Be still and keep your eyes on the Light."

With that Josh turns to walk away. His words bounce around in my brain, freezing my body in place. He's about to turn the corner into an alley when I finally move.

"Josh!" I call as I chase him. "Here." I extend some bills to him, all the cash I have. "You need this more than me."

The old man gives me a wide, near-toothless smile and pushes my hand away. "No, son, you keep it. I don't need a thing."

"Take care, Josh."

"You too, son," he replies over his shoulder. He heads down the alley, then comes back to face me. "And he knew you loved him, Sam." Josh pats his chest. "He knows."

I stagger backward and bump into a guy.

"Hey! Watch it!" he grumbles.

"Sorry," I say automatically. I pivot and run after Josh to ask him what he meant.

But he's gone.

I stumble to my car and manage to drive away. I don't know where I'm going, but I can't stay here around all these people.

I drive around town for twenty minutes or so before pulling into a park next to the Roanoke River. Not until I drop my hands from the steering wheel do I notice they're shaking. I'm shaking all over, and inside too, plugged into a power source and unable to disconnect. "God, what's happening?" I almost yell. "I don't understand. Help me understand." Maybe this is how it feels to go insane.

Still.

The same word I heard months ago. *But how can I be still when everything is blowing up? I don't know where Sarah is, and now this old guy calls me by my name and tells me he knew I loved him. Who knew? Dad? What are You doing? I don't know...*

But I do.

What?

I know. You. Sarah. The child. Your father. I know. I Am. Trust Me. Be still.

*

The shaking subsides and I cover my face. *Jesus, I've messed everything up.* I shudder as the darkness closes in again. But this time I'm not caught in the rubble of a cave-in. Instead, I'm plummeting to Earth's core, beyond the hope of rescue.

Ever since Dad died, I've worked hard to be a good man doing the right thing. But it wasn't enough. Never enough. And then I broke down and gave in to my desire for Sarah. Oh, God, I used my pain as a license to get what I've wanted for so long.

God, I am so sorry. Please forgive me.

A warmth begins in my chest and spreads out to the rest of my body. My arms fall loosely at my sides as my muscles uncoil. Now the heat is flowing out of me and surrounding me and lifting me up, like a bird carried on a current of air. Like a hawk.

Of course. *Thank You.*

"Hang on, baby," I whisper as I start the car. "I'll be there soon."

CHAPTER 19

SARAH TOLD ME she "woke up" from her post-kidnapping hibernation when her grandfather took her to Hawksbill Summit, the highest point in Shenandoah National Park. We talk about everything, so it's surprising that she's never said much about that place. I've wondered if what happened there is too sensitive to share, even with me.

I know Sarah's there. I'm as certain of that as I am that God visited me in my dreams three years ago and in my car one hour ago. He was involved with Josh's appearance too, but I'll process that later.

Now my focus must be on Sarah and the baby.

Our baby.

I say the words aloud, realizing that I want this child. Even if my life is turned upside down and every plan I've ever made gets shredded. Even if it makes no sense to my family or my friends. I want to raise this child with Sarah, my beloved Sarah.

I pray she wants that too.

The miles fly under my wheels. I'm in a hurry but not anxious. Bursting with love but not possessed. I can picture Jesus holding Sarah's hand, keeping her from harm until I reach her.

There are two trails to Hawksbill Summit. I remember Sarah telling me that she and her grandfather took the longer but gentler of the two. "Not that I believed him at the time," she said and laughed. "I was grateful each time Grandpa decided to take a break." The memory of Sarah's laughter makes me smile.

Only one car is parked in the Upper Hawksbill lot when I arrive. Sarah's.

It appears to be empty, but I check to be sure. Then I take off on the trail, as fast as my feet can carry me.

The rumbling voice tries to intrude. *You won't find her*, it growls. *She's out of hope and the only way out is…*

"Stop it!" I shout, and the dark words sizzle away like mist in the sunlight.

I'm so busy scanning the forest on either side of the path that I don't notice a rock right in front of me. I tumble forward and skid on the ground. My hands are stinging, and I'm vaguely aware that my jeans are torn. No matter. I'm close to Sarah now.

The trail has become steeper. I rest my hands on my knees for a second, then press on. I round a bend, and that's when I see it—a patch of red next to a car-sized boulder.

I'm out of breath, but not from exertion. "Sarah!" I call out, but all I manage is a whisper. I run. At least, I think I'm running. I might as well be at the bottom of a pool, fighting the pressure of the water surrounding me.

She's not moving. *Oh, God. Oh, God. Let her be okay. Just let her be okay.*

"Sarah!" I try again, and my voice rings through the forest.

She spins around and rises so quickly that she teeters against the rock for support. My legs start working properly again, and I'm beside her in half a heartbeat, catching her before she can fall.

She throws her arms around my neck and I lift her up in an embrace, then set her down so I can kiss her cheeks and her eyes and her mouth. I pause only to say her name. "Sarah, Sarah, Sarah." When I finally stop, I cup her face in my hands. "Are you all right? I was so scared."

"Shhh. I'm okay." She pats her stomach. "We're okay."

"You didn't?"

She shakes her head and the tears come. "I couldn't. I wanted to do this for you, but I couldn't."

The girl I've loved for so long would've never considered such a thing. Suddenly my relief is overwhelmed by sorrow. I fight the urge to shake her and ask what kind of man she thinks I am.

Then it hits me. *Jesus, what kind of man am I?*

Sarah pushes away and turns her back. "I guess you hate me now." She takes a ragged breath and hugs herself.

Hate her? For backing out of the abortion or for considering it? *Oh, God. Give me the right words. I have made so many mistakes already.*

I take her back into my arms and hold her close to my chest. "No, no, no. I could never hate you. I screwed up last night. I told myself it was your decision and that my only job was to support you. But that was a cop out. I left you out there on a limb, alone. I'm so sorry, Sarah." I begin to cry. "I'm so sorry."

Her shoulders heave as she sobs. "I almost…God, forgive me."

I stroke her hair. "Everything's going to be okay." I sing the words like a lullaby. "We'll figure this out."

There's so much I want to tell Sarah about this morning, things I'll never share with anyone else. But this situation isn't all about me. It is about us. All three of us.

"You deserve some answers," she whispers against me.

I stuff down a "Please." "Only when you're ready. We don't have to talk about it now."

"It won't get any easier." Sarah stares at me, and I fall into her gaze. Whatever she has to say, it won't change how much I love her.

"I knew you'd never ask me to…"—she takes a stuttering breath—"to have an abortion, but that seemed like the only way for you to have the future you've dreamed of."

"But did you think that's what I wanted?" I hope my voice isn't as strangled as I feel.

"I thought…" Sarah steps away and leans against the boulder. "I thought you love me and want me but are confused about the baby. So I figured it was up to me to make things right."

Dear God. A knife plunges into my gut and the pain is breathtaking. *Dear God.*

"I was in a very dark place when all these ideas started rushing in. It was like I was being pulled in by the gravity of a black hole and I couldn't save myself." Sarah digs into her pocket for a tissue, only to tear it apart fiber by fiber.

I want to hold her, to stop this. Instead, I stand beside her, both of us focusing on the trees across the trail.

"I was afraid I'd lose my nerve if I waited, so I slipped out early this morning. I planned to tell you after..."—she shivers—"after it was done."

I pull her toward me as gently as I can. *Please tell me what to say, Jesus. Your words, not mine.* "But you didn't do it. You chose to give our baby a chance, and that's the important thing." I brush her hair away from her face, then press my cheek against hers. "I promise I'll never leave you on your own like that again."

Sarah's body relaxes into mine and her breathing becomes more even. "I love you, Sam Russell."

I think my heart might burst, unable to contain this surge of emotion. "I love you, Sarah Winston."

Sarah places my hand against her cheek and her eyes open wide. "What's this?" she asks as she studies my scraped palm.

"Oh, yeah. I forgot about that."

She picks up my other hand.

"I tripped on a rock on the trail. Or maybe I just stumbled over my own two feet. I was in a hurry."

"To get to me." Her eyes are starting to get misty again, but she's smiling. "You know, I can't imagine going through this with anyone else."

"And I'm thankful for that, on a couple of levels," I answer.

Sarah laughs softly, and her music fills me up. "I have a little first aid kit in the car," she says. "Let's get you patched up." She tugs on my hand to lead me to the parking lot.

I don't budge. "But do you want to go on to the summit? Or were you on your way back?" I don't want to stop her from going if it's important to her.

She stares at the trail ahead before turning back to me. "I was doing okay, and I thought I'd get to the summit easily. But when I reached that rock,"—she points to the boulder where I found her—"I was suddenly overwhelmed with fatigue. I barely had enough energy to lower myself to the ground."

Without a word, I scoop Sarah up and begin carrying her back to the car. She starts kicking immediately and I set her down.

"What are you doing?" she huffs even as she grins. "I'm pregnant, not incapacitated."

"But you said you were overwhelmed with—"

She puts her hands on her hips in a mock show of temper. I know it isn't real because her gaze isn't boring through me like a laser beam. "That was then. I feel good now. Let's go." She charges off down the trail like she has an appointment.

"Hey, wait for me," I call.

We don't say much as we return to the parking lot, but I squeeze Sarah's hand now and then to confirm that all is well. She's all right, the baby's all right, and we are together.

Thirty minutes later, Sarah's dabbing antibiotic ointment on my hands and my left knee when I remember to check for a cell signal.

"What are you doing?" she fusses. "The world doesn't need you right now."

"Not the world, maybe, but several people are waiting to hear from me." I pull the phone out of my pocket with my thumb and index finger to avoid smearing the screen.

Her hand stops in midair. "Who?"

I start ticking off the names on my fingers. "I told Gavin I was looking for you before I left this morning. Then I went to your apartment and spoke to Jessie. Emilia called and said she was worried about you. Finally, I called Lissi to see if she had heard from you. I promised I'd let them know when I found you."

Sarah bites her lip and looks down. "Do they all know about the baby?"

"Gavin asked me what was wrong, so I told him. But I didn't tell Emilia or Lissi. I knew you'd want to."

She exhales slowly and kicks a pebble back and forth like a soccer ball. "Yeah, I'll tell them. I can't imagine what they'll think of me."

I take a step closer and lift her chin. "They're your friends, Red. They'll be there for you because they love you."

She leans into me, her forehead against my chest.

I hold her tight, wishing we could jump ahead a few months. Wishing we had already told... "Red?"

"Uh-huh?"

"When are we going to tell our parents?"

Sarah nearly jumps out of my arms. "I haven't even thought about...Mama and Daddy and your mom...I mean, I have thought about them a lot, but this morning the only thing on my mind was fixing things. Telling them, that's going to be...God help us."

I whisper, "But they love us too. Everything will be okay." But at the same time, I'm saying a prayer.

God, help us.

*

I tried to persuade Sarah to ride back to Blacksburg with me, that we would find a way to retrieve her car later. But she refused, which didn't surprise me.

"Don't be ridiculous," she scolded. "There's no reason I can't drive."

"But what if you get tired again," I argued.

"Then I'll pull over and you can rescue me."

I did win one concession. She agreed to stop for some lunch.

"I'll be following you," I warned. "And if you don't take the exit,

I'll honk and flash my lights and make a spectacle of myself. I might even get a ticket, but I don't care."

"Okay, okay." Sarah lifted her hands in surrender. "Whatever you say, sir."

Now, not many people are here, maybe eight customers. Back in this corner booth it feels like we have the place to ourselves. When we arrived, I scooted in next to Sarah, not wanting even a table between us.

"Separation anxiety?" she asked, patting my hand like I was a little kid.

"No." After seeing her raised eyebrow, I admitted, "Maybe. A little. Yes."

"You're too cute."

I find myself wishing we could start driving west when we finish our meal. Drive and drive and call the folks when we reach California.

Sarah turns her coffee mug slowly, like she's examining a recently unearthed treasure. "I never asked how you found me."

"It started with a dream."

Her mouth drops open. "The wolf?"

I shake my head. It occurs to me that I can use my girl's curiosity against her. "I'll tell you everything if you'll start in on your food. I'm guessing you haven't eaten anything today."

She compresses her lips into a grimace. "You sound like Mama. I'll have you know I ate some cashews last night."

"You must be stuffed." I stifle a grin.

"Oh, shut up." Sarah elbows me before spreading the mound of butter atop her pancakes. Each of us always goes with a breakfast menu if it's offered.

"You shut up."

This familiar exchange started back when we were in high school. One of us says, "Shut up," in response to a snarky comment, and the other person answers, "You shut up." Anyone overhearing us would think we are bickering, but neither of us has ever said "Shut up" to the other in anger.

"Well?"

"Well, what?" It's been such a stressful morning that I can't resist baiting her.

Sarah's knife makes a rattling sound as she drops it on her plate. "Did God talk to you?"

Enough. "Sorry, I couldn't help myself. Did God talk to me? Not out loud." Then I remember Josh. "I said I had a dream, but it was actually a nightmare."

In between bites, I tell Sarah how Emilia and I knew something awful was happening. I describe my journey to find her, from the moment I woke up to our embracing on the trail to Hawksbill Summit. I mention Josh but leave out what I have assumed was a reference to Dad. That part can wait.

When I'm done, she leans back and closes her eyes. When she opens them, they're serene. It pops into my head that her eyes remind me of Josh's. "Wow. I don't know why I'm surprised," she says in a reverent whisper. "I mean, we've both seen God do big things before, but I guess I still underestimate Him. I needed to hear your story."

I can't believe I haven't asked the obvious question until now. "But that's my story. What about yours? Why didn't you go through with it?"

Sarah reaches for her purse and coat. "Not now. More people are coming in. But I will tell you. I promise."

It's not until I turn and scan the restaurant that I notice tables and booths filling up around us. The lull is over. "Okay."

*

I texted Jessie, Emilia, Lissi, and Gavin before Sarah and I left the park, but Sarah wanted to call her friends after lunch. "I'll just be a minute," she told me twenty minutes ago. I said nothing, but a quick calculation—a woman making calls to three other women—made it clear that more than a minute would be involved.

But that's okay. The morning chill has given way to a pleasant midday. The Denny's parking lot isn't a quiet meadow, but it's not bad. I'm tempted to lean my seat back and take a nap, like a cat stretching out in the sunshine. But I can't turn off my brain.

Sarah didn't say if she planned to tell her friends about the baby. I don't think she will, only because she'd want to tell her parents first.

Her parents. My mom. The pancakes suddenly feel like a ball of clay in my stomach. The details of how they'll react to this news are unknown, but the general outline is clear. Shock. Anger. Sadness. Disappointment. Stick your hand in a sack of bad outcomes and you're likely to emerge with a winner, with the possible exception of a crime of passion.

Then again…

The scene plays out clearly in my mind. A look of undiluted hatred crossing Mr. Winston's face as I offer a feeble explanation. "Uh, sorry I got your little girl pregnant, Mr. Winston. But we were together only once and afterward we promised not to do it again. Does that help?"

It would take a couple of minutes for Mr. Winston to unlock his gun cabinet. That might give me enough of a head start.

"Somebody's a million miles away." Sarah leans in my window. "Where were you? Australia?"

"Almost. How'd it go?"

As soon as she slides into my passenger seat, all thoughts of my possible demise vanish. She has a brightness I haven't seen in days, and a lightness to her voice. More like her old self. "Actually, all three calls were good. Jessie was so sweet. I think it's possible she doesn't think you are irredeemable." Sarah grins, and I shrug in response. "I didn't tell Emilia about the baby because I want to tell Mama and Daddy first. She didn't pepper me with questions. She knows I'll tell her everything eventually. Lissi, on the other hand, had already figured it out."

"She had?" Lissi does plan to become an investigative reporter, but I didn't think she was this good already.

She nods. "She said an abortion was the only thing she could think of that could cause you to hate me."

A lump forms in my throat, and I grab both of her hands. "I could never hate you, Red."

Sarah stares at me, her eyes flickering back and forth across my face. "Maybe *hate* isn't the right word. But if I had killed this child, we would have been broken. I know it and you do too. Broken beyond repair."

I shiver as a cold, dark what-if descends on us.

Sarah squeezes my hands. "But we were saved from that, thank God. And He'll show us where to go from here."

"Yeah," is all I can manage. If only I could marry her today. I wonder if she would say yes this time. I take a deep breath. "I wish you'd ride back to Blacksburg with me. We could come back for your car. It's closer now, and we wouldn't even have to pay for another admission to the park to get it."

"You're being silly again. You can keep me under surveillance the whole way back, but we're not leaving my car here."

"You're stubborn, Miss Winston."

"And you, Mr. Russell, are persistent."

"I am when it comes to you."

*

Another sunny day. Another parking lot. This one is outside the VT Health Center. Sarah called yesterday after lunch and was able to get an appointment for this morning. I offered to come in with her, but she said I could wait outside. I tried not to let my relief show.

Although Sarah's 99.9% sure that she's pregnant, we agreed that we wouldn't go to our parents without official confirmation. This isn't the kind of revelation you can back away from later with an "Oops! Never mind."

Sarah and I are both planners. We like clear road maps showing us how to get from point A to point B to point C. But her pregnancy has dropped us into not just a new territory but a new world. The only thing we're sure of is that abortion is off the table. I haven't told

Sarah that I want us to raise this child together. She hasn't shared which way she's leaning.

Standing here in the sunshine, a bubble of optimism appears in my heart. Once the initial shock has worn off, our parents can help us figure out what to do. They've wisdom gained through hard experience and can offer guidance as we go forward.

The bubble bursts. When it comes to our folks, we're doomed. At least I am.

I look up to see Sarah walking slowly back to the car. She wraps her arms around me without speaking and holds me tight. I lean my head on hers and hug her back. I wish I could insulate her from whatever is coming next. "We're in this together, Red. Don't forget that," I murmur. "When do you want to go to Early?"

"Today," she answers, her voice muffled against my chest. "The longer we put this off—"

"The harder it will be," I finish.

We climb into my truck and wait. For a plan. For a clue, any clue, about how to proceed.

Sarah speaks first. "Do you think we should call them to make sure they're home? I can see us driving back, psyching ourselves up the whole way, only to discover that Mama and Daddy or your mom have gone someplace for the weekend."

"I don't know." Dread runs an icy finger along my spine. "Your dad might guess what's going on, and that gives him enough time to stockpile ammunition."

She punches my shoulder. "Come on, you know he loves you. You're like the son he never had."

"A son that's about to be disowned," I add.

Sarah ignores that and moves on. "And we have to make sure they all know at the same time."

I picture us sitting before a jury. "You mean, get them together?" My stomach flips.

She purses her lips, moving her mouth from side to side. "You're right. We shouldn't. That kind of puts them all on the spot. We'll tell them separately."

We both process for a moment. "So are we calling ahead or not?"

She taps her lips with her finger. "We call ahead, but just to say we thought we'd come home for a visit, not that we have any news."

I nod. "Yeah, and I'll make sure Meg is going to be there. I don't want Mom to be alone when she hears this."

"And we can decide on the way which parents are told first." Sarah's energy is returning, and so is mine. Plans do that for us.

*

We have been on the road for half an hour now, and I don't think we've said more than a few words—two dozen, tops. Sarah has been staring out her window or leaning back with her eyes closed, constantly twirling a few strands of her hair.

I'm driving, so half of my brain is adjusting my speed and scanning traffic while the other half is preparing for this trip home. *Preparing* makes it sound like I'm developing a detailed strategy, like if the Winstons say this, I'll say that. It would be more accurate to say I'm praying, although I'm not even sure what to pray for. That our parents will accept our news without a lot of grief? That Sarah and I will say the right thing at the right time? That...I don't know. I suppose all I can do is ask that everything happens the way God wants it.

I reach for Sarah and intertwine our fingers. "Doing okay?"

She smiles slightly. "I guess. The closer we get, the more nervous I become. You?"

I shrug. "About the same."

"Worried about how your mother will react?"

I wobble my head from side to side. "I'm sure she will be sad and disappointed, but she won't stop loving me." I squeeze Sarah's hand. "What about your folks?"

"I know they won't be happy..."

My mouth drops open, since that's like saying World War II was a disagreement.

"Okay, they'll be really unhappy, but I'm not worried about being disowned or anything." She gives me her troublemaking grin and tucks a bit of hair behind my ear. "If I must, I'll throw you under the bus. You're good with that?"

I slap on my best doomed martyr expression. "Why not? I'm a dead man walking anyway."

CHAPTER 20

I DROP OFF my duffel bag in my room. Mom and Megan are both out, so I can go to Sarah's house without delay.

Mr. Winston answers the door. Of course. "Well, if it isn't Sam Russell. Imagine that." He extends one hand for a shake while slapping me on the back with the other. So happy to see me.

My gut is in a knot. Sarah's dad is like a movie character laughing at a joke the moment the bullet rockets through the window. "Good afternoon. How are you, sir?"

"Very well, thank you, now that you've brought my baby girl home for the weekend."

Good Lord.

I look beyond him to see Sarah descending the stairs. My heart goes back to our very first date, when she walked down those stairs wearing a green dress. I'd never seen anything so beautiful in my whole life. And she's even more spectacular now.

"Hi," she says, her voice low. "Ready?"

I dip my head slightly, a nonverbal lie.

"Mama and Daddy? You guys have a minute?" Sarah leads me to their kitchen.

Mrs. Winston is pulling a pan of brownies out of the oven, Mr. Winston hovering behind her. She swats at him with a potholder.

"For heaven's sake, Daniel, wait a few minutes. They'll be a gooey mess if you try to eat them now, plus you'll burn your mouth."

Mr. Winston kisses his wife's neck. "Party pooper."

She pats him on the cheek. "Little boys." The two of them are so lost in each other that they seem to have forgotten Sarah and I are standing right here. My parents were like that.

Sarah clears her throat to get their attention.

"Oh, sorry, honey," Mrs. Winston apologizes. "Every time I make a dessert, I have to fend off your dad. Him and his sweet tooth." She takes her usual chair in their breakfast nook and Mr. Winston settles in beside her. "You needed something?"

Their faces are so untroubled, so content, that I feel guilty already, as if I'm holding a club over a pair of baby seals.

I slide out a chair for Sarah opposite her parents. I can't decide whether she'll feel better if I stand behind her, hands on her shoulders, or next to her. That is one detail we didn't cover. I go for what's natural and sit down.

Sarah grabs my hand under the table. "We…" She glances at me with a pale smile. "I, um…" She looks down and chews her lower lip, her grip on me tightening.

"What is it, honey?" Mrs. Winston asks as she reaches for her husband's hand. Their peaceful expressions have melted away, their eyes and mouths drawing down like candle wax.

Please help Sarah say it before they guess. Please give her that.

Sarah sits up straight and looks directly at her mom and dad. "I'm pregnant."

Mr. and Mrs. Winston don't move, and yet they seem to have been knocked backward by the shockwave of an explosion. Their eyes are wide, like victims who never saw the blow coming, their mouths open in astonishment.

Sarah and I wait for a response. Any words, even angry ones, would be better than this devastating silence. An image of a quiet battlefield littered with bodies flashes into my thoughts.

I release Sarah's hand so I can put my arm around her shoulders. "We're so sorry," I start, anxious to move on from this awful moment.

"You're sorry?" Mr. Winston says, his voice low and quivering. He jabs his index finger at me. "You should be sorry. You've ruined my little girl."

Sarah scoots closer to me and seizes my free hand. "Sam did not ruin me." She stares at her father. "We love each other, and we took things too far, but I chose to be with him. I chose him, Daddy." She looks at me, her eyes so soft and glowing with affection that I forget the situation for a millisecond. "And now you have to accept that."

"I will not," he growls, biting off each syllable and spitting it back at us.

"Daniel." Mrs. Winston speaks just above a whisper and rubs his arm.

He turns to her briefly before looking away and pushing his chair back. After resting his arms on his knees, he clasps his hands in front of him. For a moment, the only sound in the room is his breathing as he fights for control.

"What do you plan to do?" Sarah's mom focuses on Sarah, then me. "After the baby is born, of course."

"We haven't—" Sarah begins, but her father cuts her off.

"Why do you say 'of course'?" Mr. Winston stands abruptly, causing his chair to teeter. He's not yelling, but the force of his voice is stronger than a shout.

"What do you mean?" Mrs. Winston asks in an even softer tone than before.

"I mean, why do you assume Sarah will have this, this…" he stammers.

"This baby?" Sarah rises from her seat, calm and powerful, like a lioness. "My baby? What are you saying, Daddy?"

He plants his hands on the table and leans across to face her. "I am saying that you can end this now. Do not wreck your life over a mistake. Over him." Mr. Winston glares at me.

I stand to meet his gaze.

"Daniel, you can't be suggesting…" Mrs. Winston rises and turns his shoulders to face her. "We believe in life."

He jerks out of his wife's grasp. "And I do. I believe in my daughter's life, not a microscopic clump of cells." He turns back to Sarah. "God saved you from John Perkins for a purpose, and how do you repay Him? By throwing your future away like some stupid—"

"That's enough." I extend my palm to Sarah's father, then face her, blocking her view of him. I gently place my hands on either side of her sweet face. She has the same annihilated expression her parents wore moments ago. "Red," I whisper. When I don't get a response, I move in closer, until our noses almost touch. "Sarah."

"Yes?" The mighty lioness is gone and only a broken little girl remains.

"Get your bag and put it by the front door." I speak softly and deliberately, as if to a small child. "Then walk to my house and wait for me on the steps. I will be there in a few minutes. Can you do that for me?"

She nods slowly. I ask her to repeat my instructions to confirm I've gotten through.

"Put my bag by the door and wait on your steps." Her voice is flat, and I wonder if she's walked away from herself again.

Sarah goes up and down the stairs and out the door without looking at me or her parents.

When the front door closes, I turn back to the Winstons. "Sarah and I are going to tell my mother about the baby next, then we'll return to Blacksburg." I focus on her dad. "I think you need to calm down before Sarah talks to you again."

"How dare you! You can't keep me from my little girl." Mr. Winston barrels around the table, stopping inches from my face.

"Daniel!" Mrs. Winston rushes over and tugs at his arm. "You have to stop."

I glance at Sarah's mother and recall the panicked look on

Mom's face when Dad and I fought that awful night. "It's okay, Mrs. Winston," I assure her, before turning my attention back to her husband. "She's not your little girl. She hasn't been for a long time." Rage is shimmering around Mr. Winston, but I keep going. "I don't care what you think of me, but Sarah..." Saying her name touches a tender place inside me, even as it triggers something new. Something strong. "Sarah is kind and good and loves God with all her heart. You will never—and I mean, never—speak to her that way again, not as long as I have breath in my body. Do you understand me, Daniel?"

He takes a slight step back. "You can't. You have no right."

I pivot and move to the front door, then pick up Sarah's bag and lock eyes with her dad. "I have every right. I love Sarah. I am the father of her baby. And one day, God willing, your daughter will be my wife." I resist the temptation to slam the door.

When I reach the street, I see Sarah sitting on the front steps of my house, her head resting on her knees, and I run. ·

I toss her carry-on into the back of my truck without breaking stride and am within arm's reach before she even looks up. "Sam!" she exclaims, like my arrival is a surprise, as she throws her arms around my neck.

I want to hold her like this forever, but we have more work to do. "You don't have to go in there, Red," I whisper. "You can wait in the truck."

"That wouldn't be right," she answers, her head still nuzzled into my shoulder. "You were with me,"—she shudders—"so I'll be with you." She leans away, wipes her face with the back of her hand, and tries to smile. So brave, so steadfast. I wish I had punched Daniel Winston in the face.

Please forgive me. Please help me.

I breathe out as my fury ebbs. "Okay, then. Ready?"

"Uh-huh."

Megan is walking down the stairs as we come in. "Mom, Sam and Sarah are here," she calls.

"There you are!" Mom tosses a hand towel over her shoulder before embracing Sarah and me. "I was just making…" She stops speaking the instant she takes a good look at us. After removing the towel and dabbing at Sarah's face, the way she used to when I cried after a hard fall, she asks, "What's going on?"

"We need to talk," I manage to say before leading the women in my life into the family room.

Mom curls up in Dad's recliner, pulling her feet under her, as Megan balances on the chair's arm. Sarah and I sit on the sofa, huddling close together. Sarah has begun to shiver, so I wrap my arm around her and rub her shoulder.

God, help us.

Mom opens her mouth slightly, preparing to speak, but she waits. She knows. I can feel it. But the words need to be said.

"Sarah is…" I stop short of adding "pregnant." That sounds like this is all her fault and I am an innocent bystander. "Sarah and I are going to have a baby."

Mom's breath leaves her in a *whoosh*, as she leans back and closes her eyes. Megan takes her hand and strokes her arm. Dad should be here now. He should be here to hold Mom and tell her everything will be all right. Yes, he would be furious with me, and I'm sure I would walk away with an "I told you so" clanging in my head. But, oh, how I wish he were here.

Sarah intertwines our fingers and holds on tight. "We're so sorry, Mrs. Winston. We know we've let you down…"

Mom waves off Sarah's apology, shakes her head, and sits up.

Sarah and I pile our hands atop each other, preparing for another onslaught.

But when Mom's eyes open, a smile appears. A slight smile, a sad one, but a smile nevertheless. "Dad and I love…" she stutters through tears. "Dad loved you both, and so do I. But this news is…hard." She stares in our direction, but not at us. I know what's captured her attention: a picture hanging over the sofa, a portrait taken of our family when Megan and I were tiny. Megan might have been five, meaning I was two. We're lined up in a standard photography studio configuration, with Mom sitting on a bench holding me, Megan beside her, and Dad standing behind all of us. Watching over us. We're all dressed in our church clothes, but there's no Sunday-morning stress evident.

I don't recall being two, of course, but it seems that most of the Sundays of my childhood included some tears from Megan, jelly or some other edible substance dribbling down my face onto my shirt, and weary eye-rolling from our exasperated parents.

We had no idea how blessed we were.

Mom's lip quivers, and I'm certain she is thinking the same thing. *Oh, God.*

Mom rises from the recliner so quickly that Megan is almost deposited on the floor. Then my every-item-in-its-place mother pushes aside the books and candles arranged on the coffee table in front of the sofa, takes a seat, and places her hands over ours. Megan scoots in next to Sarah and stretches her arm across our backs.

Mom studies us with an intensity that makes me want to turn away. I'm not worthy of it. "We all make mistakes," she says in a soft, soothing voice. "What's done is done. Now we must focus on what's next."

Sarah's eyes flash. The lioness has returned. "I'm not having an abortion."

Mom jerks back. "Of course not! I'd never suggest such a thing."

"But Daddy...Daddy said..." Sarah's shoulders shake as the tears pour out.

I clear my throat and finish for her. "Mr. Winston thinks Sarah should."

Mom's eyes widen as Megan gasps. "I can't believe Daniel..." Mom fixes her eyes on a corner of the ceiling and shakes her head. "He's in shock. I know how it is with fathers and daughters." She glances at Megan, who nods in return. "But give him time. He'll come around."

Sarah's sobbing eases as Mom pats her cheek gently. "It will be okay, Sarah. You'll see." Mom turns to me. "But have you thought about what you want to do?"

I'm slowly regaining my footing. "Yes, ma'am, but we don't know if we're supposed to keep this child or give him or her up for adoption. We want to do the right thing, but we're not sure what that is."

Mom reaches out and combs through my hair. "Wanting to do what's right—seeking God's plan in all this—is the best place to start, Sammy."

I thought I'd settled on solid ground, but I'm faltering again. "Thank you, Mom. I—we—love you."

"And we love you," she manages to respond.

A hush comes over us. I half expect someone to begin praying, when Sarah jumps up abruptly and stumbles past me, her hand over her mouth.

"Sarah?"

The door to the powder room in the hall closes, followed by the sound of vomiting.

I rush to the door and knock. "Red? Are you okay?"

"Go away," she answers. "Please."

"Poor thing." Mom gently pulls me back. "Has she been sick a lot?"

Listening to Sarah's retching tears at me in a whole new way. I've never seen her suffer anything more than a cold. "I don't think so. I don't think she's been sick at all."

Mom turns to Megan. "You stay close by in case Sarah needs something. Sam, come with me."

I reluctantly follow Mom into the kitchen. She pulls out an insulated bag from the Super Dollar and starts rifling through her cabinets. "I keep ginger ale on hand for tummy troubles, and you'll need a sleeve of saltines as well. I think I lived on crackers and carbonation when I was pregnant with Megan."

I watch Mom as I listen for the powder room door to open. I feel utterly useless.

"I wonder if I have something else Sarah can keep down," Mom continues as she puts a box of Yummy O's in the bag. "Don't want you to forget these."

I hear Sarah's voice and hurry back toward the powder room, only to be blocked by Megan at the foot of the stairs. "Hold it, bro." She plants her hand on my chest. "Sarah's going to clean up before resting a little in my room." She lowers her voice. "I think she's embarrassed, getting sick in front of you."

"But that's silly—"

"Shhh." She puts her finger to her lips. "It is not silly to her."

I focus on the top stair and picture Sarah lying on Megan's bed, pale and worn out. "I love her so much, sis."

Megan takes my hand. "I know. Now go on and give her some space. I'll stay close for now in case she needs anything."

I turn to go.

"And Sam?"

Megan wraps me in one of her fierce hugs. "Whatever you think of yourself, I know you're a good man and I'm so thankful you're my brother. Love you."

I struggle to answer. "You, too."

When I return to the kitchen, Mom is standing at the door leading into the garage, her back to me. Her arms are moving, almost like she is kneading bread.

"Mom?" When she turns, I see she's holding Dad's old ball cap, the one he always wore when he did yard work. Dad won't be happy to see his favorite hat mangled, its bill folded in two. I almost smile.

Mom quickly hangs the hat on a hook by the door and rubs at her eyes with the heels of her hands. "How is Sarah?"

"Megan sent her upstairs to rest." I cross the room to my mother and place my hand on her shoulder. "How are you?"

Mom's eyes drift over to the door. "I told your dad a thousand times to leave that filthy hat in the garage, that I didn't want that nasty thing in my kitchen. And every time he'd give me that little-boy smile of his and stick it back on that hook." She takes a few deep breaths and trembles. "Why didn't he let someone else help that girl? Dear Jesus."

I take Mom in my arms as she begins to cry. She seems so small and fragile, like a tiny tree trying to bear up under a fierce wind.

Sarah and I did this. We didn't take Dad from her, but we have placed another burden on her, even as she struggles with the weight of Dad's loss.

"I'm so sorry," I whisper. "I messed up, just like Dad knew I would."

Mom pushes away and grabs my neck. "No, no, no. Your daddy would not want you to talk that way. That night..." She squeezes her eyes shut for a moment. "That night a lot of things were said, things that shouldn't have been said, by you and your father."

I try to look away, but Mom keeps me in a firm hold, my gaze fixed on hers. "This isn't what we hoped for you. For you and Sarah. Yes, your father would have been upset by what you've done, but that would not have changed what he thought of you. He knew—I know—the kind of person you are."

I cross the line between crying and sobbing. "I just want to do the right thing, Mama. I want to be the kind of man Dad was."

"You already are," she murmurs, before kissing me on the forehead.

"Everything okay?" Megan is in the doorway, her glance passing between Mom and me.

"It will be," Mom answers, drying my cheeks before dabbing at her own. "Sarah's still upstairs?"

"Yes, ma'am." Megan points at the bag on the table. "What's that?"

"Oh, this. A few things for Sarah and Sam to take back." Mom pulls out a chair at the table, and Megan and I follow. "I assume you're not staying for the weekend."

I shake my head. "We thought we were, but after what happened with the Winstons, I have to get Sarah out of Early."

Mom pats my hand. "We might as well have the banana bread I planned for breakfast tomorrow. Do I have any takers?"

"Sure," Megan and I answer.

We rise to do our usual tasks, wrapping normal around ourselves like a sweater. My sister makes the coffee while I pull out mugs, plates, napkins, and forks. Mom slices the bread and hums a melody I can't quite place.

None of us speaks as we savor the bread. I press the back of my fork into the moist crumbs remaining on my plate, careful to get each one.

I sense Sarah's presence before I see her. "Hi," she says softly, with a very slight smile. She's leaning on the doorframe for support. And she's pale, so pale.

"Hi to you," I answer as I hurry to her side. "How are you feeling?"

"Better. Sorry about all that."

Mom walks over and puts an arm around her. "No apologies needed, sweet girl. Have a seat and I'll get you some ginger ale."

"Thank you, but I need to leave now." Even Sarah's voice sounds depleted, as if she has just enough energy remaining to keep breathing. She places her hand on my arm. Turning to Mom and Megan, she adds, "I'm sorry, but I can't stay. Sam can, of course, but I'd have to borrow a car…"

I shake my head. "Absolutely not. We came here together and we're leaving together."

Mom gently pats Sarah's cheek. "Sam's right. We can visit some other time."

I have never loved my mother more.

*

I load my duffel and Mom's care package in the truck, and Mom gives Sarah a ginger ale for the road. The women share at least a couple of rounds of hugs before we leave.

Mom and Megan stand on our walkway to see us off, their arms around each other.

As we pass Sarah's house, we see Mrs. Winston holding on to

a column next to the steps, as if that's the only thing keeping her upright. Mr. Winston has his arms braced against the porch railing. He looks drained—of emotion, of strength, of everything. His face is blank as he watches us drive by.

I feel sorry for him until I see fresh tears running down Sarah's face. Then I don't.

CHAPTER 21

SARAH STOPPED CRYING about fifteen minutes into our drive, but she hasn't said a word. Not one. She's not a babbler, but I can't remember when we've spent forty-five minutes in total silence. I've teetered between thinking I should try to draw her out and leaving her alone.

I can't take it anymore. I open my mouth just as Sarah speaks.

"Where are we going?" She's looking straight ahead, her head slightly tilted. Confused, like she woke up here after falling asleep at her house.

Is this a test or something? "Uh, Blacksburg?"

"No." Sarah is still staring off into the distance.

"No?"

She looks at me at last and takes my hand. "I can't go home. And I don't want to go back to Blacksburg. I can't face tonight without you."

"I won't leave you, baby." Sarah might be slipping away from me, back into the darkness, even as I'm maneuvering through traffic on I-81. This is no good. I must stop. "Everything will be all right," I say to buy time. I take the next exit and pull into an empty church parking lot.

As soon as I park the truck, I hurry around to open Sarah's door. Then I lead her to the back and lift her up onto the tailgate. "Talk to me, Red."

Sarah leans forward until her forehead touches mine. "Today was so…bad. So much worse than anything I imagined." We close our eyes in unison, letting the ugliness wash over and past us. She takes my hands. "And I need to be with you. Not Jessie. We need time together. Time to talk about…everything. And not in a restaurant, not in a park, not in any public place. Someplace private."

I take deliberate breaths in and out, trying to slow my heart even as my mind dashes through our options. Like there are any.

We move away from each other at the same time. I place my hands on either side of Sarah's face. "I don't know what to do," I whisper. "Tell me what you want me to do."

She shakes her head. "I don't know either. I wish…" She looks off at the Allegheny Mountains to the west and takes deep breaths. Fighting off the pain, I guess.

I focus on my breathing too. I must be strong for Sarah. I can't dissolve into another round of tears. "What do you wish?"

Another long exhale, then Sarah turns back to me. "I wish we could go back, all the way to October. Undo all the mistakes."

"I know."

"But we can't."

"Yeah."

Sarah lowers herself to the ground and puts her arms around my neck. We hold each other and sway slightly, dancing without music.

Her phone rings.

"It's Mama." She slides the phone back in her pocket and her mouth starts to tremble. "I can't talk to her yet."

I rummage around for something encouraging to say, but nothing feels right.

"Excuse me." The man's voice comes from behind me.

I instinctively block Sarah with my body as I swivel to face him.

The man's age—I would guess late fifties—and his placid demeanor lead me to conclude that he's not a threat. A deacon or minister, maybe, who's going to tell us to move along, that this is private property. He extends his hand. "Hello. I'm Nathan Sanders, the pastor here."

I accept his handshake without hesitation, as I've been trained to do. "Hello, sir. My name is Sam, and this is…"

Sarah emerges by my side. "Sarah," she finishes.

He encloses her dainty hand in two of his. "It is so nice to meet you." His eyes quickly scan us. "Is there anything I may do for you? Anything you need?"

This nice guy probably thinks we're homeless.

Maybe he's right.

*

I waver as that thought hits me, so Sarah speaks up. "No, thank you. We were traveling back to Blacksburg and needed…" I hope Sarah can come up with an explanation because I'm empty. "A little break. We'll be leaving now."

We turn to get back into the truck, but the pastor follows me. "Are you sure?" He shoves his hands in the back pockets of his jeans and his expression shifts from welcome to concern. The way Pastor Jeff looked at my family as we planned Dad's funeral. "I don't want to intrude, but I felt the Lord pushing me to check on you. Do you have time for a prayer?"

Sarah and I read each other across the truck's bed. We're not so far gone that we would reject a prayer.

"Sure," I answer.

The pastor reaches out to me, and Sarah walks back around to join us, creating a circle. "Almighty and Merciful Father, we are in awe of You. You made all things and know all things. Nothing is hidden from You. You have told us that when we seek You, we shall find You. Therefore, I ask, in the name of Your Son, Jesus Christ, that You will fill this sweet young couple with Your peace and lead them to Your perfect way. Please make Your will plain to them and help them to rely on Your strength alone. In Jesus's precious name I pray. Amen."

His "Amen" vibrates through the air well after it is spoken, like the tone of a bell. We stand motionless in the silence. Still.

Still.

Pastor Sanders squeezes our hands, then pulls a business card from his wallet. "Please call me any time if you need anything." He smiles at each of us in turn. "Any time. Really."

I'm struggling again, so all I can manage is a "Thank you." But Sarah grasps his hand and holds it.

"Thank you for the prayer," she says, her voice soft and calm. "It was exactly what we needed."

Amen.

We're quiet as we watch the minister walk away. "Well," Sarah says, and I wait for a profound remark about the prayer. "I'm hungry."

I laugh softly. "Now that you mention it, I am too."

"Then I would like to suggest, Dr. Russell, that we eat."

I'm frozen. Blindsided.

Sarah touches my cheek. "What's wrong?"

I shake my head. Not now.

"Sam?"

My frustration bubbles up before I can stop it. "It's med school. I still don't know what I'm doing. The last time I saw my dad, we argued about it. The very last words we had were…" The memory makes me blink. I rest my cheek against hers, stubble against silk. "Maybe Dakota was right for once," I whisper. "You should be with Jack, someone who's going somewhere. But now you're stuck with me."

Sarah jerks away from me. Her eyes flash, and for a second, I brace for a slap. "How dare you!" she hisses. "Don't insult me by implying that all I want is a rich guy to take care of me. Do you think I would have led you to your bedroom that day if I didn't love you? Do you?"

Her anger hits me like a tornado dropping out of a blue sky. "No, of course not. I just want the best for you. I am so sorry—"

"Stop saying you're sorry." Sarah's fury is blazing, drying up any tears she had left. "I realized I loved you the day Smiley kidnapped me, and that love has only grown over the past three years, filling up every bit of my heart. I screwed up by pushing you away last fall, then by going off on my own to that clinic. And you pushed me away after your father died. No more." She grabs my sweatshirt and shakes me. "Do you hear me? No more. Are we a couple, or not? Are we going to work through everything—your career, the baby—together, or not?"

I'm shocked into silence, so I nod my head like a dumb animal.

"So, I'm clear?" she says, her voice suddenly soft. The seriousness of her tone competes with the slight upturn of her mouth. That soft, sweet mouth.

I shake my head slightly to collect myself. "Yes," I manage to answer. "Crystal."

We stagger into the truck. Okay, I stagger, while Sarah seems to have been recharged. We buckle up and gaze out the windshield, waiting for a sign.

I guess I could start with the obvious. "We still don't want to go to Blacksburg, right?"

"Right. At least I don't." Sarah touches my forearm. "Do you?"

"No. I could get us a room somewhere." I silently plead with Sarah to dismiss that option, because sleeping with her without being with her would be torture.

"No, that won't work. If I'm in bed with you, I'll want to…you know." A blush rises into her cheeks.

Miracles happen. This spectacular woman wants me.

I move on quickly. "So that leaves us with…"

"Nothing. Except dinner. And that's a good place to start."

I start the truck. "Then dinner it is."

Her phone dings with a text. Her sigh tells me who sent it. "Your mom?"

"Yeah." Recharged Sarah fades from view. "I guess I better tell her something, or she'll have the State Police looking for us."

My phone rings before I can suggest a response. "It's my mom. Should I take it?"

"Go ahead."

I take a deep breath and dive in. "Hi, Mom."

"Hello, honey. How is it going? Where are you?"

"Just outside Roanoke."

"You haven't made it to Blacksburg yet?"

"No, ma'am. Sarah and I stopped for a break, ran into a pastor, and talked with him."

Silence. "Oh. Okay. I wasn't worried, but then Caroline called me and said Sarah hadn't answered her phone and asked if I knew anything. She sounded really concerned, Sammy."

I feel the weight of Sarah's stare and turn to her. Her eyes are puffy from crying, and her dad is to blame for most of those tears. Her dad, not her mom, so I try to keep my voice level. "I understand. Sarah will send her a text shortly."

"A text? Don't you think she should call?"

I get out of the truck. Sarah doesn't need to hear any more of this conversation. Still, I speak just above a whisper. "Mom, Sarah has been through hell today and she is not up to talking to anyone else, especially her parents."

"But it's her mother."

I take another deep breath. "Sarah will let her know that she's okay, but I refuse to pressure her to call, not after everything she's been through."

More silence. "All right, son. I see your point. Are you headed to Blacksburg now?"

I lean against the truck and stare at the mountains in the distance. "We're figuring things out."

"Please be careful, honey. I know things look bad right now, but don't make the situation worse by being reckless."

"Yes, ma'am." I refuse to consider how things could get worse.

"I love you, son." Mom's voice is breaking.

"Love you." I disconnect before I cry too.

When I climb back in the truck, Sarah is still holding her phone. She lifts it to show me an unsent text on the screen. "This is my fifth draft. You would think I'm trying to write the Gettysburg Address. Want to hear it?"

"Sure."

Sarah clears her throat as if she's delivering a speech. "Okay. 'Hi. We are not in Blacksburg, but we are fine. I think enough has been said today, so I'll be in touch tomorrow.' What do you think?"

I think her mom will believe I wrote that text. "It doesn't sound like you, but I guess you've never had a day like this. Do you want to add 'Love, Sarah,' or something like that?"

She bites her lip and stares at the screen. "That is how I usually end our texts, like a letter. But I don't feel it right now. I'm terrible, aren't I?"

"No, you're not terrible." I stroke her head. "Send it."

Sarah jiggles the phone on her knee. "I guess I should soften it a little. Daddy is the one who…never mind. I'll add a heart emoji at the end. I can do that." She taps a few more characters before sending the text with a whoosh. "How did the call with your mom go?"

"Okay. Checking to see if we had arrived in Blacksburg."

"Like Mama."

"Yeah. Your mother called mine, in fact. Although I doubt Mom needed much prodding."

Sarah stares at her phone, but I can't tell if she is anticipating a reply or dreading it. "Nothing more persistent than a mother, huh?" She slips the phone back into her purse. "Do you think we could put all this away for a little while? Eat dinner and talk about anything else?"

"Sure. I recommend continuing south, since I'm not that familiar with what's north of Early."

"My grandpa lives in Pennsylvania."

"Uh, yeah, south it is."

Sarah laughs just as we hear the muffled *ding* of an incoming text. "Guess I should check it." Her voice is suddenly flat. "It says, 'Okay. Just remember we love you.'"

I put the truck in park. Sarah stares at the horizon, tapping her lip with her phone. I say nothing, afraid of breaching the dam she is struggling to maintain.

"She says they love me. It doesn't feel like it."

I seal my feelings for Daniel Winston in a box and take Sarah's hand. "I'm sure they love you, Red," I manage to say. "One day what happened this afternoon will seem like a bad dream."

"A nightmare." Sarah closes her eyes and rubs her forehead. "I don't know, Sam. I never imagined...I never thought...Neither of my parents has ever talked to me or Rachel that way." Her eyes widen and her mouth drops open. "Rachel! I need to tell Rachel before they do."

I pull back into a parking space. I half expect Pastor Nathan to emerge from the building to ask if we need more prayer.

Sarah gets out of the truck and starts pacing. I know I should give her some space, but I feel this need to protect her, even if that means cutting off her sister in the middle of their conversation. Rachel and Sarah have grown closer since the kidnapping, but I don't know what to expect from the Winston family at this point.

I almost jump in when I see Sarah crying, but then she smiles slightly. Her shoulders relax and her arms unwrap from her body. It looks like something is finally going right today.

Sarah confirms my guess when she climbs back into the truck. Her smile has broadened and the tears are ebbing.

"Everything okay?" I ask.

She nods. "Yes, thank God. Rachel understood, you know? She listened mostly but told me everything would work out. Nothing like Daddy."

"Did you tell her how things went this afternoon?"

Sarah exhales slowly and nods again. "Yeah. She was stunned by Daddy's reaction at first, then she reminded me that he has always been super protective of us, so in a weird kind of way what he said made sense. Not that it was right, but it made sense."

I push my anger further back into a corner. "I guess."

Sarah turns to face me and grabs my hands. "But here's the great thing. Rachel thought of a place we could go."

"Really?"

"Yeah. Her roommate's parents are vacationing in Europe. You've met Ginny, haven't you?"

I barely get a "Yes" in as Sarah's excitement ramps up.

"So, they left the key to their Smith Mountain Lake cabin with her in case she wanted to use it. She told Rachel we would be welcome for the weekend. All we have to do is swing by to pick up the key."

"Are you good with that?"

Sarah leans in for a quick peck on my cheek. "Perfect. A plan at last." She buckles in and leans back against the seat. "Maybe things are finally going our way. On to Blacksburg!"

Rachel is a senior at VT. She plans to go to the University of Virginia Law School next year. Her dad probably gave her a special waiver to enter enemy territory. While I've never talked to Rachel much, she's become a great friend to her little sister, and that's good enough for me.

Sarah deserves a good meal at a nice place after the day she's had, but we couldn't find anything like that near the interstate. So here we are at a truck stop, eating hamburgers while watching eighteen-wheelers rumble to the diesel pumps.

She leans over and dabs away some ketchup at the corner of my mouth. A simple thing, but so tender somehow. Like she cares enough about me to look out for me, even in the tiny details.

Oh, God, I love her so much.

I grab her hand and kiss her palm. I want to tell her I love her, but my throat has closed.

Sarah rests her hand on my cheek. "I know, honey. I love you too." Her green eyes have gone liquid and her mouth is curved in a quiet, serene smile.

We don't need a fine restaurant with starched white tablecloths and a wait staff hovering to fulfill every need. When Sarah and I are together, fast food can become a romantic feast.

"I still need to tell you what happened." Sarah's smile fades as she pulls her hand away.

I struggle to find my place. "When?"

"At the clinic. Why I couldn't go through with it."

I shake my head. "It can wait. We have a place to talk now, where we can have some privacy."

"But you need to know—"

"Shh. Tomorrow. You've been through enough today."

"Okay." Sarah puts on her look of mock annoyance. "You have become very bossy, you know."

"Oh, shut up."

"You shut up."

"Whatever."

Yeah, we're weird, but it works for us.

*

According to the GPS, we should arrive at the cabin in around twenty-five minutes. When we left Blacksburg after lunch, we never imagined that this day would end at a stranger's vacation home on Smith Mountain Lake, some ten hours and thousands of tears later.

Sarah drifted off to sleep around forty minutes ago. She fought to stay awake, saying something silly about abandoning me. My bossy side came out again, and she finally gave in. I glance in her direction every few minutes. Her sweet face is only dimly illuminated by the truck's dashboard lights, but I have it memorized anyway.

Things went well with Rachel. Not that I was expecting her to give Sarah a hard time, but I didn't know what kind of greeting I would get. Not that it matters, anyway.

But Rachel surprised me with a hug and told me she's looked forward to having me as a brother. Her Winston side did appear, however. Just before releasing me, she whispered, "But if you hurt her, I'll hunt you down."

"Understood," I answered.

Ginny insisted that we follow her turn-by-turn directions once we left the main road. "You might wind up in the lake otherwise."

I'm thankful I followed her advice, since we seem to be heading into the middle of a forest right out of a Grimm's fairy tale. If this place turns out to be made of candy, I'm turning this truck around.

I'm on the verge of doing just that when I spot solar lights lining a driveway, along with a solar spotlight trained on a post with a house number. I hear gravel crunch under my tires, but there's still no sign of a house. After traveling a mile—okay, maybe a hundred feet—my headlights hit the cabin.

I stroke Sarah's face with the back of my hand. "We're here."

She blinks and rubs her eyes. "Huh? We are?"

How can a woman be both gorgeous and cute? "Yes, sleepyhead. Time to stop at last."

Sarah leans forward and studies as much of the cabin as my lights allow. "I assume the place is nice since Ginny's parents are pretty well-off. But right now, I feel like we're Hansel and Gretel."

"Exactly."

"Maybe you should leave the truck running." Sarah throws a high-voltage smile at me and opens her door.

Parked in the middle of nowhere, with the darkness of a new moon night surrounding us, I feel a twinge of uneasiness. More than a twinge. I grasp Sarah's arm. "Stay here while I check things out. And lock the doors."

She grimaces. "Bossy again."

"Please."

She may not be able to see my expression, but no doubt she can hear my anxiety. "Sure."

Without my headlights, I would have to feel my way to the front door. Even so, I struggle for a second to unlock it. It opens with a creak, and I immediately reach inside for the lights. I flip every switch in unison, turning on the overhead light in the great room, a porch light, and floodlights on the roof all at once.

I'm embarrassed as I watch my fear skitter away. Scared of the dark, like a little kid. Ridiculous. I walk through the cabin, checking out the two bedrooms, the bathroom, the great room, and the kitchen. I'm not sure what I'm looking for, but it seems prudent. Like something Dad would do.

Sarah is waiting patiently in the truck when I return. "All clear."

"No wicked witches?" She is trying to suppress a smirk.

"Not this time. But I can't be too careful." I extend my hand to her. "Not where my princess is concerned."

The smirk gives way to a smile. "Oh, Sam Russell, you are a sweet talker." Her mouth drops open when we walk inside. "It's beautiful. Like something on TV." She runs her hand along the back of a leather sofa and walks to a set of sliding doors. "And look! There's the lake."

I'd been so intent on searching for potential evildoers that I hadn't noticed. "Yeah. Nice."

Sarah spins around, staring up at the beams across the cathedral ceiling. "*Nice?* We've landed in the most perfect little cabin ever and all you can say is *nice?*"

I shrug. "So I'll never write real estate ads. Sue me. I'm a sweet talker when it counts."

She shakes off her annoyance. "That you are, Mr. Russell." She turns toward the bedrooms. "Are they the same?"

"Appear to be."

"Then I'll take this one." Sarah starts walking toward the room at the front of the house.

"No, this one. That way you can see the lake when you wake up in the morning." Even in my anxious state, I saw the back bedroom had two big windows on the lakeside wall.

Sarah's eyes brighten with excitement. "Are you sure?"

It feels so good to make her happy. "I'm sure."

*

I was certain I would toss and turn, but I think I went to sleep before my head even dented the pillow. Yet I am fully awake now. The house is silent, so I can't imagine what stirred me from my dreamless sleep.

There it is. The sound of someone crying.

Sarah.

I'm not even conscious of moving. I was sitting up in my bed and now I'm kneeling beside hers. Sarah appears to be asleep, but her shoulders are heaving and tears are running down her face.

I shake her gently. "Wake up. You're having a bad dream."

Sarah's eyes flutter open. "Sam?" she whispers before throwing her arms around my neck. "Oh, Sam."

I move on to the bed and hold her, rocking back and forth and stroking her hair. "It's okay, Red. Everything will be okay. It was just a dream."

Sarah pulls away and wipes her cheek with the back of her hand. "No, it wasn't. I mean, it was, but Daddy said the same things he said yesterday. And then he walked away from me. I ran after him, but he never looked back. Then he just vanished. And I was alone. All alone."

I pull her back into my arms and hold her tight because that's the only thing I know to do. "You're not alone, Sarah. You are never alone. I'll never leave you as long as I'm breathing. And Jesus will be with you always. Just like He promised."

"But Daddy…" She sounds like the little girl I once knew.

The right words, please.

"Your father loves you and he'll come around. I'm sure of it."

Sarah's sobbing gradually ends, but we still hang on to each other. I need her warmth and she needs mine.

"Please stay," she whispers.

I take in a deep breath and let it out slowly. "We said we wouldn't—"

"No, not like that." Sarah inches away and takes my hands. "Could you just stay here with me? Until I fall asleep? Please?"

I can't turn her down. And the truth is, I don't want to, even if lying beside her becomes exquisite torture. I can't return to my empty bed. "Of course I'll stay with you. I'll stay all night." I crawl under the covers and lie on my side, my chest to her back, and put my arm around her waist.

"Thank you, honey." Her words wind down like a clock. She's already drifting off.

"Shh," I whisper into her hair, and sleep mercifully overcomes me.

CHAPTER 22

RAP, RAP, RAP.

The butterfly that landed gingerly on my arm flies away at the sound. I chase it across the field of wildflowers—flowers made of colored light—but it disappears into thin air.

Rap, rap, rap.

With each beat, another section of the world pixelates before turning black. "Wait! Stop!" I yell to…Who am I yelling at? I'm not sure.

Rap, rap, rap, rap.

I'm jolted to complete awareness all at once. Light is streaming in the windows. I glance at my phone. Eight a.m.

Sarah rolls to her back and rubs her eyes. "What is it?"

"Someone's at the door. Stay here while I check it out."

She sits up and grabs my arm. "No one's supposed to be coming. Maybe you shouldn't answer it."

I kiss the top of her head. "It's okay. I'll be all right."

Who could be here at 8 on a Saturday morning other than the owners? This could be embarrassing. I hope Ginny doesn't get in trouble.

I peek through the window in the front bedroom as I stumble into my jeans.

It can't be.

Sarah's parents.

"I'm going to check outside," I call to Sarah. "I'll be right back."

I open the door and close it behind me before the Winstons can speak. I don't want Sarah to know they're here, not yet.

Chirping fills the trees, and for a moment I see us from a bird's perspective. A peculiar group: Caroline and Daniel Winston side by side holding hands, frozen in place like reluctant door-to-door missionaries, facing me in my faded VT T-shirt, jeans, and bare feet.

"So you're living together now?" Mr. Winston asks, picking up where we left off, tone-wise.

"Daniel," Mrs. Winston pleads, rubbing his arm.

"You're right, you're right." He nods as he waves off his question. "That's not why we're here."

"Actually, I did go to Sarah's room last night when she awoke crying from a nightmare." I walk closer to her dad. "She dreamed you walked away from her, abandoned her. I held her until she fell asleep."

Daniel Winston recoils with each word, and when I stop speaking, he turns away and chews his bottom lip. Just like his daughter does. His wife puts her arm around his waist.

I don't regret telling him about Sarah's nightmare, but I feel no sense of victory.

When he turns back to me, his eyes are welling with tears. "I...I came to apologize. I need to see Sarah."

Mrs. Winston takes his hand and gives it a squeeze.

"I'll have to ask—"

The door opens. "What are you up to, Mr. Rus—" Sarah stares at her parents like they're ghosts.

Mrs. Winston moves toward her, but she backs away.

"Give us a minute," I tell them as I lead Sarah back into the cabin.

She stares over my shoulder at the door. "What are they doing here, Sam? How did they find us? You don't think Rachel—"

"I don't think Rachel said anything. We didn't think to turn off the location on your phone, so they probably tracked us that way."

"What do they want? Hasn't Daddy said enough?"

I caress her cheek with the back of my hand. "He says he wants to apologize."

Sarah closes her eyes and shakes her head. "I can't talk to them, to him, right now. I will not. He practically accused you of rape and wants me to kill the baby."

I lean in until our heads touch. "Don't worry about me, Red."

"I can't. I won't," she whispers. "Please don't make me."

"Never," I whisper back. "I would never do that. But I want you to consider one thing."

Sarah pulls away and studies me. "What?"

"I didn't get the chance to make things right with Dad, and it's been tearing me apart ever since. I wouldn't wish this on an enemy, much less the most precious person in my life."

She wraps her arms around me and nuzzles against my neck. "I get it. I'd take the pain away if I could," she murmurs.

"I know." I hold her tighter and pretend no one is waiting outside.

She eases out of my embrace, taking my hands instead. "I'll do it, but if this is some kind of trick, a ploy to convince me to—"

"I'll make them leave." I go to the door before she can change her mind. "Come in."

Sarah's mom and dad walk in quietly, carefully, like they're sneaking into a lion's cage. They perch on the edge of the sofa's cushions as Sarah pulls up a dining room chair to sit opposite them. I grab another so I can sit beside her. She laces her fingers with mine and rests her free hand on my arm. I expect her to open this exchange—I think her folks do too—but she stares at them, her mouth a firm line, her green eyes flashing with anger. Hurt in disguise.

The silence draws out to a painful length.

At last, Mr. Winston clears his throat and leans forward, his hands clasped in front of him and his arms resting on his knees. "You're angry at me, and you have every right to be," he opens, pausing for a response. When he gets none, he moves on. "I failed yesterday, Sarah. I failed as a father and I failed, I failed..." He looks down at the floor, and Mrs. Winston pats his back. "And I failed as a Christian. I have asked God for forgiveness and now…now"—he rubs at his eyes and his wife hands him a tissue—"and now I am here to ask for yours."

Sarah is squeezing my hand so tightly that I almost check to see if my fingers have gone white. Instead, I look at her. Her lips are trembling, and her eyes are filling with tears. "You accused Sam, the man I love, of taking advantage of me. You said I was stupid." She's crying again, but her words are clear. "And worst of all, you said I should kill this baby. How could you say things like that, Daddy? How could you?"

Sarah turns into me, and I put my arm around her. *Please help us, Jesus.*

Mr. Winston wrings his hands as he stares at the floor. Mrs. Winston has become a statue, as have I. We've moved from supporting actors in this drama to audience members. I can't speak for Sarah's mom, but I sense that this moment belongs to Sarah and her dad alone.

"I don't know, baby girl. I don't know," he stammers, crumbling into dust before my eyes. "I have no excuse, none. I am so sorry." He finally looks at his daughter and holds out his hands like he's begging for mercy. "I am so sorry."

Sarah slips out of my embrace and reaches for her father. "I forgive you, Daddy," she says softly.

Mr. Winston throws his arms around her, almost knocking her over. "I love you so much, baby girl. So much."

"I know, Daddy. I love you too."

Mrs. Winston, who seems to be crying and laughing at the same time, joins her husband and daughter and wraps her arms around them. I keep my seat, unsure of my place, until Sarah reaches back for me.

No more words are spoken. The four of us remain huddled together until Sarah and her dad part, each wiping away the other's tears.

Sarah's mom is the first to regain her composure. "Have you reached any conclusions about what you want to do?" she asks as we all sit back down.

Sarah is still struggling for control, so she nods at me to respond.

"No, ma'am." I assume some good manners would be especially welcome right now. "We've decided against abortion, but we don't know if we should keep the child or give him or her up for adoption."

When I say the word *adoption*, Mrs. Winston's hand flies to her throat. "You're thinking about giving up our grandchild?"

Her husband, who had been looking down as he tried to stop crying, snaps to attention. I'm unsure whether he's reacting to his wife's alarm or my statement. Then he speaks. "Now, hold on, Caroline." He turns and grasps her hand. "Adoption might be the best alternative. It would mean that Sarah could move on with her life." He then stares lovingly at his daughter, ignoring me altogether.

I wonder if he defines Sarah's moving on with her life as her moving on from me.

Not happening.

"But, Daniel," Mrs. Winston pleads, "this is our flesh and blood we're talking about. Are you saying you would be fine with someone else raising him?"

"Or her." Sarah jumps into the conversation at full strength. "Like Sam said, we haven't decided yet. That's why we came here, so we could talk things over privately." She smiles at me, and I swear I can see a rainbow forming above her.

"But surely you're going to come home now." Mrs. Winston's eyes flick back and forth between us.

"No, ma'am," Sarah answers, her voice steady and certain. "We came here to discuss things, and we haven't even had a single conversation yet."

"But your being here together, it's not...right." Mrs. Winston's voice rises. Sarah refers to her mother, a tiny thing, as a wren. But at this moment she resembles something more fearsome, like an eagle. "We didn't raise you this way."

"So you're worried about our having sex?" Sarah's voice is still calm, but her eyes give her anger away, with no hurt hiding behind it.

Would anyone notice if I drove away now?

Mr. Winston joins the discussion. "If you're trying to shock us, it won't work. But, yes, although the two of you have been having intercourse, that doesn't mean we condone it."

Maybe I could pretend to faint. Maybe it wouldn't be pretending.

"One time," Sarah answers, her voice finally matching her eyes.

No, Red. Please, no. Don't go there, I silently plead.

"We crossed the line one time," she continues, my plea undetected. "Although we knew we shouldn't have. Then we agreed that we would wait until we were married to be together again."

God, please take me home now.

The room falls silent. Sarah turns to me with a slight smile that vanishes as soon as our eyes meet. Her parents look at each other, and a wordless conversation ensues. At this point, I don't care what happens in this room, as long as it's over soon.

Mrs. Winston fixes Sarah and me with her gaze. "Still—"

"I'm staying here, with Sam." Sarah pats my hand for emphasis. "You are going to have to trust me. Trust us."

Her parents sigh in unison. "We don't have much of a choice, do we?" Mr. Winston stands, pulling his wife up with him. "You will talk to us before you do anything, though, right?"

Sarah and I rise. "Yes, Daddy," she answers, her voice soft and sweet again. "I promise."

The visit ends with an embrace between Sarah and her parents and a quick hug between Mrs. Winston and me. Mr. Winston extends his hand to me, but only after a "Daniel" from his wife and a "Daddy" from his daughter.

Sarah and I wave as they drive away—waving is a big Winston thing—and I sag against the front door after we close it.

Sarah grabs my shoulders as if to stop me from collapsing. "Are you okay, honey?"

As I stare into those bewitching green eyes, I realize that she has no idea. "Why, in the name of all that's holy, did you tell them about our love life?"

She backs away slightly. "They needed to know they could trust us. And I am pretty open with my folks. You know that."

I close my eyes. "But you've been open with them about yourself." I wave my hand toward the sofa and stare at the scene of the crime. "All that was about me too."

"Oh." Sarah covers her mouth and her eyes widen. "Oh, no. I am so sorry. I wasn't thinking." She throws her arms around my neck. "Can you forgive me?"

Her breath warms my skin, and I pull her close to me. "Just remember next time, okay?" My embarrassment dissipates in the glow of her nearness.

"Okay," she whispers before pulling away. "Do you realize we went through all of that without even a drop of coffee?"

"Because we don't have any. No food either, unless you count a sack full of crackers." Only now do I notice the rumbling in my belly.

"Then let's put ourselves together, grab some breakfast, and buy groceries."

I watch Sarah as she walks back to her bedroom. Her hair is messy, having only gotten a quick brushing. She is wearing a *Virginia Is for Lovers* T-shirt with a pair of faded sweatpants and doesn't have a drop of makeup on. And she is the most captivating creature on Earth.

She pauses at her door. "You're staring at me."

"Do you want me to stop?"

She leans against the door jamb and gives me a grin that reduces my insides to jelly. "Never."

Have mercy.

*

We grabbed a fast-food breakfast before picking up a few things at a small grocery store. Sarah hasn't felt sick today, so I wonder if stress, not the baby, was the culprit yesterday.

It's a clear blue day without a trace of haze, and just warm enough. March can be tricky in Virginia, and you can go through three seasons of clothes in one day—a coat in the morning, a sweater in the afternoon, and shirtsleeves by suppertime.

Finding rocking chairs out here on the deck felt like coming home. I think Sarah and I fell in love on her front porch, moving forward and back, forward and back, without going anywhere. Talking about nothing and everything. We're doing the same thing now. Only we're not talking. We should be, but I think we've earned the tranquility of a safe harbor.

Sarah is resting her head on the back of the chair, soaking up the sunshine. She's not asleep, since the chair's still in motion, but her face is peaceful, like she's dreaming of a Caribbean beach. I close my eyes too, only I find myself slipping into real sleep, the creaking of Sarah's rocker a lullaby.

Suddenly the creaking stops. "You want to keep the baby, don't you?"

I sit up and look at her. The peace I saw on her face seconds ago is gone. "How did you—"

She wobbles her head slightly. "I sensed it somehow. But why?"

I stare at her for a beat. This must be a test, a trick question. But Sarah's face is open and sincere. Maybe she really doesn't know. "Because it's our baby. Because I love you and you love me, and this child is the result."

Sarah drags her rocker over to mine and takes my hands. "I know, honey. But have you thought about how this would all play out?"

"What do you mean?"

"I mean, have you asked yourself how we would support ourselves at this point, much less a child? Where would we live? Would either one of us be able to finish school? And, most importantly, what's the right thing for the baby?"

Each question feels like a punch landed by a skilled boxer, a right and a left, a right and a left. I fumble my way to the deck rail, struggling to regain my equilibrium.

Sarah follows me and places her hand on my arm. "What are you thinking?" Her voice is soft and kind and warm, a sharp contrast to her questions.

"I don't have a bunch of answers. It's not like I've done a cost/ benefit analysis on this." I turn to her but don't return her touch. "I guess I thought that we would start out by deciding if we want to raise our baby together or not, then figure the rest out. But it sounds like you want to start from the other direction. Like we have to have it all sorted out first."

She clasps her hands in front of her and backs away a few inches. "Do you think I'm being cold?"

My mouth opens to say, "I don't know," but "Yes," comes out instead.

She takes another step back, staggered as if I had struck her in the face.

"I'm sorry, I didn't mean…" I reach for her.

"Yes, you did." Sarah walks farther away and leans against the rail. "And you're right. But maybe one of us must be cold here and look at the facts." She stares out at the water. "We got into this mess when we let our emotions sweep us away."

My heart is beginning to race, but not with passion this time. "*This mess?* You mean our baby? Don't you want our baby?"

When she whirls around to face me, I see a kaleidoscope of reactions sweep over her face, one color blending into another. "Yes. No. I don't know. I want things to go back to how they were. You and me and our stargazing. Planning for our future together. Just because I couldn't kill this baby doesn't mean I'm ready to become a mother. Daddy thinks we should give it up for adoption, you and Mama think we should keep it, and I don't know what I want." She plops down on the deck and lets the tears come. "Oh, God, I don't know what I want."

I sit down beside her and pull her to my chest. "I'm sorry for pushing. We don't have to decide what we're doing today, or even tomorrow." I try to let my mind go blank. I focus on my breathing, the rustle of the new green leaves on the trees, the warmth of her body curled into mine. But my brain continues to spin.

"Sam?" she whispers.

"Yeah?"

"I'm so scared."

I move so I can see her face. "Of what?"

Another tear runs down her cheek, and I erase it with my thumb.

"That this will break us. That you'll want one thing and I'll want another, and we won't be able to make it work." Sarah buries her face in my shirt. "I couldn't bear to lose you."

I push her away so I can look into her eyes. "Listen to me, Red. We're on this journey together, and we will find a way forward. I'm sure of it. Like you asked me yesterday, are we a couple or not?"

Sarah nods. "Yes. Always, I hope."

"You hope?" I cup her head in my hands and cover her mouth with mine, trying to convey the depth of my love for her in one kiss. When we part, I move my lips to her ear. "We are always."

*

The past three days have felt like one continuous contentious conversation, or a drama in a dozen acts with no sign of the curtain coming down. That's why I suggested that we drive into Roanoke for a typical Saturday night date, dinner and maybe a movie. A stupid comedy would be perfect. Sarah is still feeling good—fingers crossed—so I'm standing on the deck while she gets ready.

The lake is calm, and the setting sun is scattering diamonds across its surface. A few birds are calling to each other, but I hear no boats or cars or even voices. Sarah and I could be the only humans for miles around.

I catch a flash of brilliant red in my peripheral vision. A cardinal. It settles on a nearby branch and studies me for a moment, its head jerking back and forth a couple of times before it flies away. I follow its course for as long as I can, then return my gaze to the water.

My eyes rest there, looking but not focusing. I'm sinking down and down, almost like I'm diving to the lake's bottom. My body goes quiet.

Calm. Still.

Still.

I let the word cover me like a blanket, much like the lovey Mom says I used to drag from place to place when I was a toddler. I open my heart and listen for more—detailed instructions about what we should do would be nice—but the word stands alone.

I don't realize Sarah has joined me until I feel her head resting between my shoulder blades and her arms encircling me. I turn into her embrace.

"I shouldn't have freaked out earlier and I'm so—"

I stop her before she can go down that familiar road. "Don't you dare say *sorry*. No more going it alone, right? And that means being honest with each other. And by the way, I kinda like you too."

Sarah pushes away and gives me a light punch on the shoulder. "Yep, that's my sweet talker."

CHAPTER 23

AFTER AN "ALMOST nice" dinner—table service but no tablecloths—
we scanned the theater schedules for a goofy movie, but all we found
were slasher flicks and profound dramas. That's how we wound up
driving around Roanoke, looking for inspiration.

"We could visit my grandparents," I offer. "They play a mean game
of rummy."

Sarah stares at me, open-mouthed. "I don't think so. Your grandma
and grandpa are nice and all, but…"

I pat her hand and grin. "Just kidding. I think we've had enough
family. Any ideas?"

She looks up at the Hotel Roanoke as we pass. "I'd like to stay
there one day. I've heard it's so fancy."

I bring her hand to my lips. "And my girl deserves fancy."

She turns toward the mountains. "I know! Let's go see the Star."

The Roanoke Star was erected as a seasonal decoration in 1949
and was so popular that it's been a fixture of the skyline ever since. It's
huge—almost ninety feet tall—and its location atop Mill Mountain
means you can see its lights for miles. Grandma and Grandpa took
Megan and me there when we were little, while Mom and Dad spent
a weekend in Virginia Beach.

Megan and I kept backing up on the overlook in front of the Star, trying to take it all in, until Grandpa shooed us away from the edge. I recall his saying, "You kids aren't going to die on my watch."

We visited in the daytime, so I've glimpsed the Star's full glory only at a distance. "A splendid idea, my lady. We shall proceed."

Sarah leans across the console to kiss my cheek. "You know I love your swashbuckling talk."

Only two other cars are in the parking lot when we arrive. Good. I half-expected another ambush by Sarah's parents, or maybe Mom, with Grandma and Grandpa along for back-up.

I hold Sarah's hand tightly as we walk to the overlook in case she slips on a pebble. I have this powerful need to protect her. I don't know if that's because she's pregnant or because we're more closely connected than ever.

Another possibility brushes past my brain. Perhaps this is my inheritance from Dad—the impulse to protect those I love.

"You're being especially quiet." Sarah leans into me. "Everything okay?"

I put my arm around her. "Thinking about trying to protect you, like Dad watched over Mom and Megan and me."

She slips her arm around my waist. "I believe I'm supposed to protest that I'm an independent, self-sufficient woman who doesn't need protecting. But all I can think is that your looking out for me makes me feel warm and safe and gooshy inside."

I stop and look at her. "Gooshy?"

"Yes, gooshy. It is a technical term. Go with it."

We see the Star's glow long before we see its outline. When we reach it, we stare up, up, up at the lights, frozen in awe.

"Wow," we say in unison. Then we start giggling like two kids seeing a Christmas tree for the first time.

After a few moments, we sit on the wall at the overlook and turn our attention to a bird's-eye view of Roanoke. The twinkling lights of the city are dim compared to the structure behind us, but beautiful in their own way.

Sarah scans the view. "Somewhere down there a child is doing homework, a woman is working as a cashier in a store, and a guy is folding laundry."

I'm not looking at the scene before me. I'm studying Sarah instead. With the light playing around her and the intense expression on her face, she could be Roanoke's guardian angel, checking in on all those in her care.

"You're staring at me again," she scolds without looking at me.

"I can't help it. I can't stop staring at you anymore than I can stop appreciating a rainbow or a sunrise."

"Well, when you put it that way…" Sarah smiles at me and I forget the Star completely. "But look at this." She waves at the city. "There are thousands of stories playing out down there at this moment."

I slide closer to her. "You're right. But when I'm with you, I find it hard to think about any story but ours."

A couple who was on the other side of the overlook when we arrived walks away hand in hand, leaving us all alone. Sarah seems to take that as her cue.

"Did you know that nothing that happens to me seems real until I share it with you?"

I settle my cheek on her soft hair. "Really?"

"Yeah. It's almost like we are two halves of a whole, two sides of one brain. Does that make sense?" Sarah keeps her gaze fixed on the city, as if she's determined not to look at me.

"Sure. When we were separated, I picked up my phone all the time to tell you about something, but then I'd remember."

"Me too," she murmurs.

She nestles into my side and I assume our conversation is over. I'm good with that. I could sit here with her in my arms forever, or at least until I got hungry.

"I said goodbye to you while I waited for the clinic to open."

I straighten up, forcing her to look at me. "What?"

She turns away. "I didn't call you, of course, but I said 'Goodbye, Sam,' out loud, to help me accept losing you."

I close my eyes when the shiver hits my spine. "And yet you were still determined to go through with it."

Sarah nods. "I thought I had to, so you could have the life you deserve."

I try to beat back the hitch in my chest. "Baby, you are my life."

"And you're mine." She reaches up and strokes my face with the back of her hand. "But all I've ever wanted is what's best for you, and in my messed-up state I thought I was doing the right thing." Taking my hands, she laces all our fingers together. "We take our hands for granted, you know? The way each finger can move independently of the others to play a piano or work together to catch a ball."

Sarah pauses, and I almost ask where this could be going.

"You're probably wondering where this is going." She looks up and grins at me. "That morning I was a bundle of nerves. I felt like I was going to jump out of my skin. I didn't want to walk into the clinic on the verge of a full-blown panic attack, so I repeated the rhyme Daddy taught me. You know it. 'Breathe in, breathe out, and let it go...'"

"'There's more to life than people know,'" I finish.

"Right. I breathed in. I breathed out. Over and over. With each repetition I became more aware of the steady thump of my heartbeat and the regular, even rhythm of my breathing. I curled my fingers around the handle on my car door to open it, but I stared at them instead. My mind went blank. I can't describe it. It was almost like a trance. I'm never not thinking."

So true. I nod to encourage her.

"Then it was like my brain split open and filled with one idea—that my body is a miracle. I tapped out patterns with my fingers and marveled at how they move. I stared at a little bird pecking at the ground across the parking lot and wondered how my brain processes what I see."

"And then?"

"Then it occurred to me that this miracle—my body—started out as a clump of cells. Like this baby." Sarah gently rubs her belly. "And just like me, he or she will develop a heartbeat, and eyes, and ears, and arms and legs. I was, I was...awestruck."

I pull her into my arms and try to find my voice. "'Fearfully and wonderfully made,'" I whisper. "I think it's from a psalm."

"Psalm 139. I looked it up."

"You did?"

She turns in my embrace. "Because that phrase came to me. No, that's not right. The words did not come to me. I heard them."

I force myself to breathe. "The wolf?"

Sarah nods and the tears filling her eyes break free. "I didn't see Him, but I heard His voice. 'Fearfully and wonderfully made,' He said, as clearly as I heard you just now. You believe me, don't you? Please tell me you believe me, Sam."

"Of course I do." I gently dab at her tears. "God has always been there for us."

We look up at the stars together, drawn to their Maker. "Thank You," Sarah says softly, as if in church.

"Amen," I whisper.

*

It has been almost three weeks since we visited the Star. Almost three weeks since we were on the mountaintop, in more ways than one. Sarah has returned to her classes and I to mine, without any decisions made about our child. But the peace we experienced lingers, and I don't feel frantic about the choices facing us. I don't think Sarah does either.

The workload for both of us has been intense as we hurtle toward finals, so we haven't seen each other much. We stay in touch, of course—no more keeping each other at arm's length—but I need to see my girl. When I saw the forecast for today, I asked Sarah if she could squeeze in a picnic at a city park.

I grabbed some sandwiches from a sub shop and snagged a nice spot under a tree. Sarah should be here in around ten minutes. I like to arrive first whenever we meet because I love to wait for her. I savor the jolt I still get when she rounds the corner or walks through the door or comes over the crest of the hill.

The park is busy for a weekday afternoon, but I can spot the glow of her red hair even in a crowd. I wave her over as my heart is hit with that wonderful familiar zing. "Hey, beautiful." I take her hand to help her sit down on the blanket I brought.

"I'm not huge yet, you know," she protests, but not really.

"I know. Maybe I just like to be chivalrous."

"That's an acceptable answer." Sarah smirks, then peeks in the brown paper bag. "Is it turkey or a club this time?"

"Both. I couldn't make up my mind, so I bought a six-inch of each instead of one footlong."

Her hands fly to her face in mock surprise. "Oh my, Mr. Russell, now you've really gone crazy. Whatever shall I do with you?"

I lean over and move her hair away from her perfect little ear. "Well, if you're looking for ideas..."

I sit back in time to see Sarah blush from her neck up to her hairline. "Here I am trying to behave myself and you're sitting there looking so good and then you start whispering in my ear. You make good behavior quite difficult, sir." She busies herself with setting out our sandwiches and chips on paper towels.

I touch her hand as she slides a napkin under my Coke. "Red?" I pause until she looks at me. "The waiting will end one day. Maybe sooner, maybe later. But it will end."

Sarah sighs. "I know. The important thing is that we're together, right?"

"Right. Now we have a picnic to enjoy. Just me and my girl."

Sarah strokes her belly lightly. "And our baby."

I freeze in mid-bite. "What did you say?"

Sarah gives me a confused stare. "'And our baby.' So?"

I push our food out of the way and move in closer. "You said, '*our* baby.' Not '*the* baby,' like you have been. '*Our* baby.'"

The confused stare continues for a few more seconds, then she covers her mouth with her hand and her eyes widen. "You're right.'" She strokes her belly carefully like you would a sleeping child, but when she speaks her words run together in an excited rush. "Oh, Sam, this child is ours, yours and mine. Our son or daughter." Her voice rises as she grabs both of my hands. "We have to raise it together, honey. We have to."

Her face is blurred by my tears, but I can still see the softness in her eyes and the love in her smile. "And we will. We will."

Sarah wraps her arms around my neck, and we glide into a world of our own. The children yelling on the playground, the guys playing catch, the cars driving by—everything fades from awareness until only the two of us remain.

The three of us.

I kneel before her and hold her left hand in both of mine. "Marry me, Sarah Campbell Winston. Plea—"

"Yes, yes, a thousand times yes." She rises to her knees, and we throw our arms around each other, rocking back and forth in our embrace. It takes a couple of seconds before we realize a crowd has gathered around us. Amid the applause, a few people say, "Bravo!" "Way to go!" and "Awesome!"

We thank everyone for their good wishes—Sarah is blushing again—before the group disperses. Then she and I lean into each other until our foreheads are touching.

"I guess we better go home tomorrow," she whispers, her mischievous grin spreading across her face. "We have a wedding to plan."

*

I managed to let go of Sarah long enough for her to return to her car. But if she'd hesitated behind the wheel, I might have climbed into the passenger seat and begged her to head to Early immediately so we could grab our birth certificates and get married tomorrow.

Instead, I'm driving back to my apartment, singing Pharrell Williams's "Happy" at the top of my lungs. An old guy driving a broken-down pickup stared at me at the last stop light. I waved at him and kept right on singing. I cannot contain the joy I feel.

Oh, God, You are so good! Everything is coming together just like You promised.

"Gavin!" I call as soon as I open our door, like we live in a mansion and I must summon him from the east wing.

"Whoa. Settle down, dude," Gavin mutters as he leaves his bedroom. "Somebody stayed up most of the night studying and was hoping to get a nap between classes. Somebody is not thrilled to be disturbed." He rubs his head and focuses on me. "Hold up. What's going on?"

"Sarah and I are getting married!" The exclamation mark in my voice sounds strange even to me. Not my style normally.

He is instantly alert and crosses the room to shake my hand. "Wow. Great news, Sam. You guys have decided about the baby?"

I've talked to Gavin about the options we were considering. At first, he didn't understand our taking abortion off the table, but I think he gets it now.

"Our baby." I love the way that sounds. "Yeah, we're going to get married and raise him or her together." He opens his mouth to speak, but I hold a hand up. "And, yes, we know this won't be easy, but we're certain this is the right thing."

He shakes his head. "No, man, I wasn't going to give you any grief. I was only going to say I'm happy for you both. I know you've prayed over this, so I'm sure you're on the right track."

I pull him into a brief guy hug. "Thanks. That means a lot."

Gavin takes a Coke from the fridge and sits on the couch. "What you and Sarah have is so special, even rare. I hope I can experience that one day."

I plop into the recliner facing him. "Some friend I am. I never asked how your lunch with Kirsten went last weekend. Sorry."

He shoos away my apology. "You've had a lot on your mind, to say the least. The lunch was...good. Yeah, that's the right word. Not awkward or weird at all, not like I was thinking it would be. Kirsten apologized for the things she said before Christmas break and asked for my forgiveness."

"Really?" I force a neutral tone, but I feel my eyebrow rise.

"Yeah. And she seemed sincere. She said my telling her I loved her scared her, that she's got a bunch of issues with commitment, and she regrets letting me go." Gavin stares down at the floor, and when he looks back at me, I see hope written all over his face.

Uh-oh. "Gavin—"

He raises his palms in self-defense. "Look, I know you're worried about me. Truth is, I'm worried about myself. Kirsten hurt me really bad, and I can't go through that again."

"That's right, and—"

"So we agreed to take things slow. Really slow, like back to ground level. When we got together last time, it was fireworks from the first date. This time we're going to work on our friendship and see where it goes from there."

I nod.

"And I also told her about my faith." Gavin smiles.

"Your—"

"Faith, yeah. I asked Jesus into my life a couple of weeks ago. I haven't told you about it yet because it was still sinking in, but I know I belong to Him now. I'm sure of it."

I tear up for the second time today. "Brother, that's amazing." We stand and shake hands, then I hug him again. "Welcome to the family."

Gavin is crying too. "Thank you, man. It all started with you."

Oh, God, You are so good.

CHAPTER 24

I was still flying high when I went to bed Friday night, even though we broke the news to our parents. Mrs. Winston and Mom seemed cool with our getting married, although not over-the-moon thrilled. They appeared happy in a resigned kind of way. Mr. Winston stared at me the whole time like he was trying to gauge how big the hole in his backyard would need to be.

But now...

As I sit here in this waiting room, I feel like I've dropped into a parallel universe, a place where all good things go bad. It all started when I got Sarah's text around 3 a.m.

Something's wrong.

I traveled from a deep sleep to being fully awake instantly. *On my way*, I texted, then threw on some jeans and a sweatshirt. I clomped downstairs, not caring how much noise I made, so I wasn't surprised to see Mom and Megan peeking out from their bedrooms.

"Sammy? What's going on?" Mom hurried down the stairs, pulling on her robe as she did.

"It's Sarah. Something's happening."

I was halfway out the door when Mom touched my arm. "We'll start praying right now."

My eyes started to glaze over, but I locked away my weakness. "Thanks, Mom. Thanks a lot."

I ran down the street to the Winstons' house. It looked like every light was on, and I saw movement through the blinds. I pounded on the door when I arrived.

"Sarah called you?" Mr. Winston asked as I brushed past him into the house.

"Texted." I put my hand on the stair railing to go to Sarah, but he pulled me back.

"Let me go." I shook him off. "I need to see Sarah. She said something's wrong."

"Sam." Suddenly, his voice was so kind and soft that it took me off guard. "Sarah's mom is with her right now, and I think she needs some...privacy. Caroline called Rob Reynolds and he advised us to go straight to the ER."

I grabbed the stair rail to keep upright. "What...what's happening?" I felt the blood leave my face. "Something's wrong with the baby, isn't it?"

He closed his eyes and nodded. "Sarah woke up bleeding and in pain. Rob's calling an OB to meet us."

I turned away and stared at the door, willing myself to be tough. I told myself this was all normal, that Sarah was fine and the baby was fine.

"Sam?"

I jerked my head around at the sound of Sarah's voice and saw her teetering at the top of the stairs.

Jesus.

I ran up to meet her, taking two steps at a time.

"Sam," she repeated, collapsing into my arms. "Our baby. Our baby."

"Shhh." I carried her out to the car, shushing her all the way but offering no reassurance. I had none.

I rode with Sarah to the hospital in the backseat of her parents' SUV, holding her in my arms and gently combing my fingers through her hair. The ride only took around fifteen minutes, but it went on forever, with Sarah wincing at every bump and crying nonstop. "Our baby, our baby," she whimpered.

I tried to pray, but the words wouldn't come. I worried she would have a long wait to be seen, but she was taken straight back to an examining room as soon as we arrived. Her mom went with her. I wanted to but didn't even try. I have no standing, except as the father of her child.

I'm just a guy who would die for her. And almost did.

My phone tells me Mr. Winston and I have been waiting in these hard, plastic chairs for about twenty minutes now, but it feels like two hours—at least. A TV hanging in the corner of the ceiling is set to a twenty-four-hour news channel, and I watch for a few minutes to distract myself. Then it occurs to me that airing stories of chaos and death to people waiting in an emergency room is an awful idea.

So I try to pray again, and I succeed in asking God to take care of Sarah and save our baby. But I can't go beyond that. I can think of nothing to thank Him for, and I certainly am not going to tell Him that I want His will to be done. No. I want no part of His will if it doesn't include making things perfect again, like they were only hours ago.

Mr. Winston hasn't said a word and is only staring at his clasped hands. Maybe he's praying. I'm hit with the thought that no one on the planet loves Sarah more than he and I do.

"Daniel. Sam."

I look up to see Uncle Rob approaching us.

Mr. Winston and I jump up and rush to meet him. "How's Sarah?" He beats me to the question.

"Fine. She'll be just fine," Uncle Rob answers in his soft, bed-side voice.

"And the baby?" I ask, knowing the answer.

He shakes his head. "I'm sorry, Sam. Sarah suffered a miscarriage."

I close my eyes and sway slightly. This can't be happening. We were so happy, convinced we were doing the right thing. We wanted this baby, loved this baby. No. No. I don't believe it.

I feel hands on my shoulders and hear Uncle Rob's voice. "Sarah's going to need you, Sam, more than she ever has. She's going to need your strength. Do you understand me?"

I stare into his kind gray eyes and draw on his peace. "Yes, sir."

"When can we see her?" Mr. Winston asks.

"You can go on…"

Mr. Winston and I head for the double doors before Uncle Rob can finish his sentence.

When we reach them, I turn to face Sarah's dad. "Sarah wanted this baby. I…" I gulp some air. "I wanted this baby."

He nods and squeezes my shoulder.

Uncle Rob catches up to us and takes us to Sarah.

I hear nothing but the thrum of the blood in my head. I know that Mr. and Mrs. Winston and Uncle Rob are in the room. I know this, but they don't exist for me right now. There's only Sarah—my beloved, the center of my heart—lying in a hospital bed.

"Sam." She stretches out her arms to me and I hold her gently, as I would a porcelain doll. "We lost our baby," she whispers.

"I know, darling." I take her hands and kiss them. "How do you feel?"

She turns away from me. "It doesn't matter."

"Don't talk that way," I say, more loudly than I should. "That's not true."

"Sam's right, baby girl." Mr. Winston has moved to the other side of the bed. "You mean the world to us." He glances at me. "And we will help you through this loss. We'll help each other."

Sarah turns on her dad, a wounded lioness now. "But you didn't even want me to have this baby. Go ahead and say it. You think this is for the best."

He strokes her cheek tenderly, undeterred by her anger. "I was wrong. And I would never rejoice over the loss of a baby. Our grandchild." His eyes fill with tears. "Please believe me, honey."

Mrs. Winston appears alongside her husband. "We're here for you." She rests her hand on mine and Sarah's. "Both of you."

Sarah's eyes travel between me and her parents. "I just don't understand. Everything that's happened...I was sure God was telling us to have this baby and raise it together. And now he or she is gone. Dead. Oh, God, we never even knew what it was. Oh, God." She covers her face and cries soundlessly, tears running through her fingers.

I rest my hand on her shoulder and drop my head. *Where are You, Jesus? What are You doing? Have You abandoned us?*

I get no response. I guess we're on our own.

*

"You should eat something." I push my bowl across the table. "The chili is really good today. I think there might even be real meat in it."

I wait for a slight chuckle or a faint smile. Nothing.

Sarah has been like this since she left the hospital. I wasn't around after her kidnapping—okay, I was, but comatose doesn't count—so I didn't observe her behavior then. I don't know what her walking away from herself really looks like. But I don't think this is it.

I wonder if this is worse.

When Sarah went into hibernation, it gave her spirit time to catch up with all that had happened. Then she "woke up" and came to terms with everything. But now...now Sarah has stopped being herself.

I haven't seen her smile, much less laugh, even once since we lost the baby. Her voice is flat and robotic, and her green eyes, those sweet pools of light I have fallen into so many times, have no spark. Her outburst in the hospital was the last time she revealed any depth of feeling.

It's only been two weeks, I tell myself. *Give her time.* But I continue to flail about, searching for something, anything, to bring her back to me. Even a stupid thing, like bringing her back to this raggedy diner, one of our special places in Blacksburg.

"No, thank you," Sarah answers politely, pushing the bowl back to me. "My salad is fine." She returns to rifling through the lettuce on her plate, pretending to eat.

I take another approach. "I can't believe exams are coming up. Another semester almost gone." I prattle on like I'm trying to strike up a conversation with an acquaintance at a party. "Are you still planning on helping out your mom this summer?" Her mother is a real estate agent, and last summer Sarah worked in her office filling in for staffers on vacation.

"Maybe," she answers, examining the ham, chopped eggs, and cheese she has bulldozed to the side.

Help her. Please.

I haven't prayed much in the last fourteen days. God has moved on to other people, other problems. But I have run out of ideas.

Suddenly Sarah grabs her purse and slides out of the booth. "Sorry, but I have to go."

I process this for a second before stopping the server and asking for our check. When I get to my truck, I find Sarah leaning back against the passenger door, her eyes closed against the sun. She's crying.

"Sarah?" I want to hold her but don't know if I should.

She wipes at her eyes and climbs into the truck without answering. I get behind the wheel and wait.

With a shuddering breath, she stares out the windshield at some point in the distance. "Take me home, please."

"Red…"

She finally looks at me. "Please, Sam."

I'm useless against her grief. So I drive.

With every block, I feel my anger building. Not against Sarah, who has been leveled by the loss of our child. But against the One who could have done something about it. I rail at Him silently, screaming in my head. *I don't get it. You talked to Sarah and me, and we were sure we were doing what You wanted. Are You punishing us for something? Are You punishing me?*

Of course.

Dad.

What perfect justice. Terrible, but perfect. A bitter half-laugh escapes me.

"Sam?" Sarah tilts her head and studies me, her brows knitted together. "Are you okay?"

She doesn't need my baggage right now. "Sure."

She presses her lips together—a tell-tale sign that she knows I'm lying—and turns back to the window.

Neither of us moves when we arrive at her apartment. I've spent all my energy fighting God for the past fifteen minutes, and Sarah can't fight anyone anymore. I wonder if the tears she shed earlier were the last she had.

"Why?" The sound of her voice startles me.

"Why what?"

"Why did God let this happen?" Her eyes are focused straight ahead, as if she'll find God there. "Both of us heard Him. I even heard His voice out loud. And then He does this. It's like He is playing with us, like we're part of a bet He made with an angel." She squeezes her eyes shut. "Or the devil."

Oh, God. I have nowhere else to turn.

We can't do this here, in my truck. I squeeze her hand. "Let's talk inside, okay?"

Sarah nods.

Once we get through the door, I toss aside my uncertainty and take her into my arms. She slumps against me and begins to sob. It sounds wrong, but I'm relieved by her tears.

"I don't know, baby. I don't know," I whisper into her hair. "I was sure we were on the right path. Everything seemed so clear."

We cling to each other but find no comfort. Sarah and I are sinking, bound by grief and rage, with nothing to stop our drowning.

Suddenly I remember what Josh told me: "Focus on Him and you'll be fine, son. Be still and keep your eyes on the Light."

Jesus. Jesus. Jesus. I pray the name over and over because I have no other words.

It takes a moment for me to realize that my head is above water. I'm not gasping for air, reaching wildly for something to keep me afloat. No, more than that—I have been carried ashore, to solid ground.

"Losing our child hurts," I murmur. "It hurts so much, and I want to know why God allowed that to happen. And I am...I have been..." I pretend to search for the right word, but I have it at hand. "Angry. Yeah, I've been angry." It feels good to say it, like I have been holding my breath for a long time. "But Jesus does love us." I hold Sarah's face in my hands. "Look to Him. Breathe in and out and look to Him."

She falls back into me, and gradually her sobbing stops. "I know you're right. But I'm not there yet. I think I will be. But not yet."

"Everything will be okay." I rest my cheek against her soft curls. "I don't know how, but everything will be okay."

We sit on the sofa and Sarah curls into me. This should feel so good. So right. And it is, but at the same time we seem to be off kilter, like the world has turned on its edge and we're struggling to stand.

"I guess the wedding is off, huh?" Sarah murmurs into my side.

The wedding. Our marriage. Another stone lobbed at me. At us.

I shift so I can look straight into the eyes I love, showing signs of life at last. I touch Sarah's cheek lightly, drying one last tear. "Just because we don't have to get married doesn't mean—"

"I know." Sarah rests her hand against my face. "But we don't have to rush now."

I touch her lips lightly with mine. "Just say the word, Sarah Winston, and I will marry you within twenty-four hours."

Sarah gives me a slight smile, and my heart drinks it in. "Then I better watch my words. Right now, all I want is to feel your arms around me."

I pull her close and breathe deeply as the world resumes its balance. For the moment, anyway.

Thank You for this.

*

We survived exams, although I'm not sure how. Two years of college down, and I still have no clue about my career. Brilliant.

Sarah and I had to return home separately since each of us had a car to drive. Plus, there was all the stuff we had to clear out of our apartments. Not that much for me, really, but I'm a guy. I remember Dad renting little trailers every time Megan moved in and out of school. Girls.

It felt strange to drive back without Sarah by my side. She has seemed more like herself since the day we went to the diner, but she's still not one hundred percent, not by a long shot.

I suppose I'm not either, but I haven't been since Dad died. I must be getting used to it. I've had one-hundred-percent moments, even one hundred and ten percent, like the second time I asked Sarah to marry me and she said yes. The day I was certain Sarah and I and our baby would be a happy little family. Grief for our child sneaks up on me sometimes, like when I see kids on the neighborhood playground or a stupid ad for diapers on TV.

And now that I'm home, I can't hide from Dad's memory. I've stopped trying. The best I can hope for is that one day I'll dig out from the rubble and breathe freely.

I'm not optimistic.

I focus on cutting the steak Sarah's dad grilled for me—medium done with a touch of pink. The man is a charcoal master. Things shifted between Mr. Winston and me that night at the hospital, but I've been dreading this dinner since getting the invitation. I feared a monumental level of awkwardness. I'm no longer the nice boy from down the street. I'm the guy who got their little girl pregnant. But the evening has been okay. Not much conversation, but no tension either. Good.

"So, Sam, what do you think of Pastor Jeff's offer?" Mrs. Winston sets down her knife and fork and stares at me, hands under her chin.

"Mom!" Sarah glares at her, then turns to me. "Sorry. I meant to—"

Mrs. Winston covers her mouth. "Oh, I didn't know you hadn't..." She sighs. "I just wanted to know what Sam thought. I apologize."

I look between Sarah and her mother and wonder if my iced tea has been spiked, just like their eggnog.

Mr. Winston gives me a half grin of encouragement.

"What's going on?" I finally ask.

Sarah shoots another unhappy glance at her mother before turning back to me. "Pastor Jeff sent me a note shortly before we left school. The college student who was going to be the assistant to the director at a church camp in Tennessee this summer got a great internship opportunity. Great for her, not so great for the camp."

I think I hear the distant roar of an approaching train.

Sarah takes a breath, then picks up speed as if to fend off any further contributions from her mother. "The director is one of Pastor Jeff's best friends—they went to seminary together—so he turned to him to see if anyone from our church could fill in at the last minute. And Pastor Jeff thought of me."

I can see the locomotive now.

"For the whole summer?"

"Most of it, but I won't do it, of course."

"But, honey—" Mrs. Winston says.

"Mom," Sarah warns her off.

"Caroline," Mr. Winston intervenes. "It's a good time to clear away the dishes, don't you think?" He rises and touches his wife's elbow.

"I don't think everybody's done."

"Oh, I think we're all done," he answers, guiding his wife to the kitchen.

Sarah takes my hand. "Come on. Let's talk on the porch."

I follow her dumbly, still processing the last three minutes. Each of us takes a rocker, but there's no quiet back and forth this time. "Tell me about this job." I work hard to keep my voice soft and deliberate so Sarah can't hear Crazy Sam fighting to get out.

"It doesn't matter. I'm not going to do it anyway." She looks back through the dining room window. "I love my mother, but sometimes—"

"Why?"

Sarah turns back to me, her eyes wide with surprise. "You mean, why won't I take the job?"

I nod. I can't believe I asked the question either.

She takes my hands. When she looks at me, her eyes are soft and warm and filled with moonlight. I think my heart might burst. "Isn't it obvious?" she asks in a quiet voice. "I don't want to be away from you for eight weeks. Eight weeks, and I hear cell service is nonexistent up on that mountain. We would have to rely on occasional phone calls when I get to town, and letters." She rests her palm on my cheek. "Eight weeks. I don't think I could bear being separated from you that long."

I lean into her hand and close my eyes. I can hear her breathing and mine, and I take in the floral scent in her hair and the softness of her skin. I've loved her for so long, and my love for her only continues to grow.

Thank You for Sarah. She is so precious to me.

Then love her as I do.

I exhale slowly. I can see the right course, but I'm afraid to take it. "I don't want to be separated from you either. But what do you think you should do? You're torn. I can feel it."

Sarah rises and leans against the porch railing. "I guess you're right. Something tells me I should go. But I don't want to leave you." Her voice begins to break. "I need you. I love you."

I wrap my arms around her. "And you know how much I love you. But this could be good for you, and eight weeks isn't forever. I'll be right here when you get back." I pull away to study her sweet face, as if I need to memorize it. "Besides, you know what they say about absence making hearts grow fonder."

She stands on tiptoe to give me a gentle kiss. "Together or apart, we are always."

"Always," I whisper.

Please, let it be.

*

I wave at the Winstons' SUV until it's out of sight, smiling like an android version of myself. Then I slump as I put away the mask of Upbeat Boyfriend Who Encourages His Girl to Leave Him for Two Months. Hopefully I won't have to wear it again, ever.

"Samuel."

"Dad!" my heart cries out as I turn toward the voice. But all I see is Mr. Winston, walking toward me from his house. He didn't go with his wife and daughter because he's leaving on a business trip today.

What does he want?

"Samuel," he repeats as he extends his hand toward me. "Thank you."

I look at him for a beat before extending mine. "For what?"

"For doing the right thing." He stares down the street as if he can still see Sarah and her mom. "For letting Sarah go."

Letting her go to camp or letting her go for good? "I'm sorry. I don't understand."

He smiles slightly. "I think you do. I think you figured out that Pastor Jeff asked Sarah to do this for her own good. She hasn't been the same since…well, you know."

"Since she lost our baby." Saying the words aloud rips the bandage off.

He nods. "Yes. And Pastor Jeff thought this camp job might help Sarah move on. Caroline and I agree. And I think you do too."

I look away for a second. I'm not going to cry in front of Sarah's dad. "I do." Grabbing every bit of strength left, I look straight into his eyes. "I want what's best for Sarah. She means the world to me, Mr. Winston."

He places a hand on my shoulder. "I can see that now, son. You love my daughter."

The tears are bubbling up my throat, but I manage a "Yes, sir."

Mr. Winston's eyes are glazing over too. He gives my shoulder a squeeze, then walks away. I watch him for a moment before heading home.

"Sam?"

"Yes, sir?"

"Call me Daniel."

CHAPTER 25

SOMETIMES MY LONGING for Sarah crashes into me like a wave, leaving me breathless.

Then I slap myself in the head—figuratively, of course—and remind myself that she'll be home soon.

Sarah and I agreed that we wouldn't promise to write every day. Such a promise is too easy to break and too hurtful once broken. So we write when we can. For me, that's worked out to be almost every day. My letters are not masterpieces. No one is going to compile them into a book for readers to gush over one hundred years from now. I talk about work—I've returned to Russell Electric for the third summer as helper/picker-upper/thoroughly unskilled worker—and silly stuff, like a showdown at church last Sunday when Miss Clara faced off with Miss Frances after the latter took the former's usual seat. Tensions ran high, but the situation ended peacefully when Miss Lucille shuffled up and gushed about the beautiful dress Miss Frances was wearing, adding, "Oh, please sit with me today!" Well played.

Sarah's letters are better than mine, not only because she is a wonderful writer, but because her material is far superior. The letter I received yesterday described Sarah's attempt to lead some rising sixth graders on a hike. I say *attempt* because the group had only traveled a few hundred yards down the trail when Sarah spotted a snake in the path.

She froze, so the kids piled up like dominoes behind her, laughing and goofing off until they saw the snake too. Sarah wrote that she was quite sure it was a copperhead. She's not an accomplished outdoorswoman, but she took great care in studying snakes of the region before arriving at camp, so if she thought it was a copperhead, it probably was.

Anyway, most of the kids went berserk at that point, running back down the trail like Satan himself was charging up behind them. Sarah said the girls didn't try to hide their fear, although some seemed to add a heaping cup of drama to their reactions. The guys, on the other hand, laughed as they ran, pretending that they were too cool to be scared. However, Sarah noted, they ran nonetheless.

I chuckled as I read Sarah's description of her own response. *I tried to get the kids to slow down—I kept picturing one of them lying on the ground unconscious after running into a tree—and focused on sounding strong and authoritative. But at the same time this little voice in my head was yelling, "Run, you idiots! I think that snake is gaining on us." I half expected to see that copperhead slithering at the speed of a cheetah, its fangs reaching out for us. Sometimes my imagination is not such a good thing.*

One topic Sarah and I avoid is our feelings for each other. Both of us always close with *Love,* but we don't go on and on about loneliness and longing. I don't know how we arrived at this unspoken agreement. The way I see it, talking about what you can't have only makes the heartache worse. I guess that's selfish—I suppose Sarah would like to know how much I miss her—but she appears to have reached the same conclusion.

At least I hope she has. The alternative is something I can't think about.

My phone dings with a text from Kevin. *What's up?*

Not much. You? I reply.

Same, he answers. *Hike with Jack and me Sat?*

Hiking. As Mom taught me to say when I was a kid, "not my

favorite." But weekends are tough. Too much time to think, even with my chores around the house. *Sure.*

Maybe I'll wind up with a snake story to tell. But it still won't be as good as Sarah's.

*

"Whose idea was this?" I think my eyeballs are sweating.

Jack looks back at me and grins. "Mine, big baby. Didn't you bring your sippy cup?"

"If I had, it would be flying toward your head right about now," I grumble.

Kevin laughs. "Somehow, male bonding looks different in the movies."

I adjust my backpack and let out an involuntary sigh when air hits my soaked T-shirt.

"It is a bit warm today," Jack admits.

Uh, yeah, like ninety degrees.

"But we're almost at the overlook."

We've been out on the Mary's Rock Summit Trail for almost an hour now. I would never say so, but this wasn't a bad idea. Sure, it's the temperature of Venus. It is July, after all. But maybe that's why we haven't had much company on the trail. Except for our usual chatter, the only sounds have been those of the forest: birds chirping, bugs buzzing, leaves rustling above us. Funny how the sound of leaves scraping against each other is like waves breaking on a shore.

Thinking of the beach brings Sarah to mind, but everything does. But it doesn't sting as much out here, with one friend behind me and the other ahead.

"Here we are," Jack announces, waving his hand at our destination.

Kevin and I trudge up to join him and stare.

Peak after peak rises before us, all the way out to West Virginia. We sit down on the boulders and guzzle some electrolytes. The trees sheltered us on the trail, but out here only the ozone layer separates us from the sun. I suppose spontaneous combustion may be the price for this view. But it would be worth it.

We study the scene before us quietly—not even Jack is talking—and it feels like we're in church. Kind of like how I felt when I talked to Josh that day in Roanoke. I haven't thought about him or our conversation for a while. It's easier to focus on my job and my to-do list at home.

"How are you doing?"

I'm so lost in the view that it takes me a second to realize Kevin is talking to me. "Fine. Work. Chores at home. You know."

"Yeah," Kevin replies. "And Sarah is…"

"Staying busy at camp." As I return to the awesome view, I notice Kevin and Jack mouthing words to each other. "What's up with you two?" I ask. "Planning on throwing me off? I've seen this movie, and you will be caught."

Kevin nods at Jack, tagging him in.

"It's, uh, just that…we didn't know if you and Sarah are still, uh…" Jack stammers.

I sigh again, but not from the heat this time. While I'm grateful that my friends care about me, I am supremely annoyed. "We're still together." *I think*, I add in my head.

"Okay." Kevin speaks slowly as if he's giving me the chance to tell the truth.

Suddenly I feel compelled to tell my friends everything. It's as if days of rain have resulted in a flash flood and I'm helpless to stop it. "Sarah had a miscarriage this spring."

My friends' faces go blank with surprise. Uncle Rob, Gavin, Jessie, Lissi, and Emilia were the only people outside our families who knew Sarah was pregnant. I was waiting for the right moment to tell Jack and Kevin, but then we lost the baby.

Jack exhales. "Oh, man. I didn't know. I'm sorry."

"Me, too." Kevin shakes his head. "That must have been, I mean, I can't imagine… Is that why Sarah took that job?"

I shrug. "I think so." I struggle against telling them the whole story, but I want to. I have to. "We went back and forth about whether to give the baby up for adoption or raise it ourselves, and a couple of days after we decided to keep it—we planned to get married—Sarah had the miscarriage." I take a deep breath and study a distant ridge. "It was hard."

Jack and Kevin have clasped their hands, and each has bowed his head.

"And Sarah…" Jack prods.

"I believed she needed some time away to sort things out. I still do. It's like God is giving her some space to figure out what's next. Only…" Don't say it. If you say it, it'll come true.

"Only what?" I see my pain reflected in Kevin's face.

"Only I wish I could be sure that I'm part of what's next." Ideas that have floated through my head over the past month coalesce, revealing a picture I don't want to see. "If we hadn't lost the baby, Sarah and I would be married by now, and maybe that was never God's plan for her." I drop my head.

"Sam." Jack's voice is steady and firm. It reminds me of Dad. "Sam," he repeats, compelling me to look at him.

"I'm no preacher, and I won't pretend that I know what God's doing here." His eyes hold me, much like Josh's did. "But I don't think you do either. Stop guessing and let Him do His thing. Trust that everything will work out as it should."

I remember the compass/paperweight Sarah gave me for Christmas. "'Trust in the Lord with all thine heart,'" I recite.

"'And lean not on thine own understanding.'" Kevin completes the verse, pastor's kid that he is. He then pops Jack in the shoulder.

"Ow! What was that for?"

"'Let Him do His thing'? Did you really just say that? Almighty God, Creator of the Universe, Holy One of Israel, doing His thing." Kevin starts laughing, a low rumble that quickly spreads to Jack, then me.

"Hey, God knows what I meant," Jack protests once he catches his breath.

Kevin gives him a much gentler tap this time. "That He does, brother. That He does."

*

I must have dreamed of Sarah last night, because when I woke up, I was surprised that my arms were empty.

One more week. One more week until…

Unless…

No. Nope, no guessing allowed. Each time I'm tempted to start theorizing, I think about my compass. If I'm home, I pick it up and read the verse inside.

A familiar scent drifts into my room. Batter rising as it contacts a sizzling, buttery, metallic surface. Pancakes. Life is good.

I roll over. 9:30. Saturday, so it's okay to sleep in, but I was hoping to start cutting the grass before the sun rose to a scorching height.

"Good morning, sunshine," Mom chirps as I stumble into the kitchen. "You've been putting in some long hours this week, so I thought pancakes were in order."

Pancakes are always in order.

"Thanks." I pat her shoulder as I reach for the coffeepot.

Mom smiles, and I realize something, even in my bleary state. She is getting better.

Not that she's done with grieving. I don't know when that will stop, or if it ever will. But her smiles—real smiles, not the ones she forces for the benefit of someone else—are becoming more frequent. Dad would be happy about that.

Dad. I never think of him without his absence dropping on me like a pillar of rock. I can't go back and make things right between us. I've accepted that. But my heart has a door that can never be closed, and I must accept that too.

"Are you going to contemplate the coffee or pour it?" Mom

walks behind me to reach for a couple of plates. "Maybe somebody is sleepwalking."

"Maybe," I answer, hoping my voice doesn't give me away. "Thanks again for the pancakes. What are your plans for the day?"

Mom settles into her usual seat. "I don't have any, not yet. Perhaps I'll settle in my chair with a glass of iced tea and a good book and spend the day being lazy."

I saturate my pancakes with syrup, careful to cover every square inch of their fluffy beauty. "A lazy day for Kathy Russell? Not likely. Not that you don't deserve it."

She grins. "I might surprise you. What about you?"

"Cut the grass, do some trimming. Adventures like that." I take in another forkful of goodness.

"Well, I have an idea for you." Mom is staring at me, grinning. Foreshadowing.

I go on alert. "Which is…"

"Aunt Suzanne told me yesterday that Uncle Rob has bought a storage building for their backyard, one of those you assemble yourself out of a million pieces, with instructions written in Hindi."

"Mom—"

She holds up her hands. "Okay, sue me for exaggerating. But the fact is, for all of Rob Reynolds's talents as a doctor, he's no handyman. Your father used to chuckle when describing Rob's attempt to do things around the house. He never failed to bail him out, of course."

"Of course."

"So I thought maybe you could help today."

It's all clear now. "And that's why you made pancakes."

"To butter you up." Mom grins as she savors her awful pun.

I groan. "I'll go, but this means I get lasagna tonight."

"Deal."

*

A million pieces was no exaggeration.

When I arrived at the Reynoldses' house, Uncle Rob had all the shed parts spread out across the lawn: big boards, trim pieces, door parts, roof components, and approximately 790,000 nuts and bolts and screws. And one hex wrench. Did the manufacturer expect people to put this colossus together with a hex wrench the size of a number-two pencil?

And the instructions were not written in Hindi. No, it was worse. They consisted of hieroglyphics indecipherable to all but ancient Egyptians. No wonder Uncle Rob greeted me as if he were clinging to a piece of floating wreckage and I were the Coast Guard.

"Sam!" he exclaimed, and I braced myself for the frantic embrace of a drowning man. But then Uncle Rob's pride took over. "I appreciate your coming, but you don't have to spend your Saturday helping me. Now that I have sorted everything out, I think I'll have this thing put together in no time."

If this had been Jack, I would have replied with, "And are we talking cosmic time here?" Instead, I said, "No doubt. But I'd like to help. Saturdays are pretty long for me these days."

Uncle Rob nodded. "Sure. So, where do you think we should start?"

That was three hours ago. Even the most proficient do-it-yourselfer would need assistance on this project. In the beginning, Aunt Suzanne brought out cups of water for each of us. But after the third delivery, she dragged out this huge thermal dispenser, the kind they use at construction sites and church picnics. She even added some electrolyte powder. And yet Uncle Rob and I are still teetering on the verge of dehydration.

My eyeballs are not sweating. They're drying up into tiny marbles.

"Do you really think it needs a roof?" Uncle Rob asks. We have plopped to the ground for a break, but I'm beginning to wonder if I'll be able to get up.

I stare at the four walls finally standing straight and strong—not post-earthquake as they were earlier—and consider his question. "What are you going to store in there? I mean, as long as it's waterproof…"

We grin at each other.

He studies the unfinished structure. "I suppose a roof would look nice. Might as well go the extra mile." He struggles to his feet and offers me a hand up. "Thanks so much for your help, Sam. At times, it's felt like working with your father. Chad and I joked around a lot, but he never gave me any grief about my woeful handyman skills. Just showed up with his toolbox and plunged into whatever mess I had made."

Uncle Rob and I stand still, like we're waiting for Dad to join us. "I'd try to tell him how much I admired his ability to make or fix practically anything, but he'd brush off my compliments," he says in a hushed voice. "Said he was just a simple country boy, not a doctor like me." He shoves his hands in his pockets and looks down. "I'd come back with how everybody has different gifts, and how special his were, but he'd stop me with a 'Shut up, Reynolds. We've got work to do.' Sure do miss him." His voice cracks.

"Me too." Every day.

We give each other a minute to compose ourselves, then pick up where we left off. I try to decipher hieroglyphic number 34, forcing my brain to travel in a different direction.

"Oh." Uncle Rob sounds stunned, like Jesus Himself just showed up to drop the roof in place.

"What is it?"

His mouth has dropped open and his eyes are wide. Heatstroke?

"Uncle Rob? Are you okay?" I rush to his side, trying to remember the proper treatment.

"I'm fine, Sam. I...I just can't believe I never saw it. But now... Good Lord."

A stroke, maybe? But no facial drooping or slurred speech. Still, I put my arms around him to help him to the ground.

He waves off my assistance. "I'm fine. Really. Have a seat." He pats the grass.

I drop down and sit next to him, continuing to look for signs that something is wrong. Other than this babbling, that is.

Uncle Rob looks intently at me and his smile gets bigger. "All this time, you've been struggling with the question of whether you should become a doctor. We've talked about it and I've prayed about it, and thirty seconds ago I finally saw the answer."

"What is it?" I whisper.

"You aren't meant to be a doctor," he states with authority.

I wait. My heart races and my brain hums with possibilities, but I keep my focus on his eyes.

He rests a hand on my shoulder. "You're meant to be a nurse."

CHAPTER 26

I'D EXPECTED A revelation more in line with Uncle Rob's dramatic reaction. Something like, "You should be a missionary to Africa," or "You should become a Navy SEAL," or even, "You should become a taste tester at a potato chip factory in Pennsylvania." Not, "You should become a nurse."

But it makes sense.

I pluck a blade of grass and peel apart its sections. "Yeah, I figured my grades freshman year would keep me out of medical school."

"Samuel Russell."

I jerk my head up. His gray eyes have gone cold and the muscles in his jaw are tight.

"Yes, sir." How have I screwed up now?

"Nursing is not something you settle for. It's something you're called to. Do you understand?" He jabs his finger at me with each word in his question.

"Yes, sir. I'm sorry. That was a stupid thing to say." I am sorry, but I also want Uncle Rob to settle down before he really does have a stroke or heart attack.

"You can stop observing me." He ruffles my hair. "I'm not on the verge of a cardiac event."

"I wasn't—"

"Yes, you were, because you're your father's son. Always looking out for others."

I don't know what to say, so I return to my study of the lawn.

Uncle Rob stands up. "We need to talk, but this old back of mine requires a chair. Come on." He settles into an Adirondack chair on the back deck and I follow. "Ahh," he sighs. "Now that's better."

He's right. I lean back and realize I could be asleep in two minutes, if only I weren't waiting to learn what my future holds.

"I came down on you pretty hard, didn't I?"

I decide it's best to remain silent.

"Sorry. But I've heard that attitude so many times over the years, and I'm fed up with it. You were in the unfortunate position of being the straw that broke the camel's back." He moves his chair so he can face me. "Are we good?"

"Yes, sir. So, about my becoming a nurse…"

Uncle Rob chuckles. "Oh, yes, that. My tantrum derailed things. I was setting up the ladder, thinking for the fifteenth time today that building this shed was an awful idea, when my mind drifted back to your father. How he felt less-than. You know what I mean?"

I sense the film of that terrible night in the kitchen cueing up. *Not now. Please, not now.*

"Chad Russell was always willing to give people a break, whether it was the ex-con looking for a job or the friend with no discernible home improvement skills." He smiles slightly, remembering. "But he never gave himself one. I'm babbling again, aren't I?"

I rub my face with my hand to buy time. "No, you're not," I finally answer. "I can see it. He thought he wasn't good enough—less-than, as you put it—and that's why he pushed Megan and me to get degrees. So we would be."

Uncle Rob flicks his index finger at me. "Exactly."

"But I still don't understand…"

He holds up his palm. "Hang in there a little longer. Thinking about your father led to thinking about you and your search for your calling. I sent up a quick prayer that God would give you some clear direction. I wasn't polite. I said, 'Come on, Lord, Sam's been through so much this year. Give the kid a break.'"

"Thank you, Uncle Rob," I manage to reply.

He dabs at his eyes and clears his throat. "I waited a couple of seconds for the sky to open. When that didn't happen, I took off my cap and wiped away the sweat from my forehead, touching this scar I got when I was a kid." He pulls away his hair to reveal a pale scar at his hairline.

I swallow a deep sigh.

"And at that moment, an image of Miss Brewster flashed into my mind. And that's when I knew." He clasps his hands and rests them on his stomach as a satisfied smile spreads across his face.

Oh, yeah, of course. Miss Brewster. Patron saint of...something. Sure, everybody knows a divine vision of Miss Brewster means somebody must become a nurse. Uncle Rob, are you sure you have not had a stroke? "Uh," I say instead.

He rouses himself from his state of contentment and grins sheepishly. "Sorry, big guy. I'm on the verge of making sense." He leans forward and the grin fades. "I was in a terrible car accident when I was eight. My mother and I were T-boned at an intersection."

Annoyance gives way to empathy. "Was she...did she make it?"

"Yes, thank God, but it was touch and go for a while." The tiny wrinkles around Uncle Rob's eyes and mouth melt away as he recalls the little boy he was.

"And what happened to you?"

"I was on the opposite side of the collision, but I was still pretty busted up. A gash here"—he points to the scar again—"and a broken femur and ulna. Missed all of Little League that summer."

I wait. Patiently, this time.

"I was knocked unconscious by the collision and came to in the emergency room. I was in more pain than I'd ever known and surrounded by strangers and machines. I cried, 'Mama, Mama,' over and over. The strangers kept saying, 'Hush,' in nice voices, but they were focused on my body, not how I was feeling. I get that now, of course, but then…"

I nod. Poor little guy.

"Then this nice lady came alongside me. I can still remember her scent, something like flowers mixed with honey. She patted my shoulder—the only thing that wasn't hurting at that moment—and told me she was so glad to run into another Braves fan. I was wearing my Braves T-shirt, although it was so bloodstained that I don't know how she could read it. She asked me if I thought they had a chance at the pennant and if I played ball. When I said, 'Yes,' she asked about my position. 'Shortstop,' I answered, and that sent her into an involved explanation of why the shortstop is the key man on a team. I began to focus on her, not my pain."

"And she was…"

"Miss Brewster, yes. She wore a nurse's uniform, but that day I believed she was an angel." He rubs his eyes with the back of his hand. "I guess I still do. She saw through a list of injuries to the terrified little boy underneath." He scoots to the edge of his chair and turns toward me. "It takes more than training and skill to be a remarkable nurse, Sam. It takes a deep concern for people, the same concern you just showed for me. You want to help people, right? That's why you wanted to become a doctor."

"Uh-huh."

"Well, nursing would give you more interaction with patients, especially in a hospital setting. Doctors do drive-bys, but nurses are there for the minute-by-minute care. This may sound weird, but you could be a Miss Brewster to someone who feels scared and alone. Like I said earlier, your father had a big heart, and so do you."

I shake my head. "I don't know about that. About me, I mean, not Dad."

"Open your eyes, son." The tenderness in his voice pricks me. "Your father was not less- than, and neither are you."

"Oh, my." Mom puts down her iced tea in slow motion. "What do you think?"

I pull apart the layers of my untouched lasagna. "I don't know what to think. The idea that God would lay everything out that way… Doesn't it all seem too simple? Too easy?"

She pulls out the chair next to me, Megan's usual seat, and takes both of my hands. "Sam."

I drag my attention away from the disassembling of my pasta.

"You've struggled with your calling for a long time, probably even longer than I know. You've prayed about it, I've prayed, Megan has, the Reynoldses have. Sarah too, I'm sure." Mom's eyes are soft with her love for me, but there is something else there too. A fire. A certainty. "There has been nothing easy about this, but that doesn't mean the answer has to be wrapped in a puzzle. I can't tell you that God wants you to become a nurse. Only you can discern that. But don't dismiss the possibility just because it was presented so clearly." She gently pats my cheek. "Would you do that for me?"

I can't speak, so I lean into my mother's hand.

She pulls me to her shoulder and strokes my back. "Everything is going to be fine, Sammy. Just fine."

*

I'm tired right through my bones, and already my muscles are warning me that I'm going to feel like an old man tomorrow. But I can't sleep.

Could Uncle Rob be right? Is it possible that I've been circling around my calling all this time, staring in one direction when all I had to do was turn around and look in another?

I wish Sarah were here.

She is so many things to me, but right now I need her as my best friend. She knows me as well as I know myself. Maybe better. If she were here, we would go back and forth, with her asking questions—just as a counselor would—that would force me to examine how I'm thinking. What I'm feeling.

I suppose I should feel exhilaration now that the answer I've been searching for has been dropped into my lap. Instead, I'm still asking, still searching, still wondering. What's wrong with me?

I remember the story Sarah told me the night I lay awake in the Reynolds' guest room. The night I knocked my mother to the floor as I lunged at my father. I linger in the memory, even though pain shuffles along behind it. I listen to the velvety softness of Sarah's voice as she describes our future together, and begin to unwind. Finally, I slide off to sleep.

I awaken in a meadow. I know I'm dreaming, but I set that aside, so great is the beauty of this place. The sun is coming into view, its light turning the bellies of the clouds pink. I follow its progression as it appears over the horizon, and it takes me a few moments to realize that I can stare at it directly. If I squint, I think I can see gaseous plumes erupting from its surface.

I become aware of the world illuminated around me. Its vibrance is startling. It's as if I've been color blind my whole life. The red of the poppies. The buttery yellow of the daffodils. The rich purple of the stately irises. The cool green of the grass.

I hear the gurgle of a brook flowing on my left. The water is so clear—almost invisible—and the rocks just below the surface are the color of chocolate.

"Do you like it?"

I jump at the sound of the familiar voice. The wolf, my old friend, is sitting to my right. I didn't even hear him approach.

I throw my arms around him and bury my face in his fur. I hold on a long time, realizing how much I've needed to feel his sturdy, solid body in my arms. "Oh, yes," I say at last. "It is… Somehow *beautiful* isn't enough. Thank you for letting me see it." I scratch him behind the ears, and his golden eyes begin to glow with pleasure. "I've missed you so much."

"But I've been right here all along." The British accent is still there, and it still makes me smile. "I've never left you, and I never will."

"I know." He isn't really a wolf. I should be stretching out face down before Him, for I'm not worthy to be in His presence, much less touch Him. But He invites it. "I'm so sorry for everything." My voice fails.

"I know. You've already told Me, remember?" He nudges me with His massive head. "And I have forgiven you, Sam. For everything. Why won't you accept that?"

I sniffle and wipe my eyes. "Because…" I stop. "I don't know."

He rises. "Come with Me."

I follow Him to the edge of the meadow. Only now do I notice that it's surrounded by fog, an impenetrable wall of mist aligned perfectly with the perimeter.

"Here we are," He announces as we stop between two trees. He smiles at me. "Watch this." The wolf lets out a long, gentle breath, and the fog begins to dissipate.

I step closer to the perimeter, trying to get a better view of what lies beyond. I can almost make out someone moving in the distance.

"Oh," I gasp. "Oh, dear God." I drop to my knees.

Dad.

He's walking toward me. I can't make out his face yet, but his gait is unmistakable: the right foot turned out slightly, the easy swing of his arms, the tilt of his head.

"Dad!" I leap to my feet, but the wolf blocks my path.

"No, child. You may not cross. Not yet."

"But…" I start to argue, the longing to embrace my father overwhelming me. "Please."

The wolf leans into my legs. "No. But look. He is drawing closer."

Yes, I can see his face clearly now. It is Chad Russell—son, husband, father, and friend. But also…more. And less. There's no shadow of worry or pain or loss around his eyes. No weight bearing down on his broad shoulders. No fatigue in his stride. In their place is more of everything that made my father a good man. His smile is broader, and his blue eyes shimmer with joy.

Oh, how I wish Mom and Megan were here.

Dad stops about ten yards from the meadow. "He can't come to me?" I ask, knowing the answer.

"No." The wolf sits down at my feet and leans into me again. "Your father knew you loved him." He studies me with his golden eyes. "He knows."

All the words I've dreamed of saying to Dad, all the apologies I've repeated in my head, are stuck in my throat. All I can do is gaze at him, my mouth agape but empty, and hope he can sense the love pouring out of my heart.

Suddenly I'm filled with warmth, and I know it is Dad's love for me. He's sending it to me just as I sent mine to him. He nods and places his hand on his chest, then turns to go.

"Daddy!" I plead, my voice returning at last.

He pivots to face me. "It is well, Samuel." His voice is more musical than I remember. "It is well." Dad smiles again before walking away.

The fog is beginning to close back in, but I watch him for as long as I can. He's extending his hand. But to whom?

I strain to see. A child, maybe three or four years old, is running to him. A girl. With curly red hair flying around her. She grabs his hand. The last thing I make out is the two of them swinging their arms, the little girl skipping along.

I can't breathe. "Was she? Is she?" I manage to ask.

The wolf gives me an even bigger smile. "This is a place of beginning. And beginning again. You must wait and see."

As I study the wolf's eyes for clues, I realize they're changing color, slowly shifting from golden to blue. A deep, clear blue. I have never seen eyes that color, except for...

I want to shout when I make the connection, but I can't speak. I'm struck dumb, for the wolf's body is changing too, morphing into the shape of a man. As He transforms, light streams out of His fingers, His feet, His head, from every inch of His body—until I can't look at Him. I'm blinded by His glory.

I fall to my knees and cover my face. I want to run away and hide. I'm too small, too messed up, to be here with Him.

Two arms wrap around me, strong arms accustomed to manual labor. The desire to flee evaporates as He tosses aside the stones in my subterranean tomb. Then He gently carries my crushed spirit back to the light. His light.

"Samuel." His voice is like a song, but one composed of all songs. Of all music. Bach, Beethoven, Handel—their works were only scratchy approximations of His voice. As close as a nightlight is to a supernova.

"Yes, Lord," I answer, keeping my hands over my eyes.

"Look at me, Samuel."

I raise my head and open my eyes slowly. His light is still there but dimmed enough for me to tolerate it.

Jesus's love washes over me again as I stare into His eyes. I realize they're not only blue, but also green and brown and hazel—endless depths of compassion and kindness for each of His children, in all their beautiful variety. "I have wonderful things planned for you, Samuel, but you must trust Me." He rests His hand on my head.

Joy and peace permeate my every cell. I am whole.

"As I told my servant Isaiah, my thoughts are nothing like your thoughts. And my ways are far beyond anything you could imagine. For just as the heavens are higher than the earth, so my ways are higher than your ways and my thoughts higher than your thoughts." Jesus gently lifts my chin, and those eyes lock on me with even greater intensity. "So trust Me, Samuel. Trust Me no matter what."

"No matter what," I repeat in a whisper. I begin to fall into those wondrous eyes. Falling, falling, but not flailing.

No, I'm not falling. I am flying, skidding through wispy clouds into the sunrise.

I am free. At last.

CHAPTER 27

WHEN I OPEN my eyes, I'm surprised by the darkness of my bedroom. And disappointed. I wanted to keep flying forever.

I reach for my phone. What did He say about Isaiah? It sounded familiar. I search for "My thoughts are not yours," and Isaiah 55:8–9 pops up. I almost laugh when I realize Jesus used the NLT version. He knows—of course—that I have trouble with the King James.

Sarah! I must tell Sarah. But I can't, not yet. My heart might burst if I don't tell someone. Mom? I glance at my phone again: 4:08. Crazy early.

All I can do is write about my dream, which wasn't really a dream. But I hesitate to call it a vision, because prophets have those, and I'm not one.

I'll write a letter to Sarah but won't send it. I must share this in person, face-to-face.

Writing the letter helps me to relax, and I think I drift off to sleep around 5:15. It's 7:30 now, thirty minutes before my usual Sunday morning alarm, but I'm wide awake and refreshed. Might as well head downstairs.

Mom's not up yet, so I make the coffee and stand at the kitchen sink as I wait for it to brew. Same backyard as yesterday, showing signs of minor neglect. Rose bushes that need deadheading and tomato plants begging for water. A deserted bird's nest that fell onto the patio a couple of days ago. Loose stones on the fire pit, which has sat unused this summer. Everything appears the same as it did yesterday.

Only I have changed.

In the bright light of morning, my dream feels more like a dream—something conjured up in the depths of my brain. A tiny, sharp, snarky voice tells me nothing I experienced was real.

"But it was real," I say softly. "I know it was."

"What was real?" Mom walks up to me and peers through the window. "Did you see something?"

"Uh, no. No, ma'am. Just mumbling to myself." I'm not ready yet. "How are you this morning?"

Mom studies me for a moment. She knows my evasive maneuvers. "Fine, thank you, sir." The coffeemaker hiccups as it finishes brewing. "You made coffee? Now I know something is up, but I shall not look a gift horse in the mouth."

We drink our first cups of the day in silence. The sliver of doubt that pinched me a few minutes ago has disappeared, and a deep contentment has taken its place. I think that's the right word for this unfamiliar feeling.

And Mom continues to study me. "Did you sleep well, Sammy?" she asks.

"Yes, ma'am."

She raises an eyebrow, trying to probe deeper. "You feel better today, don't you, son? I can't define it, but something has changed."

I'm struck with a sudden surge of love for my mother, this woman who has kept her heart open and tender despite terrible loss. I can almost see Jesus smiling when He thinks of her.

I pull out the chair next to her—Dad's chair—and gently take her hand. "It's hard to explain. I will tell you one day, when everything is more settled in my head. But God did some work on me overnight, and for the first time in a long time I believe things are going to be okay for me. More than okay." My voice breaks.

Mom throws her arms around me. "Oh, Sammy, this is what I have been praying for. God is so good, isn't He?"

"Yes, He is," I whisper into her hair.

*

The contentment has followed me to work every day this week. Then, to top things off, a letter from Sarah was waiting for me when I got home today.

I gave Mom a quick hug before rushing to my bedroom, then ripped open the envelope, not even bothering to take off my grimy clothes first. I hadn't expected another letter this close to Sarah's return.

Dear Sam,

I had not planned on writing again since I am coming home soon, but I had to let you know that something has happened to me. Ms. Donaldson would call it a breakthrough, and I think Pastor Jeff would say it was an epiphany, but the bottom line is that I am finally ready to move on.

We can talk about it when I get home.

Love,

Sarah

I reread Sarah's note until I've it committed to memory. I parse the words, searching for any indication that this is not what I think it is.

A break-up.

She says she is ready to "move on," but gives no details. Sarah is a first-class person, so it makes sense that she would want to tell me to my face. She did conclude with *Love,* but that could've been automatic.

I sit cross-legged on the floor and drop my head into my hands. A voice—*the* Voice—rings in my brain. "Trust Me no matter what."

This must be the *no matter what.*

What if it is? The question floats into my mind like a cloud, and the panic creeping up on me flees, like a cockroach skittering away to hide from the light.

It will hurt. It will hurt so bad. But… I know this feeling. It's the stitch in my side and the hunger for breath and the jelly in my legs as I approach a finish line.

But?

I must press on. *But I will still trust You.*

In an instant, my thoughts pivot from myself to Sarah. She has found closure. If leaving our relationship behind has brought her peace, then that's the price that must be paid. I love her that much.

Whatever happens, I understand now that I'm not alone.

I still trust You.

*

Sarah is coming home today.

Anticipation and dread mingle in my heart. There's none of the wild-eyed desperation I've experienced so many times since last October, and I'm thankful for that. But my heart is heavy with resignation, even as it sings with the thought of seeing Sarah's sweet face.

I'm a mess, but I haven't lost my mind.

If this were a workday, my hours would be filled with lifting and hauling and responding, "How high?" when Will Cubbison tells me to jump. His delight in bossing around the boss's son would be a welcome distraction.

Instead, I have had to scrounge around for things to do. I fixed the stones on the fire pit at last. Maybe we'll use it this fall. I got Mom's car inspected even though the sticker doesn't expire until next month. I even wandered over to Uncle Rob's house to help him with some of the interior finishing of that blasted shed.

Three p.m.

Mrs. Winston—she told me to call her Caroline, but I'm not ready for that—said Sarah should be arriving around 4. If I take my time cleaning up, I might get through this last hour without breaking apart.

I clear the fog from the bathroom mirror and spread shaving cream over my face. I guess a lot of girls like beards, but Sarah prefers me clean-shaven. "I don't want to feel like I'm kissing a scrub brush," she says. I start to smile, then recall that there might not be any kisses today.

"Stop," I say to my reflection. "Don't go there."

I move the razor down my upper lip, up my neck, and across my jawline, focusing on every stroke with an intensity usually reserved for neurosurgery. As my heart rate settles and my breathing slows, a song rolls into my consciousness. "Turn Your Eyes Upon Jesus."

I wipe away the last of the shaving cream. "Okay, Lord," I say aloud. "I get it."

At 4 p.m. I sit in one of the chairs on our porch. I wish we had rockers, like Sarah's family. Rockers are better, especially when some nervous energy needs to be spent.

4:05.

4:15.

At last I spot the Winstons' SUV approaching. I'm glued to my seat, unsure whether to leap up and run to greet Sarah or wait until I'm called.

Sarah makes the choice for me. Seconds after the SUV pulls into the garage, she starts down the driveway, waving to me. Then she's running. Then I'm running. Then we meet on the sidewalk, halfway between our houses, and fall into each other's arms.

My jumbled-up brain starts analyzing what's going on, but I shut it off. I don't want to think. I want to feel.

The warmth of Sarah's breath as she nuzzles into her spot at my throat. The softness of her body next to mine. The floral scent and silky texture of her hair. The strength of her arms as they wrap around me.

We stand there for an eternity. Or a minute. Time has no meaning.

Sarah is the first to speak. "Miss me?" she whispers.

"Baby," is all I can say.

She pulls away and touches my cheek lightly. Her green eyes seem to have become even deeper in color against the slight glow of her skin. Her beauty is staggering. "We need to talk," she says softly.

I let out a long breath. *No matter what, no matter what,* I repeat silently.

"You don't need to unload your stuff?" Delay, delay, delay. Let me linger in this feeling.

Sarah looks over her shoulder at her house. "No. Daddy said he'd take care of it. He knew I'd be anxious to see you."

But why? "My porch?"

Sarah shakes her head. "No. Some place more private. Your patio?"

"Okay."

No matter what.

Sarah and I hold hands as we walk through the gate at the side of my house. Our kitchen overlooks the backyard, but Mom is out shopping. I think my caged lion nervousness drove her away.

We are alone. That is best.

Sarah stares at the fire pit. "You fixed it."

"Yeah. Today, in fact. I got tired of looking at those loose stones every time I stood at the kitchen sink."

"I guess we should add handyman to your resume." She gives me her biggest, most heart-melting smile, and I sway a little. The afternoon sun reflects off the claddagh necklace around her neck.

I point to it. "You're still wearing it."

She touches the pendant instinctively. "Of course. I never take it off unless I'm swimming or something."

"I didn't know you were coming back." The words tumble out unexpectedly, then hang in the air between us.

Sarah draws her brows together and tilts her head one way, then another, as she studies me. "Uh, of course I came back. You've known—"

"To me. I didn't know if you were coming back to me."

Sarah draws closer but stops when she's an arm's length away. "What are you saying?"

I take a deep breath. I must get this all out in one shot since I don't know how long I'll be able to keep myself together. I shove my hands in my pockets to hide their trembling before I realize they are still.

Like me.

"In your letter, you said you're ready to move on. And I'm so happy for you, Red. Really, I am." The words are coming more easily than I expected. "I have always wanted what's best for you. And you're not tied to me in any way, not anymore, so—"

Sarah takes a small step toward me. "But—"

I lift my palm. "Please, let me finish. You know I'll always love you and I'll always be your friend, whatever—"

She moves closer. "Stop."

I'm almost done. "But—"

She places her hand over my mouth. "Shut up."

I reply without thinking, mumbling behind her fingers. "You shut…"

In a breath, Sarah covers the last of the distance between us, moves her hand to the back of my head, and pulls me down for a kiss.

It is like no kiss we have ever shared before.

Not a careful, uncertain first kiss. Not a hungry lover's kiss. It's both and neither—a claiming kiss. "You are mine," she breathes into me. "And I am yours."

I rake my hands through her hair as raw emotion consumes me. "I love you, I love you, I love you," I repeat as I claim her mouth, her cheeks, her throat. "My darling Sarah."

When we part at last, neither of us can speak. Sarah gives me her soft, makes-me-weak grin, and I smile back. I can tell it is a goofy, that-guy-is-stoned smile, but I can't help it. I do feel kind of drunk right now.

"I've always loved that," Sarah whispers into my ear.

"What?"

"The way you smile after we kiss." She combs my hair away from my face before trailing her fingers along my cheek. "It's sweet and vulnerable and so sexy I almost faint."

"I doubt—"

She covers my mouth with her hand again. "Don't you dare argue with me about this. It wouldn't be polite."

"Yes, ma'am," I answer with as much politeness as I can muster. Along with my goofy smile.

"See? You're doing it again," Sarah sighs before pulling me in for another kiss.

"Red?" I murmur as I rest my cheek against hers.

"Uh-huh."

"If not me, what are you moving on from?"

Sarah leans her head into my chest and releases a shuddering breath. "Grief. Longing for the baby I'll never hold. Anger at God for allowing that to happen." Her voice wavers, and I hold on tighter, as if there were any space between us. I hear the echo of my pain in hers. But when she looks up at me, her green eyes are quiet. "Day after day, I begged God for answers. Then one night I was talking to the chaplain on staff, and he said that we have to recognize when to give up."

"Give up?"

"Yeah, that was my reaction. Giving up sounds a lot like quitting, and Winstons don't quit." Sarah lowers her voice in an impression of her father, an attempt so far off the mark that we cannot help but laugh softly. "But what he meant is that we must accept that some things won't make sense until we get to heaven. Our human hearts and minds can only go so far."

I remember my dream. "'My ways are higher than your ways,'" I whisper.

Her eyes widen with surprise. "That's exactly what Pastor Bill said. I knelt beside my bed that night and told God I was giving up, that I was tired of fighting with Him all the time. And He gave me peace, Sam." Her eyes fill with tears. "Peace like I haven't felt in a long time. I will never forget the child we never knew, but I'm certain that he or she is safe in God's arms."

I can't speak, so I nod and gently kiss her forehead.

Sarah frames my face with her hands. "You let me go away even though you thought I might not come back to you."

I nod again, unable to stop my own tears.

"My sweet, sweet love." She kisses one cheek, then the other. "But something has changed." She stares at me. "Even when you thought I was breaking up with you, your eyes were calm behind the pain. Like, like…" Her face opens in delight. "You've found peace. Is that it?"

I place my hands over hers. "The wolf came to me."

*

Sarah started crying as soon as I mentioned Dad. Sitting knee to knee beside the fire pit, I can see the glow build in her eyes, like a body of water filled with bioluminescent algae. "So beautiful," she manages to say. "Seeing your father, talking to him. What an incredible gift."

"But that's not all."

Sarah's hand flies to her mouth as I describe the little girl who joined Dad. I wait quietly for her response. I've had days to think about what I saw, and I'm still not sure what it means. "Do you think…" She looks up for a moment, searching for her words. "Was she… Do you think she was our baby?"

"I assumed she was." A new idea comes to me as I speak. "But now I wonder. Jesus said that I was in a place for beginning and beginning again. If Dad is beginning again, then the little girl might be…"

"Beginning." Her voice is hushed. "So she might be waiting to be born. To us." Sarah grabs my hands and leans in until our foreheads touch. "Our daughter, Sam. Is it possible?"

"All things are possible," I whisper.

The world goes still and falls away, until only Sarah and I remain, held in the strong embrace of One who never lets go.

Never.

Ever.

All at once I know. I see. I've been blind, groping around in the dark, but now the light is pouring in. I back away just enough to gaze into Sarah's eyes.

"There's one more thing, Red. I'm not meant to be a doctor."

Concern and hope swirl across Sarah's face. "You're not?"

"I'm meant to be a nurse."

CHAPTER 28

I PULL THE plastic cover off my suit and notice that the dry cleaner's tag is dated a year ago. I guess the last time I got dressed up was for Hannah Riley's wedding. That was a good day.

Hannah was painfully shy in high school, a sweet girl who was one of Kelsey Abbott's frequent targets. Sarah and I were amazed by her transformation when we ran into her during Christmas break our freshman year. Hannah had blossomed in her new environment at the University of Mary Washington. She was still quiet, but not timid, and she and Sarah wound up going shopping together. They stayed in touch after that.

I take the pants off the hanger and try them on. I hope they fit. I run every day to fend off the effects of Sarah's cooking. We muddled through the first year of our marriage, with each of us taking turns preparing our meals and neither doing an especially good job. Sarah announced shortly after our first anniversary that she'd resolved to become as proficient in the kitchen as our mothers. She delegated the job of dishwashing to me.

Deal.

Sarah started reading cookbooks like they were novels. There were a few failures— something called Hot Chicken Salad still haunts me. But Sarah never gave up, and I'm the beneficiary of her persistence.

Her apple crisp is the sweetest thing this side of heaven, a fact I will never share with Mom, given her pride in her desserts.

The metal fastener slides into the waistband without a struggle. Thank goodness. Now for the coat. It slips on easily. No surprise there since I haven't gone to the gym as much as I should.

I stand in front of the mirror above our dresser. Not bad. I hope suits don't go in and out of style like women's clothes, because I have no intention of rushing out and buying another before tomorrow.

I remember buying this one six years ago. The suit I'd worn on my first date with Sarah and to Dad's funeral didn't fit anymore. The pants were okay, but the coat didn't even come close to buttoning.

I started lifting weights while working on my BSN degree at James Madison University. It was hard to leave Virginia Tech and even harder to move away from Sarah, but Uncle Rob's advice and my own research convinced me it was the right thing to do. Going to the gym became a welcome distraction. Until he graduated, Kevin and I often went together, competing like guys do. Getting stronger was almost an afterthought. Still, trying on that old suit made me wonder what Sarah ever saw in me, scrawny kid that I was.

I smile at my reflection. Am I the most blessed guy in the world, or what? I sit on the edge of the bed and settle into my memory. Six years evaporate and I'm planning a special date with Sarah.

Megan insists on going shopping with me. "I love you, bro, but you have the fashion sense of a snail," are her exact words. She goes into full personal-shopper mode, picking out a charcoal-gray suit, crisp white shirt, and a blue tie. "It's a jacquard pattern, and the blue will bring out your eyes," she comments, like she needs to sell me on it.

I wipe my sweaty palms on my legs as I wait for Sarah to answer her door that night. I'm more nervous than I had been on our first date, and that is saying something, considering I'd been as twitchy as a cat in a tree.

When Sarah answers the door, all the oxygen is squeezed out of my lungs. I can only stare at her, my mouth agape.

As Megan would attest, I am no fashion guru. I can't describe what Sarah is wearing with fancy terms about the style or the material. What I see is a vision straight out of a fairy tale.

The dress is deep green, with sleeves that stop just below Sarah's shoulders. The neckline scoops below her collarbone, offering the barest glimpse of her breasts. The fabric flows to a perfect fit around her tiny waist before stopping an inch or so above her knees.

Sarah plunges directly into self-conscious mode. "I told Rachel I wasn't sure about this dress. I don't know what I was thinking. I can change." She's halfway to the stairs before I find my voice.

"Stop." I grab her hand and pull her toward me. If we weren't in her parents' foyer, I would wrap my arms around her and kiss her for a long time. Instead, I caress her cheek. "You have absolutely no idea how stunning you are, do you?"

She blushes and tries to look away, but I move my hand to her chin to keep her gaze on me. "You think so because you love me, but…"

"I do love you," I croak, still struggling for breath. "But it is a fact that you're incredibly beautiful, and every man in that restaurant tonight will wish he were in my shoes."

"I told you he would like it." We turn to see Rachel peeking around the corner from the dining room, wearing a Cheshire cat grin. "When Sarah said you were taking her out for a nice dinner, I dragged her off to the store. Big sister was right once again."

Sarah rolls her eyes in mock exasperation. "Yes, oh wise sibling, you were right."

"Yes, she was," Caroline says as she and Daniel join Rachel. I wonder if they have all been waiting just inside the kitchen, giving Sarah and me this moment. Giving me a chance to catch my breath.

As I look at Sarah's family, I realize the four of us are part of a sweet conspiracy, with only Sarah unaware of what's going on. For the first time, I feel more than kindness and acceptance from them. I feel love.

Sarah's eyes flick back and forth between us, and panic swishes past me for a second. I knew talking to her dad was a risk, but it was also a necessity. I can only hope that Sarah's powers of perception have been dimmed somehow.

"Okay, this is getting weird," she says at last. "Maybe the aliens have finally taken over. Mr. Russell, do we have a reservation?"

"Yes, ma'am," I answer, trying to stifle a sigh of relief. As I help her with her coat, I glance back at the three Winstons.

All three give me a thumbs-up.

My dream of dinner at a five-star restaurant crashed and burned when it collided with my college-student budget. But Megan turned out to be more than a personal stylist. She also found a well-reviewed little French restaurant located in a converted farmhouse about forty-five minutes from Early.

I had checked out the place in the daytime and thought it was okay. But that night it's a perfect Christmas card—evergreen garland draped across the railing, candles glowing from every window, and the branches of a Christmas tree sparkling through the sidelight in the front door. We even have a few flakes of snow to complete the effect.

Sarah stares out the windshield like a kid seeing fireworks for the first time. "It's magical," she breathes. "Oh, honey, thank you so much." Her smile fills my heart, and for a moment I wonder if you can die from an overdose of bliss.

My pragmatic side is pleased to note that Sarah's skeptical vibe has disappeared completely.

According to Sarah, dinner is spectacular. She raves over the Boeuf Bourguignon and makes soft moaning sounds with each spoonful of the chocolate mousse. Dessert for Sarah equals torment for me. The best kind. I can't taste anything. We might be eating plain oatmeal as far as I'm concerned. All my senses are consumed by the woman before me.

"Didn't you like your dinner?" Sarah asks after scraping the last of the mousse from the dish. "You're making me feel like a pig over here."

"It was nice, but I'd rather sit here and look at you." Her eyes seem to absorb every ray of light from each candle and Christmas bulb in the room and amplify it.

She places her hands under her chin. "This has been such a lovely evening. Like something out of a movie. But what is going on?"

I reach across for her, and she gives me her hand. "Well, first, it is a bit of a celebration. You're heading into your last semester at Tech. I only wish I were graduating with you."

Sarah pats my hand. "Me too. But you will be right behind me. You're still on track for commencement next December, right?"

"Right. Second, I wanted to give you a reason to wear a dress like that. Have mercy." I add my goofy smile.

She blushes and leans toward me. "Stop that. You know how that smile affects me."

I take in a deep breath and let it out slowly to regain my balance. "And finally, because it is Christmas."

Sarah's eyes take on additional sparkle. "Am I getting a present?" Her love of gifts hasn't abated over time, with the anticipation and surprise far more important than the present itself.

My heart thuds and I force myself to stick to the plan. "Maybe." I glance at the time. Eight thirty. "Ready to go?"

"Yes, sir." Sarah grins and I almost drop to the floor.

She starts asking questions when we take I-81 to Winchester, then north toward the West Virginia line. "We're not going home? Are we going to a movie? For coffee someplace?"

Sarah's interrogation stops when we leave the interstate, and she catches a glimpse of the lighted trees in Clearbrook Park. We've talked often about coming to this annual display. The county park is illuminated with hundreds of thousands of lights, and you can walk through at your own pace. But family activities have taken over our calendars every year. "We finally made it!" She almost giggles like a little girl. "And it's as beautiful as I thought it would be. How can you top this? More chocolate?"

I bring her hand to my lips. "You'll see." Then I reach behind the seat and grab a tote Caroline gave me earlier. "You might want this."

She says nothing as she pulls out yoga pants and some winter boots with socks. I worried this part of the plan would seem ultra-weird, so I start babbling with an explanation. "I didn't want you to get cold, and I figured you could slip the pants on under your dress. I'll block the door, you know, to give you some privacy, and…"

Sarah caresses my cheek, and I'm surprised to see her eyes glazing over. "That is the sweetest, most romantic thing ever." She blinks and touches the corner of her eye. "Rachel will kill me if I ruin her makeup artistry. Now go on while I suit up."

We take our time touring the park, pausing to appreciate every illuminated scene. Sarah likes the animated extravaganza best, with a computer coordinating lights with music. When we find a booth selling hot chocolate, she makes that soft moaning sound again, adding that she can die a happy woman.

Families clear out as the night goes on, and we find ourselves alone in a tunnel of light.

It's time.

I lead Sarah over to a bench and take both of her hands. We fall into each other's eyes, and the bliss overtakes me once more.

Breathe in, breathe out…

I've written—yes, written—a whole speech, but it dissolves in the warmth of Sarah's gaze. "I realized I loved you when I saw John Perkins placing you in his trunk. But I don't know when you became more than my best friend. I might have loved you my whole life and even before."

"Me too." Sarah's voice cracks. "The worst part of being trapped in Smiley's basement wasn't wondering what was going to happen to me." Her green eyes are shining. "It was wondering what he had done to you." She reaches up to put her hands on either side of my head. "And I think I love you even more now than I did then."

My voice falters under the weight of the moment. "Sarah, you and I have already been through a lifetime together. Loss, grief, and separation. But faith and grace and joy too." I drop to one knee before her and pull the velvet box from my coat pocket.

Sarah covers her mouth with her hands, her tears flowing over them.

"I don't know what the future holds, but I do know, with everything I am, that I want to travel there with you. Sarah Campbell Winston, please give me the great honor of being your husband."

"Yes, yes, yes!" She throws her arms around my neck before I can even put the ring on her finger. "Always, always yes."

My first proposal was rejected. The second was accepted, then set aside.

The third time is the charm.

"I thought you'd disappeared," Sarah announces as she walks into our bedroom. "You said you were going to try on your suit and then, *poof.* You're not trying to get out of washing the dishes, are you? Because I've been baking for the thing tomorrow, and there are approximately seventy-eight bowls, measuring spoons, cups, and pans in the sink."

I rise and wipe away a smudge of flour from her cheek. "No, ma'am. I would never renege on our agreement. It works to my benefit."

"Okay, then," she answers, backing down from an irritation that never existed. "I'm so glad we moved back here, especially now. I hope I have enough food for everybody."

"We'll have enough food for all of Early, although I hope they don't come." I put on my horrified face. "You didn't invite them, did you?"

She smiles. "Not all of them."

Sarah and I lived near Richmond after we married, and I thought we would put down roots there. But then a counselor position opened at Monte Vista High, and I learned Sarah had dreamed of returning to Early. Nurses are in high demand, so my finding a new job was never a concern. Living close to our parents? I wasn't as certain about that, but I wanted my Sarah to be happy. So we moved.

We bought an older two-story home about fifteen minutes away from where we grew up. I admit I was more than a little nervous when we signed the mortgage papers. But the proximity of our families has been a blessing, especially in the last three months.

I draw Sarah close and press my cheek to hers. "Is Little Bit still asleep?"

"Uh-huh," she says softly. "But there's so much to do. Not just the dishes, but cleaning the house and—"

I give her a gentle kiss. "We'll get everything done. We're a team, right?" I move to her throat while pulling the elastic from her hair. "But first things first." I give her my best goofy smile.

Sarah brings out the grin she saves for me alone. "Sweet talker."

*

"Dear Lord!" I exclaim. I think only He can sustain me through this.

Sarah sticks her head into the nursery as she buttons her blouse. "That bad?"

"I never...I mean, how can our angelic daughter produce something straight from the depths of Hades?" A medical professional should be impervious to such things. I am not.

Little Bit gives me a big toothless smile, thrilled with my reaction to her, uh, "gift."

"Poor Daddy." Sarah pokes out her lower lip in mock sympathy.

"Shut up," I call after her.

"You shut up," she replies before reappearing in the doorway. "We're going to have to stop saying that, you know. Little ears pick up everything."

"Yeah, I guess." This might be more upsetting than Little Bit's diaper. "But what if we shortened it? Like, one of us says *you* in one way and the other responds with *you* said in a different tone?"

Sarah's expression softens. "Don't worry about it, honey. We'll figure something out. Let me know when she's ready for her baptismal gown."

"Thank goodness you're a beautiful little girl," I tell Little Bit. "Because if you'd been a boy, your mother and I would've had a lively discussion about your wearing that thing."

"I heard that."

I finish changing our daughter, restoring her sweet vanilla baby scent, and place her on my shoulder. "Let's hope you only have sisters," I whisper into the perfect whorls of her tiny ear.

Then we begin our morning dance.

We start every day with my rendition of "Red River Valley," an old song Dad used to sing as he worked around the house. Little Bit is a wonderful partner, following my lead perfectly as we do a box step around her room. These are holy moments for me, set apart for gratitude.

This time I sense Sarah watching us. "Sorry to interrupt," she says quietly, "but it's almost time to go."

Sarah slips Little Bit into the baptismal gown worn by her great-grandmother. Grandma Winston passed away when Sarah was ten, but she left a legacy of faith and love behind, along with at least a dozen carefully crafted quilts. When we learned we were going to have a daughter, our first impulse was to pass on her name, Charlotte.

We had agreed to name a son Daniel Charles, after our fathers. Sarah wanted to make him a junior, but one Sam Russell is enough for this world. I was thrilled to learn a little girl was on the way—we had expected as much—but at the same time I was a little sad Dad's name wouldn't live on.

"Maybe next time," Sarah told me. She wants a houseful of children, but I have suggested we take it one baby at a time.

Mom started crying when we told her about our choice. "Thank you. Thank you so much. Your daddy would be so proud," she said between hugs.

Sarah and I didn't get it. When the hugging finally stopped, I had to ask what was going on.

Confusion passed over Mom's face. "Well, honey, I assumed you chose that name because you knew."

"Knew what?"

"That Charlotte is the feminine form of Charles."

*

The church is almost full this morning. Standing next to the pulpit, I can see only two or three empty spots in each pew. Not to brag or anything, but the Winston and Russell clans make up a fair percentage of the congregation. I was surprised by how many friends and family members told us they would be here for Little Bit's dedication.

All our grandparents and aunts and uncles are here. Mom and Megan are seated with Caroline, Daniel, Rachel, and Rachel's fiancé, Brendan. It took a while for Daniel and me to warm up to him, but we've decided he is okay. Sarah and I keep trying to find a good match for Megan, without success. Yes, even I, sensible man that I am, have waded into those treacherous waters.

I see Kevin and Rebecca in the third row from the front. I can't believe those two have never gone further than being best friends. Sarah says to give it time, but it's already been years.

Jack flew in from Seattle last night. He said his wife had to stay behind for work, but his eyes told me there was more to that story. A familiar spark appeared when I told him Lissi had arrived from New York, but now they're sitting on opposite sides of the church. I don't think they've even spoken to each other.

Gavin and Kirsten drove up from Roanoke yesterday. They got married a couple of years ago. He hopes to complete his residency in pediatrics soon, and she is a youth minister. They plan to go on a medical mission trip this summer.

Only God could have seen that coming.

Only God could have seen any of this.

Pastor Jeff is talking about the meaning of baby dedication. He's explaining that Sarah and I will promise to teach our daughter about Jesus Christ, with the goal of her becoming a believer herself one day.

Then he tells the congregation, especially our family and friends, that they will be asked to pledge to do the same.

My pastor's words are good and true, but I can't focus on them. My arm is wrapped around my wife and our sleeping daughter and my heart is singing to a tune I can't hum with words I can't pronounce.

I feel the light of my dream returning. Jesus's light. It zings through the hearts of our loved ones in the room, ricocheting from person to person, before shooting up to heaven itself. There it flows through Dad, Pop, Grandma Winston, and the baby we lost. Then the golden torrent pours back to Earth, to this platform where we stand. It travels from me to Sarah and then on to our precious daughter.

Pastor Jeff reaches for Charlotte and shushes her tenderly as she utters a faint cry. "What name do you give this child?" he asks.

Sarah and I decided on her middle name long ago, sitting knee to knee on my patio after we reunited for good. We smile at each other, and I wonder if we are too filled with the Light to speak.

"Charlotte," we manage to say in unison. "Charlotte Grace."

Your feedback is very valuable to me; it helps me improve my writing and provides fuel for future stories. It's also much appreciated by your fellow readers. So, please review *Always, Never, Still* if you have a few moments. Thank you!

ACKNOWLEDGMENTS

Only God could have brought this book to fruition. Left to my own devices, I would have moaned and meandered, never moving beyond the first chapter. I am overwhelmed by the Father's faithfulness, the Son's mercy, and the Holy Spirit's guidance.

I give thanks for everyone who has supported me in my writing journey. To my husband and our sons and daughters-in-law: Your love and encouragement pulled me out of countless ditches, enabling me to brush myself off and return to this story.

To my editor, Christy Distler: Your work not only improved this story, but made me a better storyteller.

To those who read *Chrysalis* and took the time to write a review or send a note or speak to me about what the book meant to you: You have no idea how much you touched my heart. Your responses led to the writing of this book. I hope you found the ending satisfying.

Visit www.ritafinchpettit.com to sign up for free exclusive content from the Shenandoah Stories, more information about my novels, and the latest posts from my blog, "A Moment's Notice." You can also get in touch with me at ritapettit@ritafinchpettit.com. I'd love to hear from you!

Grace and peace,
Rita

Made in the USA
Middletown, DE
26 November 2021

53463075R00189